SUSPICION OF MALICE

Also by Barbara Parker

Suspicion of Betrayal
Suspicion of Deceit
Criminal Justice
Blood Relations
Suspicion of Guilt
Suspicion of Innocence

BARBARA PARKER

SUSPICION OF MALICE

A DUTTON BOOK

DUTTON
Published by the Penguin Group
Penguin Putnam Inc., 375 Hudson Street, New York, New York 10014, U.S.A.
Penguin Books Ltd, 27 Wrights Lane, London W8 5TZ, England
Penguin Books Australia Ltd, Ringwood, Victoria, Australia
Penguin Books Canada Ltd, 10 Alcorn Avenue, Toronto, Ontario, Canada M4V 3B2
Penguin Books (N.Z.) Ltd, 182–190 Wairau Road, Auckland 10, New Zealand

Penguin Books Ltd, Registered Offices:
Harmondsworth, Middlesex, England

First published by Dutton, a member of Penguin Putnam Inc.

First Printing, May, 2000
10 9 8 7 6 5 4 3 2 1

 REGISTERED TRADEMARK—MARCA REGISTRADA

LIBRARY OF CONGRESS CATALOGING-IN-PUBLICATION DATA:
Parker, Barbara (Barbara J.)
Suspicion of malice : a novel / by Barbara Parker.
p.   cm.
ISBN 0-525-94542-3
1. Connor, Gail (Fictitious character)—Fiction.   2. Women lawyers—Fiction.
3. Miami (Fla.)—Fiction.   I. Title.
PS3566.A67475 S875   2000
813'.54—dc21   00-023136
Printed in the United States of America
Set in Sabon
Designed by Leonard Telesca

PUBLISHER'S NOTE
This is a work of fiction. Names, characters, places, and incidents either are the products of the author's imagination or are used fictitiously, and any resemblance to actual persons, living or dead, business establishments, events, or locales is entirely coincidental.

For Laura,
who deserves that first-class cabin on the QE2

SUSPICION
OF MALICE

CHAPTER

1

It was the dog that awakened her, the strange noises he made. A yelping whine, then a bark. Then nothing, and she drifted back to sleep with the soft whirr of the air conditioner. Rain tapped on the roof of the cottage, and dim light came through the window. Then the barking started up again.

Diane thought Jack might come down from the house and see about it, because after all, Buddy was his damned dog. She remembered that Jack had thrown a party last night, and he'd been happily drunk when she'd gotten home at midnight. It had been three in the morning before the music and laughter had quieted down.

Roof-roof-roof. Roof-roof. Hyeeeeeeee—

Diane shoved the pillow off her head and squinted at her clock. 6:45. "Oh, great." In plaid boxers and a camisole, she stumbled out onto the small wooden porch. Nothing stirred in the yard. All she could see of Jack's house was some white clapboard and the steps to the screened porch. In the other direction, past the mildewing seawall, lower Biscayne Bay gleamed as dully as an old nickel.

No dog anywhere in sight. "Stupid mutt."

A walkway ran across the yard, vanishing under a cedar trellis and into a thick stand of palm trees. He was in there. *Roof-roof. Roof.*

"Buddy! Come!" What was he doing? Diane thought of bufo toads—huge, slimy creatures with poisonous skin. Buddy would taste anything. She ran down the steps and across the yard, then under the trellis. Vines decades old kept out the rain, and the light dimmed. Dead leaves stuck to her bare feet. There was a fountain farther on, and Diane could hear it. The path turned, then opened up to a semicircle of teak benches, beds of bromeliads, and hanging baskets of orchids.

Jack's black Lab stood right in the middle of the path. He turned his head and looked at her, and his tail wagged. Diane came closer, then stopped. There was something just past him. The low, overcast sun barely penetrated the shade, and the thing—whatever it was—lay halfway under some bushes. Gradually the details became clear. A man's legs in tan slacks, feet pointing upward. An arm.

Barking, the dog loped toward her. Diane stumbled, caught herself, and raced back the way she had come, along the path, under the trellis, and across the wet grass to Jack's house, then up the steps. Her hair fell from its knot and into her eyes. Buddy danced in circles around her. She flung open the screen door, leaving him in the yard.

A spare key was hidden in a conch shell. She retrieved it in trembling fingers and jammed it into the lock. The back door opened into the kitchen. "Jack! Jack!" She ran through the hall, slipping as she rounded the corner. Dim light came from a globe held aloft by a bronze nude.

"Jack!" Her feet thudded up the stairs. "Jack, get up!"

His door swung open and Jack came out in old hiking shorts. "I'm *up*! What in the name of God's little angels is going *on*?" He was pulling a faded green T-shirt down over his belly. His eyes were puffy, and his big sandy mustache was turned up on one end, down on the other.

"There's a man by the fountain. On the path—oh, my God, Jack—he's dead. I heard Buddy barking, and I went to see—" Diane steadied herself on Jack's shoulder. "And there was a man lying on the ground. I think he's dead."

"What do you mean, dead?"

"I mean not breathing, Jack! Not moving."

"Maybe he's sleeping."

"No! Buddy's been barking forever."

"Well, who is it?"

"I don't know! I was afraid to look!"

"Calm *down*." Jack rubbed his face. "My. How inconsiderate, right in my backyard. He's probably asleep. Wait for me downstairs. I'm going to get some shoes on."

"Do you want me to call the police?"

"No. If you want to be helpful, *ma petite*, go make some coffee."

The door closed. Diane heard a woman's voice. Then Jack's low murmur. A few seconds later he came out in his old leather boat shoes. The door closed, but not soon enough to cut off a view of tangled red hair and a sheet clutched to somebody's breasts.

Jack's stern glance admonished Diane for not being downstairs already. At the landing she whispered, "That was Nikki."

"Shhh. You saw nothing, child." He nudged her along.

Jack looked out the kitchen window as if the wild landscaping would part and reveal whatever was there. He held aside the curtain with one hand and with the other twirled the ends of his big mustache into points.

"I had hoped, on this drizzly Sunday, to spend the day in the sack. No hope of that now." He dropped the curtain. "If my guest ventures downstairs, tell her to stay in the house. I'll go have a look-see."

"What about the coffee?"

"Of course. Start the coffee—not that I need it after this jolt."

Jack pushed open the back door. The dog rose from the mat, and its swaying tail tipped over a beer bottle. More of them littered the porch. The ashtrays were full, and a roach clip lay on a side table. Dead? Dead drunk was more like it. Guests had occasionally been found in the yard, sleeping it off, but not, he had to admit, this time of year, not with mosquitos chewing on exposed flesh and humidity so high one could work up a sweat breathing.

The drizzle was turning to rain. Jack touched his .38 snub-nose through his pocket. The neighborhood was generally safe, and he didn't expect to see any strangers, conscious or otherwise, but one never knew. Buddy trotted along beside him.

The main walkway from the house, paved with old keystone, arrowed to the seawall and a boathouse, where Jack kept his fishing boat raised on davits. Stepping-stones curved left toward the cottage, and another path meandered through a collection of rare plants and palm trees to the grotto. That had been his cousin Maggie's mad creation. She had piled up coral rocks and studded them with tacky Florida souvenirs, then set a bronze manatee on its tail. The sea cow's hippo-like mouth spurted water into a pond where fat carp wove among purple swamp lilies.

Jack could hear the splash of water as he took the path under the trellis. It blocked the rain, and intermittent drops spattered onto the keystone. Jack swept a spider web off his face. Then he saw it—a man's legs and feet. White canvas deck shoes with leather laces. Khaki pants, soiled with dirt and bits of rotten leaves. The rest of the man lay just beyond a clump of elephant-ear philodendron.

"Hey!" Jack knew already, but called out, "Wake up!"

Drops of water fell from the trellis onto a philodendron leaf, which moved slightly, as if shuddering. Buddy whined through his nose. Jack pointed toward the house. "Go home!" The dog circled, panting and wagging his tail.

Walking closer, Jack felt a sharp crunch under his shoe—a snail, smashed like a tiny brown porcelain cup. Slime trails crisscrossed the path. Standing alongside the man's thighs, Jack slowly peered around the huge leaves of the philodendron, holding the edge of one to pull it aside. He saw the other arm—muscled, golden-haired—and at the end of it a hand covered in blood. The shattered bones of the wrist gleamed purplish through the skin.

Without his volition, Jack's eyes traveled upward, quickly taking in details that mounted in horrific impact. A torso in a white knit shirt, neat little red holes in it. And so much blood. Not on the shirt. On the face. The left half was bathed in red, and streaks of it ran into the man's ear and matted his hair. One blue eye gazed upward. The other was a pulpy mass of glimmering black. It seemed to be moving. Then Jack saw the ants. Swarms of them.

"Oh, sweet Jesus," he moaned, letting go of the leaf, which gaily bobbed and dipped. Hands on knees, he waited for the dizziness to pass, then stood up. "Buddy, come!" His voice cracked.

Walking slowly through the rain, he gathered his thoughts. Water dripped off his eyebrows and chin, and his T-shirt clung to his back. Diane was on the porch. She pulled open the screen door, and her eyes took him in, finding the answer. She whispered, "He's dead, isn't he?"

Jack went inside, shaking his head when she asked who it was. He grabbed a dishtowel and ran it over his face and neck. The smell of coffee filled the kitchen, but he had no taste for it.

Nikki sat at the table, green eyes open wide. Jack absently smoothed his mustache and stared across the kitchen.

Diane spoke again. "Jack? Who is it?"

He beckoned to Nikki. "Come with me into the study for a sec. Diane, be a good girl and tidy up the back porch, will you? Don't go anywhere. I won't be long."

He took Nikki down the hall, their footsteps reduced to soft thuds on an ancient oriental carpet gone to threads at the edges. The house was too cold. He had turned the air conditioner down to sixty-something before Nikki had slid into bed, giggling. In the study, gray light filtered through wooden blinds.

"What is going on, Jack? Say something. What happened out there? Somebody died?" Her glossy pink mouth was open.

He set his hands firmly on her shoulders. "I want you to be very calm. Can you do that?" Nikki nodded. "It's Roger. He's been shot."

She stared, then blinked. "Roger? Roger is . . . *dead*?" She dropped onto the sofa. "Oh, my God."

He sat beside her. "This is a mess, baby."

CHAPTER

2

Rain hissed under the tires, and the windshield wipers swept back and forth and back. A drizzle here, a downpour farther on. Ragged clouds tumbled across the sky. This had to stop soon. Or it might not. One couldn't be certain of anything this time of year.

Anthony Quintana set his elbow on the window frame, arched his hand across his forehead, and squeezed. Long fingers moved upward on his temples as if testing the bones for cracks. He would rather have been in bed. Asleep or simply horizontal, it didn't matter. Unless he had a trial scheduled the next day, he didn't like to waste his Sundays working. The Cresswells weren't even clients—yet. They could have come to his office during normal business hours. He could not remember why he had agreed to do this.

Ah, yes. Nate Harris had asked him to.

The deejay on the doo-wop show spun another one. *Ooo-wah-wah, bop-bop-aaaahhhh*. Nate's lips moved, and he tapped the beat on the steering wheel. He watched the road through round tortoiseshell glasses.

Coño cara'o. Ten-forty-five in the morning, listening to that idiot music, sailing along in Nate's white Ford Taurus sedan toward the far northeast corner of the county—an area Anthony detested for its glutted roads, endless malls, and pretentious condominiums elbowing each other for a view of the Atlantic.

Porter and Claire Cresswell lived in one of them. Porter's company built boats, and he had money. Boatloads of it, Anthony assumed. Porter had been in and out of the hospital, and he'd put his son, Roger, in charge. A close call with cancer had rattled Porter's brain, or so Nate had explained to Anthony. Porter was sure that his son was embezzling money or secretly selling off assets or—God only knew—plotting to turn the company over to a multinational that would start making lawnmowers. Porter feared the IRS would freeze his bank accounts. He feared FBI agents at his door. Porter had begged Nate to find him a good criminal lawyer.

Anthony knew little about Porter and Claire, except that Nate had remained close to his in-laws since his wife had died three years ago. He was especially fond of Claire, Maggie's mother. Nate was a judge on the criminal bench. A good man, a scholar, a rare light in the courtrooms of this county. He liked to hand out special projects to the lawyers who practiced before him. Programs for community awareness, for immigrants, for battered women. It had always been hard to say no to Nathan Harris.

Nate turned down the radio. "What's the matter? You have a headache?"

Blinking, Anthony dropped his elbow from the armrest. "What? No." He unbuttoned his collar and loosened his tie. "I don't need this, do I?"

"I don't know, Porter and Claire are pretty formal. Where are your gloves?"

"*No me jodas.* Do I take off the tie or not?"

"You see me wearing one?" Nate asked. "What does that phrase mean, exactly?"

"It means . . . 'Don't play games.' " Anthony folded his tie.

"No, the precise meaning."

" 'Don't fuck around with me.' You know what it means."

"You ought to write a book," Nate said. " 'How to Cuss in Spanish.' I want an unexpurgated edition. I'd like to know for sure what the defendants are saying about me at sentencing hearings."

"I hope you told Porter Cresswell, when you volunteered me to handle this, that if it becomes drawn out, he may have to find another lawyer."

"What are you talking about?"

"I might not stay in the area. I mentioned that, no?"

"In passing. Don't tell me you were serious about New York."

"Why not? I was a federal public defender there for several years, and I still have contacts. My son is in New Jersey with his mother. I could easily move to New York."

"And your daughter just moved here to start college." Nate's round glasses made him look like a gray-haired owl. "What is this? Nobody moves from Florida to New York, it's unnatural. You're leaving because of Gail."

"Who?"

"*No me jodas,*" Nate said.

"It has nothing to do with her."

"You and she break up, then you disappear to Spain. Now you're thinking of relocating to New York. And it has nothing to do with Gail."

"No."

After a moment Nate returned his gaze to the road. He sighed. "Let it go, my friend. God knows, it hurts and you grieve, but this too shall pass."

Anthony might have laughed but for Nate's doleful expression. "Nate . . . no one died. I got my ring handed back to me. *Que lástima.* Too bad. I was saved from my own stupidity, marrying that woman. Believe me, I am not crying about it."

"Listen to that. You can't even say her name."

"Gail. All right?"

"A little snappy this morning, aren't we? Out partying last night?"

"Yes, with a box of files from my office."

"Was it fun?"

"No."

Rain streaked the passenger window. Through it Anthony gazed out at U.S. 1, which had been widened and prettified with palm trees and flowers. Welcome to Aventura. The cars were expensive, the faces were white, and the conversations would all be in English. The Taurus turned at a massive shopping mall and headed east toward the water.

"Listen," Nate said. "If I get the appointment to federal court, there's going to be a vacancy in the circuit court. You should run for judge."

"I don't have the patience to put up with that shit."

"Sure you do. Don't underestimate yourself. You'd have no problem getting elected. Good connections in the Cuban community, an excellent reputation in the bar. You know the law. On the bench you have a chance to do some good. The job doesn't pay what you're used to, but I suspect you've accumulated enough not to worry about it."

"I have accumulated enough not to worry about anything." Anthony leaned against the headrest and closed his eyes. "When I was in Spain, I considered not coming back. It's different there, Nate. Not so rushed, so nervous. They don't have a federal regulation for every damned problem, and you can smoke your cigar in a restaurant or compliment a woman without being accused of harassment. It's a beautiful country. The people are polite. They have pride in themselves, in their history, not like Miami. Hot as hell this time of year, but I'm used to that."

"You're kidding."

"Am I?" Anthony gazed out at the low hills of a golf course, which once had been mangrove swamp. "Sixteen years as a lawyer. Maybe it's enough. I'll be forty-three next month. Incredible. Even so, it's not too late to start over. I could do anything. Go anywhere."

"Sure, but Spain—"

"Why not? I speak the language. Where do you think Cubans came from? Look at this." He pushed his coat sleeve up his forearm. "Three weeks on the Costa del Sol, I look like a gypsy. I could buy a house on a cliff and lie in the sun. Come over and visit me. The women are gorgeous. You live like a monk, that's your problem."

Nate put on his turn signal and waited for traffic to clear. "I could use a little debauchery. Sign me up."

They were nearing the ocean, marked by a line of condominiums that completely obscured the view. Beyond them, patches of blue showed through white-topped clouds.

"Tell me about Cresswell Yachts. What they do. Who runs it. I want to pretend I know something."

The Cresswells' condo had a view from twenty-six floors up of the winding intracoastal, the curve of the Atlantic, and the skyscrapers of downtown Miami. The housekeeper led Anthony and Nate Harris over antique oriental rugs on tile floors, past silk-upholstered chairs and gilded tables on which sat orchids in porcelain pots. Finally they were taken into a wickered and rattaned sitting area that opened onto a glassed-in terrace. Ceiling fans twirled, and green plants cast tropical shade.

A slender blond woman in casual slacks and a pastel blue blouse hurried toward them. Smiling, she pressed her cheek to Nate's. "Hello, you sweet thing. I haven't seen you in *weeks*!" Her bright smile swept around. Anthony knew her age—sixty-one— but she dazzled. Her hair was cut youthfully, feathering on her cheeks. If there were tucks at her ears and jawline, they were too discreet to be noticed.

"Mr. Quintana, I'm so pleased you're with us. I'm Claire." She took his hands.

He smiled down at her. "No, no, call me Anthony. Will you?"

Her cheeks went pink. "All right—Anthony. My goodness. Porter? Come meet our guest."

Her husband studied the newcomer with gray eyes set in a square, sunburned face. A cleft divided his chin.

Driving the last half-mile, Anthony had learned that Porter Cresswell owned the company with his brother, Duncan, whom everyone called Dub. Porter was president, and Dub was in charge of sales. Dub's wife, Elizabeth, who had risen from within the company, oversaw scheduling and production. The three of them had maintained a fairly good balance until Porter's illness. Porter persuaded his son, who ran a related yacht leasing business, to sit in the president's chair for a while. He had made him a ten-percent owner. This new arrangement had not pleased Dub and Liz, but Porter was used to having his way. Now Porter was well again, but Roger refused to step down.

Porter's handshake was strong. One corner of his thin mouth rose. "Nate tells me you're a pretty good lawyer, Quintana."

"I wouldn't want to argue with a judge," Anthony said.

Claire was closing in on Nate, who had come in carrying a flat package about two feet by three. "Now what can *that* be? You said you were bringing us a little surprise, but what is *this*?"

"It's to say thank you. You and Porter suggested I apply for the federal bench. You pushed me and cajoled and wouldn't let me say no. If I get the job, well, a lot of the credit goes to you."

Porter shook his head. "Come on, Nate. This isn't necessary."

Nate held the package and Claire pulled off the tape. The brown paper fell away, revealing a canvas framed in gold. "Maggie painted this," Nate said. "It's from before we were married, so I'd never seen it before. I mentioned to Jack that I was looking for something, and he showed me this. He says it's the only portrait Maggie ever did."

Anthony came closer. Nate had told him he was bringing his in-laws a painting. A young ballerina with silvery hair stood alone in her tutu in the darkened wings of a stage. Her body was flat-chested, very long and thin, almost sexless, and yet compellingly beautiful. An odd blue light made her skin glow.

Claire stared down at the girl. "Why, it's Diane. She's just a little girl here, isn't she?" Claire looked at Anthony, explaining, "Diane is Porter's niece, Dub and Lizzie's daughter. She's twenty now, a soloist with the Miami City Ballet."

"Is that so?" Anthony said, "My daughter, Angela, is taking classes with them this summer."

"Then they might know each other. What a small world." Claire smiled at Nate. "You're giving us this. Oh, it's too *much*. We can't."

"No, no, Claire, it's my sincerest pleasure."

"Why, aren't you the sweetest thing?" Claire set the painting upright on the rattan sofa and came back to kiss his cheek. "Porter? Don't you want to thank Nate?"

"Damn nice of you, Nate." Porter clapped him on the back.

"Hey, who wants a drink? Claire won't let me have any, but I like to play bartender. What about you, Quintana? Got some rum. You're Cuban. I make a damn good daiquiri."

"Ahh . . . a Bloody Mary? Skip the celery."

"Good choice. I make an even better Bloody Mary. Nate?" Nate said to make it two, and Porter Cresswell crossed the sisal rug and went around a carved mahogany coffee table to get to the bar.

Anthony walked over to the windows to gaze down at the intracoastal waterway. "An impressive view."

"They were going to put in another building over there." Porter Cresswell indicated the spot with a jerk of his chin. "We had to file a lawsuit. You know anything about condo law?"

"No, I specialize in crime."

A chuckle rasped out of Cresswell's throat. He came around the bar with the drinks in tall crystal glasses. "Here you go, gentlemen." He growled near Anthony's ear, "You and I can go in the study after we eat. Leave Nate and Claire to gab."

Anthony decided he did not like this man, and he began mentally to add digits to his bill.

A small hand curled around his elbow. "Porter, darling, talk to Nate for a minute. I'm going to show Anthony the gallery."

"Have a look at our newest acquisition," Porter said. "I bought it from a collector in Chicago. You wouldn't want to know how much."

"Oh, tell me." Anthony smiled at him.

"One hundred and thirty-five thousand bucks. My daughter's last big piece. That's how much her paintings are worth, and they say the prices will only go up."

"Amazing." He added another thousand or so to his fees.

Claire said, "It was on the cover of *Art in America*. They did a whole article on her. I have the magazine if you'd care to look at it later."

"Yes, I would."

"Never mind Claire. She has a stack two feet high of that magazine. You aren't obligated."

"I'd like to," Anthony said. He left his drink on the bar.

*   *   *

A wide corridor had been turned into a gallery devoted to the works of Margaret Cresswell. The floor was black slate, and the ceiling was dotted with lights. Claire stood gazing at her daughter's art, two dozen or more pieces. The centerpiece was a huge abstraction of black with splotches of color showing through. It was spiky and jarring.

"This was my birthday present from Porter." Claire laughed. "Don't ask me which one! Sometimes I just . . . come in here and look at it. Maggie was such a beautiful, talented girl. Not always easy to understand, as you can guess from her work. She was never known as a Florida artist, because she spent her adult life in the Northeast. She met Nate at my nephew Jack's gallery when he showed her works, and Nate was so taken with her. He flew up to New York for her first single exhibition, and they married a year later. I'm so glad, or we'd hardly ever have seen her. One always thinks that time will just go on and on." She hesitated. "You know about Maggie's suicide, I suppose?"

"Yes. Nate told me."

"He's a sweet man," Claire said. "He wanted to blame himself, but she was fighting her demons long before they met. He gave her some happiness before the end. She was . . . only thirty-three." Claire fell into silence. The bright, unforgiving surroundings revealed the sagging skin of her neck that her luxurious Hermes scarf failed to cover. She looked up at Anthony with a smile. "It's all right if you don't like the painting. Not everyone does."

"No, I wouldn't say I don't like it, only that it is, as you say, hard to understand." He walked closer. The paint had been applied in intricate layers. "The first time I met your daughter, we argued. I said art had to mean something. She said no, the observer is the one who gives it a meaning. Without the observer, it doesn't exist. I can't look at any painting without remembering what she said. She was a person of rare genius and warmth."

"Thank you for saying that." Claire's eyes glistened. She took Anthony's arm. "Listen, I have to apologize for Porter. The situation at the company is causing such stress. I guess Nate explained. Porter let Roger handle things while he was sick, and before you knew it, everybody was at each other's throats. Porter decided for the sake of the company he had to go back, but Roger says, 'You're too old, Daddy. You're too stuck in the past.' Well, when it's your son, you don't just *fire* him. Porter is beside himself. If you could just set his mind at ease, he'd feel so much better."

Anthony didn't say anything right away. What did they expect him to do? Recite prayers? Make the sign of the cross?

He took Claire's hand and kissed it with great respect. Then he held it close to his chest. "You mustn't worry. I'll make sure everything is all right."

When they came back, Porter and Nate stood at the windows talking about the list of candidates for the vacancy in the federal court. Nate was one of three. Porter was giving reasons why Florida's senior senator would send Nate's name to the White House for official nomination.

"You don't want to know how much I contributed to that cocksucker's last campaign."

"Do me a favor, Porter. Don't remind him."

"Might do some good." Porter gave a raspy laugh. "He stopped that fucking condo down there in its tracks, I'll give him that much. Money talks, bullshit walks. Remember that."

"It's on a plaque outside the courthouse," Nate said.

Porter looked at him sideways and caught sight of Claire and Anthony. "There you are. What were you doing, playing lovey-dovey with my wife? Her face is all red."

Claire's eyes closed. "Porter, please."

"The man can take a joke, honey." He put an arm around her shoulders and kissed her cheek so hard it pressed her eye closed. "Smile. Come on. Let's see it."

She smiled, then pulled away, patting his chest. "Isn't everyone hungry?" There was a phone on a table by the sofa. She pressed a button, waited, then told someone named Maria that they were ready for lunch. She hung up and flashed a smile. "Okay. Soup's on in five minutes!"

Porter splashed some plain club soda over the ice in his glass. "A toast. To United States District Judge Nathan Alan Harris."

"Hear, hear," Claire said. Anthony raised his Bloody Mary as the muted chime of a doorbell filtered into the room.

Porter said, "You do a lot of drug cases, Quintana?"

"A few. All my clients have been wrongfully indicted, of course."

"You bet." Porter grinned, then gestured with his drink to Nate, who sat at the bar eating salted peanuts. "They say the only damn cases down there in federal court are drug cases. I remember this one guy wanted us to make him a fast boat. That was back in the good old days of the Cocaine Cowboys. Guy says, name your price. I told him to get lost. You remember the Don Aronow case, don't you, Quintana? I knew Don. Used to build racing boats. Nice fellow, but ran with a bad crowd. Ended up filled full of holes."

The doorbell was still chiming. "Who the hell is that? Where's Maria?"

Claire said, "Maybe I should go answer it."

"We've got a fucking housekeeper so you won't have to. Sit down." He bellowed, "Maria!" His face turned red. "Get the goddamn door!"

Anthony could hear quick footsteps on the marble floor. A few moments later a heavyset man in a green knit golf shirt appeared in the doorway, and the housekeeper's footsteps receded back toward the kitchen.

Porter frowned. "You should've called. We've got guests."

Claire began the introductions. "This is Duncan Cresswell, Porter's brother. Dub, this—"

"Why didn't you call?"

Duncan Cresswell shook his head, and his jowls moved. "I need to talk to you and Claire right now—in private." He glanced at Nate. "Hello, Nate. Sorry about this."

Claire's hand was at her throat. "What's the matter? Dub? What happened?"

Anthony stood up. "We'll be in the living room." Nate nodded, and the two of them walked into the hall. Anthony said quietly, "Do you have any idea what that was about?"

"None."

A woman's scream came from the patio, turning into a wail. "*No, no, no—*"

They spun around just as Duncan Cresswell came out. "Maria! Maria, get in here!" The woman was already on her way from the kitchen, asking what had happened, what was the matter? The man grabbed her shoulder. "Their son—he's been killed. Go get Claire's pills from her bathroom. Go on! Hurry." White-faced, the woman vanished.

Nate stopped him from going back inside. "Dub! What did you say?"

The answer came in a whisper. "Roger was shot to death last night at Jack's place." Nate stared at him, too stunned to speak. "The police won't say anything, but it looks like a robbery. His wallet's gone, his watch—Diane found him. She'd been up at Jack's all night, and after breakfast she was going back to the cottage and heard the dog barking, and found Roger's body. They called 911 right away, but it was too late. I mean, Jesus, he was lying there all night. Diane called us about an hour ago. I didn't want them to hear this from the police."

"Oh, my God. What about Nikki? Does she know?"

"Not yet. The cops sent somebody to the house. The neighbor says she's up in West Palm Beach for the weekend. They're trying to find her cell phone number. Oh, Jesus." He turned toward the door. "This is terrible. Maggie's gone. Now Roger."

"Let me talk to them," Nate said.

Anthony moved closer, not wanting to stare, but shock and sorrow had erased his presence. He might have been a shadow, for all the notice they paid him. Porter Cresswell's arms were wrapped tightly around his wife, who sat on the sofa and moaned. Nate crouched beside them. The housekeeper ran in with a pill bottle and leaned over Claire, weeping, touching her shoulder. Dub handed her a glass of water. "Claire. Claire, honey. Take these."

Giving them privacy, Anthony walked into the living room and stared at the view till Nate came out. "Stay with them," Anthony said. "I'll get a taxi."

Nate wiped his glasses on his handkerchief. "No, it's better if we leave. Claire wants me to apologize to you for the disruption.

That's Claire. Always the lady. I promised Porter I'd find out what's going on. Dub's going to call the rest of the family. It's a damn, miserable shame, isn't it?"

Outside, the rain had stopped, but the smell of it lingered in wet earth. They waited for the valet, and finally the Taurus squealed to a stop on the cobblestoned driveway. Anthony was just opening the passenger door when a shout came from the parking lot.

"Nate!" A man in a white Panama hat ran toward them, face hidden by sunglasses and a wide blond mustache. He leaped over a low hedge and stopped, breathless.

"I just heard," Nate said. "Dub came over. He's upstairs."

"Fuckin' cops. They're all over the place. I had to slip out the back. How's Claire?"

"Bad. Go see her, but don't stay. The police could give you some problems for leaving the scene, Jack."

"I'll deal with that later." The sunglasses turned toward Anthony. Introductions were made. The man was Claire's nephew, Jack Pascoe. The body had been found on his property. Nate repeated what Dub had said about a robbery. "Do they have any idea who did it? Or when? Did you or Diane hear anything?"

Pascoe glanced over at Anthony, then said, "Not the first. Anyone could have wandered in from the street. My security arrangements last night were somewhat porous. Who expects something like this?" Pascoe's mustache curled onto his round cheeks. He moved closer to Nate. "Lucky you're here. Could we chat? I left a message on your voice mail about an hour ago. Ignore it. Would you excuse us, Mr. . . . ."

"Quintana. I'll wait under the portico."

Anthony paced slowly, hands in his pockets, pretending disinterest, but on his first turn he noticed Jack Pascoe gripping Nate's upper arm. Their words were obscured by the rustle of palm fronds. A minute later, Pascoe rushed toward the double glass doors, which swung open, then shut, swallowing him into the cavernous marble lobby.

In the car, Nate said nothing. He gripped the top of the steering wheel as if he'd aged thirty years. At the end of the driveway, he abruptly stopped, swung the wheel to the right, and parked under some trees. The radio played at low volume. Nate turned the knob and it went off. "Mind if I ask an opinion?"

"Go ahead. I assume this is related to the conversation you just had."

"I was at Jack's house last night. He had some people over." Nate lifted the tortoiseshell glasses to rub the bridge of his nose. "Jack's father was Claire's brother, so Jack and Maggie practically grew up together. Anyway, she had her studio in the cottage behind his house, and that's how I came to know him. He called me last week and said why don't you come over Saturday and look at that painting we were talking about? Jack's an art dealer. I'd told him I wanted something to give Claire and Porter, and he suggested the portrait. I paid him five thousand dollars as a down payment."

Anthony made a small laugh. "What's the total price?"

"Twenty."

"*Alaba'o*. You're a generous man."

"Oh, it's a steal, I swear to you. It would cost fifty in a Chelsea gallery. Jack let me have it for less because he wanted to make sure it went to Claire and Porter. It was Maggie's only portrait, after all."

Anthony waited. "I don't see the problem, Nate. Unless the painting is hot."

"No, no, nothing like that. Jack just told me back there that the police asked him for a list of his guests. I wasn't on it."

"Why not?"

"Jack. Oh, God. He was trying to do me a favor. You see, Jack had a fairly offbeat collection of acquaintances at his house last night. He didn't want my name to be found among them."

"Nate, I wouldn't describe you as offbeat."

"No, I'm the most boring of the lot."

"What kind of offbeat acquaintances are we talking about?"

"Aside from Jack's sailing buddies and their girlfriends, there was a poet who got drunk and made up limericks about his erection. A Brazilian samba dancer who turned out to be a guy— Jack's little joke. And a couple of musicians from the blues bar

Jack goes to. Jack assured me that no one would even remember my face." Nate smiled. "This could be true. It wasn't a group that had much interest in judges."

"Nor a crowd that judges would normally hang out with. Particularly a judge who wants a federal appointment."

"Correct." Nate's mouth twitched, either from nerves or a bizarre sense of hilarity.

"Did you see Roger Cresswell last night?" Anthony asked.

"I saw him with Jack around . . . nine-thirty? They were going into Jack's study. Roger wasn't there long, maybe ten minutes. I was in the living room at the time watching people dance and looking through Jack's old record collection."

"Did you speak to Roger?"

"I did. I said, 'Hello, Roger,' but he didn't make eye contact, so I'm not sure he heard me. He went right out the front door and slammed it. I asked Jack. He said, 'Oh, it's the usual shit.' You see, Roger and Jack have a problem about Claire. Jack's her only other relative, and Roger thinks Jack is after Claire's money. I don't believe that and I never have." Nate added, "I guess I should say . . . they *had* a problem."

Anthony asked if Nate had heard the men shouting.

"No, nothing. Jack didn't seem angry. It's been going on for years."

"How long did you stay at Jack's?"

"I arrived about eight o'clock and left about midnight."

"It doesn't take four hours to put a down payment on a painting."

"True, but . . . Jack throws the most interesting parties. It's hard to pull yourself away. Try not to watch a drag queen giving samba lessons. But generally, I listened to music and watched the other guests. I had a few drinks—maybe more than I should have."

"Apparently. So you bought a painting, you saw Roger Cresswell come and go, you got drunk, and you learned the samba from a Brazilian transvestite. And if all this came out, the consequences for your nomination to the federal bench would be cataclysmic. Nate, if you're not leaving the circuit court, I won't run for that vacancy after all." Anthony raised his hand, forefinger upward. "But wait. Jack Pascoe says not to worry. No one will ever know you were there."

Nate smiled slightly. "I didn't actually learn the samba. Yes, Anthony, I am aware of my legal duty. I should call the homicide division and offer to make a statement. No. I should tell *Jack* to call so they won't charge him with obstruction of justice."

"Nate, your integrity is commendable." Anthony mimed a telephone at his ear. " 'Hello, detective, this is Jack Pascoe. You know—this is so crazy!—it completely slipped my mind that Judge Nathan Harris was at my party last night!' "

Nate chuckled, then laughed. "We'll hear it on the news. 'Federal nomination withdrawn. Noted criminal court judge and transvestite samba dancer attend wild orgy the night before heir to yacht fortune is found shot to death.' " His laughter trailed off. "Roger Cresswell dead, his mother and father in pieces, and all I can think of is how to save my own ass."

"Don't beat yourself up," Anthony said. "It's a normal reaction."

"I've never been afraid of anything, but I'm afraid people will think I told Jack to lie. I didn't, but they'll think so. I want to be on the federal bench. I deserve it. God help me, I do, but if this gets out, I'm finished."

"We'll try not to let that happen."

"Do you have any suggestions? *Are* there any?"

"We'll talk about it," Anthony said. "Let's get out of here. You're buying me lunch."

CHAPTER

3

For a pick-up performance, mid-week, and with most of the principal dancers still away for the summer, the theater was unusually full. One of the women made that observation as the lights dimmed.

Gail Connor glanced to her right. Her mother was leaning around Betty to hear what Verna was saying.

"It's because of the murder. They're all here to see Diane Cresswell." "*We* bought our tickets a week ago," Irene corrected. Betty whispered, "She found the body, you know. Her own cousin! Imagine dancing the night of the funeral." "Are Roger's parents here?" "Oh, I shouldn't think so. Claire was just devastated." "I heard they didn't get along with Roger's wife." "It's no surprise to me. Have you met her?"

"*Shhhhh.*" The command hissed from the row behind them, and the women quickly faced forward.

Canned tango music swelled from the speakers, and red velvet curtains parted on a barroom in 1930s Argentina. The men were in white shirts and black pants, the women in low-cut chiffon dresses, their hair held back in tight buns. When the blond ballerina in sequinned red twirled toward the men, Irene tapped Gail's wrist. Gail took this to mean that the dancer was Diane Cresswell. She tilted her head to see around the person in front of her.

The Cresswell name had been in the news since Sunday. Occupied with work, Gail had not paid much attention, but each morning her mother, dressed in a parrot-green robe and slippers, would read aloud from the newspaper, pausing to stir the eggs or butter the toast. The heir to a yacht-building fortune found in his cousin's backyard with seven bullet holes in his body. No suspects, few clues. Wallet and Rolex missing. The widow away for the weekend. A wild party the night of the murder. But who in attendance had wanted to kill Roger Cresswell? Or had it been a random robbery? The police wouldn't speculate. A frightened neighborhood had hired armed patrols.

Gail would sit there at the table, not to hurt her mother's feelings, but more often than not she would only pick at her food. *That's fresh-squeezed juice, don't you like it? You have to eat. I'll make you a boiled egg, then. Or milk toast with cinnamon. You'll make yourself sick on just tea.*

Strange, living at home again at thirty-four. Home. That concept had been rather fuzzy lately. The house she'd lived in with her fiancé—*former* fiancé—was empty and on the market. Before that, she'd been married, living with her husband and their daughter. Dave now managed a marina in the Virgin Islands, and Karen was visiting him for the summer. When she came back, where would home be? Gail wanted to find a house in a good neighborhood, but it would have to wait until her savings account recovered.

Sweat tickled the back of Gail's neck. The air was too heavy, too warm. She fanned herself slowly with the program, wondering if she could last till intermission.

At last the music ended, and applause swept through the audience. The dancers came forward, each man leading his partner by the hand, each woman making a low, graceful bow, costume glittering. Someone in the front rushed forward with five cellophaned bouquets of roses and tossed them awkwardly onstage. In the center, Diane Cresswell picked hers up, blew a kiss, and curtsied.

Gail stopped applauding, afraid to jostle the bubble that threatened to burst into nausea. If she were very still and breathed slowly it might go away. The curtains closed. The house lights came up slightly, and Irene held the program in front of her mouth. "Gail. Five rows ahead. The couple on the aisle. She's chairman of the Heart Fund. At intermission I might go speak to them. Want to come along?"

"I don't know them."

"I do. They're good contacts for you to have. I could introduce you."

"Not tonight."

The lights dimmed, and bright, lively music lilted from the speakers. A moment later the curtains opened on a painted olive tree and a hanging bit of tile roof. Two dancers came out dressed as Italian peasants, the girl in a short striped tutu, the man in a loose white shirt and black tights to the knee. Ribbons decorated their tambourines. They smiled at each other coyly, like lovers. Their feet were blurs.

Elbow on the arm rest, Gail leaned her forehead onto her fist.

The young man leaped into the wings, leaving the girl to her solo. Her striped tutu bobbed and dipped, and she pirouetted around and around. The ribbons on her lacy white hat swung out behind her. A minute later the man soared back into view. A series of spinning leaps took him across the stage.

The music pounded straight into Gail's head. Her skin was cold and damp, and her stomach had climbed to the back of her throat. Fumbling for her purse, she whispered, "Mom, let me out." She stumbled over Betty's foot and nearly fell on Verna. Glares and huffed exhalations came from people farther along the row. "Sorry," she murmured. "Excuse me." She hurried up the aisle, through a black velvet curtain, past the disapproving frown of the usher, then across the lobby and into the ladies' room. She threw up in the nearest stall.

A minute later heels tapped across the tiles. Gail guessed who it was before seeing a confirming flash of red hair through the space in the door. She flushed the toilet, patted her mouth with a tissue, and unwrapped a breath mint.

"Gail? Honey?"

When she came out, her mother was standing there. "Were you sick?"

"I had to go to the bathroom." She washed her hands. "Go on back. I'm fine."

"No, it's a short dance, and the second intermission is coming." Her mother watched her in the mirror, worried.

Gail uncapped her lipstick. "I know, I look like hell."

"A little pale, that's all." Irene drew a yellow silk scarf through her fingers. "Do you want to leave, darling? I could take a cab home with you. They won't mind."

"I'm sure they'd understand." Gail tossed her lipstick into her purse. "They know all about it, don't they? You gossip about everything. Were they shocked?"

"Shame on you for such an attitude. I didn't have to tell them. They aren't blind. They care very much for you."

Gail leaned on her hands, bowing her head. "I know. I'm sorry."

The door creaked on its big metal springs, and an elderly lady thumped in on a walker, accompanied by a younger woman carrying her bag. Applause from the theater faded as the door swung shut. It opened again, and more women came in, filling the room with their chatter.

Irene picked up her purse. "Well. I'm going to find Betty and Verna. Coming?"

"In a minute." Brush in hand, Gail watched her mother march out, quick little steps in her patent leather pumps. Gail wanted to scream, to get out of here, to walk on Lincoln Road until the performance was over. *Of course* they knew. What a juicy piece of information. They were just too polite to bring it up in front of her. They were talking about her right now.

If they weren't blind, what did they see? Moving around the other women at the mirror, Gail turned sideways and studied her body. The sleeveless black dress still skimmed over her tall, thin frame. She smoothed her dark blond hair back from her ears. Nothing had changed.

In the small lobby she stood in line for a soda. The small theater was restored Art Deco, all curves and red carpet, brushed steel, and frosted glass. Her gaze swept over a group of girls, then backtracked. One of them was looking at her with wide brown eyes. Angela Quintana. In that moment of recognition, Gail caught her breath. It was too late to turn around, too late to slip back to her seat.

The girl hurried across the lobby, dodging around people in her way. She was all legs in a short black skirt and chunky sandals. Angela put a polite kiss on Gail's cheek, then smiled again and hugged her, an unhesitating gesture of affection that took Gail by surprise.

"Hi, Gail. How are you?"

"Great." Unsure what else to do, she continued to smile. "Well. What's up? Have you started college yet?" Angela had been living with her mother in New Jersey since her parents' divorce, but she would attend the University of Miami. Gail remembered hearing Angela's father say she needed to be close to her Cuban heritage, and where else but Miami? Exiled parents often said such things, Gail had noticed.

"School doesn't start for a couple of weeks," Angela said. "I've been taking classes with the ballet."

"Oh, yes, that's right. How's it going?"

"Wonderful. *Really* hard, but I love it."

"And your brother? How's Luis?"

"Okay, except for having to attend summer school, so he didn't get to go to Spain with Dad. I couldn't go either because of ballet. Dad just got back with this dark tan and about ten rolls of pictures—the whole tourist thing. I had to stay with Nena because, well, you know, he wouldn't let me stay by myself."

"Your great-grandparents are well?" Gail maintained her smile. At some point they would run out of conversation.

"Oh, sure. Getting old, but they're so sweet." Angela wore a blue top with little cap sleeves, and her waist seemed as narrow as a flower stem. A tiny gold crucifix hung just below the notch in her collarbones. As she looked at Gail, her brows slanted downward. "My dad told me you guys split up. I didn't believe him at first. Gail, I'm so sorry."

For an instant Gail wondered just how he had explained it. He must have been fairly vague, may even have pretended a certain regret, or Angela would never have crossed the lobby to say hello. Her dark eyes shone with curiosity.

Gail made a dismissive wave. "Well, you know. Really, we're both fine with it." The line moved toward the concession stand. "Oh, can I get you something to drink? A soda?"

The girl shook her head and came closer. "Gail, there's something really important I have to ask you. It's a favor—not for me, but for a friend of mine. He's one of the dancers—Robert Gonzalez. He's the one who did *Tarantella*?"

The Italian dance that Gail had walked out on, halfway through. "Oh, yes. He's very good." Gail told the attendant to give her a club soda, no ice. She laid two dollars on the counter, then turned back to Angela. "I'm sorry. This friend of yours—"

"Bobby Gonzalez. He wants to talk to a lawyer, and I saw you in line, and I'm like, wow, it's Gail. Could you see him after the show? He needs some advice."

"I can't stay afterward, I'm afraid." Gail picked up her soda and threaded her way toward the windows through the crowd. "What's this about?"

Angela glanced around before saying in a low voice, "You know the man that was killed? Roger Cresswell? Bobby was at that same party. The police are talking to everybody, and they came around to Bobby's apartment, and he *told* them he doesn't know anything, and now they want to ask him more questions."

"He was there when Roger Cresswell was murdered?"

"He didn't see it. Nobody did. He doesn't know anything about it."

Gail angled her straw into her soda. "Then why—if I might ask—is he reluctant to talk to the police?"

"Bobby says they don't have any suspects, so they're after him because they know where he came from. He grew up on the streets in East Harlem. Well, not *on* the streets, but in a tough neighborhood, mostly Puerto Rican, you know? I promised I'd help him, and then I saw you right *there*. It's fate."

"Angie, this is a criminal investigation. You know who to ask."

"My dad? Well . . . he's busy."

"Not too busy for you. He can't be."

"Okay. The thing is, he doesn't like Bobby. I went out with him once, and Dad totally freaked. He's like, *no*, you're not going out with him again ever, he's nobody. Wait till you're in college, find some nice guy from a good family." She rolled her eyes. "He doesn't approve of *anyone*."

"So . . . you don't want him to know you're still seeing Bobby."

"We see each other at the studio. We're friends."

Gail knew that lie when she heard it. "How old is he? Just curious."

"Twenty-one." Angela gazed up at Gail. Two gold barrettes held her center-parted hair back from her face. "Can you help him? It wouldn't take much time. And he'd pay you. I know he has some money saved." Delicate brows drew together, making a small crease in smooth skin. Seventeen years old. Gail could see Anthony in the straight nose and full lips. His eyes were darker, hers a soft velvet brown with long lashes.

"Please? You could talk to him, couldn't you? On the phone, even. I won't tell my dad I spoke to you. You don't have to see me again."

"Oh, Angie, it isn't that. I've done a few criminal cases, but when it comes to a murder investigation, well . . . Bobby should find someone who specializes. The ballet has lawyers, surely, who could recommend someone?"

"He doesn't want to tell them about this." Such desperation on that face. In a small voice she said, "Do you know anybody else?"

Gail glanced away, a hand on her hip. So. Anthony Quintana would toss this kid overboard, not a second thought. A poor Puerto Rican, not good enough for *his* daughter. Ballet dancer? Even worse. Gail set her cup on the windowsill and opened her bag. "All right. This is my card. Give it to Bobby and tell him to call me tomorrow morning. I'll be in the office till noon."

"How much do you think it will cost? He'll want to know."

Gail smiled and shook her head. "Nothing. It's on me. He does a great *Tarantella*."

"Oh, thank you! He'll be so relieved." Angela pressed the card to her small bosom. She kissed Gail's cheek again before running back through the lobby to her girlfriends. Her dark hair swung on her shoulders, and she moved as lightly as a bird.

Before the fiery crash of their engagement, Gail and Anthony had bought a house in Coconut Grove. Now that it was on the market, both sets of keys had been given to Anthony's law partner, who was handling the details so the owners wouldn't have to speak to each other. Gail would get nothing from the sale because, by her reckoning, what she owed to Anthony exceeded her share of the equity. He hadn't asked for repayment, but she—in a gesture of pride that she had almost come to regret—told his partner that she didn't want Mr. Quintana's money, and if he didn't either, he should stack it up and strike a match.

Until she was able to buy her own place, she and Karen would live in her mother's house near downtown Miami. The rear of the property faced Biscayne Bay, and the gated, walled neighborhood was shaded and quiet. For Karen's room, Irene had bought new curtains and a matching comforter and had arranged on the bookcase all the books, Beanie Babies, art supplies, rocks from her travels, and other junk an eleven-year-old girl could accumulate.

In ten days Karen would be home from her summer with Dave. He lived in a small apartment on the island of St. John with a balcony overlooking the town of Cruz Bay. There were banana trees and goats along the winding dirt road that led up to it, and green hills in the background. Karen had sent pictures. Dave made enough to live on, but not enough to pay for Karen's private school in Miami, or her clothes, or the braces she soon would need.

In hindsight—achingly clear—Gail could see how wrong she'd been to turn down a partnership at one of Miami's most prestigious law firms. She had been too sure of herself, too eager to set her own hours, to choose her own direction. She'd wanted more time with Karen and Anthony. She'd wanted a *life*. So she had rented an office near a major shopping mall and burned up her savings on furniture, books, equipment leases, salaries, and simply staying afloat until the business took off.

It hadn't—not yet. Bills were getting paid, but without much left over. If she failed, it meant starting over, finding a salaried position. This would not be easy in a town where the old firms were hiring more Hispanics, and civil practice lawyers like Gail were in plentiful supply. She might be forced to take a job farther north, perhaps Tampa or Orlando, where an Anglo last name was no liability.

If she could just hang on, just a little while longer, it would be all right.

In pajamas Gail knocked at the open door of her mother's room. Irene was sitting cross-legged on her bed writing letters, using a book as a desk. She looked over the top of her glasses.

"I should go online. Everybody else is. Nobody sends letters anymore, do they?"

"You can use my computer," Gail said. "I'll show you how."

"Okay, but let's do it before Karen gets back. I want to show her how smart her grandma is. She thinks I'm over the hill. Well, I guess I thought my grandmother was decrepit when she was fifty-nine. That isn't *old*. Is it?"

"You're a kid." Gail sat on the side of the bed. "Mom, I am so sorry for speaking to you the way I did at the ballet. I can't explain it, except that . . . it seems that all I have in my head these days are thorns and scorpions and spiders. So ugly. And sometimes they get out. Forgive me?"

"Always." Irene squeezed her hand.

"Hey, I got a client tonight. It's a freebie, but great PR. He's one of the dancers. His name's Bobby. He was at the party where Roger Cresswell was killed, and the police want to talk to all the guests, of course. Bobby is reluctant to get involved, and he wants some legal advice."

"He was *there*?"

"Yes, but he didn't see anything. The police are talking to everyone. I think they'll just draw a line through his name and move on. You'll never guess how I got this one. Angela Quintana is his girlfriend. She saw me in the lobby and we talked about it. I don't do criminal law, but this is only a quick phone consultation. I thought I'd run upstairs and see Charlene Marks before Bobby calls. She's a former prosecutor. Five minutes' worth of advice from Charlene, and I'm ready."

Irene folded her glasses. "Why didn't Angela ask her father to handle it?"

"Señor Quintana doesn't like Bobby. Angela doesn't want him to know they're going out."

"Is that what you call him now? Señor Quintana?"

"It's either that or 'jerk.' "

Her mother carefully set her glasses in the box of stationery on her nightstand. "You know very well that Anthony's going to hear about it sooner or later."

"She won't tell him. And if she does, so what? If it annoys Anthony that I'm helping Bobby Gonzalez, then tough bananas."

Her mother looked at her. "You're not over him, are you?"

Gail laughed. "Over him. Well, maybe not. I think of him and want to throw things. Mother, I'm helping Angie because I like her, not because of some repressed desire to keep in contact with her father. Can't I want to help someone? Lawyers do that occasionally. This kid is being hassled by the police. Dancers don't make much money, and for him, a lawyer would cost a fortune. There. My good deed for the day. If it gets complicated, I'll give it to Charlene."

Irene was silent for a moment, then said, "Are you still planning to have her drive you to the doctor's tomorrow?"

This conversation was about to head in a bad direction. Gail kept her tone light. "It's convenient if she takes me. And then . . . well, I'll probably spend the night at her house. I'll call you." She stood up and kissed her mother's cheek. " 'Night, Mom."

"I could go with you and bring you home."

"No, it's fine. Charlene and I are such pals." She started to move away, but Irene held firmly onto her arm.

"I'm going to say this again, though you don't want to hear it. Talk to Anthony. It would be different if he knew."

Gail shook her head. "Good night, Mother."

"You're only *assuming* what would happen."

"I *know*. Forget it." Gail laughed. "He doesn't want to see me again, talk to me, hear from me, and I feel exactly the same way.

I've made my decision, and I'd be very grateful if we could just drop it. You said you understood."

"I don't. I don't understand at all."

"No, because you were raised Catholic in the fifties. It's a different world now. Women have choices."

"We always did! This is selfish and cowardly." Irene started to cry. "I could take care of the baby while you work. I could help."

"For God's sake. There isn't a *baby*."

Irene yanked a tissue out of the holder. "Well, it's not some goddamn blob, it's your *child*. It's my grandchild, and it may be the last one—"

"Oh, *don't*! That's not fair!" Gail pressed her hands to her forehead, then let them drop. "I've got to go to bed." At the door she turned around. "Are you going to keep crying? You won't make me feel guilty. Mother, would you please stop that?"

Irene lay down and turned her face to the wall. "Go on. Do what your conscience tells you. I have nothing more to say."

Gail cried out, "How can you presume to judge me? How? You've never worked for a living. You didn't have to worry about a place to live that was yours, or whether Renee or I would have clothes to wear or a decent school to go to." Gail flung her arm out, encompassing the house and all that was in it. "You had a great marriage. Daddy loved you till the day he died. He took care of us. He never called you a whore and told you to get out of his sight." Her throat ached. "Don't you think I hate this? I hate every minute of it, but it's my decision, it's my life, and I'm doing the best I can!"

The room fell silent. Then her mother said, "I know you are, Gail. Go to bed. I'll see you in the morning. Love you."

Gail stared at nothing, then nodded. "Love you too."

In her room she ripped the cellophane off an aromatherapy candle. The label said SERENITY. She lit it and shook out the match. Next she pressed a button on her portable stereo. A drawer slid out, and she dropped in a CD. Native American flute music.

Then she turned off the lamp by the sofa bed and settled herself in with a cold glass of chardonnay. They had ended it on the

Fourth of July, an appropriate day for fireworks. She had been about six weeks pregnant at that point, but her powers of denial were in excellent shape. Then she noticed a tenderness in her breasts. She locked herself in the bathroom with an at-home pregnancy test, hoping that her symptoms were due to something less drastic, like cancer.

In the flickering candlelight, with notes from a wooden flute echoing off the red rock walls of a canyon somewhere, Gail leaned against her pillows and sipped the wine. Not good for women in her state, despite the fact that before such things were known, her own mother had downed pitchers of martinis through two pregnancies. But it didn't matter what she drank at this point.

How had this happened? They'd been careful. Her doctor had shrugged. "It happens."

Once the shock had faded, she'd considered telling Anthony. Of course she had thought of it. She had pondered the range of outcomes. If a letter had reached him, although his partner had instructions not to accept any letters or phone calls from Ms. Connor, would he deny it was his child? He was capable of believing that. Would he send a check to ease his conscience?

She had wondered, briefly, and usually in her dreams, if he would want to see her. If he would try to talk her out of it. Not even that would change the essential fact: This was her problem, not his. The outcome would have been exactly the same. Tomorrow would be the same.

Her eyes fell on the small black velvet box on the end table. She had put it there earlier tonight intending to make a decision on what to do about it. The box contained a pair of earrings—three-carat aquamarines surrounded by diamonds. Anthony had bought them to go with her wedding dress, a silvery blue Louis Feraud gown that he'd also paid for. Gail had canceled the order for the dress, and she had tried to leave the earrings at Anthony's office, but Anthony was gone, and no one would take them. So she'd brought them home. Seeing Angela tonight, Gail had considered giving them to her, but they seemed too sophisticated for a girl of seventeen.

Save them, then. Insurance for hard times.

Gail set down her wine and picked up the box, holding it on her upraised knees. She pressed the gold catch, and the lid slowly came up. Even in the dimness of her room the earrings sparkled like sunlight on the ocean.

Lindísima, he had said, when she'd put them on. *They're beautiful, like your eyes. Like the water off Varadero Beach. I'll take you there one day.*

CHAPTER
4

With another splash of scotch over ice, Anthony Quintana returned to his chair. Soft leather sighed as he sank into it and crossed his sock feet on the ottoman.

The chair gave him a view all the way to the door. At any moment he expected to hear the jingle of keys, then his daughter's footsteps in the tiled hall. She was late. The ballet should have ended—according to Angela—around ten o'clock. With a few minutes to say good night to her friends, then twenty minutes home, she should have arrived an hour ago.

Eyeing his portable telephone on the coffee table, Anthony considered trying again to reach her. He wondered if she had deliberately turned her phone off. Perhaps she had only forgotten. He trusted Angela, but anything could happen. A prowler in a dark parking lot. Drunks on the road.

He took a sip of scotch, then returned to the notes on his lap. Late this afternoon a courier had made a delivery from Nate Harris. The envelope contained, among other things, a letter about progress so far in the investigation of the Cresswell murder. Nate had asked one of the prosecutors in major crimes, a man he had known for years, to find out, discreetly of course, what was going on with the case—not an unusual request by a friend of the victim's parents, who happened also to be a judge of the criminal court.

Oh, Nate! To take such a risk! Even so, Anthony was glad for the information. It would tell him where the police were headed. Did they have any viable suspects? The moment an arrest was made, Nate's problems would be over.

On Sunday, Anthony had been forced to think of what Nate could do that wasn't illegal, unethical, or suicidal. Of course Nate should tell the police that he'd been at the party, even if it wrecked his chances for the federal bench—but only *if* he had anything material to add to the investigation. Anthony had asked him three questions. Do you know who killed Roger Cresswell? Do you know anyone at the party who might have? Do you know anything about it? The answer to each having been no, Anthony advised him to go home and keep his mouth shut.

As for Jack Pascoe, Nate was to thank him for trying to help, but advise him to see his lawyer. Jack was to tell the lawyer exactly what he had done. If the lawyer told Jack to go to the police to amend his statement, so be it.

Would Jack see a lawyer? Anthony doubted it. He thought he could deflect possible charges of impropriety, but Nate's chances of getting to federal court would be DOA if anyone found out where he'd been that night. This was unlikely, unless one of the other guests remembered him, this quiet, gray-haired man who had sat in the shadows, hardly speaking to anyone, watching the goings-on with bemused, scholarly detachment. Nate was out of danger, at least for the present.

Shuffling through the papers, Anthony found a rough sketch of the property, a large lot near Old Cutler Road, south of the city. High wood fence on three sides, fifty yards of seawall. Anyone could easily have gained access by walking through a gate in the wood fence that bordered on a vacant lot used for overflow parking. The victim's Porsche had been found a block away. Had the killer followed Cresswell in? Or waited for him to return? Small landscaping lights illuminated the path.

The *pop* of a .22 would not have been heard over the music. Gunpowder on Cresswell's shirt indicated that the killer had fired at close range. Two bullets to the chest, then a third at an angle in his upper arm. One in his back. Blood on the path showed that Cresswell had run several yards before collapsing. The killer had stood over him, still firing. Cresswell had lifted his hands instinctively to ward off further damage. A fifth bullet went through his right wrist. Cresswell had been dead by then, or dying. The killer had put six and seven through his left eye. The bullets had spun around in the cranial cavity, ripping apart his brain and cracking the bone. The ground had been drenched with blood. Before leaving, the killer had pulled the plug on the lights, discouraging guests from wandering through and finding the body.

Wallet gone, watch gone—a Rolex worth over six thousand dollars. No shoe imprints on the walkway. Rain had obliterated the footprints in the dirt area just outside the fence, along with the tire treads of the cars that had parked there.

Tossing the papers to the coffee table, Anthony finished his scotch and stood up. Where was Angela? His imagination was alive with dark possibilities. He listened intently for the purr of a VW Beetle. He had wanted to buy her something heavier, but Angela had been entranced by the idea of putting a fresh flower each morning in the little vase on the dashboard.

He got up and poured the last of the scotch into his glass. He dialed Angela from the phone in the kitchen. No answer. It was difficult, living with a teenager. Five years ago his ex-wife had taken Angela and Luis back north. He had missed them terribly, his children, but not for one moment their mother. He'd been a student at Columbia Law, enduring the frigid loneliness of icy streets and early darkness, when they'd met at a salsa club. Rosa had been lively and pretty, and at twenty-four he had not looked beyond that.

In the living room he put Jack Pascoe's guest list on the coffee table, sat on the ottoman, and read over it. He had told Nate not to speak to anyone about the case, but here was a list, courtesy of Jack Pascoe, scrawled on lined paper, a long column of names. Anthony assumed that the police would do background checks on each of them, looking for a criminal past. They would ask them to account for their whereabouts that night. The exact time of death could not be determined, but it had to be sometime after ten o'clock. Roger had arrived at Pascoe's party around 9:30, stayed about ten minutes, and had come back. The police had found in Roger's car a receipt from Walgreen's Liquors, stamped 10:03 p.m., and a fifth of Johnny Walker Black with several ounces missing. They had also found $1,000 in cash and a withdrawal receipt for $2,500. The balance had probably been in the wallet.

The police were looking at a young dancer with the Miami City Ballet, Robert Gonzalez. Unless there were two of them, Anthony had met him. *Hi. Mr. Quintana? I'm Bobby Gonzalez. How're you doing? So . . . is Angie ready?* Gonzalez had sat on the edge of the sofa clearing his throat and looking around while Angela finished dressing. A springy, muscled five-eight or -nine, curly black hair, and a scar across his knuckles. *This is a very nice place you have, sir.* Polite, but they were all polite with a girl's father.

What had this father learned? That Gonzalez was twenty-one, born in New York City, lived in East Harlem, moved to Miami at thirteen with his mother and four siblings. He'd never attended college. He rented an apartment with two other dancers on Lenox Avenue in Miami Beach, and he drove a faded black Nissan with the tints peeling off the windows. Anthony had not embarrassed Angela by refusing to let her go out that night, but he told her, when she returned, that it was the last time. As far as he knew, she hadn't seen Bobby Gonzalez again.

The police had good reason to suspect him. He had worked for a few weeks at the Cresswell boat yard over the summer. The night of the party, witnesses remembered a confrontation. Cresswell poking Gonzalez in the shoulder, Gonzalez asking him if he wanted his ass kicked.

Jack Pascoe had paid Gonzalez to help with the cleanup, but Gonzalez disappeared around midnight, sticking Pascoe with the bulk of the work. Police wanted to interview him, but he was avoiding them.

Gonzalez had an arrest record: carrying a concealed weapon, possession of marijuana, resisting arrest with violence. As a defense attorney, Anthony knew that such charges could be bullshit.

These had pleaded out to misdemeanors, but it made him nervous. "Concealed weapon" usually meant "knife."

When his portable phone rang, he nearly tipped over his drink getting to it. "Angela?"

But it was his sister, Alicia. She spoke in Spanish, the more intimate language of family. She hoped she wasn't calling too late. Was he in bed?

"*No, no. Espero por Angela. ¿Qué pasa?*" He told her he was waiting for Angela. Had something happened?

"Not really. I wanted to talk to you, that's all. I was just saying good night to Grandfather. He wanted to know where you were. He asked me, 'Where's Anthony? I am dying, and he doesn't come to see me.' There were tears in his eyes! Thank God Nena was asleep in her room."

"He isn't dying, Alicia, he's playing his little games again."

"I told him you were still in Spain, that you would be home soon. He made me say it twice before he let go of my hand. Anthony, you have to come see him."

At eighty-four years of age, with a wheelchair and a pacemaker, Ernesto Pedrosa still knew how to manipulate. There were a houseful of relatives, a full-time nurse, and he had begged Alicia to leave her husband and children in Texas to come home for a few weeks to help take care of him. Alicia had never refused his demands.

Anthony sighed. "You know we argued. I don't want to talk about it."

She laughed. "An argument? Oh, I heard about it from Aunt Fermina. You were shouting at him in his study with the door closed, then you told Nena you would never set foot in the house again. Why?"

"Alicia, I am closer to you than to anyone in the family, but there are things that I can't discuss, not with anyone."

"Nena told me that all this happened after you broke up with Gail. Maybe you went crazy. Is that it? You won't talk about that either. Why did you call off your engagement? Or did she? Who was it?"

"It doesn't matter. It's over."

"She adored you. I could see it in her face when she looked at you. And in yours too. What happened, Anthony? Please. What is going on with you?"

"Alicia, I have to go. Angie will be home soon, and I have work to finish."

"Oh, Anthony. My poor brother. Your pride is going to kill you someday. I love you, but you're breaking my heart."

When he hung up the phone, Alicia's words echoed in his ears. *"Me estás rompiendo el corazón."*

Propping his forehead on his fists, Anthony closed his eyes. After a moment, he got up and paced to the glass doors that looked out at the inlet behind his house. Past the patio and the screen he could see the quiet black water, bright windows on the other side, and the silhouettes of boats tied to docks.

The old man was at it again, using Alicia this time. For thirty years—since the day Anthony had been dragged out of Cuba against his will—Ernesto Pedrosa had tried to control him. As a boy, Anthony had felt the sting of his grandfather's belt, but he had never cried, enraging the old man even further. At twenty, he'd been thrown out of the house for reading socialist literature. In adulthood he had made his own way, asking for nothing—unlike his cousins, who had grown rich taking whatever shit the old man had handed them. It was Anthony who threw it back at him. They fought. They disagreed about everything. Cuba and the American betrayal, the food at dinner, the fall of the Soviet Union, the Miami Dolphins, the *Miami Herald*, the embargo, Anthony's divorce, the venality of local politicians, whether the grass needed more water.

After each fight, they would refuse to speak to each other. Anthony would appear only for holidays and family occasions. Then his grandfather would start sending emissaries. A cousin, to invite him to dinner. Nena, to ask if he'd accompany them to midnight mass. After years of this maneuvering, the arguments had worn thin, and peace was declared. Ernesto had not become soft, but he had become old.

He had offered Anthony everything—businesses worth hundreds of millions of dollars, a sixteen-room mansion, bank accounts not even his wife had been told about. Ernesto Pedrosa would have given him all this, but he would have kept his grip on the strings. Anthony might have cut them—Ernesto must have expected him to try—but one moment, one hideous revelation, and the game was over.

A simple act, but impossible to tell Alicia about. Not her, or Nena, or any of them.

Ernesto Pedrosa had arranged for a murder. A man had been shot and dumped into the river on his orders. No money had been paid. It had been done out of loyalty, respect. Love for an exiled patriot who for forty years had fought for *la causa*, the cause above everything. He had sacrificed his only son, Tomás, dead at the Bay of Pigs, for the cause. He had financed terrorist acts for the cause, had warped American foreign policy, had divided a community. When Pedrosa asked a favor, it was done. A certain man had threatened his grandson—his life, his flesh, his heir—and so he had to die. Ernesto had not first asked permission from the beneficiary of this service, no, because he'd thought Anthony didn't have the *cojones* to see that it had to be done.

Confronted, the old man had admitted everything. Anthony had cursed him to hell and back, had ripped the bullet-riddled Cuban flag off the wall and thrown it at him. From his wheelchair, Ernesto had laughed. *Call the police. Have them take me away. You have the backbone of a woman. I should have left you in Cuba.*

Anthony had walked out and had kept going. In saving him, Ernesto had killed everything else between them. Anthony could not go on as before. To condone a murder, to forget that the dead man had a family—Anthony might as well have pulled the trigger himself.

His sister had been wrong. This had nothing to do with Gail Connor. She had only been the catalyst, telling him what Ernesto had done, and daring him to do something about it. What? To wreck a family by turning an old man over to the police? She had not understood that. She had said he would cover for Ernesto to protect his own position. That he wanted power more than truth. That he and his grandfather had become exactly alike.

There it was: her quick accusations, her lack of trust, her willingness to believe the worst. Of course he'd been angry, but not for long. They were equally unsuited. He felt the relief of a man who'd been kicked off the elevator just before the cables snapped.

He went back to the kitchen, picked up the bottle on the counter, and held it to the light. Empty. When had he bought it? Monday. He couldn't remember drinking all of it, but someone had. He threw it into the trash.

The front door opened, and he turned toward the sound. "Angela, ¿estás tú?"

"I'm home. *Estoy a casa, papi.*" She had an American accent. He was trying to improve her Spanish, but she spoke it reluctantly. "Hi, Dad."

"*¿Dónde has estado? Es tarde, niñita.*"

She turned and looked at him. "I wish you wouldn't call me that. I'm not a child."

"You're late." He spread his hands wide. "I may say that, no? Where have you been?"

"We went for something to eat afterward."

"Who are 'we'? You and . . ."

"Some of the girls in my class."

"Haven't I asked you to call if you expect to be late? I tried to reach you. Did you have your phone off?"

"I didn't notice. It was off in the theater, then I forgot."

"We have orientation at the university at eight o'clock in the morning. Did you forget that too?"

"*Papi,* don't yell at me, please. I'm sorry." She came over and leaned against his arm. The part in her hair ran straight and clean, and the delicate curve of her forehead and cheeks made his chest hurt. "I'm really sorry to be late. I won't do it again."

He could never remain angry with her. He kissed the top of her head. "All right. I was worried. Come sit down. I want to talk to you."

She seemed not to hear him. Then she raised her eyes. "What if I don't go to school this semester? To tell you the truth, I don't think I'm ready for college."

"Not ready? What would you do instead?"

"Audition for the ballet. They always need extra people for *The Nutcracker*, and auditions are in a couple of weeks. The thing is, I need to work hard to prepare, and there are all the rehearsals and performances. If I make it, and they like me, they might hire me to be in the company. And if not, I could go to school in January. Doesn't that sound reasonable?"

"No."

"Why not?"

"Sweetheart, listen to me. Don't you think maybe you're just a little bit infatuated with all the lights and the glamour?"

"That's a very patronizing thing to say."

"Angela."

"It is! I've been dancing since I was seven years old!"

"You never said anything about dancing as a career. Now suddenly this is what you want?"

"I'm a good dancer, better than anyone in my class. Edward Villella himself saw me this week. He picked me out to show the others what to do. He said, 'Look how well she moves, look at her line.' He chose *me*."

"And on the basis of a compliment, you would throw away your college, your place in the dormitories, the tuition that I have already paid—"

"We could get a refund!"

"*Olvídalo*. Absolutely not. It isn't the money. I don't care about that. Of course you're a good dancer. You're a very talented girl, but you said yourself, a dancer has a short life. Then what? You'd have no education, no way to earn a living. Do you expect me to support you? I won't. You'd be spoiled like so many kids whose parents have money."

"But Dad, just to audition—"

"No. I can't allow it. Don't look at me like that, Angela. You're only seventeen years old. You must grow up a little. Get an education first. Or dance in your spare time—as long as it doesn't interfere with your studies. Have I ever been proven wrong in my advice to you? Have I?"

"No, *papi*."

"All right, then." With an arm over her slender shoulders, he guided her toward the living room. "Sit down. There's something I need to tell you." He sat in his chair, she on the ottoman with her back straight and her hands folded, waiting. Her mouth was in a firm line. She was still angry.

"This young man who came to the house. Robert Gonzalez. You haven't seen him again, have you?"

She blinked. "At the studio—"

"Socially. Have you seen him socially? Have you been alone with him? Has he talked to you?"

"Why are you asking me that?"

"Yes or no?"

"No."

"Do you recall ever hearing him mention the name Roger Cresswell?"

"I—I don't think so. Who is Roger Cresswell?"

"He was the man murdered last weekend at a house off Old Cutler Road. Don't you remember it on the news?"

"I haven't been watching much TV."

"Well, there was a party, and someone shot him and took his money. An acquaintance of mine, connected to the investigation, told me that Bobby Gonzalez is a suspect." Angela stared at him. "I know this is a shock to you, sweetheart, someone you know, and so forth, but it's true. Promise me, Angela. Don't speak to him. Don't be alone with him."

"It isn't true! Bobby couldn't do that. He *couldn't*."

Anthony took her hand. There were little gold rings on two of her fingers, a silver one on another. So innocent. "I am sorry to tell you this, *cielito,* but people are full of surprises, not always pleasant ones. This young man refuses to answer questions, he threatened Roger Cresswell at the party, and he has no alibi. He's been arrested before—possession of drugs and carrying a concealed weapon. One has to wonder what's on his juvenile record."

She stared back at him.

"Bobby didn't mention this, did he?" She shook her head. "He could be very dangerous. Stay away from him. Do you promise?" Her mouth opened. "Angela? An answer, please."

She bit her lips, then nodded. "Yes. I promise."

"You must be careful with young men. Most of them want only one thing from you. This is true. Many girls have been ruined, believing their lies and flattery. You know what I'm talking about, don't you, *preciosa?*"

She stared at the hands clasped in her lap. "Yes, *papi.*"

"Good. Now go to bed. We have to be on the road by seven to beat the traffic. I'll wake you up at six o'clock, all right?" He touched her cheek. "Don't be angry. *Te quiero más que nada. Tú lo sabes, ¿sí?*"

"*Sí, papi.* I know you love me more than anything."

"Sleep well." He held out an arm.

She kissed him goodnight. "*Buenas noches, papi.*" From the hall she looked at him with dark, mournful eyes, then ran up the stairs.

CHAPTER

5

After he saw the number on his beeper, Bobby took Sean Cresswell's portable across the bedroom and sat on the floor under the windows. The only noise was the click of buttons on the PlayStation. Sean's mouth would go into strange shapes when he jerked on the joystick. Sean was listening to Wu-Tang through his headphones, but Bobby would have to keep his voice down. If Sean's mother knew he was here, she'd probably kick him out. He was a bad influence on her little boy—nineteen years old, on probation for jacking his cousin Roger's Porsche out of the boat yard parking lot. Roger had gotten the car back but pressed charges anyway, teaching the young man a lesson.

He entered Angela's number, and she picked up on the first ring. "It's me, baby. What's up?" She started crying. "Angie? What's the matter?"

"Where are you?"

"Sean's."

"Oh, great."

Bobby knew that Angie didn't like Sean, but there wasn't much he could do about it. "Why are you crying, *mamita*?"

"I have to talk to you. Can you come over? I'll sneak out."

"It's thirty miles. What's going on? What happened?"

"My dad . . . He said . . ." Her voice was small and tight. "He said the police think you killed Roger Cresswell."

"That's bullshit. Why'd he say that?"

"He has this friend or something who knows about the investigation. He wants to make sure I stay away from you. Bobby, I *know* you didn't, but he told me other stuff too. He said you were once arrested for having drugs and weapons. Is that true?"

"What?"

"Is it?" She didn't say anything else, and he could hear Lauryn Hill singing in the background.

"No. It was some weed and a little pocketknife." She still didn't say anything. "Angie, I swear to you, it was nothing. Me and some friends were at a concert at Bayfront, okay? They told us to leave, and I told them no. So the cops beat me up and searched my pockets. They charged me with resisting with violence, plus the other stuff. Three felonies."

"Did you go to jail?"

"A couple days, then I bonded out. They put me on probation for a year."

"Is that all you ever did?"

Bobby draped his arm across his knees. "It's the last, if I want to keep dancing."

"What about before that?"

"It doesn't matter, baby. That was back in the day."

"I want to know," she said. "I tell you everything, don't I?"

"Yeah, but you don't do anything." He laughed. *"Mi angelita."*

"Was it bad, what you did?"

"No, not . . . *bad.*" He closed his eyes and put his forehead on his arm. "It's not the same now, Angie. I'm not with that anymore."

"Did you go to jail?"

"No, baby. A little time in detention, that's all. Mostly my uncle took me home and beat my ass." All he heard was Lauryn Hill on the stereo. "Angie? Your old man's trying to scare you, is what I think. Hey, it's me. Remember me? Bobby?"

"Oh, it was so awful, what he said." Her voice was a whisper.

"He was drinking tonight—*again*. I could smell it on his breath. And he was really mad at me."

"Did he hit you?"

"Well . . . no."

"If he did, I'll take you out of there. Nobody does that to you, not even your father."

"Bobby, it's okay. He doesn't ever hit me. He was just mad because I got home late."

"I'm sorry about that. It's my fault."

"No, no, it was mine. God! He is so unreasonable. He wants to control my life. He refuses to let me audition for the ballet. He goes, no, you can dance in your *spare time*. Oh, sure."

"Try out anyway. Don't let him all up in your face. You gotta be strong."

"He'd kick me out. He said if I don't go to school, he's not going to support me anymore."

"I'd take you in."

"You would?"

He laughed softly. "You know I would."

"Bobby?" She had her mouth close to the phone, probably with her hand cupped around it. "There's something else. The night Roger Cresswell died—my dad said you don't have an alibi, but you *do*. You were with me."

"Forget it. I'm not getting you into this."

"Bobby! I want to."

"No, it's okay. I'll get Sean to back me up. Really. Don't worry."

"What are you going to say to Gail Connor? You should tell her the truth."

"I won't tell her about *you*."

"She knows we're going out."

"And like she's not going to tell your father."

"She said she wouldn't."

"How come they split up, anyway?"

"I don't know. It's probably my dad's fault. She's very nice. You'll like her."

"Hey, Angie, don't be so afraid of your dad. Okay? You're not a child."

"He treats me like one." Her sigh warmed his ear. "Bobby, do you think Edward meant what he said?"

"I told you ten times already, yes. The man does not hand out bullshit."

"You think I have a chance to get in?"

"Didn't I say that? Have some faith. Look at me. I mean, of all the guys in the world *least* likely to do ballet—"

"I love you, Bobby."

"*Te quiero, mamita.* You're the best thing in my life."

"Better than dancing?"

"Well. That's different. Apples and oranges."

"What am I? The apple or the orange?"

Every time she did that sexy-voice thing, his brains shut down. "Hmm. You're the apple."

"Am I the apple of desire? You want to take a bite right now?"

"Oh, man." He laughed softly. "A big one. Real juicy."

"What would you bite first? Maybe . . . this? Or . . . let's see . . . this?"

He held the phone closer to his mouth. "Angela. You trying to make me come over there and show you?"

She pulled in a breath and whispered, "Oh, shit, it's my dad. I gotta go."

When Bobby dropped the phone back on the desk, Sean was still sprawled out on his lounge chair playing Street Fighter, watching the TV screen past his bare feet up on the foot rest. He took off his headphones. "Who was that, your woman?"

"Yeah." Bobby watched Sean's player, a black guy in a bandanna, silently fire at a kung-fu fighter. Blood spattered the street, then vanished, and the figures suddenly faced each other again.

Sean said, "You want to go out tonight, bro?"

"Why do you play that game? It's boring."

"You want to go out? I've got some cash. We could go over to the Beach."

"No, I need to get up early." Bobby watched Sean's hand jerk on the joystick. He was supposed to be studying for his final in algebra at Miami-Dade. Going to summer classes was part of his probation. He was smart, but he couldn't get into a regular college, the way he'd messed up in high school. Too bad, because his parents could have sent him anywhere, even Harvard.

Bobby heard voices from downstairs and went over to the door, easing it open a crack. Diane was screaming about something. A condo on South Beach, closer to the ballet.

"Then work for it!" her mother yelled. "I never had things handed to me on a silver platter the way you have."

"I work! I have a job!"

"Five hundred a week, and you expect us to subsidize it, and we do. But all we hear is, 'I want more, more.' Whose new car is that in the driveway? You want a down payment, sell the car."

"How am I supposed to get around without a *car*?"

Sean's father got into it. "Hey! Shut up, both of you. Liz, we can lend her the money."

"Lend? We're not lending her another dime. She has to learn some responsibility."

Diane yelled, "You give Sean and Patty whatever they want, and I get shit!"

"Maybe if you *asked* instead of *demanding*—"

"I'm getting out of here. I'm going back to Jack's."

"Go."

"Fine! You're a selfish, pretentious bitch."

"What? What? Say that again. Say it." Then some screaming and slapping noises. "Filthy mouth . . . As much as we've done for you . . ."

"Stop it! Don't!"

"Liz! Leave her alone. Jesus, right in the middle of Jay's monologue, every goddamn time."

Then the oldest girl, Patty, running down the hall, her voice moving toward the stairs. "Shut up! Why can't you all be *quiet*? I'm trying to sleep!"

Diane was crying. "I hate it here! You can go to hell!" Footsteps came up the stairs then stopped. A door opened and hit the wall.

Dub shouted, "Are you satisfied, Liz? Are you?"

"Patty, go back to bed. I'm sorry, honey. Go back to sleep."

A minute later, Diane's footsteps went the other way, then down the stairs. The front door slammed.

Bobby quietly closed Sean's door. He used to think these people were all right. Huge house, new cars, everything clean, big refrigerator never empty. One girl in college, another in the ballet, Sean an athlete at Gulliver Prep—before they expelled him.

"Diane just left."

"Yeah. They're always scrapping about something. Mom says she's tired of Diane sucking money off of them. Dad just wants it quiet so he can watch TV." Sean jerked the joystick. "We could go to the Grove. It's closer. I got the keys to Dad's Vette."

"No, man. I'm tired."

"You only live once, bro."

Bobby sat on the end of the bed, blinking a little with fatigue. His left ankle was hurting. He'd come down wrong on it tonight, though no one had noticed. He'd been up too many hours, been rehearsing too hard. When he stayed over, Sean let him sleep in the recliner, but right now Sean was in it, still playing his game. The light of the TV screen was on his face. He looked like his father—chubby cheeks and a big forehead. Sean had a ring in his ear, one in his navel, and another he wore in his eyebrow when he went out. He kept his hair buzzed short, except on top. Bobby used to cut his that way, but it looked ridiculous onstage, so he'd grown it out before auditioning for the company.

He and Diane had been in the ballet school together, and about five years ago, he'd met Sean. Sean had noticed Bobby's tattoo, which was gone now. They started hanging out. Lately Liz had made it clear that she didn't like Bobby around. Bobby wouldn't be here now if he hadn't been afraid of going home or to any of his friends' places on the Beach.

"Hey, Sean." He leaned forward and tapped Sean on the arm. "I need you to do something. Last Saturday, when Roger died, the cops want to know where I was after I left Jack's. How about if I say I was with you?"

After a few seconds looking at the screen, Sean said, "With me?"

"Yeah. My car was in the shop, so Angie dropped me off at

Jack's and picked me up later, about a quarter till twelve. Nobody saw her, but if her dad finds out we were together, she'll get in trouble. What were you doing? Were you with anybody the cops could check out? Pay attention, Sean." Bobby's hand shot out and ripped the joystick away. "This is important."

"What the fuck? Give me that back."

"You going to help me or not?"

"You made me lose." Sean dropped his bare feet to the floor and leaned over to turn off the PlayStation. "Yeah, I left here about eleven and went over to the Beach. Mom hid my fuckin' keys, so I used my spares. You were with Angie?"

"Yeah. We went and had coffee."

"Is that all you had, bro?"

"Come on, Sean. Let's say you beeped me at eleven-forty, and I called your cell, and you said to meet you on the Beach. Far as Jack knows, I had my car. Okay. So say we met up about twelve-thirty at my house and we went out. Where? Where's a good place we could've gone?"

"I don't know. Liquid. Cameo. Whatever. No, it was Amsterdam. I used my fake ID. The bouncer was this fat bald dude, remember? We met those bitches from Germany. Fritzi and Mitzi. Or was it Helga and Olga?"

"Don't try to be funny, okay? If they ask."

"I got your back, man. We were at Amsterdam. What time did we stay till?"

"Like, a quarter to three, 'cause I got home at three o'clock. You got all that? Sean?"

"Yeah, bro. I beeped you at eleven-forty, we hooked up at twelve-thirty, went to the club, and left at a quarter to three. By the way—Sonic Boom was playing that night, then they went to disco. We got bored and split. It was mad crowded. And I really did go by there. Are we straight now?"

"Fine. Just keep Angie's name out of it." Bobby dropped back down on the end of the bed. "Hey, Sean. I have to see a lawyer in the morning. Do you have any cash? I can pay you back next week."

"How much you need?"

"I don't know. Three hundred. Have you got it?"

"No problem." Sean stood up and moved some books around on a shelf over his desk. He turned around with some hundred-dollar bills and fanned them out. Bobby counted eight or nine. Sean said, "Take what you need."

"Whoa. Where'd you get all them benjamins?"

"My dad." Sean sounded bored. "I've got some mutual funds I can't have till I'm twenty-one, but he let me sell some. My mother doesn't know, so I keep it out of sight."

"Oh, yeah? You didn't jack it out of his wallet, did you?"

"No." Sean shoved three bills at Bobby. "Don't be stupid, take it. Just pay me back, yo." He put the rest of it behind the books.

"I'll get it back to you next week." He stuck the bills in his hip pocket.

Sean was doing his little smile—sleepy eyes, one side of his mouth going up. "The cops are after you for Roger?"

Bobby shrugged. "They want to talk to me."

"You could've done it. You hated him."

"So did you. Wasn't for Roger, you wouldn't be doing algebra like back in high school."

"So? He called you a faggot, man."

"And I busted his face for him." Bobby flicked a punch on Sean's shoulder.

Laughing, Sean aimed one back, which Bobby deflected. "You the one who shot him, man?"

"What?"

"Did you cap him, bro?"

"Did I cap him? *Bro?* Look at you, rich white boy, talking street." Bobby clenched a fistful of Sean's polo shirt and shoved it into his stomach. "Homeboy from Gables Estates. Look at that computer, the TV and shit. You busted up two cars, your old man lets you drive his fuckin' Corvette, and you so hard. You go to my street, they'd crack up laughing."

Sean went after him jabbing, kidding around. Bobby swerved away. Sean was big, but Bobby was fast. Sean came across the room laughing.

Bobby held his hands up. "Shut up, Sean, your folks are gonna hear. Listen, you know if Jack has any friends named Alan? He's got thick gray hair and round glasses? Taller than me, kind of skinny. You ever see anybody like that over at Jack's?"

"I don't think so. Why?"

"Well, he was at Jack's party, and the cops say he doesn't exist. They asked me where I was, right? This one cop goes, 'Can you account for your whereabouts during the entire course of the party?' And I said, 'Sure, I was inside the house washing glasses and tying up the garbage mostly, or out on the porch. Ask anybody.' And he goes, 'You never went out in the backyard at all?' "

Grabbing his toes, Bobby arched his foot then stretched it the other way, testing the pain. "I wasn't trying to play with these guys, but you gotta be careful. One of Jack's friends he goes fishing with slipped me a joint, so about eleven o'clock I took a break and went down to the water. I told the detective, 'Yeah, I was sitting on the seawall with this guy named Alan from about eleven to eleven-forty.' The detective was like, 'How do you know the time so precisely, Mr. Gonzalez?' And I go, 'I just remember, okay?' Well, I remember because Angela beeped me at exactly eleven-forty, but I can't tell him that. Then he asks me what was Alan's last name, and I said I didn't know the last name. Just Alan. I described him, and then the cop says there was nobody like that at the party, nobody named Alan. Then he asked if I still had the clothes I wore that night, and could they have them. He goes, 'It's routine so we can get this matter cleared up.' "

Sean had turned his desk chair around to sit facing Bobby. "Did they take your clothes?"

"No, man, they didn't have a warrant, they couldn't do shit. I said, 'Look, you better leave, I'm late to rehearsal already.' The main detective gave me his card and told me to call. I didn't, so yesterday they were waiting for me outside the studio. He goes, 'Mr. Gonzalez, don't you want to help solve this crime and ease the suffering of Roger Cresswell's family?' It was so funny, man, the way he said it, I had to laugh. Then the other guy gets in my face. He goes, 'You're lying to us, and I don't like that.' And I go, 'Well, I don't like your bad breath, dude.' The older guy pulls him off of me and says, 'We'll be seeing you.' "

"Did they get a warrant?"

"Maybe. They might be there right now, ransacking the apartment. My roommates will be pissed off."

Sean gave Bobby's shoulder a punch. "You were with me, bro. We can say I beeped you at eleven, and you left then."

"No, they don't like it when you change your story. Besides, I went back in the house and told Jack I was leaving. I'll ask the lawyer what to do." Bobby put his elbows on his knees and dug his fingers into his hair. "Alan. He was there, bro. I saw him. Jack fuckin' *knows* him, and when I called, he goes, 'Sorry, man, I can't talk about the case.' "

They heard the knock on the door and froze. Sean exhaled. "Shit."

"Sean? Sean, let me in."

"I'm studying, Mother."

"Who's in there with you?"

"No one. I have the TV on. Is it disturbing you?"

The doorknob rattled. "Open this door. Now."

"Go in the bathroom," Sean whispered.

"No. Open it." Bobby started putting his sneakers back on.

Under his breath Sean said, "Bitch." He flipped open his math book and picked up a pen. Twiddling it in his fingers, he opened the door a few inches. "Yes?"

His mother pushed him out of the way and came in, looking around. Her dark brown hair swung at her shoulders. Elizabeth Cresswell was one of those older women who looked good in makeup, but most of it had worn off. It was smudged under her eyes.

She smiled at him. "Bobby, I'm going to have to ask you to leave."

Sean said, "Why does he have to leave?"

"Because it's late, and I said so."

"He doesn't have to leave. I told him he could stay the night."

"Sean, dear. Whose house is this? And please put your father's car keys back where you found them."

"I don't have his fuckin' keys. Ask him, or is he too drunk to remember what he did with them?"

His mother crossed her arms. "Now, what was it your probation officer said about cursing? Remind me."

Bobby swung his backpack over his shoulder. "Let it go, Sean. I'll catch you tomorrow."

"Later, bro."

They did the hand slap as Bobby walked past. "Later."

Elizabeth escorted him down the curving stairs, through the living room, then into the foyer. She opened one side of the double doors. The neighborhood was quiet, only the crickets and the splash of water in a fountain in the driveway. A line of lamps led out to the front gate. His own car was parked around the corner.

"Good night, Mrs. Cresswell." He trotted down the wide steps.

"Bobby."

Letting out a breath, he stopped and turned around.

She was standing in the light of the doorway, a hand on her hip. Gold bracelets dangled from her wrist. She had a nice body for her age, and she knew it. "Stay away from my son. I don't care how good you look in tights, you're still a worthless little punk. If I see you around here again, I will have you arrested for trespassing. Are we perfectly clear on that?"

He wanted to slap her, the bitch. He would have—back in the day. He smiled, ran up onto the porch and skidded on his knees, arms extended. "I'm gonna miss you, mama!"

She stumbled backward. "Get away from me."

The door slammed behind her, and the lock turned.

CHAPTER

6

She found Dub in bed already, lying on top of the satin comforter watching CNN, holding a glass of bourbon on his belly. He always wore V-necked white T-shirts to bed, and they rode up at the waist. Cigarette smoke drifted through the shade on the cut-glass lamp.

"Did you give him the heave-ho, warden?"

Liz kicked off her sandals and shoved them into her closet. "I *told* Sean I didn't want him associating with Bobby. Every time they're together, Sean starts in with the mouth, like some . . . ghetto kid. He never got into trouble until he met Bobby Gonzalez. He's a menace. If I could think of a way to send him back to Puerto Rico, I'd do it."

"I think he was born in New York, Lizzie."

She tossed her bracelets and watch into her jewelry box. "You don't take this seriously, do you?" Gold earrings followed.

"Bobby's all right, except . . . don't you think it's a little weird, a kid from his background, running around in ballet slippers?" Dub waggled his fingers.

"He isn't *gay*. Diane assured me of that."

"Since when is she sleeping with Bobby?"

Liz shook a cigarette out of her husband's pack. "They dated a couple of years ago. Don't you pay attention to anything? Now she apparently likes older men. Where's the lighter?"

Dub switched channels, pausing at an ESPN replay of a Sammy Sosa home run. "If you mean Jack, I don't buy it."

"She ran back over there in a damned hurry, didn't she? And the night Roger was killed they were in his house together. Talking? Please." Liz clicked the gold lighter and stared at the flame. "Maybe Diane lied to the police." She inhaled smoke and tossed the lighter back on the nightstand. "Do you think that's a possibility, Dub?"

Ice cubes rattled as Dub sipped his bourbon. He put the glass back on his stomach. "What do you mean? Jack might've killed Roger?"

"Hasn't it crossed your mind?"

"Can't say it has." Dub pressed the remote through several commercials. "Why would Jack do that?"

"Oh, twenty or thirty million dollars." Liz lay her cigarette beside his in the ashtray and pulled her red knit shirt over her head. "Claire's rich in her own right, and she'll inherit all of Porter's money, too. Who's she going to leave it all to, now that Roger is dead?"

"Not good enough. Claire's going to be around for a long time."

Liz unhooked her bra. "Porter won't. Jack will start working on Claire to let him sell Maggie's paintings. Think what it would do for his business." Liz tossed shirt and bra to the chaise longue, then unzipped her pants. "It's just my little theory, and Jack certainly isn't the only one who could have done it."

When she stepped out of her underwear, Dub's glance didn't waver from the television screen. It annoyed her. Even at fifty-four, a man should at least have the courtesy of looking. Dub drank too much, she reminded herself. The doctors had told him to stop, and he wouldn't. He had bottles stashed all over the office. At least he had never been violent. He didn't yell at her or the kids. He would just get drunk and go to sleep.

Liz knew about alcoholics. Her mother had been one—the violent kind. At sixteen Liz had moved out and put herself through night school. At eighteen she'd gone to work at Cresswell Yachts sanding pieces of fiberglass. No air conditioning in the boat sheds, fans going, eating her lunch out of a bag, listening to loud Cuban voices. She learned Spanish quickly, did her job without complaining, and moved up to shift supervisor. Then one day she stayed late, and Charlie Cresswell followed her into the tool shed and closed the door. She got her revenge by demanding a job in the sales department. She had noticed his younger son working there.

"Are you going to share your little theory with the police?" Dub asked.

Naked, Liz pulled a green silk kimono off its padded hanger. "God no. Let them figure it out. They don't need my help." Belting the robe, she looked at the floor by the closet again. The gold-framed painting she'd propped against the wall was gone. "Hey, where's that painting? It was right *here*. Did you move it?"

"I haven't seen it, Liz."

"Goddamn it. She took it. Diane came in here and stole it on her way out!"

"So what? You said it didn't look like her."

"That's not the point! Porter *gave* it to us, and she stole it! Don't you *care* if that girl is a thief?"

Dub took a sip of his drink. "Jesus."

"I do my best for this family, and all I get from her is sarcasm and hostility. Sometimes I think she hates us."

"She was mad because we didn't go to her performance tonight."

"I'm surprised *she* went. It showed such disrespect for Porter and Claire. Oh, I don't want to talk about it. It's been a hideous day. I hate funerals." She scooted across the bed, sliding on satin. "Pass me the ashtray, will you?" He put it between them.

Lying crossways, propped on her elbows, Liz watched Bette Davis in a big-shouldered coat and a hat, knocking frantically on a locked door in a seedy hotel. *Richard! Richard, let me in! It's me, darling. It's Helen.* Dramatic music played on the sound track.

Dub asked, "What do you mean, 'Jack isn't the only one'?"

Liz tapped her cigarette on the ashtray. "Only one what?"

"The only one who could have done it. What did you mean?"

"Oh, I don't know. Roger was such a prick. Even Porter was outraged. He double-crossed his own father, for God's sake."

"Double-crossed?"

"Roger promised him he wouldn't make any big changes, but the minute Porter was gone, bam. No more of these wallowing luxury boats, no sirree, let's make them lighter and cheaper and sell twice as many! A good idea in theory, but my God, you just don't stop a production line in its tracks! The money we lost! Porter was absolutely livid. 'I could kill you! You're trying to destroy everything our family stands for.' Yes, I could believe that Porter had shot him."

"The only kid he had left?"

"He's a lunatic. If he can't have it his way, he destroys it. Remember last month the men found a crack in one of the fuel tanks? They could have fixed it, but Porter came after it with a fire axe!"

Dub was apparently still chewing on her previous remark. "Not everybody looks guilty, Liz. Claire couldn't have done it."

"I agree with you there. Claire couldn't see Roger's faults. Claire is the queen of denial. A pretty little windup toy. 'Yes, Porter. No, Porter.' " Liz rolled over to lie on her back. Her silk kimono came open, only the belt spanning her bare waist. "Let's not talk about this anymore."

"You started it."

"I'm sorry I did. Turn off the TV. Please, Dub."

"What about Nikki?" He flipped to another channel. David Letterman was making jokes with the bald guy who led the orchestra. "The wife is the first person the police look at when the husband gets whacked. That's what I've heard."

Liz made a low laugh. "Watch yourself, Duncan." She stretched out, arms over her head. The kimono slid off her breasts. Cool air from the vent made her nipples stand up.

Colors flashed on the ceiling, and the speakers popped every time Dub pressed his thumb on the remote.

He had considered hiring someone to follow his wife, see if she was cheating, but *knowing* would be worse. Which one of the engine salesmen or sunburned lift operators? Who was getting sawdust or machine oil in his wife's panties? Who was looking at Duncan Cresswell and smirking? It was more peaceful not to know. He wasn't even sure he cared.

In five years he had accumulated over two million dollars. He'd never made as much as Porter, so a little creative accounting was his way of evening things out. Roger had started sniffing around, but he hadn't known how to read the books.

Dub considered it his rainy day fund. If one day Liz tried to fuck him over in court, or if he woke up and decided he couldn't stand hearing Spanish or fighting traffic anymore, he could pack a bag, grab his passport, and . . . go. He had the destination picked out. Anguilla, in the French Antilles. He'd been down there fishing last winter. As the boat had headed back to the marina, he'd looked out at the white spume off the stern and thought of Liz. He'd seen her slipping overboard. He'd seen her getting smaller till her head was a black dot. Then nothing.

He took his cigarette out of the ashtray. "I could fire you. Do you realize that, Lizzie? Maybe Roger was right. It would be a lot more peaceful in the office if you weren't around."

"Would you fire me, Dub? Would you?"

She scratched her nails along the waistband of his shorts. What she ought to do, Dub thought, was show him a centerfold photo of his bank statement from Caledonia Bank and Trust, Ltd., on Grand Cayman.

On the television, Jay Leno was talking to an actress with long curly hair, someone he didn't recognize, plugging her new movie, which he'd never heard of. Jay saying, *Let's show a clip, can we?* Dub thumbed the remote. A music video from India, women singing in warbling voices, dancing in a line in flowing saris. He pressed buttons at random. The Nashville Network. HBO. The Weather Channel.

Her hand was moving on him, squeezing, long nails occasionally catching his flesh, but nothing was happening down there. Dub lifted his cigarette to his lips. He wanted to touch the end of it to the sleeve of that silk robe, see what she'd do.

First time he'd seen her she'd been polishing fiberglass with a disk sander. Face mask on for the dust, gloves, long smock, hair all white, nothing showing but those cocoa-brown eyes. Within a year she'd been wearing a short dress and high heels, running a calculator in the sales department. He still didn't know how she'd managed that transformation. She did a boat show with him, and he wound up in the forward stateroom with her head in his lap. Six months later she was pregnant with Patty, and they got married.

She'd picked up the boat business fast, and she'd known how to get the most out of the workers. Any idea she had, she let Dub take the credit, and when the old man died, he'd given Dub a share—only a third, but without Liz, he'd have gotten zip. Now he had half—on paper only. Porter still made the decisions. Dub didn't care. He had his bank account.

"Turn the TV off, Dub."

"In a minute."

She grabbed the remote, jabbed at it, then flung it across the room. It hit the armoire, and the batteries fell out.

Dub stared at the blank screen. "I guess I don't get any tonight."

"Up yours."

"What about you, Lizzie? Why did you want Roger dead?"

"I didn't say that."

"Come on. You started this game."

Her hair was in her eyes, and she swept it back and held it. "Me. Well, why did I want him dead? His ideas weren't bad, but he was such an asshole. Roger never listened to me, and I've been there for twenty-four years! Does that count, Dub? Wanting to kill someone because he ignores you?"

Dub reached into the drawer for his pint of bourbon. "Roger wanted to fire you. He said you were overstepping your authority."

She hooted a laugh. "Let's call it saving the company from bankruptcy."

Liquid flowed into the glass. "Lady of leisure. What would you have done all day? Get yourself a regular massage. Go to ballet parties with Claire. Maybe find a tennis instructor who likes mature, foxy women."

"Maybe just find a man who can get it up."

"Where were you that night, Lizzie?"

"I was here with Sean and Patty, as well you know."

"Couldn't have jumped in the car and run over to Jack's? It would have taken five minutes to get there. Find Roger, plug him a few times. You could've told the kids you were soaking in the tub. Or said you were going over to give the neighbor a blow job. 'Now, don't tell your dad.' 'Okay, Mom.' "

"Stop it, Dub. That isn't fun."

"Sure it is. You can do whatever you want now. Shit, when Porter's gone, you can even be president."

"Let's finish the game. Where were *you* that night, Dub?"

Dub tilted the glass, sliding the last ice cube into his mouth. "With Roger and Porter at the Black Point Marina. We took those Canadian CEOs out for a cruise. I sold two boats, just doing my job. As soon as we landed, Roger split. I don't know where the hell he went."

Liz rolled onto her stomach and slithered up till her mouth was at his ear. "No, Dub. That's what you told the police, but you told *me* that Roger was going over to Jack's. Did you find him? You didn't get home till two in the morning."

"I took the guys out to the Strip Mine. They wanted to see some firm young bodies."

Her breath was hot on his neck. "Nobody would have missed you for an hour. I believe you even have a .22 pistol in your gun locker."

"I had no reason to shoot him, Liz. I had no quarrel with Roger, not like you."

"But you *did*. What better way to get back at Porter? Poor Dub. Always in second place. Porter got an M.B.A., but you didn't finish college. Porter is president of Cresswell Yachts. You're the lowly director of sales."

"So I was jealous and shot his son?"

"More than jealous." She burrowed closer. "Why did you rush all the way up to Aventura to tell Porter and Claire about Roger, when Diane *told* you that the police wanted to inform the family? Why, Dub?"

"Not because I hated him."

"Oh, yes. You wanted to see his reaction. You wanted to deliver the news yourself. 'Oh, boy, I get to tell Porter. I get to see him bleed.' "

"Elizabeth, you are one cold-hearted bitch."

She whispered into his ear. "It's why you married me." She left tooth prints on his ear lobe, then sat up, kimono falling off one shoulder. "It's late. I'm going to take a shower. Set the alarm for six o'clock, will you? I have a meeting with the Detroit Diesel rep at seven-thirty." Her kimono belled out behind her as she crossed the bedroom.

In the shiny curve of the blank TV screen Dub could see a distorted image of Lizzie going into the bathroom. The water went on. The shower door slid shut. A minute later steam started rolling out.

What if she fell? Slipped on some soap and hit her head on that gold-plated tub faucet that cost a thousand bucks for the set. Would she drown? How deep would the water have to be?

Dub closed his eyes and drifted. He thought of his island. A warm-skinned brown woman with breasts ripe as mangos. The breeze in her black hair. A small house painted yellow and turquoise. Water clear as gin, warm as blood.

CHAPTER

7

"Never do favors for *anyone* not on a time sheet." Charlene stood at her desk shuffling through papers. "There is no such thing as a five-minute phone consultation, don't you know that? It's like five-minute sex. They always want another one, and they never respect you for it."

Gail had caught Charlene Marks just as she was preparing to leave for a hearing downtown. Charlene handled divorces for sports figures, entertainers, politicians, or anyone else with enough money to fight over. Before that, she'd been a prosecutor, slamming prison doors on murderers, rapists, and assorted armed thugs. Gail specialized in civil trial practice. Of criminal law, she had a fairly good grasp of where to find the county jail. She assumed that Charlene would be able to supply the guidance needed to field a simple telephone call from Angela Quintana's boyfriend.

"Come on, Charlene. What do I tell him?"

Sliding files into a slim leather portfolio, Charlene looked over her glasses. The silver frames repeated the strands in her salt-and-pepper hair. "You don't *need* five minutes. It takes five seconds. 'Bobby, if the police contact you, tell them to call me. Tell them you are so sorry, but your mean, nasty lawyer has *ordered* you not to say a *word*.' See how easy that is?"

"For him. What do I tell the police?"

"What you *should* do," Charlene said, "is to send this kid to a criminal lawyer. But since you've already promised to give him a quickie— Who's the victim, by the way?"

"Roger Cresswell. It's been in the news. Have you heard about it?"

"Good God. Yes, I have heard about it. I've been particularly interested because about two months ago, Roger Cresswell came to see me. He sat right in that chair. He thought his wife was cheating on him. Then he called a week later and said never mind, so I never minded." Charlene folded her glasses. "They're quite wealthy—his family, I mean. Roger would have inherited everything if someone hadn't pulled his plug. May I ask *you* a question? *What* are you thinking? This isn't just any old murder case. The media are all over it. This kid—Bobby, right?—if there's even a chance he could be arrested, leave it alone. You don't have the experience."

"All right. If it gets sticky, I'll refer it out. You know, Charlene, this isn't just any kid, either. Robert Gonzalez dances for the Miami City Ballet. They have scads of donors and board members with business contacts, and if it gets around that I've done a creditable job with one of their dancers, well . . ."

"Ahhhh. I see. Assuming he's innocent." Charlene lifted a slate gray, raw silk jacket off its hanger behind the door. "Not to throw ants on your picnic, but I was in the system for fifteen years, and believe me, ninety percent of them are guilty as hell."

"But he hasn't even been arrested, much less indicted. If I can show that Bobby couldn't have done it, they'll leave him alone. He'll be happy, the ballet will be happy, and I might pick up a few clients."

"You mean represent him solely for purposes of striking him off the list of suspects. Yes, you could do that, but be prepared to dump him the moment you hear the words 'arrest warrant.' Not to worry. I have a referral list of criminal lawyers." Charlene put the narrow strap of a black Gucci bag over her shoulder. "Follow me out, we'll talk."

Charlene's skirts were hemmed several inches above her knees, and the slit in the back revealed an incredible pair of legs. Even with her mane of gray hair, men thirty years younger would stare. She waved goodbye to the receptionist, and pushed through the heavy paneled door.

"Okay, here's what you do. Debrief him on everything he did for several hours either side of when Roger Cresswell was last seen, and when they found his body. Where was your client during all this time? Who saw him? Witnesses, witnesses. And have him tell you what he knows about Roger Cresswell to sniff out a reason somebody else might have whacked him—but a gold Rolex is motive enough."

"So is getting rid of your husband before he can file for divorce." At the elevators Gail pressed the down arrow. "You wouldn't mind sharing your notes, would you? The prospective divorce client is now dead."

"What a waste. He was so blond and buff, with pretty blue eyes. He gave me distinctly unmaternal urges. I'm such a bad girl. What was his wife's name? Something silly. Nikki, that's it. He paid for her breast implants, and she was nagging for lipo on her butt."

The doors opened and the women went inside, facing their own images in bronze-tinted mirrors. Light jazz played on hidden speakers.

Charlene leaned closer to the mirror to check her makeup, pinching a piece of mascara off her lashes. "Ask Bobby what he told the cops. Defendants always run off at the mouth. They just have to explain themselves. That tendency was of great help to me as a prosecutor, but it can screw up the defense. How's my hair?"

"Fine."

At the lobby the doors slid open, and Charlene put a foot across the track. "I'll be back from court by eleven-thirty. We'll leave at noon. Are you okay? Did you bring everything you need? You're still spending the night at my place, aren't you?"

"Got my toothbrush and jammies," Gail said.

"Good. We'll bring home some takeout and a bottle of Dom Perignon and get smashed. Tomorrow's Saturday; you can sleep as late as you want." Charlene smiled and gently squeezed Gail's hand. "It's going to be all right."

*   *   *

Sitting at her desk, Gail worked through the correspondence and pleadings and assorted junk that seemed to sprout like weeds on her desk every night. She typed notes into her computer, pausing every now and then to nibble a soda cracker. The nausea was easing, but mornings were still iffy.

Calls came in during the morning but none from Robert Gonzalez. By 11:15, Gail had given up on him. Then Miriam buzzed her that he had arrived.

"He's here? As in, standing on the other side of my door?" She looked at her watch and quietly cursed.

Miriam brought him in. Bobby Gonzalez did not walk—he moved in a combination of lope and glide. A baggy green T-shirt hung from square shoulders. He wore loose cargo shorts, and the muscles in his legs were so sharply defined they looked chiseled.

"I know I was supposed to call, but I wanted to meet you, so I took the bus—my car's got a radiator leak—and you have to make like two transfers, then get on the Metrorail, and by the time I got to the Dadeland Station I said, well, I'm here now, no point calling." He sounded as if he'd just stepped off the subway from the Bronx.

Gail gestured toward a chair. "Yes. Well, we have a little time. I'm sorry, but I absolutely must leave at noon."

"No problem. I can't stay too long, either." He dropped his backpack on the floor and set a Yankees ball cap on top of it. Black curls fell onto his forehead. "It's very nice of you to talk to me, Ms. Connor." Thick eyebrows arched, and his wide mouth hovered in the smile of a person who wasn't quite sure what to expect. He sat forward, then back, then on the edge of his chair, glancing around the room, taking in the plants on the windowsill, the maple wood furniture, the certificates and licenses on the wall.

Gail said, "I enjoyed you last night in *Tarantella*."

"Yeah? Thanks. I'm hoping to do it in the season, if they make me a soloist. It's a gut-buster. That's what Edward calls it."

"Edward . . ."

"Edward Villella. He's the director. He *started* the Miami City Ballet."

"Of course. He's from New York."

"Right, so am I. East Harlem. He's Italian, from Queens. I'm the same height as him, and we have the same body type. What I really want"—Bobby knocked his knuckles on the arm of the chair—"is to dance *Rubies* someday. It was choreographed for Edward by Balanchine. You know who *he* is, right?"

"Of course. Well, I should come see you. When does the season start?"

"Our first performance is in late October. Hey, anytime you want tickets, you let me know. I'll get you some house seats."

Gail caught sight of her clock on a shelf across the room. "I suppose we ought to talk about why you're here."

"No problem." Bobby sat on the edge of the chair, clearing his throat, bouncing his knees.

"Angie told me that the police have been asking you questions about the Cresswell murder, and you prefer not to talk to them. You don't have to. If they have questions, you can refer them to a lawyer. To me, if you wish, but you should know that I'm not an expert in criminal law. My specialty is commercial litigation— trial work for business cases, personal injury, things like that."

"But you're a regular lawyer, right?"

She smiled. "Yes."

"Ms. Connor, I really appreciate this, your time and everything, but I don't expect you to do this for nothing. I brought some cash with me."

"No, keep your money for now, and let's just see what we've got. And remember, whatever you tell me stays here. We take an oath of confidentiality."

He nodded. "Sure."

"First, a little personal information." She took down his full name, his address, his telephone number. Date of birth. Contact number at the Miami City Ballet.

Bobby sat forward, an arm on her desk. "What I'm worried about is, they might arrest me, even if I didn't do anything. It happens. They put people in jail because they want to say they solved the crime, and then you have to prove you didn't do it. If that happens, I can't make bail. My family doesn't have the money, and I don't think the ballet would pay it."

For a few moments Gail looked for words to correct this amazing ignorance. Did he truly believe what he'd said? Police throwing citizens in jail on no evidence solely to clear a case, then making them prove their innocence? But Bobby had stumbled on one truth: Whoever was arrested for this crime would be staying in jail. There was no bond in capital murder.

Gail said, "Why do you think they're after *you*, in particular?"

He made a quick shrug. "Because they keep coming back." His thick-lashed, puppy-brown eyes seemed completely guileless.

"Well, that certainly explains things." A few crackers were left on the napkin by the telephone, and Gail broke one in half and ate it. "Oh, I'm sorry, would you like one of these?"

"No, thanks."

"Lunch." She took a sip of soda. "Let's talk about Roger Cresswell. He was shot to death last Saturday night at a house near Old Cutler Road—"

"Outside, in the backyard," Bobby corrected. "The owner is Jack Pascoe. Jack is Roger's cousin. He hired me to help him out at the party, and Roger showed up, then they found his body the next morning, back in the trees."

"How well did you know Roger Cresswell?" She broke another cracker and brushed away the crumbs.

"Not real well. I'm friends with his cousin, Sean. Sean's sister, Diane, is in the ballet. Sean got me a job at Cresswell Yachts for a few weeks this summer, and I'd see Roger around. Their families own the company, but I think Roger was running it since his father got sick. They put me in the glass shop—that's where you make the boat hulls out of fiberglass. Roger fired me after the security guard found a disc sander in my locker, but I didn't put it there. I think Roger did. They keep spare keys in the office."

"Why would he do that?"

"Because I wouldn't kiss his butt. If he was wrong, I said so. Nobody liked him." Bobby shrugged. "I was about to quit anyway. It was only temporary, to make some money till rehearsals started."

"When did he fire you?"

"Last week, on Thursday."

"Two days before he was killed?"

"That looks bad, right?"

"Do the police know about it?"

"Probably, if they talked to anyone at Cresswell. I didn't tell them. They came to my apartment, and I told them what I knew, trying to be cooperative, but then they came back with more questions, and I didn't want to say anything else." Bobby leaned over to unzip a pocket in his backpack. "One of the detectives gave me his card."

He laid it on Gail's desk. SGT. FRANK BRITTON, HOMICIDE BUREAU, MIAMI-DADE POLICE DEPARTMENT. "Well, look at this." In explanation, she waved a hand and said, "We've met in the past. What did Sergeant Britton ask you?"

"Did I know Roger, did I know who might've wanted him dead, could I account for every minute at the party? I can, but they don't believe me. I got to Jack's at eight o'clock, and I was in the house—you can ask anybody—from eight to eleven, and at eleven I went down by the seawall to have a beer, and I was talking to this guy named Alan. Then Sean beeped me at eleven-forty, and I walked back to the house and called him, and he said to meet him on South Beach. So I left Jack's at a quarter to twelve and met Sean at twelve-thirty at my place. It's twenty-eight miles, and you'd have to drive like a maniac to get there in less than forty-five minutes. We went to Club Amsterdam, and I got home at three o'clock and went to bed. My roommates saw me."

"Sounds like you're covered."

"Except the cops say there wasn't an Alan. They say Jack never heard of him, which is weird because Alan knows Jack. I called Jack and he doesn't know what I'm talking about. What a lie. I *saw* him in the living room looking through Jack's old record collection."

Gail reached for another cracker. "Someone else must have seen him—unless he was a ghost. When you and he walked to the seawall, no one saw you together?"

"I don't think so. There was this black drag queen from Brazil with a red wig on, and she was showing people how to do the samba." Bobby laughed. "I said to myself, man, I'm outta here before she grabs *me*, so that's when I left. It's about fifty yards to the water, but you can't see it through all the trees and bushes, then it clears out. The moon was straight up, just about full. So I sit down with my feet hanging off the edge, and about a minute later—not even—I hear somebody say, 'Oh, hello!,' like he didn't know I was there."

"Are you saying he followed you?"

Bobby's foot was on his knee, and he flexed it one way, then the other. Under the fuzz of dark hair, muscles bunched and released. "I think so."

"He's gay?"

"He was pretty drunk, I know that. He said he used to be married, but I've had married guys hit on me. You can't always tell. It doesn't bother me, unless they push it. Alan stood kind of far away at first, like, oh, I'm not really here, we're not having this conversation. But he was cool. I think he'd back me up, if you could find him."

"Tell me what he looks like."

"Uhhh . . . bushy gray hair. Round glasses. About five-ten, kind of skinny."

"How does he know Jack?"

"He didn't say."

"What did you and he talk about?"

"Jeez." Bobby let out a breath. "I remember he said he was getting away from the music, which was pretty loud. I said, yeah, me too. He went to school in Chicago, and he said how much weed they used to smoke back then. Pot. That's what he called it. And . . . oh. He said his wife was an artist, but she passed away. Then he starts talking about the meaning of life and death and all that. He recited this poem about athletes dying young, then he cracks up laughing. Hey, maybe he's a professor. That could be. Jack knows some professors at UM."

Gail twirled her pen by the ends, then lifted her eyes. "That beer you were drinking—"

He looked back at her. "Yeah?"

"You sure it wasn't a joint? I don't care, but I'd like to know."

He made a guilty smile. "Somebody gave it to me. A friend of Jack's. But I wasn't, like, hammered. I remember everything."

"You shared it with Alan?"

"He took a few hits. He said he doesn't do it anymore. I don't either, but this guy gave it to me, and—"

"It's okay. Is there anything else? Really, you have to be up front with me."

"No. That's it." Bobby cleared his throat again—only a nervous gesture, Gail thought. Bobby Gonzalez seemed as healthy as a young stallion. What else was he holding back? Gail had interviewed enough clients to know that they routinely skipped over awkward details. Not a lie, exactly. They simply wanted the attorney to like them, not even aware, sometimes, of this filtering process.

"All right. Did you and Alan go back up to the house at the same time? Maybe someone saw you then."

"No. Sean beeped me and I said I had to make a phone call. Alan just, like, rolled back into the grass and looked up at the sky and said good night, take care of yourself, young man. That was it. I didn't see him again."

"And would Sean confirm that you called him at a certain time?"

"Definitely."

Gail tapped her pen on her notes. "Tell you what. You sit right there for a few minutes and write down names of people at the party, as far as you can recall them. Write down everything you said to the police. And everything you know about Roger Cresswell. Put that down too."

"I'm not a great speller."

She tore her pages off the pad. "That doesn't matter in the least. If you need anything, ask Miriam. I'll be right back."

In her office a few floors above Gail's, Charlene Marks sat at her desk with minestrone soup from the deli downstairs, delicately eating, avoiding drips on her skirt. "Did I not tell you so?"

"Charlene, Bobby's in the clear. He has an alibi for every moment. He arrived before Roger Cresswell, he was busy in the house, and when he wasn't, he was with this man Alan."

"Who either doesn't exist or doesn't want to be found. A man, possibly a university professor, probably in the closet, who was smoking dope with a twenty-one-year-old ballet dancer at a wild—very wild—party." Charlene tapped her watch with a perfectly manicured nail. "It's eleven-thirty. Just a reminder."

"Yes, all right." Gail stole a piece of her bread. "You know more about the Cresswells than I do. You've talked to Roger. You've been following this case in the news."

"I don't know who Alan is, and don't even try to get the guest list from the police. They won't give you *bupkis* in an open investigation."

"Alan said his wife was an artist, and she died. Wasn't there something in the paper about Roger Cresswell's sister? She was an artist, and she committed suicide?"

"Yes. She overdosed on pills. You're correct, it was in the paper. 'Tragedy again strikes Cresswell family.' You think Alan was married to Roger's sister."

"It would explain how he knows Jack. What was her name, Charlene? I need the last name. If she used his, we've found him."

"What was it?" Charlene lowered her plastic spoon. "An artist. Cresswell. Something Cresswell." Rolling her chair back, Charlene stood up and looked around her office. "Wait a minute. Wait a minute." She strode across the thick carpet to one of the bookcases and ran her finger along a line of magazine boxes. She tilted one out.

"It's funny what sticks in your mind, isn't it? I spoke at a seminar a few years ago on battered spouses, and there was a judge who did a section on restraining orders. He wrote an article about it for the *Florida Bar Journal*." Charlene sat in an armchair and flipped open one magazine after another, dropping the discards in a disorderly pile. "His wife had recently committed suicide, and by way of condolence, I suppose, I mentioned that I'd seen her obituary in the *New York Times*. She'd been an artist, apparently quite well known. Where in hell—? Ah!"

She flipped pages as she walked back across the room. Folding the magazine open, she thrust it in front of Gail, who saw a page of text and a small, black-and-white photograph of a man in his forties with graying hair and tortoiseshell glasses. The caption read, NATHAN A. HARRIS, JUDGE, ELEVENTH JUDICIAL CIRCUIT.

"He transferred into the criminal division after I'd left, that's why I didn't immediately hear bells going off." Charlene tapped the photo. "You do notice the middle initial, don't you?"

"A is for Alan. I've met him, Charlene. He was at a cocktail party that Anthony's office threw last Christmas. He was on our invitation list for the wedding! Anthony said his wife was deceased. Oh, my God. A judge. He's going to be just *thrilled* to talk to me."

"It gets worse." Charlene's brows rose. "Nate Harris is on the short list of candidates for federal district court."

"You lie."

"Don't you keep up with anything? Tricky, tricky. Cause problems for a judge, he will never forgive you, and his friends in the civil division, before whom you appear, will never forgive you either."

"What do I do now?"

"Oh, it's simple." Charlene laughed. "Send Bobby to some other lawyer."

Bobby Gonzalez studied the photograph, then looked up, open-mouthed, at Gail. "Where'd you get this?"

Gail had cut out the photo—minus the name—and taped it to a plain piece of paper. "Never mind that now. Are you sure it's him?"

"I'm positively sure."

"How are we coming with those notes?" Scratchy handwriting filled two pages, and continued onto a third.

"Fine, but I need to go pretty soon. I have rehearsal, and it's a long way back to the beach."

A hand on his shoulder, Gail said, "I'll be right back. Maybe I can drive you." Leaving Bobby in her office, she went around the corner to her secretary's desk. Miriam had gone to lunch, and her size-two sweater hung on the back of her chair.

Gail sat down and picked up the telephone, dialing a number from memory. When the receptionist answered, Gail told her that an emergency with a client had arisen. "I'm so sorry, but I can't possibly come in this afternoon. . . . Yes, I realize that, but there's nothing I can do. Please tell the doctor I'm sorry. . . . Well, could I come in early next week?"

The voice reminded her that if she rescheduled to next week, the procedure would cost more.

"Yes, I understand. That's no problem."

Did she really want to do it? Was she having second thoughts?

"No, it's just not convenient *today*. Could you hold on a minute?"

Quickly Gail flipped pages in the desk diary, seeing what was on the schedule for next week. Something would have to be shifted. "God, what a mess. I'm going to have to call you back later."

She hung up and sat for a minute with her fingers pressed against her lips. Her breath had stopped, and a tremor had worked its way to her knees. She stared at a box of pastel paper clips. A pencil jar Miriam had decorated with lace. The heart-shaped photo frame with her husband's picture in one side, their toddler, Berto, in the other. A little stuffed teddy bear to Miriam from Danny held up a rose. *I love you.*

Karen would be home on Saturday, flying in with Dave on a flight from Puerto Rico. By then everything would be fine. Back to normal. As if this had never happened.

Gail picked up the phone and called Charlene. Her secretary said Charlene was on another call, but hold on—

"No, don't disturb her. Just say . . . my appointment's been rescheduled. I'll call her later."

Gail drove Bobby Gonzalez to the ballet's rehearsal hall on South Beach, and he asked if she'd like to watch. He put a folding metal chair in the corner of the large, high-ceilinged room. The wood floor gleamed, and one wall was mirrored. A TV and VCR were pushed to one side among the portable barres the dancers had used for their warmup. Sunlight poured through big uncurtained windows. A few pedestrians walked by, some pausing to look in.

The accompanist was playing runs of bright notes. He stopped when the ballet mistress clapped her hands. She explained a combination of steps by walking through them, then called for one of the women to demonstrate. The dancers tried it. She nodded, then told them to find their positions for partnering work. The accompanist turned a page in the sheet music and brought his hands down on the keys.

Four men moved in a diagonal line across the floor, the women coming toward them from the opposite side. The lines shifted, split apart, and dancers broke into pairs. Their eyes were glued to the mirror. With no audience to play to, faces frowned in concentration. Lips moved, counting beats.

The dancers' clothes were rag-tag and worn. The ballerinas were thin, long-legged creatures. Their toe shoes were frayed and stained, and one girl had a rip in the side of her leotard. Nothing matched. The men wore tights or knee-length gym shorts, and soft, faded T-shirts, a few with gaping holes. Their bodies were gorgeous, Gail decided. Powerful arms and legs. And fabulous backsides. It was hard not to stare.

Gail found herself smiling. They were all wonderful, but she felt a keen pleasure in watching Bobby. He was just as good, she thought, as the most accomplished male dancer in this group, who must have had ten years' more experience.

Leaving her building, Gail had offered to buy him lunch, but he'd wanted only a Diet Coke at a drive-through to go with the granola bar he'd brought in his backpack. In traffic, the drive to the Beach had taken forty minutes, and Bobby had talked about how he got into ballet. At the studio he introduced Gail to one of his former teachers, a woman about fifty whose career as a principal dancer with the San Francisco Ballet had ended with a hip replacement. While Bobby and the others did their warmup at the barre, the teacher came over to where Gail sat and unfolded another chair. Bobby had confided in this woman, and she knew who Gail was.

Robert Gonzalez was the fourth of five children. His parents had rented a fourth-floor walkup in East Harlem. Gloria had worked in a hardware store on Second Avenue, and Willy had taken the 6 train downtown before dawn every morning to work as a street cleaner. Bobby had gone to Central Park East Elementary.

Bobby had never considered dancing a particularly feminine art. His father and uncles danced the *merengue* or mambo right in the small living room, and every weekend they put on silky, open-necked shirts and gold jewelry and took their wives to a ballroom on West Fifty-eighth. A man who can dance, his father said, will always have women. One floor below lived a man with the Dance Theater of Harlem—a very beautiful black man with elongated muscles, who had seemed eight feet tall to the boy. He had laughed when Bobby imitated his movements, and lifted him high in the air.

Not a perfect childhood. They were poor. Gloria explained away her bruises as a fall on the stairs. When they had to take food stamps, she wept. Bobby's oldest sister became pregnant at fourteen. Bobby shared a mattress on the floor with his brother, and in the winter they slept in their coats.

A man by the name of Eliot Feld, a former dancer and choreographer for the American Ballet Theater, offered tryouts in elementary schools. He wanted to pull out the ones with potential and give them a chance at his ballet school. One afternoon, with nothing better to do, Bobby tagged along with one of his sisters. The next week Feld himself showed up, ignoring the sister and calling Bobby aside. What had they seen in this child? His energy, his speed, his body type—long supple limbs, a certain proportion of torso to leg.

At ten years of age, Bobby Gonzalez started formal training in ballet. His bones were still soft enough. A dancer who starts too late will not develop turnout. The foot must arch properly, the hip sockets must be mobile enough to allow for the outward rotation of knees and thighs. Without this, he might become a modern dancer, but he would never succeed in classical ballet. At twelve Bobby went to Harbor Junior High for the Performing Arts, where he was known as a show-off. The girls fought to dance with him. At thirteen he was the young prince in a local dance school's production of *The Nutcracker*.

In January of that year, Willy Gonzalez was fired from his job. He came home drunk, and when Gloria yelled at him, he broke her jaw. Willy spent a few weeks in jail, then left for San Juan. Gloria's brother in Miami offered to take them in, and they moved to his old two-story stucco house in a largely Puerto Rican section of the city. Gloria promised Bobby he could continue his lessons, but he knew it was hopeless. There was no money, even if there had been a ballet school in that neighborhood.

The first time Bobby mentioned ballet on his street, the other boys laughed, and the biggest attacked him. Bobby scarred his knuckles on the boy's teeth, but never talked about dancing again. He threw away his practice clothes. He acquired tattoos, a swagger, and a string of arrests. The police had his photo on file at the station.

At fifteen, on the point of being sent to the alternative school for delinquents, Bobby was herded with the rest of his homeroom into the auditorium at Edison High. The Miami City Ballet was giving a demonstration of classical dance—girls in tutus, men in slippers and tights. Some of the kids in the audience slept. Boys snickered. Girls whispered to friends and passed notes. What must Bobby have thought, sitting in the dark auditorium, eyes fixed on the stage? One of the male dancers took a microphone and talked about the ballet school. There would be tryouts for scholarships in a month. When the students clattered out of the auditorium, had Bobby lingered behind? Had he gone outside to watch the dancers leave through the stage door, get into their cars, and drive away?

He let a week go by, in which he hardly slept. One night, telling no one, not even his mother, he took a bus to Miami Beach. He looked through the windows of the old studios on Lincoln Road, seeing a rehearsal of what he knew was the *pas de deux* from the last act of *The Nutcracker*. When it was over he walked to the beach a few blocks away. It was cold that night, and a wind blew off the ocean. He stood on the firm part of the sand and stripped to his boxers. And danced. If anyone saw, he didn't care.

Two years away from ballet, how hard had it been? His legs must have ached. How tender were his feet? He wouldn't have practiced where anyone could see. He'd have waited till late at night and gone behind the house, or he'd have sneaked into an empty building.

He showed up at the school three weeks later to try out for one of two places open, and borrowed a pair of slippers from a box of discards in the dressing room. The teacher who talked to Gail had been there that day.

She said, "There were twenty boys trying out. Some had been dancing steadily for years, and they were all good. Bobby fell a couple of times simply because he was trying so hard. He had such a raw edge. So tough. It was quite compelling, really. We all started watching him. Here was this boy we'd never seen before, with a tattoo and a horrible haircut, but with this perfect body, perfect proportions. Very strong, very quick. Other boys in the group had more finesse, more training, but Bobby . . . when it's there, you *know*. Someone must have called Eddie, because he came downstairs to see."

Laughing softly, the teacher leaned closer to Gail. "When Bobby was trying out, he was so serious. At the first class, after he'd been accepted in the school, he couldn't stop smiling. There was a discoloration on his front tooth, and I asked him, what is that? You should get that fixed. The next day, that one tooth was so white, and I said, Bobby, come here, let me see. He'd painted it with Liquid Paper because he didn't have money for a dentist. Well, we have a dentist on the board of directors, and he fixed it. But that's Bobby. He makes do—sometimes to his own detriment. He doesn't eat well. I feed him sometimes. He doesn't get enough rest because he's always working. His mother has some kind of disability, and his sister is on her second or third baby, and the younger ones are always after him for things. The men in the family think he ought to get a real job, and Bobby has that to contend with. We pay better than most regional companies, but it's still hard. He makes a little extra money teaching in the outreach program. The students like working with him, I suppose because he speaks their language. He's lucky he came to Miami. It's hard to get noticed in New York, even when you have a great deal of talent, as Bobby does. The top of the pyramid is so tiny. So few of them make it."

For a while she watched the dancers, then said, "Bobby's going to have a good career, if he can survive long enough."

In the corridor behind them Gail heard voices and the thumps of heavy shoes and dance bags hitting the floor. The teacher glanced at her watch, then excused herself. Time to start class.

She paused with a hand on Gail's shoulder. "Take care of him, will you?"

CHAPTER

8

Through the glass wall of his office, Jack saw Nikki come into the gallery. Her black linen dress showed a good bit of bare leg, but the color was right for a widow. Likewise the dark glasses. Then she pushed them into her wavy red hair, spoiling the effect.

This was Tuesday, and Jack hadn't seen her since the funeral last week. He hadn't phoned. He hadn't wanted to hear that breathy little voice: *Hi. What's up?*

Jack turned to Diane, who had not noticed his lapse of attention. She was still studying the portrait of herself, which he had propped on a shelf. A young girl in tutu and pointe shoes waited to go onstage. Her pubescent body shone in blue light against the enveloping blackness of backdrop and curtain. Her face repeated the curves of Diane's face, the small mouth, and upturned nose, and they both had cornsilk hair.

Staring at this painting, Jack wondered what in hell he should do. He had bought it from Roger Cresswell, then had sold it to Nathan Harris as a gift for Claire and Porter. Then Porter, outrageously ungrateful, had given it to Dub and Elizabeth. Diane had taken it—rescued it—from her Philistine parents, and here it was again. Diane wanted to sell it. It made his head spin. Jack supposed he should start by sending Nate's down payment back.

"I could find a buyer," Jack said, "but without proof you own it, you'll take a hell of a discount."

"How much do you think I could get for it?"

Jack wound one end of his mustache around his finger and contemplated the shadow market for art, which he preferred to stay out of. "Ten thousand, no questions asked. As much as fifty to a serious collector of Margaret Cresswells."

Diane's voice became wistful. "I'd like to keep it, but I need to live closer to the ballet. It would be so great to have a condo where I could see the ocean."

"You will," Jack said. "It's time you had your own place."

"I'd miss you and Buddy. I'd miss the cottage. I love it there."

"It's always yours to come back to." He smiled at her. "My advice is, talk to your parents. Grovel if you have to. Maybe your mother is simply trying to show you who's boss."

"She doesn't even like it! I heard her tell Dad it's dark and depressing. She just wants it to show off to her friends. She says if I don't bring it back, she'll call the police. Why does she hate me so much? What have I done that's so terrible?"

"Nothing, *ma petite*. She's jealous. You're Princess Aurora."

Diane reached out to slide her fingers along the edge of the frame. "I remember one day Maggie was visiting from . . . oh, God, wherever she was living then, and she wanted to see me dance. I took her to a dress rehearsal, and this is what I was wearing that day, a white tutu. She got it so perfect, even the pearls. I never knew how good she was." Diane made a little cry. "Jack! How could I even think of selling this? She meant me to have it. I know she did."

"Tell you what. You work on ownership. Maybe you should ask a lawyer for some legal advice. Meanwhile, I'll take some photos in case you change your mind." He took his camera out of a drawer. If Dub and Liz loosened their tentacles on this portrait, Jack would send slides to potential buyers and scan a print for his website. "You can always say no," he added.

Shifting out of the way, Diane glanced into the gallery. "Guess who's here."

"I saw her come in."

Diane's voice dropped to a whisper. "You're crazy for being with her, Jack."

"It's over, pumpkin." He focused and pressed the shutter.

"Thank God." Diane turned her back on the door. "The police talked to me again. They think you and I are lovers."

"And you told them—"

"I said that's ridiculous, we were just staying up late talking, and I wouldn't lie for you anyway."

"Good girl." Jack came in closer on the portrait and took one more. "Let me take this home, all right? You don't want to leave it in your car."

"Thanks. Listen, do you have a friend named Alan? Last week Bobby said he'd met someone named Alan at your party, but he didn't know his last name."

"Alan? I haven't the foggiest. Bobby must have gotten it wrong. Or maybe this guy came to the party and I didn't see him."

"Maybe so. Don't say I asked you, okay? Bobby got a lawyer, and he's not supposed to be talking about the case." Diane picked up her bag. "I'd better get to rehearsal." She kissed him on the cheek and tugged at his mustache. "Love you."

"Love you too, kid."

She walked, in her graceful, splay-footed way, out of his office. Her baggy jeans hung over thick-soled sneakers. When she passed Nikki, the two women glanced at each other but neither spoke.

Nikki held onto the door, swinging around, leaning in. "Hi. What's up?"

"You tell me." Jack hit the button on the camera to rewind the film.

"Well. Mr. Friendly. Why was Diane here?"

"No reason. Passing through town, paying her respects."

Nikki glanced through the door to make sure Jack's assistant was out of earshot. "Is she still okay with . . . everything?"

"She's fine. I told you not to worry."

"I can't help it." Nikki's glossy pink lips parted. The two front teeth were slightly longer than the others, and when Jack had first met her, he'd thought of a rabbit. Fluffy hair, white bunny-teeth— and a centerfold body.

Jack put his camera away. "How's your friend in West Palm holding up?"

"Oh, she's been great. We're used to covering for each other."

"She cheats on her husband too?"

"Ha-ha." Nikki had a habit of moistening her lips. "I left three messages. Why didn't you call me?"

"Perhaps I am wrong," he said, "but a period of grief for a widow is usually customary."

"Jack, I have to talk to you. Don't worry, I'll keep my hands to myself."

Letting out a breath, Jack walked past her into the gallery. He told his assistant to come back in half an hour. He locked the door and turned over the CLOSED sign, resetting the hands on the little clock. Through the windows he could see the surf shop and a Cozzoli's Pizza. There had never been more than one or two serious galleries in Coconut Grove, and they had departed years ago.

Nikki's narrow black heels tapped on the slate floor, and a tasseled purse bounced at her hip. "Wow. Every time I come in here, you've got new things. It looks nice."

A remark like that made Jack's jaw clench. Had she been sincere or sarcastic? He preferred sarcasm. Sincerity meant that Nikki was too stupid to see that the pieces in this gallery were, for the most part, crap.

He sold uninspired abstracts one might find at an outdoor art show, assembly-line watercolors of beaches and tropical fruit, prints of Key West cottages with a cat on the porch. Buy any of these, another would appear from the storeroom. He carried the usual cartoonish Romero Britto pieces so beloved by tourists. There were oil paintings of pears that resembled freckled yellow butts, and the obligatory thatch-hut-and-palm-tree landscapes for the Cubans. In the office was a third-rate Picasso that somebody, sooner or later, would purchase to say they had a Picasso.

Until a year or so ago, Jack had owned a gallery in Coral Gables, where he'd shown high-quality pieces acquired from private collectors. He'd been a consultant for banks and corporations. He'd done appraisals for the Miami Art Museum. Clients had sent him to New York for auctions. Purchasers of yachts from the Cresswell boat yard had turned to Jack Pascoe for help in choosing the perfect DeKooning or Kline for the stateroom. And then disaster.

At Aunt Claire's last birthday party, Roger got stinking drunk. She scolded her son and compared him to Jack, his older, more sensible cousin. When Jack left the party, Roger was waiting for him in the parking lot. He'd accused him of sucking up to his parents, of using them to find clients, of drooling over their money. Jack had pushed him into a hedge and kept walking. Still drunk, Roger had lurched after him. *You're dead, Jack-O.* Jack-O had told him to go fuck himself.

The disaster began shortly thereafter. How had Roger done it? He'd known Jack's clients because Jack had talked too much. It would have been easy—a few words to a certain society figure. A hint dropped to the president of this or that bank. One client withdrew her collection of Bonnard lithographs. Then a curator for a Texas museum, looking for a choice Wifredo Lam, had told him they'd decided to buy it elsewhere. A friend told Jack he'd heard rumors of bad-faith dealing, of fraud, of kickbacks from major galleries in New York and Chicago. Jack lost his corporate clients. Within three months his phone stopped ringing, and no one would take his calls.

Jack's reputation was trashed, and without proof of Roger's perfidy, there had not been one damned thing Jack could do except keep smiling, bide his time, and wait for the right moment.

The infuriating thing was, Jack had made money here, across the street from a pizza parlor, next door to a T-shirt shop. He'd made lots of money, more than in Coral Gables. And with each fat bank deposit, his stomach churned.

Nailing Roger's fluffy little snookums had helped, but not much.

She had walked into an area near the front of the gallery where pieces of any value were displayed. Smash-proof plate glass windows extended from floor to ceiling. The portrait of Diane had hung there for several weeks. People would stop on the sidewalk and gaze at it, forgetting to lick their ice cream cones. Mothers would pause with children tugging on their hands. The luminous beauty of that painting had even caught the attention of mouth-breathing college students heading for happy hour at the Irish pub.

That particular spot on the wall was empty now, and Nikki asked, "Why do you have the picture of the ballerina in your office?"

Jack spread his hands palms up. "Why not?"

"Do you have a buyer?"

Seeing no reason to explain the portrait's circuitous journey during the last two weeks, Jack simply said, "No."

Nikki laughed softly and bounced her little purse on her knees. "Don't take this the wrong way, Jack, but I'd really like to move it to some other gallery. One that's a little more . . . high class?"

"What?"

"Well, it's been here a long time, and you haven't sold it, and I need the money."

Jack squinted at her. "What are you talking about?"

"You were selling it for Roger, and I need the money, Jack. I just came from the probate lawyer, and I'm broke. Roger let his life insurance lapse, he took out loans on his stocks, and there's hardly anything left in the bank! Oh, sure, there's his interest in Cresswell Yachts, but it's going to take *forever* to sell."

"Ahh." Comprehension. Jack patted her shoulder. "Nikki, I am sorry. Honest to goodness I am. The painting wasn't here on consignment. I bought it."

Nikki blinked. "How much?"

"Ten thousand. Cash." He added, "Since it was a cash transaction, we . . . dispensed with a contract and sales receipts. Although I do have a bill of sale, proving my ownership. Well, actually, I sold it to someone else. Never mind. The point is, Roger sold it to me about two months ago."

A year or so after Margaret Cresswell's suicide, Porter and Claire had given the portrait to their son, Roger, who had promptly reframed it in hideous black metal and hung it over his pool table. A couple of months ago, Roger had needed some quick cash. His profligate lifestyle had caught up with him. Jack had offered ten grand for the portrait. He had sworn to sell it back if Roger ever came up with the money. And then Nate Harris had wanted a little something as a thank-you present. Jack had let the painting go for under half its value for the delicious pleasure of imagining the result, next time Roger paid a visit to his parents' house. But his parents had given it away, and Roger was dead.

Nikki's purse was still bouncing on her knees. "If you sold the painting, what's it doing in your office?"

"Well, it's for sale again. Perhaps."

"How much did you sell it for the first time?"

Jack could tell where this was going. "Nikki, my transactions are confidential."

"I bet you made a profit, though, didn't you?" Her eyes had narrowed. "A big one. That painting had a price tag of seventy-five thousand dollars."

"A *suggested* price, Nikki. I sold it for quite a bit less. Hardly anything."

"What if we split the profits? How about that?"

"Sorry."

"Jack, if I don't get some money soon, I could lose the house!"

Half expecting her to break into tears, he said, "You have a job."

"Freelancing for an ad agency? I can't live on that! This is totally unfair."

"It's not my fault. Blame Roger. He sold it."

"Because you cheated him, that's why."

"He was a big boy."

"I ought to sue you, Jack! Roger was right, you're nothing but a cheat and a liar." Her voice became shrill, and her flame-red hair seemed to sizzle.

Anger set Jack's teeth together. "Go ahead. Sue me. The police might find out about your lapse of marital fidelity."

"So we had an affair. So?"

"Let's be precise. You were going down on me the same night someone was pumping bullets into your husband."

"You're disgusting! It was *your* idea to lie to the police, not mine. You even got Diane involved. Here's something to tell them. The night Roger was killed, I called you at ten-thirty. Nobody could find you. Where were *you*, Jack? With Roger? Explain that to the cops. So don't threaten *me*." Nikki whirled around and walked through his office door. "It's *mine*, and I'm taking it with me!" She reached onto the shelf and grabbed the frame with both hands.

"Stop that!" Jack rushed for her wrists. "Let go! I will break your fucking arms."

"It's *mine*!" Her lips drew back, exposing her rabbity incisors. She stamped a heel on his instep, and he howled. He caught her in the gallery and dragged her around the corner, out of view of the street and into a grouping of knock-off Boteros—fat men in fedoras, fat-thighed women in flowered dresses.

He held her with one arm and ripped the portrait away. It clattered to the floor, landing facedown. Jack breathed into her ear. "Oh, yes, Nikki, call the police. Tell them where *you* were that night. When you knocked on my door at eleven, was he already dead? I think you lured him to my house, you shot him, and then you suckered me into giving you an alibi."

"Oh, brilliant!" Nikki was laughing so hard she bent double. "Oh, my God. I shot Roger?" She twisted around, breaking into giggles. "That would have been dumb. Roger had nothing but debts!"

"You didn't know that till an hour ago, did you?" Arms spread, Jack stood between her and the portrait on the floor behind him. "Did you do it yourself or hire somebody?"

Her laughter had stopped, and she drew herself up, raising her chin. "You know what? This may be really hard for you to understand, but I cared for Roger."

"Sure you did."

"Okay, we had some problems, but I *cared*! I didn't know that till it was too late. When the police told me, I cried."

"Give this girl an Oscar."

"I *cried* and it was *real*! Roger loved me. Not like you." With the heel of one hand she wiped the tears off her cheek. "You only wanted to fuck me to get back at him." Nikki picked up her purse from the floor and put on her sunglasses. "You're a real shit, Jack."

She ran to the door, turned the lock, and was gone. The little sign swung back and forth.

CHAPTER

9

Theodore Stamos, sitting by the second-floor window in Porter Cresswell's office, noticed the fifty-ton high-lift rolling across the yard. It would pick up one of the new boats and carry it to the river. Ted should have been down there. In his mind he listed the things he wasn't getting done while he was stuck in this meeting, listening to Porter ramble on about how his old man had risked his last dollar on a prototype of the Cresswell Cutlass. How Charlie Cresswell turned the company into a leader in power boat design, and they should all be proud to carry on the tradition. . . .

What Porter ought to be talking about, Ted thought, was how the company was going to recover from the various fuckups of the past six months, the biggest fuckup being Porter's son, who had thought a business degree was a substitute for getting his hands dirty.

This was Porter's first day back since the funeral, and he'd aged about ten years. His wife, Claire, sat in the corner reading. She'd been driving him around lately. With his money, Porter could have hired a limo and a chauffeur, saved her the trouble.

All the top people in the company were here. Porter's brother, Dub. Dub's wife. Management from sales and marketing. And the production supervisors, including Ted, who was in charge of wood and fiberglass. Ted was thirty-seven, and he'd been getting his hands dirty at Cresswell over half his life.

Porter rocked back in his chair. "My dad—and Dub's—started this company in a shop no bigger than a garage. It's still down there, right by the river. Humble beginnings and a grand vision."

No mention of Ted's father, Henry Stamos, who had built the first boat. Henry's only assets had been his hands.

Ted noticed the yellow Porsche come through the open chain-link security gate. It sped across the parking lot, swerved into a visitor spot, and skidded to a stop. Roger Cresswell's car. Leaning closer to the window, Ted saw the driver's side open. A woman's long legs swung out, black dress up her thighs. Then a mop of red hair and big sunglasses. Nikki Cresswell. She slammed the door and disappeared under the roof overhang at the entrance to the building, apparently in a hurry about something, not bothering to park in the garage, leaving the car baking in the sun. It was another day in the nineties, and heat waves shimmered off the metal roof of the main assembly shed and glared on the hard white ground.

Ted heard Elizabeth Cresswell's voice and looked around.

"Porter, I'm sorry to break in, but I've got a meeting with Personnel in five minutes." She didn't sound sorry to break in. She stood up, and her back was to Ted. White shirt and slim khaki pants. Dark hair tied with a red scarf. He wanted her to turn around, give him the front view.

People shifted, started remembering things they had to do.

Hands gripping the arms of his chair, Porter pushed himself out of it. His jacket hung loose on big shoulders. He lifted one side of his mouth in a grin. The man looked like a cadaver. "I talk too much. You should've stopped me fifteen minutes ago, Liz. It's good to see you people again. I'm glad to be back, damned glad. Claire and I are grateful for your sympathy . . . your friendship." His voice broke, and he waved them toward the door. "All right, let me get to work."

There were some handshakes as people filed out. The leasing manager squeezed his shoulder. Porter said, "Stamos! Wait a minute. Close the door and come back in here."

Ted did, then walked over to Porter's desk. Dub was still sitting in a chair to one side, a can of Coke on his thigh. Probably had a couple ounces of liquor mixed in. He'd gained weight, and his belly hung over his belt. Dub's job as director of sales involved entertaining vendors and boat buyers, taking them out for steaks, then to strip clubs, if they wanted. Ted knew this because Dub would take him along to keep these people out of trouble.

In the corner, Porter's wife turned a page in her magazine, inconspicuous as a sofa cushion.

"A couple of homicide detectives came by this morning," Porter said. "Sit down, will you? They wanted to talk to you, but you weren't around. Your crew chief said you were doing a water test."

"Yeah, I was out on one of the forty-six-footers. Why do they want to talk to me?"

"They've got some questions about a kid who used to work here, Bobby Gonzalez. Friend of my nephew Sean's. He worked for you. Isn't that right?"

"More or less. He was in the glass shop for about a month." Bobby Gonzalez had been put to work laying down fiberglass and pressing in the liquid resin with rollers and brushes—a tough job, and hot this time of year, even with industrial fans blowing into the boat hulls. Ted said, "I believe Dub arranged the job as a favor to Sean."

"I should have known better." Dub took a swallow of whatever was in his Coke can. "He has an arrest record. He was in a gang. Did you know that?"

"No. I thought he was a dancer."

"He is. He's a ballet dancer. If I wasn't sure Sean liked girls, I'd worry." Dub laughed, and his stomach moved.

Porter said, "Now, listen, Ted. The cops asked me about the relationship between Gonzalez and Roger here at the company. I said that Roger fired him for stealing some tools, and Gonzalez attacked him. That's true, isn't it?"

Ted could see that Porter wanted it to be. "Well, they had some problems. I think Roger resented having to add another worker on the shift, so he made it real tough on Bobby, trying to make him quit, I guess. Bobby started backtalking Roger in front of the men, and Roger told me to fire him, but I said, 'Well, Roger, you better learn to deal with the employees,' so I wouldn't do it. Then security found one of our sanders in Bobby's locker. I never pegged the kid for a thief, but Roger brought Bobby up to the shop office and fired him. I got there about the time they were tangling, and I pulled them apart." Ted added, "The kid's a hothead, but I can't see him shooting anybody."

Porter pointed at Ted. "Nobody asked you that, did they?"

Ted didn't reply immediately. The finger was still pointing. He said, "That's the question, isn't it? If he could have killed your son?"

"The cops think he did. The night Roger died, people at that party heard Gonzalez threaten him. Everyone there can provide an alibi—except Gonzalez. Last week the police found a shirt in Gonzalez's trash can with blood on it the same type as Roger's."

Claire looked up from her magazine but said nothing. The sun came through the window, lighting her pale blond hair.

Ted said, "I'm not clear on . . . what you're saying."

Porter laughed, and a crooked smile remained. The loose skin of his jowls settled onto his shirt collar. "Just tell the cops about that fight. Tell them you saw it all, how Gonzalez attacked Roger, and I don't want to hear how you tried to excuse his behavior. When I ask for your help, I would hope that you have enough loyalty to give it, and keep your fucking opinions to yourself." Porter was still smiling. "Is that clear enough for you?"

Feeling his neck getting hot, Ted thought about what to say. He wondered if Porter had gone crazy. He wondered what would happen if he got up and went back to work. Both the brothers were looking at him, Porter from behind his big desk, Dub with his fat belly and booze-red face. Ted nodded. "Yeah. It's clear."

Then he stood up and said if there was nothing else, he had to get back down to the shop. He was reaching for the door when somebody knocked, and it opened. He had to dodge out of the way.

Nikki Cresswell came in, walking like she was about to fall off her high heels. Her eyes were red, and her mascara was smeared.

Porter's secretary was right behind her. "I'm sorry, I *told* her you were in a meeting, but she wouldn't wait."

Claire put aside her magazine. Dub started to get up.

"No, don't bother," Nikki said. "I'm not staying. I just came by to talk to Porter, but it's lucky you're here, Dub, because you might be interested in this. Wow. Ted's here too. Maybe I should put a notice on the bulletin board." She made a little laugh.

Porter said, "What is it you want, Nikki?"

"I have to sell Roger's shares in the company as soon as possible." Nikki sounded like she had a cold. "Roger was so far in debt. I mean, I had no idea. He didn't even have life insurance, or retirement, or anything like that. I don't have enough to get by on till the probate goes through. Anyway, the shares are for sale. No reasonable offer refused!"

Silence. Everybody looking at her. Ted Stamos knew he ought to slide on out the door, but this was too good.

"Porter, you ought to buy them back, then you'd have more than Dub again. If Dub buys them, he'd have almost sixty percent." Nikki made a big smile in Dub's direction. "Think about that. You'd be in control. Or maybe I'll sell them to the employees."

"What the hell are you talking about?" Porter demanded. "You have no interest in this company."

"Yes, I do. The lawyer handling the estate said that since Roger didn't leave a will, anything he had is now mine."

"Are you crazy?" Porter laughed. "Those are *my* shares. You don't own any part of this company. Jesus. It can't be inherited by spouses or sold piecemeal to outsiders. Dub's and my father set up the business to make sure it stays in the family. Roger knew that. He should have explained it."

Nikki's mouth was open for a few seconds before she said, "What?"

Claire murmured, "Porter, please. Not now."

A stiff forefinger accented Porter's words. "Pay attention, Nikki. Children inherit, spouses don't. You have *no interest* in this company. None."

"No! Wait, that's not true. Roger said he owned ten percent of the company, and his shares were worth twenty million dollars!"

"You've got *nothing*, don't you listen? I told Roger he was making a mistake to marry you. Gold digger. My son's warm in his grave and you're picking his bones."

"Don't you dare say that!" She clenched her fists at her sides. "I loved Roger! You never did. You treated him like dirt. All his life, nothing was ever good enough—"

"Go on. Get out of my office, you sleazy little tramp."

Claire was trying to calm her down, and Nikki was batting her hands away. "You can't do this. It's a lie! I'm going to see a lawyer!"

"Go ahead, see your lawyer. See what you get." Porter was laughing.

"You dried up old fuck. I hope you *die*! I hate you *all*!" She backed toward the door. "You're going to be sorry, I swear."

When she slammed the door, the wood paneling on the wall shook.

The Cresswells looked at each other. Dub finished off his drink and squeezed the can flat in the middle. "Well, well."

Ted Stamos said, "I've got to get back downstairs."

Porter pushed out of his chair, stumbling a little, then standing upright, straightening his jacket. "How'd she get in? I want security notified. She isn't allowed in here. Did you hear what she said? That little bitch. I came back to work one day, just out of the fucking hospital, and she's sitting on Roger's lap in my chair, and they're talking about what they'd do when I was dead. Well, I didn't die, did I? Greedy. Both of them. Sharp as a serpent's tooth—what's that quote, Claire? A child's ingratitude is like a serpent's tooth . . ."

At the door Ted glanced back into the office. Porter's wife was looking out the window as though this wasn't happening. She could probably see a yellow Porsche tearing across the parking lot.

Ted Stamos and the other production supervisors—engines, electrical, and mechanical—had offices overlooking the floor of the main assembly building, where the boats were constructed. Two lines were pulled along like circus elephants hooked together, sixty-to-eighty-footers on one side, smaller boats on the other. The lines began where layers of fiberglass were laid into molds for the hulls. Hoists ran overhead to lower the decks, shafts, and engines. Steel scaffolding supported a wood floor at gunwale level, workers going back and forth. Carpenters, plumbers, electricians, engine mechanics. Each team in a different color T-shirt. Every boat made by hand. Up to three months per boat.

When a boat reached the end of the line, a high-lift would carry it to a slip and lower it into the water. Someone from Cresswell would take it a few miles out in the Atlantic with a rep from the engine manufacturer and run it wide open. Assuming no bugs, the boat would be trimmed out with carpet, furniture, and audiovisual systems, then trucked or piloted to the buyer.

The main building was open at both ends, metal roof on concrete I-beams. If Ted stood on the catwalk at the east end, he could see the narrow Miami River, lined with rusty freighters, snaking toward the buildings downtown, a couple of miles away. Below him, spread over ten acres and bounded by chain link fence and cyclone wire, were the various warehouses and shops at the Cresswell yard: the wood shop with stacks of fine teak, cherry, and maple; a metal shop with lathes and bandsaws and racks of sheet metal, rods, and pipes; and storage areas for galley equipment, heads, and shower stalls; sonar, GPS, and shortwave radios; bait tanks, fuel tanks, drive shafts, propellers, portholes, dozens of rolls of fiberglass, and hundreds of miles of cables and wiring.

Ted spent as little time as possible in his office. He preferred to be on the floor with the men. Sometimes he'd pick up a wrench, or get inside a hull with a resin gun, or tinker with a new cabinet design. His father had said, *If you act too much like a boss, the men won't care about nothing but the paycheck.*

Whenever Ted needed to think, he would go to his father's workshop. He still called it that, although Henry Stamos had been dead for fifteen years. It was a small room, twelve feet square, around a corner from the wood shop, where the big saws and routers and planers were located. Henry had used the workshop for putting together smaller pieces, like fine built-in cabinetry.

Henry's tools still hung on pegboard above the scarred work-bench. A step stool with peeling red paint was pushed under-neath. Henry had made it over thirty years ago so his son could stand on it and watch him work.

Charlie Cresswell had talked about giving Henry a piece of the company, but never did, and Henry wasn't the kind of man who would push. Time went by. Charlie was killed in a boating acci-dent, and the company went to his sons. Then Henry got cancer—too many years breathing acetone. He'd not left much more than his carpentry tools, and Ted wasn't sure who they belonged to—him or the company. Until recently it hadn't mattered. Then Roger Cresswell asked why the hell that room was locked. He wanted it opened and cleaned out. Ted asked him did he want his teeth readjusted.

After getting the hell out of Porter's office, Ted headed for the workshop. He closed the door behind him, pulled a high stool over to the bench, and sat down. He had a portable phone on his belt if anyone needed him.

The conversation with the Cresswells weighed on Ted's mind, and as he sat there he mulled it over. What bothered him most, he decided, was that he'd just been reminded of who he was. A hired worker. An employee. Porter could go back on his promise to put him in charge of the floor. He could be let go.

Ted knew he could find other work if he had to, but that wasn't the point. He had almost twenty years in this job. That meant something. The people who meant something were here. Ten years ago his ex-wife had remarried and gone to Ohio with their two daughters, teenagers now. He sent cards, and he paid child support, but they rarely wrote back, and for the most part, he had put them out of his mind.

Being president of the company meant that Porter Cresswell could do what he wanted, fire anybody who pissed him off. He could turn the business over to anybody, even a blue-eyed golden boy who didn't have shit for brains.

Roger had talked about saving money. No more teak or cherry. Panel the interiors in reconstituted wood with plastic veneer. Re-con wood was a fraction of the price. In a meeting on that topic

Ted had said it would turn the Cresswell name into a seagoing joke. Roger had backed off. Then Roger decided to make a new hull mold in four days. It could have been done, but Roger told the men to lay down the next layer of glass when the previous layer hadn't yet hardened. The mold crinkled and was ruined. Worse, it ruined the plug—the form underneath. Production was set back for weeks.

Roger had blamed the men, who should have known. He'd blamed Ted Stamos, who stood by and let it happen. *You're trying to fuck me over, aren't you, Stamos?* Ted had known that sooner or later, Roger would get even.

There wasn't a Cresswell in the bunch worth a damn. Something bad in the family. Except for the girl, Maggie. The one who had killed herself a few years ago. Ted was only surprised that she'd lasted as long as she had. He'd known her once, way back. How the hell old had he been? A teenager, anyway. She'd been a quiet girl with long honey-brown hair. Sweet as honey too. He'd told her that, first time he'd kissed her.

The Cresswells had lived in Miami Shores, a big two-story white house with columns. Ted knew his way around power tools even at that age, so Henry had sent him over to build a deck and trellis. Ted had worked stripped to the waist, and he'd seen Maggie's face at the window. Finally she came out with some iced tea, and things progressed from there over the next couple of weeks. Then her brother saw them together and told. Porter grabbed Maggie by the arm and dragged her away. Called Ted a piece of trash and ordered him off his property. That night, Henry had said to leave the girl alone, don't make trouble with the boss. Ted had hated that most of all, his father caving in. Now he was older, he understood. So Ted had stayed away from Maggie Cresswell. He thought about her sometimes. How if they'd stayed together he might be running this company.

Ted reached across the workbench and took a wood plane off its hook. The steel blade and the box were still shiny under a light coating of oil. The hickory handle was dark where his father had touched it. Henry Stamos's big hands had been raspy as sandpaper, thick with calluses, wrinkles criss-crossing leathery skin. There had been a fading tattoo of an anchor and flag on his right hand, and his left index finger was nicked off at the first knuckle. He could turn a sheet of teak into a galley table in less than two hours, all the lines straight and true.

Henry's people had been sponge fishermen. They'd come from Greece to settle just north of Tampa, and they'd fished the Gulf. Henry had met Charlie Cresswell in the Navy, then moved down to Miami when Charlie needed a marine carpenter. He wanted to make good boats. Build them right. That still had to mean something, even these days.

Ted heard a noise behind him. The click of a key in a lock. He turned around.

Elizabeth stood in the doorway. "Want some company?"

"Sure. How'd you know I was here?"

"You weren't anywhere else."

He watched her come toward him, the movements of her body, breasts wobbling a little under her white knit shirt. It was tucked in tight at her waist, and her hips moved like they were greased. She stopped an arm's length away, looking at him sideways, bangs level with her dark eyebrows.

Ted grinned at her. "Come on. Come over here."

She said, "I don't know. Maybe I shouldn't get any closer."

"Yeah, you should."

She reached out and ran a finger over his cheek, pulling away before he could catch her wrist. "Did Porter talk to you about Bobby Gonzalez? He said he was going to."

"Twisted my arm is more like it."

"You know how Porter is. Just humor him."

Ted turned the plane over and tested the blade on his thumb. "How's it going to look to the men, me shading the truth like that? They hated Roger."

Elizabeth said, "They won't know what you tell the police. How can they?"

The plane moved slowly down the edge of the workbench. A curl of wood appeared. "I could be history too, just like that kid. You know that, sugar? They could boot my ass right out of here, fuck that I spent my life in this company."

"Stop it. That won't happen. I promise." She leaned against him, reaching around, rubbing the muscles in his chest.

Ted made another pass with the blade. "What do you want, Elizabeth? Just tell me. Okay?"

She put the point of her chin on his shoulder. "Just do what Porter says."

"What if they arrest the kid?"

"At least he'll be out of Sean's life for a while."

"Out of whose life, Elizabeth? I caught you a few times looking at him from the catwalk. Yeah, you did, don't lie."

She gave him a play slap on the head. "Oh, shut up, you. I'm serious. You don't know the effect he's had on Sean. 'My homey.' 'Bro.' That's what Sean calls him! Bobby keeps turning up at our house, no matter how often I tell him to go away. Sean's language is horrible, he's failing his classes, and I found a baggie of pot in his closet. Someday Sean will take his place in this company, but he won't make it if he doesn't straighten up. Oh, God, Ted, I don't know what to do."

"It's a phase. I did the same shit. Put him to work in the glass shop. See how he likes rubber gloves and a face mask eight hours a day."

"Porter's going to talk to him. Maybe that'll do some good. Dub is no help. I don't think he even cares. He sits in his recliner and drinks, oblivious to everything."

"Hey, Elizabeth?" Ted set the plane back on the bench. "I don't want to hear about your family situation. Okay?"

"Okay." She kissed him under the ear, then ran her tongue inside.

He pulled her around between his knees. "Where have you been, pretty thing?" She undid his buckle and tugged to release the belt. He sat up straighter so she could get to the button on his jeans. There was a small scar at the corner of her upper lip, and he liked to imagine he'd put it there. He felt his zipper go. "Go lock the damn door."

"I did already."

He reached around and pulled off her scarf, and her hair fell into his hands.

CHAPTER

10

At 7:45 A.M. on Thursday, as Gail was pulling out of the drive-way at her mother's house, her cell phone rang. Bobby Gonzalez told her that the police had just arrived at his apartment with a search warrant. Could she come over? Gail told him to stay out of their way and be quiet. She would be there in fifteen minutes. "As if I know what the hell I'm doing," Gail muttered to herself.

Bobby rented the spare room in an apartment near Lenox and Seventh, a relatively quiet area where the architectural blandness was mitigated by shade trees and tropical plants. The small, two-story building was not streamlined Art Deco but the flat, blocky style of the fifties. A school of gray and pink bas-relief dolphins swam across the end of it.

Gail parked illegally at the curb in a residents-only zone and hurried along the sidewalk, passing two patrol cars and a plain sedan with a blue light on the dash. The men they belonged to were, she assumed, busy tossing her client's apartment.

A cracked concrete walkway extended at right angles from the sidewalk, and a walk on the second floor formed a roof over the doors on the first. Four up, four down, each looking out on a narrow stretch of grass, a hedge, and the whining air conditioners of the adjacent building. Gail dodged around curious neighbors. An old man with a white beard and a yarmulke peered over the painted metal railing. Two women rattled away in Spanish. The aroma of frying bacon came through someone's open jalousies.

At the last apartment, portable barricades and yellow tape marked the door. Gail looked for Bobby and found him seated on the edge of a brick planter, dressed only in a pair of jeans. Two other young men sat beside him, equally as rumpled. Bobby's friends from the ballet company, she assumed. It was their apartment.

Gail grabbed Bobby's elbow and pulled him out of earshot. "Are you all right?"

"Yeah, fine. They went through my car already. They said if I didn't give them the keys they'd break the window. Can you go see what they're doing?"

"In a minute. Did they give you a copy of the warrant? Let me have it." He took some folded sheets of paper from his back pocket, and Gail looked them over.

The warrant gave the police authority to enter Apartment 4, 690 Lenox Avenue, Miami Beach, and to search for a weapon, instrumentality, or means by which a felony, to wit: murder, had been committed. . . . She scanned farther down. One gold Rolex watch, engraved RCC; one black leather wallet belonging to Roger C. Cresswell and contents of same. Driver's license. Credit cards. A .22-caliber pistol and/or ammunition for same. Clothing, footwear, and/or any other item of evidentiary value—

Gail flipped the page, finding an affidavit signed by Frank Britton, Miami-Dade Homicide Bureau. An enumeration of facts that justified a search. That Robert Gonzalez had worked for Roger Cresswell. That on August 14, after Cresswell fired him from his job, Gonzalez physically attacked him. That on August 16, the night before Cresswell's body was found, Gonzalez threatened him—

"It says you attacked Roger Cresswell. And threatened him the night he died." Gail looked at him. "Is that true?"

"When he fired me, we got into this scrap, and I hit him. He saw me over at Jack's and, you know, we had some words, but it was more like he threatened me."

"You didn't tell me about that."

"Well . . . I didn't think it mattered."

Gail gave him a hard look then went back to the affidavit, reading aloud in a murmur. "Failed to produce credible alibi for period encompassing time of death. . . . On August 22, a dark blue T-shirt was taken from the trash discarded from Apartment Four"—her voice rose—"and that bloodstains on the shirt were found to have the same blood type as the victim, B positive?" Her eyes rose from the page.

Bobby said, "That's the shirt from when I got in the fight with Roger. His nose was bleeding. I tried to explain to the detective, but he's like, shut up, I don't want to hear from you."

"You *admitted* it was your shirt?" When Bobby only stared back at her, Gail said, "I told you not to talk to the police."

"Sorry."

She let out a breath. "Stay here. I'll be back."

At the perimeter of yellow tape she spoke to the officer standing guard. "I'm Bobby Gonzalez's lawyer. If Sergeant Britton is in there, could I speak to him?" She extended her business card. After a second, he took it and leaned into the apartment. "Sergeant? Some lady out here wants to talk to you." Through the crack in the door Gail could see the arm of a green sofa and an empty pizza box.

Frank Britton hadn't changed much from the last time they'd met—gold-rimmed glasses, short brown hair, a stomach settling toward forty. He could have passed for a high school math teacher.

"Gail Connor. My goodness, it's been a while." They shook hands across the tape. He glanced at her card. "Mr. Gonzalez said you might be dropping by to join us." Britton had a deceptively friendly smile and folksy Florida Cracker accent. "I thought you did civil trial practice."

"Generally, yes." She smiled back at him. "Since Bobby isn't in handcuffs in the back of a patrol car, I assume you don't have enough evidence for an arrest."

"Not yet, but we're working on it."

"By going through his trash?"

"Anything thrown out is considered abandoned, Ms. Connor. Fair game."

Two Miami-Dade officers came out of the apartment, each carrying a cardboard box. The other detective, a younger Hispanic man, gave Britton a clipboard. "We're done in there, Frank."

Britton took a pen out of his pocket and signed it. "This is your receipt, Ms. Connor, for things we're going to take with us." He tore one copy off the form and handed it to her. "Keep in touch."

"You bet." Walking back toward Bobby, Gail read it. Master bedroom: one .22-caliber semiautomatic Ruger pistol, one partially empty box of Remington .22-caliber bullets. Bedroom #2: Six pairs of pants, four shirts, three T-shirts, and a pair of Nike sneakers. And $300 in cash.

Gail whirled toward the street and caught up with Britton by his unmarked sedan.

"Wait a minute. What's this? You took a pistol and bullets from his roommates' bedroom. The warrant doesn't give you the right to search their room."

Britton finished adjusting his clip-on sunglasses, then said slowly, "Well, Ms. Connor, we can search anywhere the occupants give us permission, which they did. They were real cooperative."

She detested her own uncertainty even more than his patronizing tone. "The money, then. Why did you take money from Bobby's room? You can't possibly tie that to Roger Cresswell. And why are you taking his clothes?"

Smirking, the other detective set the boxes inside the trunk and closed the lid.

Britton said, "The day Roger Cresswell died, he took a little walking-around money out of his bank—twenty-five hundred dollars in cash. We found the withdrawal slip in his car. I want to know if those new, sequentially numbered hundreds we took from your client's dresser might be traced to Mr. Cresswell's bank. As for the clothes, we're going to run them through some tests. If we find any blood, a sample goes to the lab. They've already started a DNA check on that shirt that came out of the trash. Bobby can have his clothes back if they come up negative. The money too, if it belongs to him. And the pistol—well, his buddies are going to need to get a court order."

Britton came a little closer, brow furrowing, showing his concern. "You know, I'd hate to see the boy charged with first-degree murder. They had a fight. Maybe it was self-defense. Why don't y'all come with us, and let's talk about it?"

"I think not."

He let out a sigh and shook his head. Gail watched him go, then turned around, staring in Bobby's direction. The neighbors were dispersing, and Bobby's roommates were going back inside the apartment. And from somewhere, a dark-haired girl in a short skirt had appeared. Angela Quintana.

Gail motioned for Bobby. Angela came along too, hanging onto his hand. "Hi, Angela. Let me borrow Bobby for a minute, may I?"

Bobby squeezed Angela's shoulders. "Be right back, baby." His jeans hung off his hips far enough to show a muscled lower abdomen and dark, feathery hair at his belt line. "Don't worry, Gail's taking care of everything." He kissed her quickly on the lips and turned her toward the apartment.

He and Gail headed toward the end of the block. She gave him the receipt. He held it with both hands, and his eyes moved across the page. "Shit! They took my clothes? My *money?* I was going to pay you with that!"

"They'll give it back. Where'd you get it?"

"I borrowed it from Sean Cresswell."

"Okay. Did you notice the .22 semiautomatic on the list?"

"Yeah. It's Jason's." Bobby seemed surprised she would ask. "That's not the gun that shot Roger. No *way.* Twenty-twos are everywhere. My uncle has one."

"Please don't say that to the police. All right?" Gail said, "Tell me. Why did you keep a bloodstained T-shirt for more than a week, then throw it out after the murder?"

Bobby shoved his thick black hair off his forehead. "I didn't notice! There wasn't that much on it, and the shirt's so dark. Last week I was getting some clothes together to wash, and I saw these, like, stains, and I go, whoa, that's blood, so I threw it away."

His explanations made sense. Gail realized that she'd been afraid he had lied to her. Or worse.

At the corner they turned back, walking in silence. No cars passed. The only movement was the sway of branches overhead. Dappled light played on the street. A shiny yellow Volkswagen was parked along the curb. Its bumper sticker read: BALLERINAS Do It on Pointe. Angela's car.

"The T-shirt. You obviously didn't wear that same shirt to the party at Jack Pascoe's, did you?"

"No, I had on this funky old Hawaiian shirt and some shorts."

"Good. He has to remember that," Gail said. "It isn't as bad as I'd thought."

They had reached the walkway leading to Bobby's apartment. Gail stopped him with a hand on his arm. "On Tuesday I called Judge Harris's chambers and left a message for him to call me. Supposedly he's in trial. He didn't call yesterday, so as soon as I leave here, I'm going to track him down."

"He'll say he never saw me."

"No, I don't think so. I've met him a couple of times. Some people just strike you as decent. I hope I'm right."

"Yeah, if we get Alan, I'll be okay." Bobby nodded, then broke into a smile. "Stay and have breakfast with us. Angie brought some bagels."

"Maybe some other time. You aren't telling her about any of this, are you? About Judge Harris?"

"I just said we found who it is, but not his name."

"Well, don't tell her anything. What's she doing here?"

"We're going to go to the studio for a couple of hours and work. The ballet's auditioning next week for *Nutcracker*. I'm helping her practice." A smile turned up the corners of his wide mouth. "You have to see her dance. She's so beautiful. There are some things to work on, but she's got a lot of talent. Her father doesn't know how much. He's an idiot."

"Does he know she's trying out?"

"No way. If he knew I was helping her, he'd probably break my legs."

Gail's mind spun on visions of what Anthony would do, finding his *niñita* in this rundown apartment, which a gay couple shared with a boy from East Harlem who might be arrested for murder—if Gail didn't persuade a circuit court judge to risk his career by telling the truth.

"I want to give you a check," Bobby said. "You came all the way over here, and now you're going to see Judge Harris—"

"Forget it. I agreed not to charge."

"No, really. I'd feel better. How about I give you a hundred now, and more when I get paid? Is it okay if I postdate the check?"

She sighed. "Sure." A man had his pride.

He opened the door to his apartment. The living room was a mess—sofa and chair cushions tossed aside, books removed from shelves, desk drawers pulled open. A poster of Rudolph Nureyev in a turban gazed back at Gail from above a TV resting on concrete blocks. No sign of the roommates. She assumed they had gone back to sleep.

Bobby fixed the sofa cushions. "Here, sit down. I'm going to get dressed."

Looking out from the kitchen, Angela said, "Is everything okay?"

Gail went to speak to her. "Angie, listen. Bobby and I can't talk about the case. I'll do what I can for him, I promise."

Angela gave her a quick hug. "Thanks, Gail. It means a lot."

The kitchen was no more than a narrow corridor leading to an exit door, and the sun streamed in through glass jalousies. Yellow daisies lay in their wrapper of paper on the worn countertop. The dish drainer was crammed with mismatched plates and cups. Apparently Angela had just washed them. A small coffeemaker hissed on the stove. She stirred the milk that steamed in a bent saucepan. With her small breasts and long, slender limbs, she looked about fourteen. Pink butterfly clips held back her hair. The gold chain of her crucifix made a thin line of light on pale skin.

"You like *café con leche*, don't you?"

Gail took a moment to assess the state of her stomach. "Sure. Is there a soda? A Coke or something?"

"Look in the fridge." She moved aside so Gail could open the door.

The refrigerator was nearly empty. A carton from a Chinese

restaurant. A bag of limp carrots. Nonfat milk. A mango. Gail shifted some beer cans and found a Sprite. "Bobby told me you're trying out for *The Nutcracker*."

"Next week, and I am so nervous."

"He says you have a lot of talent."

A smile brightened her face. "Oh, I hope so. I've studied for ten years. The last two summers, I've taken classes at the American Ballet Theater, but I never believed, till now, that I could have a career in dance. The problem is, I can't do that and go to college at the same time. A dancer's life is very demanding, you know." The coffeemaker was bubbling, sucking the water through the grounds, and Angela turned off the heat.

Gail reached into her pocket for her rolls of Tums and peeled back the paper. "You should probably mention this to your father."

"I *can't*."

"Well, you'll have to at some point."

Angela thought about that. "I'll tell him after tryouts." She poured the thick, dark coffee into an old glass measuring cup and added sugar, stirring vigorously. "I'm supposed to be moving into the dorms this weekend. He says if I drop out of school, he won't support me. I don't care. Look at Bobby. He doesn't have a lot of money, but he's happy. That's what matters in life, isn't it? If a person is happy or not? Well, I want to dance, and I'm going to, no matter what *anybody* says."

Angela's chin went up, and she looked at Gail through her lashes. The full lips, pressed tightly together, turned down at the corners. Gail felt a jolt of recognition: Anthony's expression exactly. But while he might accompany that look with an order, his daughter wanted approval. If not from her father, then from a reasonable substitute.

Nibbling her Tums, Gail nodded. "Then do it. I believe that a woman should always do what she wants as long as she has no encumbrances. Opportunities might not come around a second time."

"Exactly." Vindicated, Angela accented her words by thumping three mugs onto the counter. She filled them with hot milk.

"Where would you live?"

"Well . . ." Her brown eyes shifted to Gail. "They're about to promote Bobby to soloist. He'd be making more money, so he could afford his own apartment. We could share. That's not wrong, is it?"

Gail laughed. "Who am I to judge? Just be careful. I hope you are."

Angela's cheeks colored. "I *am*. Bobby is so respectful, you wouldn't believe. Oh, my God, if I moved in with Bobby, my father would kill me."

"No, he wouldn't."

"I know, but . . . he always has these perfect responses to whatever I say, and it makes me feel like I don't know *anything*. Like if I make my own decisions, they've got to be wrong, and if he doesn't keep me under surveillance twenty-four hours a day, I might get pregnant or end up on drugs, and totally ruin my life."

Gail nodded.

"He's so *Cuban*, and I can say that because I'm one, too." Angela sighed. "I just have to think of how to tell him so he doesn't freak out."

She set the bagels and coffee on a tray and Gail carried it to the table. Angela followed with cream cheese and napkins, then went back to arrange the daisies in a wine carafe. Just then Bobby came out of his room. He'd put on a clean T-shirt and sandals and combed his hair. He gave Gail a check for one hundred dollars and apologized that it wasn't more. Angela told them to sit down and eat before everything got cold.

Bobby came around to pull out Angela's chair and kiss her cheek. Smiling at him, she topped the hot milk with espresso. Bobby told Gail to help herself to the bagels. Angela asked Bobby what kind he wanted. Onion, please, *mamita*. She put it on a plate and spread it with cream cheese.

Gail couldn't look at them anymore. They were too beautiful. She wanted to cry.

The criminal courts were housed in a gray building with a view of the expressway that arched over the Miami River. Gail could count on one hand the times she'd gone up the wide, pink-marble steps, passed through the X-ray machines, then taken the narrow escalators packed with lawyers, police officers, court personnel, witnesses, the accused, and extended families of the accused.

Voices echoed on tile floors in long, poorly lit corridors. Judge Nathan Alan Harris presided in a courtroom on the fourth floor. Gail went inside the glassed-in anteroom and looked through a narrow window. The courtroom was full, and she could hear the buzz of conversations, but the judge was not on the bench.

She went down the hall a bit, finding a plain oak door. It was locked. She stood back and waited, glancing around to see if anyone was watching. When a man in a suit came out carrying a stack of files, Gail went through before the door could close behind him. He barely glanced at her, this tall blond woman in a slim skirt and fitted navy jacket, a row of gold buttons down the front. She was obviously someone with business here.

She found Judge Harris's office, marked by a nameplate affixed to the wall. Flexing her fingers on the strap of her shoulder bag, Gail took a breath and went in. The assistant's desk was straight ahead, but male voices came from the judge's chambers. Someone laughed. Gail wandered closer. The judge came into view—a lanky, gray-haired man in a long-sleeved striped shirt. He was taking a black robe off a hanger.

Gail realized that the judicial assistant was speaking to her.

She went back to the desk and stated her name, and that she was a lawyer. "It's urgent that I speak to Judge Harris." When the woman asked her what it was about, Gail shook her head. "I'm sorry, but the matter is confidential."

"And I'm sorry, but the judge is about to go on the bench. I don't see you down for an appointment. How did you get in here?"

He came out of his office buttoning the top of his robe, continuing his conversation with the other man, a lawyer whom Gail recognized from Florida Bar meetings. She placed herself in their path. "Judge Harris, I'm Gail Connor. I tried to reach you earlier this week—"

"Gail. This is a pleasant surprise." He held out his hand, shaking hers with a warm, firm grip. "Yes, you did call me, and I'm

sorry for not calling you back. I was swamped. Don't go away."
He turned to speak to the other lawyer, arranging a meeting next
week. *Input from the commission . . . Third DCA . . . jurisdic-*
tional issues. Their voices intruded into Gail's head, threatening to
turn what she'd planned to say into incoherent mush.

Judge Harris touched her arm. "Sorry. Walk with me. I'm
wanted in the courtroom." In the hall he nodded at a colleague
going the other way, then inclined his head closer to Gail. "Does
this have something to do with a mutual acquaintance of ours?
Anthony Quintana?"

Gail, who had been on the point of speaking, released a small
laugh. "No. It's about a client of mine."

"Is it? Oh. I assumed . . ." He made an apologetic grimace. "I
thought you might ask me for some . . . oh, some advice, or . . .
God knows. I'm sorry, you said—"

"A client of mine, a young man named Bobby Gonzalez—"

"Not an open case, I hope. It wouldn't be ethical for me to—"

"You don't recognize the name?" The judge shook his head.
"He's twenty-one, about my height, black hair. A dancer with the
Miami City Ballet. You met Bobby Gonzalez at a party two weekends ago at the home of Jack Pascoe, where Roger Cresswell was
shot to death. Bobby is now a suspect in the murder."

Gail waited for a reaction. There was only a blank stare
through the tortoiseshell glasses. She went on. "Bobby couldn't
have done it. He had no opportunity. He left the party about a
quarter to midnight and met a friend. During the forty minutes
prior to leaving the party, he was with you. We need you to explain that to the police. I realize that this puts you in a delicate position, but we should be able to work this out in a way that—"

"No, your client is mistaken. I do know Jack Pascoe, but—"

"—a way that protects your privacy, but we need to prove that
the police suspect the wrong man."

"As I *said.*" The judge waited for Gail to stop talking. "Yes, I
know Jack—he was my late wife's cousin—and while I have visited his home on several occasions, I did not do so on that night,
and to my knowledge, I have never seen or spoken to your client."

"But you must remember him. A young man with black hair.

He speaks with a New York accent. He was wearing a Hawaiian shirt."

"How can I remember if I wasn't there?"

"You and he sat on the seawall talking for forty minutes—"

"He may well have, but not with me."

"He said you'd had a lot to drink—"

"Ms. Connor, I repeat, I was not there."

Angrily, she retorted, "Please don't expect me to believe that."

"You accuse *me* of lying?"

She swallowed. Her mouth was dry as cotton. "I think your first reaction is to protect yourself, but a young man's freedom depends on your courage."

"This is outrageous."

His bailiff called from the door of the courtroom. "Judge? They're ready."

"Yes, I'm coming." Nathan Harris made a chilly smile. "If you will excuse me?"

Gail followed him along the corridor. "Bobby remembers you clearly. He can describe what you look like. He said you told him you'd gone to school in Chicago. Your wife was an artist, and she died—"

"He could have learned that anywhere. I have nothing more to say to you."

She held onto his arm through his robe, forcing him to stop and look at her. "If you walk away, there will be six TV reporters outside your chambers in time for the evening news. What will the judicial nominating committee have to say about that?"

He stared at her.

The bailiff said, "Judge, is there a problem?"

"One moment!" He turned his back on the open door to the courtroom and spoke through clenched teeth. "What do you want from me?"

"To get this resolved as discreetly as possible. Judge Harris, I understand your situation." Gail pulled a business card from her pocket. "Call me on my cell phone. The number's written on the back. We'll arrange to meet this evening, perhaps at my office, or wherever you feel comfortable."

"That's impossible. I'm in trial."

"A phone call. Thirty seconds. Just call to say where I can meet you."

"I—I have to think about this. Give me till Monday."

"I can't. Bobby could be taken into custody before then. You can have until six o'clock today. No later."

Nathan Harris studied her business card. Thin lips pursed outward, and a pulse beat in his hollow temple. With a stiff nod, he said, "I'll call you." His black robe swirled behind him as he walked into the courtroom. The bailiff looked at Gail, then closed the door.

The corridor was empty. Gail heard a quick, rasping noise and realized it was the sound of her own breathing. She put a hand on the wall to steady herself.

CHAPTER

11

Anthony Quintana's grandmother, Digna Maria Betancourt de Pedrosa, counted among her forebears a prince of Castille and a mistress of King Carlos V. Her grandmother had married the first president of Cuba, her uncle had founded the Havana Yacht Club, and her father had owned a shipping line. Digna's marriage, at age eighteen, to a young banker, Ernesto José Pedrosa Masvidal, had been attended by the island's business and social elite. They had honeymooned for three weeks in Europe.

Forty-some years ago, the family—including aunts, uncles, and cousins—fled Cuba, believing they would go back in six months, a year at most. They were still waiting. As matriarch, Digna kept alive the dreams and illusions of old Havana in the Pedrosas' house on a shady street in Coral Gables. She knew the birthday and saint's day of each child in the family, collected food for the poor, and took care of servants who became too old to work. She said her confession, attended mass twice a week, and carried her rosary everywhere. Although ladies of her class did not believe in *santeria*, she had a corner shelf in her bedroom, and on it she kept a yellow candle, a strand of blue and white beads, some tobacco, a vial of rum, and a small statue of the black virgin of Caridad del Cobre. She took no chances.

Anthony had never hesitated to oppose his grandfather, but Nena was another matter.

She had called yesterday to invite him to lunch at a new French restaurant on Salzedo Street. If conditions were normal—if he hadn't vowed never to speak to Ernesto again—Anthony would have gone to her house, but Nena arrived at his office at a quarter till twelve, accompanied by his sister, Alicia, who drove. He had not seen his grandmother since his return from Spain.

As always, she was elegantly dressed. She wore a plum-colored two-piece suit with ivory hose. Big gold earrings matched the buttons on her suit. Her platinum hair was thinning, but stylishly coiffed. She clung to him for a moment, the top of her head barely clearing his shoulder. "I have missed you, my dear heart," she said in Spanish.

He kissed her rouged cheek. "You are well, Nena?" He addressed her as *usted*, out of respect, not *tú*, which applied to younger relatives.

"Well enough, thanks to God."

She came into his office, noting with approval the modern furniture and soft leather chairs, all of which she had seen before. Halogen lights shone on built-in bookcases and a black cantilevered desk. She lingered over the framed photographs of Angela and Luis. They spent a few moments discussing the children's health, and their studies.

Alicia hung back, and her glance slid away when he looked at her. She had thick, curly hair and the deep blue eyes of their late mother. Anthony had inherited their father's dark eyes.

Digna set the graduation portrait of Angela back on his desk. "She starts school soon, no? You are sending her to live in the dormitories."

A reflection not on the child, but the father. Anthony said, "My house is too far away to be convenient."

"You know the child could live with us. We are very near the university." Digna smiled at her grandson. "But then you would have to visit her, and you have sworn not to enter my house again." Before he could respond, she turned to Alicia. "My dear, do you think you could bring me a cup of tea?"

Anthony reminded her that they would be at the restaurant in ten minutes, but she wanted her tea immediately. "My secretary can make it for you," he said.

"No, no. Alicia knows just how I like it. Nice and strong, not too much sugar. My doctor says my blood is already sweet enough. Take your time, Alicita."

So. Nena wanted to corner him about something. Anthony asked his secretary to show his sister to the office kitchen. He added, "Hold all my calls."

Digna had wandered to the far end of his office, where a sofa and two armchairs faced a private atrium. She carefully lowered herself down and crossed her legs at the ankle.

What would she say? That he should apologize to his grandfather. That he should make amends for the disastrous Fourth of July party, at which Gail Connor had embarrassed the entire family by packing her bags and walking out, in view of everyone. That he must come back, or the family enterprises, forty years of sweat and blood in this country, would crumble to dust.

Digna watched him come toward her, tilting her head as if taking inventory—dark brown Hugo Boss suit, gold cufflinks, silk tie. "When was your last haircut?"

"Pardon?"

"It's very long."

"Is it?" With both hands he pushed it back from his temples. "Not really."

"I see some gray there, my dear."

"Well earned, I assure you."

"But in general, you look very well. Not so pale as before. Spain does that, no?" Digna patted the sofa. "Sit here next to me."

Still standing, Anthony smiled down at her. "Nena. I think I know what this is about. When Grandfather became ill, you agreed that Elena and Bernardo could act as guardians, running his businesses. Now he is better, but they refuse to give up control. Alicia has told me everything. The family is in turmoil, and you find yourself in the middle. I admit that if I hadn't left, this wouldn't have happened. Everything would be in my hands, as Grandfather had planned. I am sorry. My advice to you—most respectfully—is that you take care of your husband, enjoy your life, and let the others do as they please. You shouldn't spend one moment worrying about it."

Digna Pedrosa's silvery brows rose, creating lines on her forehead. "How impressive that you can read minds."

Anthony nodded. "In any event, I may not be here much longer. I have tentative plans to move back to New York."

"And why would you go to such a cold and foreign place?"

"There's more opportunity in New York. And I'd be closer to Luis. A boy needs his father around. I've made inquiries about a job, and it looks promising. I'll tell the children when everything has been arranged."

Digna stared up at him, then said, "One of the few privileges of age is to say what one thinks. May I?"

Anthony made a slight bow. "You have always done so."

"Run away to New York if you wish, or to the moon, but don't expect to leave your problems in Miami. They will follow you like dogs and howl under your window." Digna looked at him steadily for several more seconds, then sighed. "It wasn't the guardianship I wanted to discuss with you. It's your grandfather."

Anthony's groan was so soft he didn't think she could have heard, but her ears were still sharp. She said tartly, "You should be grateful. He rescued you from that wretched island. If not for him, you would have nothing, nothing, not even food for your children."

"Of course I would. I'd have come out on a raft, and we'd be having this same crazy discussion." Anthony pulled his cuff back to see his watch. "Where is Alicia? Our reservation is for noon."

"I canceled it. Don't worry about me, I already ate."

He stared at her.

"My dear heart, please listen. Ernesto has not always been wise, but he has always loved you. More than any of the others. You know this. If he was hard on you, if he lost his temper—"

"Because I'm the son of a communist traitor."

"Oh, be quiet. Ernesto expected more from you than from the others because you could give it. If the hope was greater, so was the disappointment, every time you turned away. He demanded from you no more than he would of himself. You are so much alike, you know."

"Forgive me, Nena, but I am not like my grandfather. I have never wanted to be." Anthony stared through the sliding door into the atrium. Light from the second-floor skylight dappled the ferns and miniature palms. Water sparkled on coral rocks and lapped at the sides of a small pool. He wondered if he could find an office in Manhattan that would accommodate something similar.

His grandmother's soft voice mixed with the muffled burble of the fountain. "How is Gail Connor?"

Taken slightly off balance, Anthony looked over his shoulder. "I haven't the least idea. Why do you ask that?"

"You're not seeing her again?"

"No, Grandmother, I am not."

"Thank God. I had resigned myself to your marriage, but I was never in favor. American women are too independent. They make decisions for their husbands, I have heard. Is this true?"

"They try."

"You need a woman like your sister. You see how Alicia supports Octavio."

"Octavio is an ass."

A ripple of humor played across her face. "Yes, but Alicia doesn't let him know it. American women always criticize. To them, the individual comes before the family, isn't that so? Has Gail Connor poisoned your mind? Turned you against us?"

Anthony found himself in the odd position of defending a woman he had no wish ever to see again. "No, she didn't do that."

But Digna went on, "Then why do you hate us? Ernesto is a part of me, like my eyes or my tongue. If you hate him, you hate me too." She fumbled at the clasp of her purse and withdrew an embroidered handkerchief, which she pressed to her nose.

He sat down and put an arm around her. "Nena, don't say such things."

"Will you see him? I swear to the Holy Mother I will never ask another thing of you as long as God grants me breath."

The phone rang. Anthony ignored it and held onto his grandmother's hand. The age-spotted skin was soft, and her nails were
beautifully tended. After sixty years, her wedding ring had worn
thin. "I'll think about it, all right? Not today. Give me some time.
A couple of weeks."

"Ernesto may be dead by then."

"I doubt it. The old man has another ten years in him, at
least."

The phone was still ringing. Anthony turned his head, frowning. "What does she want? I told her, no phone calls."

It continued to ring. Perhaps Angela had been in a traffic accident. She was unconscious. The police had found his number in
her wallet.

"One moment." Anthony stood up to reach the extension on
the end table. "Yes, what is it?" His secretary apologized for disturbing him, but Judge Harris was on the line. He wanted to
speak to Anthony. It couldn't wait. Extremely urgent. Anthony
told her he would take the call in the conference room. His grandmother still clasped the handkerchief on her knees.

"Nena, I'm sorry. It's a client. An emergency. I'll be right
back." The glassed-in conference room was just down the hall.
He closed the door and picked up the extension on the credenza
under the windows.

"Nate? This is Anthony. What's going on?"

The voice on the other end was measured and clear, but he
could hear the tension in it, and as he listened, his hand tightened
on the receiver.

"*Ay, mi Diós.* . . . You didn't tell me you saw Gonzalez at the
party! . . . What do you mean, *forgot*? . . . Yes, Nate, it is most
definitely a problem."

Anthony paced as far as the phone cord would allow. "When
do you go back on the bench? . . . I'll be there in fifteen
minutes. . . . Listen to me. If by some chance she calls, do not talk
to her. Don't talk to *anyone* about this. . . . No, no, it's going to be
all right, I'm sure of it. We'll think of something."

When he replaced the handset it rattled slightly. Had she gone
mad? To threaten a judge? And how had she come to represent

Bobby Gonzalez? Had she sought him out? Had he come to her? Why would she take a homicide case? She knew nothing about criminal law.

He was halfway to the lobby before he remembered that he had left his grandmother in his office.

His sister had come back with the tea. Alicia and Digna were both seated on the sofa. Their hushed conversation broke off as he came through the door.

He found himself speaking English, already creating a distance between himself and the women. "Nena, Alicia, please forgive me, but I have to leave. A client just called with a problem. An emergency situation. Very serious."

Alicia stood up. "How convenient."

Digna's cup clicked into its saucer. "Hush, Alicita. Your brother has to go save someone. It's his job, no?"

Anthony felt his pocket for his car keys. "Stay here, please. Finish your tea. I'm going to be gone for at least an hour."

His grandmother said, "Will you call me? Soon?"

He rushed back across the office and kissed her. "Within a few days, I promise."

She reached up to pat his cheek, a touch as delicate as a butterfly wing. "Thank you. *Te quiero, mi corazón.*"

"I love you too, Nena."

Alicia's deep blue eyes poured reproach.

CHAPTER

12

The judge requested that Gail meet him at eight o'clock at his condo on Grove Isle. The island was a private enclave a hundred yards or so off Coconut Grove, accessible by a bridge with a security checkpoint. Gail recalled a private marina, a flashy lobby, and a four-star restaurant. Otherwise, her memory was hazy, as she had been there only once, a black-tie dinner party for the newly installed Brazilian consul. Her former law firm had represented the Banco do Brasil, and she had just settled a case worth millions. What glittering days those had been.

At home, there was a note stuck to the refrigerator under a palm-tree magnet. *Have gone to movie with Verna, home ten-ish. Love you.* Gail suspected that her mother had cleared out to avoid the temptation of asking how it had gone at the clinic today. It had not gone. Afraid to miss Judge Harris's call, Gail had canceled. Again.

She grabbed a cup of yogurt and ate it on the way to her room, fearing that anything heavier might make her throw up on the judge's shoes. She showered and changed into a sleeveless beige dress and short jacket. Clipped on gold earrings. Brushed her hair sleekly behind her ears. The effect was businesslike but not butch. From force of habit she turned sideways in her dresser mirror. *Stop that,* she told herself. She set out fresh water for the cats, then wrote a note for her mother—where she would be, with whom, and what time to expect her. *Love you.* She stuck it under the magnet.

On the front porch, popping up her umbrella for the drizzle, she realized why she had been so detailed. The note had been prompted by subconscious concern that Judge Nathan Harris, whose spotless reputation and rising career she had put into jeopardy, would suddenly snap. He would seize her by the throat, pull out a gun, come at her with a lamp raised over his head . . .

At five minutes to eight, her car turned off Bayshore Drive onto the short bridge that led to Grove Isle. The headlights picked up flashes of rain in the fading gray of evening. Heavy trees gave way to a view of two buildings, each about fifteen stories high, brown-painted terraces making horizontal stripes on beige stucco walls. The style had been popular in the late seventies, an era when cash from drug profits had flooded Miami like a tropical downpour.

The buildings were joined by a common entrance. Judge Harris had told her to leave her car with the valet. She pulled out of the rain and turned off the wipers. A middle-aged couple, dressed for the evening, got into their Jaguar, and the valet jogged in Gail's direction.

How odd, Gail thought, that Nathan Harris would live *here*. A measly salary of a hundred grand a year wouldn't be enough, unless he had inherited money from his wife. That was possible. Aside from the value of her paintings, Margaret Cresswell had been born into a wealthy family. Gail made a note to ask her mother about that. With her charity work and contacts, Irene had access to every society tattle-tale in Miami.

A doorman held open a heavy glass door, and Gail entered the lobby, where she checked in at the desk. With a practiced smile, the guard directed her toward the elevators. Top floor, apartment two. And go right in. The door would be open.

Gripping her purse in both hands, she watched the indicator flash from floor to floor. What did she really know of him? His wife had overdosed on sleeping pills at age thirty-three. Why? Had he driven her to it?

The good judge could be living a secret life, Gail thought. Why had he gone to that party the night Margaret's brother was murdered? He'd gotten smashed, had smoked a joint with a twenty-one-year-old kid. Such a strange crowd—drunks, artists, old hippies, a transvestite teaching the samba. Gail's imagination flashed with wild scenarios. Perhaps the judge couldn't confess that he'd been there because it was he who had shot Roger Cresswell. But why? What had Roger known that had ended his life? What if he had been blackmailing the judge? What if—

The elevator stopped, and the door slid back. Gail peered into a carpeted corridor illuminated by a chandelier in a long gold oval. Audubon prints of spoonbills and egrets decorated the walls, and an arrangement of fresh flowers sat on a mahogany table. No one was about. She stepped off the elevator just as it started to close. There were four sets of double doors, and from one of them a patch of light fell into the hall. She walked closer. A view of the living area was blocked by a divider paneled in exotically grained wood. Recessed lights shone in pools on white travertine marble. Her heels tapped, then sank into carpet as she moved around the divider. She rapped her knuckles on one end of it.

"Judge Harris?"

The large room contained sleekly modern leather furniture and more polished wood. Hidden lights glowed on glass shelves. Several oddly shaped vases with twisted black branches had been placed along the wall of windows facing east. Through them she saw the darkening sky.

A light shone from a hallway near the dining area. She went halfway into the living room and called out, "Hello?"

From behind her came a noise—a click and a hollow thud—the sound of a closing door. She whirled around, and a moment later a man appeared beside the divider.

Inhaling a gasp, she stumbled back a step. Quick images flooded her mind—dark hair and eyes, the white vee of an open-collared shirt, a coffee-brown suit.

Anthony Quintana.

He stopped a few feet away, out of range for a handshake. His casual stance showed no sign of tension. "I apologize for frightening you, and for the subterfuge, but you might not have come otherwise."

Gail's hand was clenched over her heart. "What are you doing here?"

He smiled slightly, then added, "I'm representing Nate Harris."

"Oh, really." Anthony hadn't materialized out of nowhere, she realized. He'd been standing behind the divider, waiting for her to go around the other end of it. After Gail was sure she could speak calmly, she said, "Where is he?"

"He's not here. In fact, this isn't his apartment. It belongs to a client of mine who comes in the winter. He owed me a little favor. I thought it would be private. Convenient for both of us." The soft Spanish accent made his words seem intimate, charged with meaning.

Her heart was still slamming at her ribs. "What did you do, pay off the security guard?"

"Again, my apologies." Anthony gestured toward the long sofa facing the windows. Gold circled his wrist and shone on his cuff. "Would you care to sit down?"

She didn't move. "No. I prefer to speak to Judge Harris."

"With regret, that's impossible. He asked me to handle this."

"Looks like he picked the wrong lawyer." She walked toward the door.

A few long strides took Anthony there first. "Nate won't talk to you. I ordered him not to."

"Get out of my way."

In a smoothly placating tone he said, "Gail, you made a demand on him this morning. I think we should discuss it."

She calculated the odds of pushing him aside. "Kidnaping opposing counsel is a rather extreme method of representing a client, Mr. Quintana."

"Of course you can go." His hands rose level with his shoulders, palms out, a surrender. "I won't stop you. But if you do leave, what will you have accomplished for Bobby Gonzalez? If he is arrested, what will you have gained?" Eyebrows went up, furrowing his forehead. "Yes, I admit that neither of us wants to be here, but let's try to put aside our differences for the sake of our respective clients. That's reasonable, isn't it?"

She had heard this routine in the courtroom, asking an adverse witness a few innocuous warm-up questions before the claws came out. She knew he wanted something, and that she wouldn't like it. But he was right: Leaving now would accomplish nothing. She sent him an icy stare. "What do you suggest?"

Another polite smile. "We'll see what we can work out. Sit down, please."

Turning her back on him, Gail walked across the living room as if to check the place out, but her vision was so dimmed by rage she barely avoided running into the furniture. She wandered to one of the built-in display cases, where rows of clay figurines sat on polished glass shelves, as if in a museum. Fat little creatures with oversized heads, stubby arms and legs, and jutting breasts and bellies.

Anthony's voice said, "They're from Guatemala. Olmec, I think."

She tossed her purse into one of the leather-and-chrome Eames chairs. "You do have a talent for picking solvent clients."

Another sidelong glance brought more details. He still wore his hair combed back from his forehead, but now it fell into waves at the nape of his neck. His skin glowed with a rich tan, and she remembered what Angela had said: Her father had vacationed in Spain. This annoyed her. She had wanted to see evidence of dissolution. Of loss and decay. Circles under his eyes. Anything.

"May I offer you something to drink?"

"No, thank you."

"I hope you are well. And Karen? Your mother?"

She mirrored his emotionless smile. "We're wonderful. How kind of you to ask. It must be so distressing, having to see me again, after you ordered me out of your sight."

Finally a reaction—a tightness in the lips, a little flare in the nostrils, just a ripple on the surface. "It would be better—don't you think?—if we agree to leave the past where it is? It's not relevant."

"Oh, I don't know. It makes this whole thing sort of fun.

Maybe we can just agree not to throw each other off the balcony." She found the latch and pushed open one of the glass doors. The buildings downtown, a few miles to the northeast, were vague towers of lights in the rain. The ocean was an endless expanse of gray. Legs still shaking, she pulled in a deep breath of moist, heavy air. Bougainvillea, potted palm trees, and hanging baskets had turned the long, narrow space into a jungle.

Anthony's silhouette appeared, moving across the terra cotta tiles and up the low wall of the balcony. Standing just out of arm's reach, he leaned an elbow on the wall and interlaced his fingers. He obviously hadn't noticed how damp it was, or the patches of mildew that would grind themselves into the fine wool-and-silk fabric. She recognized the suit. He'd bought it off the rack at the Hugo Boss store in Bal Harbour. On sale—$1200.

He said, "How did you come to represent Bobby Gonzalez?"

The unexpected question surprised her. She remembered the promise made to Bobby not to involve Angela. She shrugged. "I know people at the ballet. One of them told him to call me. Someone in administration."

"Did he mention my daughter?"

"Oh, that's right, Angela's taking classes at the ballet this summer. Such a coincidence."

"I'm not certain I believe in coincidences."

"What difference does it make where I find my clients? I certainly didn't ask for this one, knowing it would bring me *here*. Can we get to the point? Bobby Gonzalez is a suspect in a homicide, and he needs Nathan Harris's help. This isn't complicated. It shouldn't take five minutes."

He replied with a sigh of endurance. "Well, it's not that easy."

"Why not?"

Turning toward the city, he rested both elbows on the wall. For Anthony Quintana to do that, unaware, showed a state of extreme mental distraction. His cool demeanor was a fat lie. But Gail remained tense, like standing too close to a purring but uncaged panther. Her eyes, now accustomed to the darkness, glided over his profile, searching for a clue to his thoughts. She studied the planes of his face and the angles of cheekbone and temple. The long straight line from brow to the tip of his nose, then the curves of full lips and rounded jaw.

Finally he said, "The situation for Nate Harris is . . . delicate, even dangerous. You understand that. The morality police on the committee would kill his nomination if there were the least suggestion of impropriety, regardless of truth."

"If it's handled discreetly, I don't see why they'd find out."

Anthony went on, "Nathan Harris is a good man. A fine judge. You've talked to him. You said you admired him."

"Yes. I did say that."

"He has done nothing wrong. He's completely blameless. It would be a loss to the federal judiciary if he were kept off the bench. To Miami as well, because if this turns into a scandal, he could be forced to resign."

"I doubt that. A judge in this circuit can do anything but insult the Cubans."

Anthony let that pass. "What you want—if I understand fully—is a statement from Nate Harris that he was with Bobby Gonzalez for a period of about forty minutes during a certain party on the night Roger Cresswell was shot to death. Yes?"

She nodded. "Not necessarily a formal statement, as long as he makes it clear to the police that Bobby couldn't have done it."

"But Gail, he can't make that assurance. He might recall a conversation with Bobby at some point during the evening. He might recall where it took place. But when? He isn't certain. Nor could he vouch for what Bobby did before or after the alleged conversation. You see the problem."

The pushing was still at the subtle stage, but Gail had felt a distinct bump. She looked at him, then said, "Alleged?"

"Until we reach an agreement on the facts, I can't allow my client to admit anything."

"Fine. The *alleged* conversation took place between eleven and eleven-forty on the seawall behind the home of Jack Pascoe, who hosted a party that your client and mine both attended. Witnesses saw when Bobby left the house and when he returned. Bobby says that Judge Harris appeared within a minute of his having sat down on the seawall, and that Nate remained there when Bobby went back to the house. Forty minutes. Or thirty-nine, if you want to be picky. Judge Harris had been drinking, but was he so drunk that he doesn't remember any of this? Bobby has an alibi for the entire night except for that period. That gap is what we need to eliminate."

Anthony leaned forward as if she might say something more. He prompted, "And after those forty minutes?"

"Bobby left the party at eleven-forty-five and drove to his apartment on South Beach, where he met a friend, Sean Cresswell, Roger's nephew, at twelve-thirty—the travel time checks out. They went to a night club, and Bobby got home at three o'clock, which his roommates can verify."

"Ah. Then you haven't heard. Sean Cresswell's parents took him by police headquarters this morning. Sean admitted that Bobby asked him to lie. Sean was at home the night of the murder, and his mother confirms it." Anthony made a slight shrug—palms out as if asking her to drop into them some explanation for this discrepancy.

All she could think to say was, "That can't be right."

"I'm afraid it is. Bobby was lying."

"Where did you get this alleged information?"

"From someone who knows." Anthony went on quietly, "It doesn't make much sense, does it, to demand an affidavit from Judge Harris when the truth is, Bobby could have killed Roger Cresswell after midnight, not before."

A hip against the wall kept Gail steady. If Bobby hadn't been with his friend, then who— Gail closed her eyes for an instant, seeing a slender girl with long, dark hair. A girl he'd want to protect, and who would be in deep caca if her father ever found out.

She crossed her arms. "I'll talk to him. There has to be an explanation. There is no way he killed Roger Cresswell. I would never believe that."

"You know he was in a gang? That he was arrested for stabbing another boy with a knife?"

"That was years ago! He grew up."

Anthony leaned closer. "This morning the police seized a .22–caliber pistol from his apartment."

"From his roommates' bedroom. It isn't his, and he didn't use it. Let them test it. There won't be a match."

"They also found a bloodstained shirt in the trash outside Bobby's apartment. The blood is the same type as Roger's. Explain that."

"It's Roger's blood. It got there because on the day that Roger falsely accused Bobby of stealing tools from the boat yard, Bobby hit him in the nose. He finally threw the shirt out, and the police found it. He was wearing a different shirt entirely the night of the murder. There are witnesses."

"What about Sean Cresswell?" Anthony demanded. "The false alibi."

"I don't know, but I'm going to find out. Meanwhile, forty minutes or four hours, I need to establish where he was. I need Judge Harris."

There was no reply as Anthony gazed back at her, eyes black in the shadows. When he spoke, his voice was controlled. Polite again. "This isn't the kind of case you usually handle," he said. "I think you'd prefer—if you had a choice—not to be involved."

"How insightful," she said.

"You're a commercial litigation attorney—an excellent one, I would be the first to say it—but in criminal law . . . well, most lawyers in your position might feel . . . uncertain. Criminal law is constantly shifting, and procedure can be a trap. But you want to do your best for Bobby. Don't you?"

"Of course."

"As I do for my client," he said. "Yes. I think we agree that both our clients deserve effective representation." He waited.

Gail exhaled. "Yes. And?"

"And you would probably agree that a lawyer with more experience and more . . . how can I say it? Recognition in the field. Someone with clout. That person is more likely to do a good job for his—or her—client."

When his eyebrows lifted again, she said, "All right, a lawyer with clout. What's your point?"

"That you don't have it. Not in criminal law. For Bobby's sake, and for Nate Harris, please. Let someone else do this. A lawyer who has experience dealing with the police and the state attorney's office. Someone they know and respect. I can suggest several names, and you could pick one you approve of. I believe that's a reasonable accommodation."

She thought of Anthony Quintana cartwheeling down the side of the building. She couldn't decide which was worse—the patronizing insult to her abilities or his blatant attempt at manipulation.

"You want me off this case," she said.

As if she had never replied, he went on in the same superior tone. "Of course you'd be reimbursed for your time so far, which is . . . I'm guessing . . . ten hours, at a rate of . . . two hundred an hour? Two-fifty?"

She nearly laughed. "You're paying me to get off the case."

"No, no. Are you listening to what I'm saying? Your inexperience could hurt both our clients."

"Oh, bullshit. You want me to go away, that's what this is about."

His even white teeth were set together. "If I may, what you should be thinking about—rather than your own injured pride—is your client."

"I *am*, Mr. Quintana. What if Bobby is arrested? Then what? Are *you* going to pay for a murder defense? How much does it cost these days? A hundred and fifty grand? Two hundred?"

He was beginning to crack around the edges. "If this is handled properly, Ms. Connor, it won't get to trial. But if it did, are you up to it?"

Her temper flared. "I didn't pass the bar exam yesterday. I have been investigating, negotiating, and trying cases for *eight years*, and I am *not* going to turn him over to some hand-picked *flunkie*! The only thing complicating this case is *you*." She pressed the heels of her hands against her forehead. "I can't stand this."

Furious, she slid the door open and went back inside, Anthony behind her. She turned on him. "Do the right thing, Anthony. Bobby is innocent, and you know it. I want a statement from Nate Harris by five o'clock Monday."

Color had flooded his cheeks. "It can't be kept quiet," he said. "It would be on CNN in twenty-four hours. Nathan Harris is a good man, a man of moral strength and intellectual courage. I will not—I promise you—allow him to be sabotaged by lies and innuendo."

Gail laughed. "Well, why don't you ask this tower of moral strength about that joint he was smoking with Bobby Gonzalez?"

Anthony stared at her.

"He didn't tell you about that, did he? Bobby went down to the water to smoke a joint, and Nate showed up, so they shared it."

"Impossible." Anthony laughed in disbelief. "That's insane. Nate Harris doesn't smoke grass, and if he did, he wouldn't do it at a party with people he barely knows. It would be professional suicide."

"Ask him. If he's so honest, he'll admit it. Miami is a weird place, and politicians and judges have done even stupider things. A few tokes on a joint? That's nothing. People will believe it. And you know what else? They're going to ask what Judge Harris was doing with a young male ballet dancer."

Anthony leaned into her face. "Repeat that publicly, I'll see you sued for slander."

"I want his help! I want *you* to stop standing in the way."

"How would you like to see Bobby Gonzalez fired from the ballet? It could happen."

"That's a complete bluff. The ballet wouldn't do that."

"No? The Cresswells are on the board. They're major donors. If they believe that Bobby is responsible for Roger's death, he would be gone. No big deal. He's in the back row. He could be replaced tomorrow." He dusted one hand against the other. "Believe it, Ms. Connor."

Gail stared at him. The claws were out now and Bobby was caught between them. "Could you really be that vicious? Oh, of course you could. Why even ask? I put nothing past you. No underhanded, ruthless act would be too low."

He came within inches, lowering his head, the whites of his eyes showing under irises dilated to black. "Consider your own actions. You allow Nathan Harris only two disagreeable choices—either to perjure himself or to say he was smoking grass with a male dancer half his age. That is not acceptable. Take that road, and your client will suffer the consequences of your poor judgment."

Gail was nearly tall enough, in her heels, to look him squarely in the eyes. "If Nathan Harris is destroyed, blame yourself. You're turning him into a coward and a liar."

Anthony's eyes snapped with fire. "Why are you doing this? Why this . . . death grip on an inconsequential case that you don't have the skill to handle?"

"Because he's my client. Because I promised him."

"How much is he paying you? Anything?"

"None of your effing business."

"You would do it for free, wouldn't you? Because you get a chance to say to yourself, oh, goody, now I can stick it to Anthony Quintana."

"Are you that much of an egoist? If I'd known you were involved, I'd never have taken this case!"

"So leave it."

"Why don't *you?*"

Suddenly he swiveled away, pacing, breathing through his teeth. She heard him mutter, *"Ay, esa mujer es increíble."*

Her head throbbed. Afraid she might faint, she sank onto one end of the sofa, cream-colored leather squeaking softly. He paced back to her, and with averted eyes she saw his trousers and his gleaming, unscuffed Italian shoes. She hoped he stepped in dog shit in the parking lot.

"Well. A standoff," he said. "Which one of us is going to pull the trigger first?"

"Leave Bobby alone. Dancing is all he has."

He paced away, then back again. "You don't want a drink? Some water? You look a little—I don't know—pale."

"I'm fine. You can bring me a glass of water. I'll drown myself in it."

"Do you want it or not?"

"I said yes!"

"All right, then."

He went to the wet bar on the wall near the dining table. A cabinet opened, then slammed. Water gurgled from a bottle.

He came back with a heavy Baccarat tumbler tinkling with ice cubes, which he put on a coaster on the immense coffee table. On the table. Not in her hand. Maybe his flesh would fall off if he touched her.

Gail lifted the glass carefully and sipped while he stood watching.

His jacket was pushed back, and his hands rested on narrow hips. A better manicure than she had. No clear nail polish—no, he was too macho for that. Brown alligator belt, gold buckle. He would be wearing his twenty-dollar briefs. She tried to imagine they were pink, and failed.

"I have a suggestion about what to do," he said.

"I didn't like your last one."

"Listen. What you want is not so difficult. You want the police to leave Bobby Gonzalez alone. If they do that, you don't go after Nate Harris."

"Must you put it that way? 'Going after' him."

He was thinking aloud. "If we could find an alternate suspect. If the police had a better case against someone else."

"Great. Just find out who shot Roger Cresswell."

"That's not necessary. We don't have to prove it."

"What if the police arrest Bobby Gonzalez before we give them an alternative?"

"No, I don't think they will, not on what they have now. It isn't enough. They'll wait for the DNA results on the blood-stained shirt. That could take eight weeks."

"But the blood wasn't from the night Roger was killed."

"You told me that, but I need the names of witnesses who can prove it. Meanwhile, we investigate everyone involved, and if we're lucky, there will be someone else for them to look at besides Bobby. We have an advantage: Nate knows the Cresswell family. He was married to Roger's sister, Margaret."

"I know."

Surprised, Anthony said, "How?"

"Small world. Charlene Marks has met Nate Harris." The tension between them had dissipated, but Gail's hands were still trembling. "And a couple of months ago Charlene talked to Roger

Cresswell about a divorce. He thought his wife was cheating on him. I don't think the police know about it."

"Good. Follow up on that." Anthony went to slide shut the terrace door. "I've met Roger's parents and his uncle. Nate and I were at the Cresswells' house the morning the news came of Roger's death. I went because Porter Cresswell wanted advice from a criminal lawyer. I think he may be mentally unstable, but he knew there were problems. When he became ill early this year, he let Roger take over. Porter's brother, Duncan, is part owner, and Duncan's wife, Elizabeth, is in management. They didn't agree with Roger on most issues, and the operations were paralyzed with jealousy and power struggles. Porter wanted Roger to step down, but he refused. Motives already, you see?"

"You think his murder came from inside the family," Gail concluded.

"I do. Roger wasn't involved with drugs, and he didn't gamble. He'd had no arguments with his friends." Anthony smiled. "We have a good chance of success."

Gail looked at him. "I still want a written statement from Judge Harris."

"Why?"

"If you want to play private eye, fine. But if the police come after Bobby, I'll have something."

"You didn't hear what I told you," Anthony said. "A statement covering forty minutes won't help you, if Bobby can't prove where he was after midnight."

She rested her forehead on extended fingers. "This won't work."

"I have a good investigator. We could use him."

"Who's going to pay for that? Bobby can't afford it."

"I will. I can't ask Nate. It would be improper."

"But it's proper if his lawyer pays?"

"I have no choice." An edge sharpened his words. "You should be grateful and stop complaining. Giving Nate Harris's name to the police at this point would be reckless. You'd destroy him for nothing. If you do that, I will take action. Trust me."

For a long moment she returned the intensity of his unblinking stare. The pulse beat in her neck. She said, "I'll give it a week. Then we'll see. And I want to know what's going on. Everything you find out."

He made a single nod of his head. "Of course, you should be informed."

"*Involved,* Anthony. I will be *involved.*"

He made an exaggerated lift of his hands. "Fine. All right. Involved."

"Thank you."

Turning his back, he muttered, *"Jesucristo, me vuelve loco."*

Gail set the glass back on the table. The crystal sparkled as she turned it around on the coaster. "Let's talk about logistics. How do we handle this? Where do we meet? Not your office. Or mine. Does it have to be in person?"

"You want to do it by video-conference? Then we don't have to be in the same room."

She laughed softly. "Sure. Why not?"

His steps slowed as he approached the sofa, where she sat playing with the glass. He was silent so long she looked up at him. He said, "You despise me, don't you?"

Their eyes held. Then she couldn't bear it any longer and turned her head. "As you said . . . leave the past where it is. Don't mention it. Ever. I won't either."

"*Bueno.* That will make it easier for us to work together."

Silence stretched out. Gail could see that his cat's-eye ring was back on Anthony's left hand. He had taken it off, waiting for a wedding band. The faintest hint of his cologne reached her consciousness, and a memory burst into her mind. How he'd smelled the first time she had pressed her mouth to his bare chest.

His hand tapped on his thigh, then reached for her empty glass. "Well, that's all we can do for now. I'll call you tomorrow."

"Morning is better." She went to retrieve her purse. "I'm taking the afternoon off to shop for Karen. She's coming home on Saturday."

"Ah. Summer vacation's over already."

"Yes. She spent most of it in the Virgin Islands with Dave."

Purse in hand, Gail looked around, hoping to see some kind of reaction to that, but there was only a rush of water from the mini-bar. Anthony was rinsing her glass in the sink.

He called across the room, "I'll phone you at ten o'clock. Is that convenient?"

"Fine." She went toward the door. "Good night. I'll see myself out."

She made it into the corridor, but decided not to wait for the elevator and ran for the exit stairs. Then the pain in her chest let go, and she leaned against the concrete wall and cried. A great hiccup of a sob, then another. Hot tears dropping off her chin. Fingers against her mouth, hiding the noise. Making her way down fifteen flights in her high heels because the doors didn't open from the stairwell. The echoes of her footsteps accompanied her.

In her misery Gail felt as if a knife were being plunged into her heart. Even her bones ached. *You despise me, don't you?* Yes. Yes, I do. Arrogant, stone-hearted son of a bitch.

Hanging on the railing with one hand, she pressed her other fist into her belly and doubled over, wanting it gone immediately, now. Out of her, gone. She cursed herself for not having kept the appointment. It would have been easy. Judge Harris hadn't called till five-thirty, and she could have kept the damned telephone in her hand at the clinic.

She had wondered, until this moment, why she'd waited so long. Why she'd felt relief every time she'd had to cancel, gloom as each new date came nearer. Moral queasiness? Fear of pain? Not really. Then why?

Because she hadn't wanted to let things slip away from her anymore, not even this. She'd wanted to salvage something from the wreck. To be able to say, even after seeing her marriage dry up and her daughter tossed back and forth between them, and watching her career turn to shit and a love affair go down in flames, that there was at least one thing in her life she could do.

No, there was an even worse reason for not having ended it. This . . . thing inside her that she still couldn't call a child was part of a man she had once loved beyond reason. He had entered her brain, her lungs, the marrow of her bones, so deeply that when he pushed her away and called himself a fool for ever loving her, she hadn't believed him, not in her soul. It was like watching someone die, the breaths still coming, slow and shallow, one tiny, flickering spark of irrational hope still remaining.

That spark had at last gone out.

On the fifteenth floor, Anthony Quintana walked onto the terrace with a glass of ice and a bottle of his client's best single-malt scotch. He had left his jacket inside and rolled up his shirt sleeves. It was too humid tonight. The air conditioning pouring through the open door helped.

He set the glass on the edge of the balcony and poured. He wondered how in hell it had all turned out this way. Gail should have accepted with grace the fact that she was in over her head. He had thought—he had *known*—that after one look at him, she'd have been happy to throw this case to some other lawyer.

Now what? He had to find a murderer. How had he been cornered into this? How? It had happened before, with that woman. Suddenly finding himself in a place he'd not wanted to be in, with no knowledge of how he had gotten there. Very strange.

In some way he couldn't define, she seemed different. She'd lost weight, perhaps, though she was already thin. Or had gained a few pounds. Or her hair was combed differently. She was too pale, and he had made out faint tracings of blue under the delicate skin of her neck. He had seen the flutter of a racing heartbeat.

Anthony leaned to see over the balcony, not touching it because it was wet, and he didn't want to ruin his shirt. The driveway was down there at an angle, and at long intervals a car would come out from under the portico and move slowly toward the bridge. There had been two BMWs and a Mercedes. So far no small silver Acuras. This was what Gail Connor drove now. He knew this because a month ago, just before leaving for Spain, he'd seen her in traffic on Flagler Street near the courthouse. His car had been at a cross street, and he had watched her until horns had started blaring behind him. Three days ago he had seen another silver Acura and a woman with blond hair, and his breath had caught in his throat until he realized that it wasn't Gail at all, and he'd felt stupid.

He drank his scotch and watched the driveway, but her car never appeared, or he had missed it somehow. He watched the bay for a while, but the rain had kept the boats from going out, and there was nothing to see. He remembered how the plants hanging from the edge of the roof had swung in a sudden breeze, and the light had flickered on her hair, and even in the darkness it had shimmered with gold.

CHAPTER

13

Gliding on pointe, arms floating outward, Angela noticed in the studio mirror that Bobby was walking toward the door. A girl from the office had come in. Angela made a pirouette and stopped, a hand on her hip. With *The Nutcracker* on the CD player she couldn't hear what they were saying. Bobby looked around and said to keep working. He would be back in a few minutes.

As soon as he was gone, Angela ran over and peered into the corridor, then hurried toward the exit. She came out at one end of the lobby. At the far end, big photographs hung on the curved wall, and windows gave a view of the plaza. There were two figures in silhouette, Bobby in his sweat pants and baggy T-shirt, Gail Connor in pumps and a suit.

One of the doors at the main entrance opened, and Angela saw Diane Cresswell come in. They said hello to each other, then Diane looked around to see what had held Angela's attention.

"Who's that with Bobby? His lawyer? What's going on?"

"I don't know. She just showed up."

Diane knew about Bobby. He had told her everything. They had gone out a couple of years ago—which Angela didn't like to think about—and they were still friends. Diane was beautiful, with her milky-white skin and silvery blond hair. And a beautiful dancer, strong and quick. She'd never had to audition. Edward Villella had seen her in New York and had invited her to join the company.

Bobby was staring at the carpet, then up at the skylight as if Gail were lecturing him about something. Their voices were muffled. Diane said, "Do you think she'd talk to me for free, like she did for Bobby?"

"Do you need a lawyer?"

"I might."

"Gail would probably help you. What's it about?" Angela waited, but Diane said nothing more. Diane was watching Bobby and Gail come across the lobby toward the glass doors at the entrance. Gail continued outside, vanishing past the corner of the ticket window.

Bobby turned and saw the girls, and Angela could tell by the stiff way he moved that something was wrong. "Hi, Diane."

"Hi." Still looking toward the street, she said, "See you guys later, okay?" She went out the same way Gail Connor had gone, leaving them alone in the lobby.

Angela said, "What did Gail want?"

His mouth was tight. "Sean sold me out." Bobby started toward the studios, and Angela had to hurry to keep up, clattering in her pointe shoes. Bobby looked to see if anyone was around before saying, "He told the cops I asked him to lie. I can't believe he would *do* that. Gail wanted to know if your dad talked to you last night, and I said I didn't think so, because you didn't say anything to me."

"Bobby, slow down."

He pulled open the door to Studio Six and let her go in. The music was still playing. He went over and punched a button. Silence.

"They met last night—your dad and Ms. Connor. He's the lawyer for Judge Harris. They're *friends*, would you believe? That's how your dad got into in it. He's supposed to call Ms. Connor this morning, so she wanted to talk to me first. She guessed I was with you, Angie. She said if I wasn't with Sean, where was I?

Damn Sean. Why'd he do it? I'd never have ratted him out like that."

"Oh, my God. She's going to tell my father?"

"She has to. They're working together, and she has to explain where I was after midnight. But she won't tell him today. I made her promise. That gives you time to talk to him yourself."

Angela pressed her hands against her cheeks, which were burning. "I *can't.*"

"You have to. You want him to find out from her?"

"If he finds out I was with you till *three o'clock in the morning*—Oh, God."

"People stay out all the time. Jesus. You're in college, not junior high. Tell him we were at Denny's."

"He wouldn't believe that. He'll send me back to New Jersey."

"How? Tie you up and put you on the plane like a piece of luggage? There's nothing he can do. If he breaks anybody's neck, it's gonna be mine. If he cuts you off, so what? Get a job. I told you, you can live with me."

Angela sank to the floor and sat with her legs straight out, face in her hands. "Oh, my God."

Bobby stood over her. "You said you would."

"You don't understand!"

"Sure I do. I'm not good enough for your *papi*, the big important lawyer, and all your stuck-up relatives. I never even seen that house you're always talking about. Every time your dad comes over here, you tell me to get lost. You're ashamed to be seen with me, aren't you?" He pulled her hands away from her face. "Aren't you?"

"No! Bobby, don't say that. I love you."

"Yeah? You don't know what that means. You love somebody, you stand up for them. If you can't do that for me, then leave. Go on. Be his baby girl the rest of your life."

Hands falling limply into her lap, Angela started to cry. Through the shifting light of her tears she could see a pair of white socks and worn practice shoes, gray at the toe and heel. They moved away, then came back. He stood on one foot, then the other.

"Hey. Would you stop it?"

She drew in a breath that tore at her throat. "I *do* love you, I'm just scared. Please don't be mad at me."

Bobby dropped down cross-legged beside her and pulled her head against his chest. "I'm not mad at you, *mamita*. I'm *tired* of it, you always taking shit from your old man." He stroked her hair and kissed her. "You have to decide, girl."

Angela wiped her eyes on the hem of his T-shirt. "Okay. I'll talk to him." Bobby hugged her tightly. She said, "I'm moving to the dorms tomorrow anyway. I might call him from UM. I can hang up when he starts yelling at me."

"Angie, listen. Your father has no right to judge you. How to live your life, what to do. Like he was so perfect. I'm going to tell you something I noticed, okay? About Ms. Connor. I could be wrong, but I don't think so. Yesterday at my apartment, she's eating Tums and drinking a Sprite, you remember that?"

"Yes."

"Same thing last week. I go to her office, and she's eating saltines and a soda for lunch. Plus the Tums. I *know* what that is, because I've seen my sisters and their girlfriends do it. And while I was there? I overheard her talking to a doctor's office, canceling her appointment because she had a client—me—and she couldn't go that day. So tell me. What does that mean?"

"She's sick?"

Bobby smiled at Angela as if she had said something funny. He kissed her forehead. "*Mi angelita.* You're too sweet. She's pregnant."

Gail was driving slowly down the ramp in the parking garage when she saw a girl running toward her from the other direction. She waved for Gail to stop.

Pulling to one side, Gail pressed the button to lower the window.

"Ms. Connor? I almost couldn't find you." She took a breath. "I'm Diane Cresswell. I apologize if you're in a hurry. . . ."

"No, it's fine. Wait. Let me park the car." She pulled into an-other space and turned off the engine. When she got out, Diane

Cresswell extended one finely boned hand. Her yellow tank top hung loose outside a miniskirt that showed off her legs. The muscles were slim and smooth, but Gail thought a tuning fork might make a nice ringing noise if tapped on her thigh.

Gail said, "I'm glad to meet you. I saw you dance on Lincoln Road last week. It was lovely. And please accept my condolences for your cousin. I know it's hard to lose someone in your family."

"Thank you. We didn't know each other that well, Roger and I. He was a lot older. I feel so sorry for his mom and dad."

"I think my mother might know your aunt Claire," Gail said. "She belongs to the Ballet Guild."

"Mmmm. Then I may have met her. Aunt Claire is in the Guild, too."

Waiting for whatever would come next, Gail studied the girl who had found Roger Cresswell's bullet-riddled body. She was different from the ballerina at the theater, but there she had danced in full makeup. Her platinum hair was tied with a bow at the nape of her long neck, and her brows were delicate curves.

She said, "It's good I saw you, because I was thinking I might need a lawyer. Not for anything *major*, just a question—if you have a minute?" Her words were soft and perfectly enunciated.

"Yes, of course. We could find some coffee if you like."

"That would be nice, but unfortunately, I have a costume fitting at nine o'clock."

"Well, then. How can I help you?"

"It's about a painting my cousin Maggie did—a portrait of me when I was twelve years old." Diane paused. "You know who she is, right?" When Gail nodded, she went on, "It was at my parents' house. My uncle Porter gave it to them, but they didn't like it. They only wanted it because Maggie was famous, so I took it to my cousin's gallery. That's Jack Pascoe. Well, he's not really my cousin, but—"

"Yes, I know who Jack Pascoe is," Gail said.

"Okay. Jack says if I can establish ownership I could sell it and buy an apartment on the beach. I don't think I *want* to sell it because I'm sure my cousin Maggie meant it for me. Anyway, my mother says if I don't bring the painting back, she'll call the police. I don't know what to do. Jack says I should get some legal advice."

"Surely your own mother wouldn't have you arrested."

A smile played at the corner of her mouth. "You don't know my mother."

"No, I don't." Gail wanted to pull this girl by the elbow to the nearest bench. *Tell me about your mother, your father, your aunt and uncle. Tell me about Jack Pascoe. And tell me about Roger. Who wanted him dead?*

Gail said, "Well, I'd need to have the facts before I give you an opinion. We should talk about it. Would you like to come by my office?"

"Angela Quintana said you might not charge. I have to be careful with money."

"There's no charge for a consultation." Gail smiled at her. "I'd love to see the portrait sometime. Where do you keep it?"

The answer was what Gail had hoped for. "At my place. I live in a cottage behind Jack Pascoe's house. Where the party was."

There was a quick intelligence behind Diane Cresswell's cool blue eyes. Gail said, "Maybe we could talk there. Save you a trip?"

"Today?"

"This weekend. I can't on Saturday, but maybe Sunday. Would that be convenient?"

"Sure. What time?"

"Give me your phone number. I'll check my schedule and let you know." She went back into her car for a pen and notepad. As Diane was writing, Gail said, "Bobby must have told you quite a bit. He really should be careful about that."

"We're very good friends." Diane lifted one shoulder in a small shrug. "Discretion is a virtue, they say."

"Yes, it is. We should all practice it."

"I agree."

After another moment or two, Gail said, "I'll call you."

"Thanks."

Diane Cresswell shouldered her dance bag and hurried toward the exit.

*   *   *

Traffic in Miami, barely tolerable in off-hours, was so snarled at nine, even heading south, that it took an hour for Gail to get from the beach to her office. Jammed behind a landscaper's truck with a flapping load of palm trees, Gail reached for her portable phone. With one eye on the road and a knee bracing the steering wheel, Gail quickly punched in Charlene Marks's number.

The receptionist said Charlene was on her way to court.

Gail disconnected and tried her cell phone, and Charlene answered. She said, "My God, I'm on U.S. One, too! Wave as you go past. What's up?"

Gail filled her in.

A laugh came over the line. "I don't *believe* this!"

"I should have predicted it," Gail said. "He and Nate Harris are friends. If the judge gets himself into a little problem, of course he's going to go to the one man devious enough to pull him out of it."

"Can you trust him?"

"Of course not, but it's the best alternative for Bobby. He gets the benefit of an investigator on the case. It could work." Gail adjusted the vent on the air conditioner to blow more directly on her neck.

"Are you going to tell him about seeing Diane Cresswell?"

"Why not? I won't let him go with me, but we need to share information. Charlene, I need a favor."

"Oh, dear."

"Your notes on Roger Cresswell. *Por favor.*"

Charlene promised to call her secretary and have the copies waiting when Gail came to get them.

There wasn't much—a client intake form and two handwritten pages torn from a legal pad. Gail scanned them in the elevator, trying to puzzle out cryptic symbols and nearly illegible handwriting. Charlene had not been happy to give up her notes, but Gail had pointed out that a dead client was not likely to raise the issue of attorney-client privilege.

Gail found her door unlocked, meaning that her secretary had arrived. Before she could cross the small waiting area, the inner door opened, and Miriam Ruiz's wide-eyed face appeared.

"*Ay,* Gail! Guess who just called."

"Who?"

She trotted after Gail into her office. At twenty-two, Miriam still had the enthusiasm of a teenager, and her corkscrew hair bounced on her shoulders. "No, you have to guess."

Gail tossed her purse to her desk. "Anthony Quintana?"

Large brown eyes blinked. "Yes! How did you know?"

"We sort of . . . ran into each other last night on opposite sides of a case. He's representing Judge Harris."

"No!"

"*Que sí,*" Gail replied. "What did he say?" She put a hand on her telephone.

"He asked if you were here, and I said no, and he said call as soon as you get in." Miriam twisted her fingers together. "What are you going to do?"

"Call him back?"

"Do you need the number?"

"I seem to remember it."

At the door Miriam said, "He sounded exactly the same. He asked how I was. And if I got my degree yet in my accounting program. He asked about the baby. He remembered Berto's broken tooth!"

Gail picked up the handset and smiled at her. "Yes, isn't he just charming? Go on. Let me call him. I'll tell you all about it."

"Oh, sure. Sorry."

The door clicked shut. Gail looked at the handset for a moment, then dropped it back on the telephone. It was still early, only 10:15. Better to read Charlene's notes first. Then write a memo, which could be e-mailed to him. But before anything, some coffee, lots of it. She'd had a bad night. The window had lightened to pale gray before she had finally slept.

A month ago Gail had leased a larger suite upstairs, which had its own compact kitchen. Now the coffeepot sat on a small refrigerator in the secretarial area, and they got their water from the ladies' room down the hall. But Gail bypassed the pot in favor of the Styrofoam cup of *café cubano* that Miriam had bought in the cafeteria. She lifted the lid and poured some into a one-ounce plastic cup.

Miriam was watching her from behind her computer. "Did you call him?"

"I'm fortifying my nerves."

"Was it okay last night?" Miriam was looking at her like a puppy left out in the rain. "Did you . . . talk about things?"

Gail sipped the *café*. "No, and I don't plan to." She gave Miriam a quick smile. "The man is a complete asshole. My only regret is that it took me so long to see it."

"Wow. You're in a mood."

"Rotten," Gail cheerfully agreed. "If he calls again, I'm not here." She tossed the empty cup into the trash. "I'll call when I'm ready."

At her desk she kicked off her shoes and sat with one leg under her, reading. Most of Charlene's notes had to do with money. Making a joke—or maybe not—she had once told Gail, *The first two questions for any potential client are How big a check can you write me? and Will it clear the bank?* Gail didn't particularly wonder why he hadn't come back. Charlene's initial retainers started at $10,000, and Roger could have been shopping around.

Roger Charles Cresswell. Only son of Claire and Porter Cresswell. Age thirty-two. Worked at Cresswell Yachts, executive V.P., making $250,000 a year. Before that, he ran the company's leasing operation. An entire page was devoted to assets and liabilities. Stocks, bonds, mutual funds—all highly margined. Condo in the Grove, owned by Roger and Nikki—big mortgage. His Porsche and her BMW were leased. They had a few thousand dollars in a savings account. They owed a staggering amount on their charge cards. Charlene had written, *Wife a spendthrift.* Gail wanted to add, *What about you, Roger?*

They had been living large, but it was all show, except for the shares of Cresswell Yachts, a ten percent ownership, which Roger had acquired along with his new job as company V.P. Charlene had lovingly written, and underlined several times, the figure of $20,000,000.

Gail mentally filled in the blanks left by Charlene's abbreviated style. Daddy had drawn Roger back to the family fold by giving him ten percent of the business. Roger had alienated Uncle Duncan and Aunt Elizabeth. Daddy had wanted his job back. Charlene had written, *Old man going mental?* Roger's opinion, anyway. Had the old man been crazy enough to shoot his own son?

The juicier details were on the other page. Nikki Cresswell, age twenty-six. Married four years. They'd met when the ad agency she'd worked for had done Roger's boat leasing ads. *Possible adultery?* Gail wished Charlene hadn't put a question mark after the word. She wished Roger had said with whom.

Roger's first Christmas present to Nikki had been a set of breast implants. Then the other enticements—cosmetic dentistry, ladies' Rolex, Caribbean cruise (first-class cabin), set of Ping golf clubs, weekends in New York, membership at a health spa. Then the diamond engagement ring. *Wife refuses to work full time.* Well, duh.

What if Nikki had found out that Roger had seen a divorce lawyer? Had she looked in the Yellow Pages under HIT MEN?

Gail pushed aside the notes and came out of her office for a follow-up mug of American coffee. She avoided Miriam's inquisitive glances. She went back inside, closed the door, and stared at the telephone. Buzzing on caffeine, back in control of her confidence, she punched in Anthony's private line. She did not want to speak to his secretary.

"*¿Quien habla?*"

"This is Gail. I just got in. Miriam said you'd called?"

"Gail, hello. I didn't expect you on this line. How are you today? Better?"

"I'm fine. I was fine last night." Realizing she'd begun pacing, she said, "Well, how do we do this? I suppose we could discuss strategy, but first, it might be a good idea to pool our information. That would save time. Each of us could do a detailed memorandum bringing the other up to date."

"You're still angry."

Momentarily confused, Gail stopped walking. "What?"

"If I made you angry last night, I'm very sorry. It was all . . .

maybe a little intense. I was thinking of my client first, as you were. I promise you, we aren't enemies. We have to work together for this to succeed, and anything I can do, I will."

He had never been able to erase the soft Spanish accent, and it gave his words a quiet intimacy that told Gail immediately how bitchy she'd sounded. She leaned against the edge of the desk. "You're right. And I'm sorry for being so . . . uncivil just then. Let me start over. I just picked up copies of Charlene Marks's notes from her consultation with Roger Cresswell. Should I fax them over with a memo?"

The little exhalation on the other end of the line might have been a chuckle. He said, "No memos. Just tell me what Charlene says. Roger Cresswell's wife had a lover. Do we know who it was?"

"Unfortunately, no. I'll double-check with Charlene, but Roger may not have known either. Maybe he was suspicious for nothing."

"How long had they been having marital problems?" Anthony asked.

"Let me see. . . . Her notes don't say. They'd been married four years. Nikki was twenty-two at the time. He was twenty-eight. Oh, get this. He bought her a set of boobs for Christmas, before they got married."

"What? Some books? I didn't—"

"Boobs. Implants. Fake *tetas*."

"*Feliz navidad*," Anthony said.

"He gave her whatever she wanted, then complained she expected too much." Gail read from the previous page. "They had the usual condo, cars, boat. Stocks, mutual funds, *et cetera,* but liabilities exceeded assets, except for Roger's stock in the family company, worth about twenty million dollars. I don't know if that's gross, net, or wishful thinking."

"Not much for a company of that size. There must be some debt."

"Don't make Roger sound so poverty-stricken. His parents were loaded. Okay, how do we do this?" Gail asked. "We can't send out subpoenas for depositions. We aren't the police. We can't make anyone talk."

"Neither can they," he said, "but people do talk. If you go after them in the right way, they open up to you. My investigator can do background checks, but he can't get close to the family. I can. Nate is my contact, and I hope to be able to talk to them personally."

"Shouldn't I be there?" Gail said.

There was a long pause, then a slight tapping noise as if he were bouncing a pen on his black granite desk. "No, you're Bobby Gonzalez's lawyer. If they found out, they would be suspicious of your motives."

"All right," she said grudgingly. "What about alibis? We can't send the police after someone who wasn't *there*."

"You assume that our suspect pulled the trigger himself. He could have hired someone else. Unfortunately, the police won't give us their reports, so if we want to know about alibis, we'll have to start from zero. No, I remember hearing that Roger's wife was spending the weekend with a friend in West Palm Beach. So Nikki has an alibi. Jack Pascoe told Nate that he was with Diane Cresswell after the party was over. She's Roger's cousin, a ballerina with the Miami City Ballet. She lives in the cottage on Pascoe's property, and supposedly they were up all night talking in his kitchen—if you can believe that."

"Anthony, she's only twenty. How old is Jack Pascoe?"

"About my age. You know, Gail, this has been known to occur."

"Yes, but they're cousins."

"No, no, they aren't related by blood, only by marriage. Jack was Roger's cousin. Roger was Diane's cousin."

Gail began drawing a chart on another page, then put an X through it. "Nate Harris knows who's who, doesn't he? Could you ask him to do a list?"

"I have one. I'll fax it. Here, write this down. Nate told me that Roger came to Jack's house that night around nine-thirty, and he and Jack went into the study. Ten minutes later, Roger came out, walked right past Nate, and slammed the front door when he left. Nate asked, and Jack told him it was nothing. Quote, 'the same shit.' He was referring to their long-standing competition for Claire's affections. In wealthy families, this usually comes down to money. Roger was Claire's only child, but Jack was her only other relative. Aside from millions of dollars' worth of other assets, Claire has an art gallery in her home devoted to her daughter's paintings. Jack is an art dealer, and . . . well, you can see."

"Talk about motive." Gail added, "This is getting a little sticky for you, isn't it? If the media find out Nate was at the crime scene, and that you advised him not to talk—"

"Nate had nothing relevant to add."

"So you thought."

There was a long pause, then he said, "Maybe I shouldn't have told you about that. I don't know—are we co-counsel or adversaries?"

His question, so simply phrased, echoed with complications. Gail said, "I think whatever we discuss between us is confidential. We have to start there."

She could hear his pen tapping on the desk. Then his breath in her ear as he sighed. "Yes. We'll start with that. You've always been discreet. There was nothing I ever told you that you didn't hold in confidence. If I implied otherwise, I'm sorry."

Feeling the conversation sliding away from her, Gail said, "So let's not worry about it. When are you going to see Jack Pascoe?"

"As soon as possible," Anthony said. "Nate is setting it up, otherwise I wouldn't expect much cooperation. I hope to see the crime scene early next week."

"I'd like to go along."

"No, I'll do it."

"Why can't I go?"

"Gail, didn't I just explain that you shouldn't investigate the case?"

"You were talking about interviewing witnesses."

"No," Anthony said firmly. "If you want to be involved, why don't you be responsible for putting everything into writing and keeping track of details?"

Gail had put Diane Cresswell's telephone number on her desk. She took the piece of paper and turned it over. "So what you want me to do, basically, is to stay home and keep the place tidied up."

"Could I be so lucky?"

"Ha-ha. Please bear in mind," she said, "that if we don't come up with something within a week, I'll have to get Bobby off the hook myself, and saving Nate Harris is not my priority."

"Tell me, Ms. Connor, was your client able to explain where he was after the party, now that his alibi witness has recanted?"

Gail picked up a paper clip and twisted it open. "Oh, that's right. I need to see about that, don't I?"

"When can I talk to him?"

"Is that necessary? He may not want to talk to you."

"I don't care what he wants." Clearly enunciating each word, Anthony repeated, "When can I talk to him?"

With the phone still tucked under her ear, she bent the paper clip into a crank shape and turned it. "When can I talk to Judge Harris?"

"For what reason? He isn't a suspect."

"Does he have information about the Cresswell family? Was he at the scene?"

A sigh of forbearance preceded Anthony's reply. "I'll see what I can arrange. And Bobby? What about this weekend? Oh, you have Karen coming home. Of course you want to spend some time with her. Shall we say Monday morning?"

"Monday is Labor Day."

"Good. You have nothing else on your schedule. Do you want to bring him to my office, or for me to come to yours?"

"Why don't we just do it on a conference call?"

"You're kidding."

"No."

"*Ay, mi Diós.* Yes, maybe we should write memos. I agree. Memos and faxes. Is that how you want to handle it? To avoid contact? We can send e-mail. No, let's go into a chat room right now, on our computers. Why don't we do that?"

"Anthony—"

"We could put one of those little cameras on the monitor to see with—unless you object to that too." When she didn't reply, he said, "What do you think will happen if we talk face to face? Tell me. What would happen?"

"We would start screaming at each other?"

"I'm not screaming at you."

"Yes, you are."

"I am not."

"Are too."

Then he laughed. "If I was—and I don't think so—then I apologize."

Gail said the word again in her head. *Apolozhice.* "Am I being difficult?"

"Yes, but I'm used to it."

"Oh, thanks. All right, what about Nate?"

"At my office. Is late Tuesday afternoon good for you? Or we could have dinner together, the three of us. I think he would enjoy seeing you again."

Gail wanted to take the phone from her ear and stare at it. She said, "You don't mean that, do you?"

Several seconds ticked by.

"No." The silence went on until he said, "You know something funny? I forgot we don't do that anymore. Have dinner together. It's true, I forgot. We were talking as if . . . as if we . . . My brain must have slipped backward. No, I didn't mean to say it. Never mind. What else do we need to discuss, because I have a client waiting for me."

The room went out of focus, and her breath stopped.

"Gail?"

"Oh, sorry. I think that's it for now."

"Good. Let me know about Monday, the time and so forth." He laughed. "And don't forget to fax me your memo."

There was a click, then nothing. Still staring across her office, Gail finally heard the telephone company's announcement: *If you'd like to make a call, please hang up and try again—*

She put back the handset and sat for a while longer trying to figure out exactly what she was feeling. Finally she pinned it down. The same sickening rush of terror that had accompanied her only hot-air balloon ride, when at two thousand feet the gas jets had clogged, and the pilot couldn't get the valve cleared, and a gust of wind had pushed the balloon, rapidly sinking, toward the Everglades, and on the horizon lightning had danced among gathering clouds.

CHAPTER

14

The instant his conversation with Gail Connor was over, Anthony stood up from his desk so quickly that his leather chair wheeled backward and slammed into the credenza, knocking over a perfectly balanced, abstract metal sculpture. He recovered the fallen piece from the carpet and set the nail-like point back on its vertical support, where it bobbled and dipped. What must she have thought, listening to his lapse, and worse, his inane attempt to explain it? With the flick of a finger, he set the cantilevered metal into a swooping spin.

He had said too much, but he had not told her everything. At noon he would have lunch with Claire Cresswell. Only Claire; her odious husband, Porter, would be out on the water with his brother and a few people from the yacht company. If Gail knew that he would be speaking to the murder victim's mother, she would make up some excuse to go along. He preferred not to argue about it.

His day was already jammed. After lunch there would be a plea negotiation with a federal prosecutor. A quick bond hearing. An appointment with a stockbroker accused of bilking his clients. He would probably refer the case to some other lawyer, rather than become involved in a lengthy trial that could complicate his move to New York. That decision was still to be made, but among the papers on his desk were two letters and three phone messages regarding positions in or near the City. He was taking very little new work. His desk was stacked with files to close out or reassign.

Anthony swept his jacket off the back of the chair, put it on, and noticed a piece of dark green thread protruding from one of the sleeve buttons. He tugged gently. *"Ño."* His favorite Armani. He opened his top drawer for the small pair of scissors he used for such emergencies.

As he unzipped the leather case, the phone rang. His private line again. Was she calling back already? He picked it up. "Yes?" But it was only his sister, and he took a breath. "I can't talk now. I'm on my way out."

She told him that she needed to see him. It was important, about their grandfather.

"Alicita, I saw you and Nena only yesterday. Give me some time to think about it. I told Nena I'd call her." Anthony hesitated, then said, "What happened? His heart?"

No, not that. Alicia said she had just found out why Ernesto wanted to see him, and she thought Anthony should know about it before he called their grandmother.

"I am past caring what the old man wants. For the first time in my life I am truly free of him. When I walk back into that house— if I do—it will be because I choose to, not because of Ernesto Pedrosa's manipulation."

In a torrent of words, Alicia accused him of not caring for her, for Nena, for anyone but himself. That if fifteen minutes out of his day was too much to ask, maybe he belonged in New York, just go, forget he had a family—

"Enough!" Anthony looked at his watch. "What does he want from me? Just say it. Why does everything require a big discussion?"

Not on the telephone. She couldn't just *say* it. It would sound crazy. When could they meet?

"I don't know. I have no time this afternoon. Maybe after work, six o'clock. I'll call you in a couple of hours." Anthony hung up. *"Ay, que pena."*

His eyes fell on his desk diary. His daughter's name was written in at six o'clock for dinner. *"Cara'o."* He had suggested Caffé

Abbracci or Les Halles, but Angela had wanted The Cheesecake Factory—overcrowded, overdecorated, and loud. That way, she could eat and run out the door to the movie she'd already arranged to see with her girlfriends. At 7:30 this morning, still in his bathrobe, he'd watched her bright yellow Volkswagen disappear down the street. Off to spend the day on the beach. Tomorrow she would take the rest of her things to the dorms. No, *papi,* don't bother yourself, my roommate has an SUV. He hadn't objected. It was her last weekend of freedom. And perhaps girls that age didn't want their fathers around. He had consoled himself with the thought that once she was settled in school, he could continue with plans for his own future.

Buried somewhere among the files on his desk were notes for an agreement to sell his interest in Ferrer & Quintana, P.A. The folder had floated from one spot to another for nearly three weeks, but he'd not been able to get to it. Raul hadn't pushed. Raul didn't *want* to dissolve the partnership. He had even suggested that if Anthony hadn't drafted the agreement by now, his heart wasn't in it. Not so.

In a cliff-top villa in Marbella, dozing in a chaise under the rustling fronds of a date palm, Anthony had seen the answers laid out as clearly as the blue Mediterranean two hundred feet below. Go back to New York. Resume his life where he'd left it ten years ago, before nostalgia had sent him home to the stifling *cubanidad* of Miami, that illiberal swamp of intrigue, with its lunatic politics and slavering fixation on money and power. But Ernesto Pedrosa, his Machiavellian wits still intact, was plotting to keep him here. What game, Anthony wondered, was the old man playing? What in hell did he want now?

He dialed the main line at the Pedrosa house, and when elderly Aunt Fermina answered, he spent thirty seconds inquiring about her health, then asked to speak to Alicia.

When she came on, he said he was sorry, but six o'clock would be impossible. He was meeting Angela for dinner. Perhaps tomorrow—

No, she had too much to do tomorrow. Why couldn't they meet right now? They could talk outside the house. It was less than a mile from his office. Park down the street, for God's sake. Five minutes. Was that so much to ask? Then it would be off her mind, and she wouldn't bother him again.

"All right. Five minutes."

Anthony hung up and grabbed his briefcase and cell phone. On his way down the corridor he paused to tell his secretary when to expect him back. He had his hand on the side exit door when he heard his partner call his name.

Raul Ferrer was a compact, balding man with an amiable nature, five children, a devoted wife, and an uncanny brilliance with multimillion-dollar real estate development deals, in which Anthony had wisely invested.

They stepped into an empty office. Raul said, "This morning I received an offer on the house in Coconut Grove."

"What house?"

Raul's mustache twitched. "Yours and Gail Connor's. On Clematis Street."

"You don't need my approval," Anthony said. "Just sell it. You're the trustee." They had given Raul this power to avoid any discussion.

"Yes, but I want to run this deal by you. The buyers can close immediately at four hundred thousand. This will take care of the real estate fee and give you back what you have in it."

"Fine. Sell it."

"On the other hand, if you wait, you could make a good profit."

"I don't need a profit."

"Perhaps not, but Gail does. She says she borrowed some money from you, so whatever she gets, to let you have it, up to $125,000, plus interest."

Anthony frowned. That was the money he had given her when she'd fallen into a financial emergency at her office. Given, not loaned. She knew that. They were no longer engaged to be married, but that didn't change the facts. "She doesn't owe me anything."

"She says she does."

"When did you speak to Gail?"

"There were several occasions in the past month."

"Why didn't you tell me?"

"Why?" Raul arched his brows. "Before you left for Spain you gave me specific instructions. I was to transmit nothing to you from Ms. Connor. No letters, no phone calls, no third-party messages. Nothing. You said, 'I don't want to know she exists.' But now that you and she are talking again, I thought—"

"No. We aren't *talking*. We're working on a case together."

"Have you been putting something funny in your cigars?"

Anthony took out his car keys. "I have to go. Sell the house and send her a check."

"She won't take it," Raul said.

"What do you mean? She has to take it."

"She won't. She says she would tear up any check unless she's certain you were repaid."

"You see how unreasonable she is, Raul?"

Raul gave him a long look. "What do you want me to do? Accept the offer? Reject it?"

"I'm not sure." Then he remembered that he would see Gail on Monday. "I'll let you know by Monday afternoon."

"I won't be here," Raul said. "Monday is Labor Day, and I'm taking the family to the Keys."

"Tuesday, then."

Raul pointed. "Oh, by the way. Your button is loose, there on your sleeve."

Anthony waved a dismissive hand as he opened the door and went out to the parking lot. He put on his sunglasses. The glare was intense.

What an impossible woman. She would starve before accepting a piece of bread from him. With the house on Clematis Street, she had insisted on paying half the expenses, when he could easily have outspent her ten to one. Yes, there was the problem again. He had called it love, to do things for her. She had called it control. She had thrown his help—his love—back in his face the same way she had thrown his ring at him.

The Pedrosas lived in a sixteen-room, two-story house on Malagueña Avenue, where banyan trees arched into a shady green tunnel.

A wall with decorative ironwork permitted a view of a fountain in front, balconies at the upstairs windows, and a red tile roof. As he slowly drove past the gate, he saw his sister waiting under the vine-covered portico.

He made a U-turn at the corner and parked on the grass between street and sidewalk. Alicia got in and closed the door, giving him a look that left no doubt what she thought of this. Even so, she presented her cheek for a kiss before sinking into the leather seat. Her dark, curly hair was up in a short ponytail, girlish for a woman over forty, but it suited her. She was still pretty. Twenty years ago she had wanted to become a doctor. Then she had married that miserable husband of hers, given him four children, packed on twenty pounds, and never again spoken of medical school.

Alicia asked brightly, "How's Angela?"

"Very well, thank you. She's moving into the dorms tomorrow. She said she would come say goodbye to you before you leave and give you some presents for your kids. How are they?"

"Crazy to see me again. I've been away too long. Octavio cries to me on the phone. I miss him so much. I tell him, be patient, sweetheart, just a few more days."

He wanted to say, but didn't, that his sister was a fool. He leaned an elbow on the armrest. "Alicia, I have an appointment."

"Yes." She looked through the windshield as if the words she wanted might be dangling from the trees. "Last night, after Nena had gone to bed, Grandfather knocked on my door. He was in his walker, and I thought he might be a little better, so I took him downstairs and we had some milk and crackers. Then, right there in the kitchen, he started to cry. And he asked for you again. You see, he knows you aren't still in Spain, so I couldn't fool him with that lie. He said I had to get a message to you. He said it was something that only you could do for him. And I said, 'Grandfather, my sweetheart, what is it?' He made me promise not to tell anyone but you. Do you know what he said?"

Anthony waited, then said, "No, I don't."

"Grandfather said, 'I want him to take me to Cuba before I die.'"

Anthony tilted his head, not sure he had heard it right. "Pardon?"

"He wants you to take him to Cuba before it's too late."

Wavering between laughter and shock, Anthony said, "He's gone totally insane."

"He didn't sound at all incoherent, as he sometimes does." Alicia shook her head. "No, he meant it."

"That proves he's crazy."

"You have to talk to him, Anthony. He won't live much longer."

"That's not true."

"It is. I've spoken to his doctors. He's dying. His pacemaker helps, but he's eighty-four years old, and so depressed. He doesn't want to eat. He lies in his bed all day. If he believed that he were going to Cuba—"

"Believe in a delusion? When he finds out the truth, what then?"

"He wouldn't. He might die before the arrangements were made—it could take a year or two—but he would be happy."

"Alicia, no. Are you as crazy as he is? How can you suggest such a thing? Listen to me. Ernesto Pedrosa can't go to Cuba. He cannot. No arrangements in the world would allow him entry. They'd arrest him as a traitor as soon as he got off the plane. He's a wanted man. He would be put on trial. He *knows* this."

"He wants you to take him in secretly."

Anthony let his head fall back on the headrest. "Jesus Christ."

"You've done it, Anthony. You do it all the time, to go visit *papi* and Marta and the kids."

"I don't sneak in. I go through Mexico. I get off a plane at José Martí Airport in Havana, where Ernesto Pedrosa's name is on a list. If our father weren't a decorated hero, I would probably be arrested."

"But people do sneak in, don't they? Tell him there's a way. It would make him so happy."

"Alicia . . ." He laughed in disbelief. "Does Nena know about this?"

"He says he hasn't told her. She would never let him go."

"Good. Then someone is thinking clearly."

"Anthony, talk to him. Tell him you'll go with him."

"Absolutely not."

"Did I say you really have to do it? Did I? Just tell him you will."

"I won't lie to him."

"Yes! He needs to believe it's possible. He needs hope. Imagine how he feels, facing death knowing that he will never see home again. Ever."

"What of his promises? He swore—swore on the sanctity of the virgin and the blood of Christ—that he would never go back as long as the regime was in power. He financed acts of terrorism. Was his life a lie? Everything he believed in?"

"I know, I know."

"He threw me out of the house. He called me a communist. I had to move out of Miami so I could breathe. Now you tell me that none of it *mattered*?"

Alicia was still looking at him patiently. "Will you see him?"

"No."

"Anthony." Gently Alicia took his arm and hugged it. "Some things must be done because they're right, and we have to put aside how we feel. You need to forgive him. And yourself. You're my brother, and I know you. At heart, you're a good man."

He stared at the street. "I'm not good, Alicia, whatever that may be. I'm not like you. My sweet sister. You are the best woman in the world. An angel. Why do you stay with Octavio Reyes? What does he do to deserve you?" Anthony looked at her fiercely.

Her eyes widened. Blue as the sea. "Octavio doesn't have to *do* anything. I love him. He's the father of my children. Love doesn't depend on whether we deserve it or not. It's just . . . given."

Anthony dropped his forehead into his palm. He wanted to weep.

"Oh, what's this?" Alicia pulled at the string on his sleeve.

"Don't—"

The button came off in her hand. "I'm sorry. Leave your coat with me. I can sew it back on."

"I'll take it to my tailor."

"For a button?" She laughed. "You're so useless." She pushed his jacket off his shoulder. "Come on. Let me have it."

"No, Alicia, I have to be in court this afternoon. It's all right." He took the button from her and dropped it into his pocket.

His sister folded her hands in her lap. It seemed she had run out of words.

Anthony said, "I don't know what to do about Ernesto."

She leaned over and kissed his cheek. "Remember I love you, whatever you decide."

Stopping to talk to his sister meant that Anthony had to hold his Eldorado on eighty miles an hour until the exit for Aventura. Speeding tickets were only a minor risk. Highway patrolmen were generally absent from the expressways in Miami until rush hour, when they were hardly needed, since it was impossible to go over thirty.

The valet who took his car told him that Mrs. Cresswell could be found at the marina. Anthony left his coat and tie in the car and rolled up his shirt sleeves. A brisk wind on the intracoastal waterway ruffled his hair as he walked around the corner of the building. There were a few dozen sail and power boats at the docks that fingered into the water, and a sleek white yacht was tied along the seawall. The bow jutted toward him, and the bridge was a curve of tinted glass. Coming closer, he could see four or five people onboard, one of them a big, gray-haired man with a crooked mouth and wide jaw. Porter Cresswell.

His wife stood in the shade of a tiki hut on shore. Her white cotton hat turned in Anthony's direction. The brim sparkled with rhinestones, and sunglasses hid her eyes. She extended her hands. "Anthony. It's good to see you again. Thank you for your kindness. The flowers you sent, and the lovely letter."

"All too inadequate," he said. "Are you going boating?"

"No, I'm having lunch with *you*. The boys are going out, Porter and Dub and some men from the company. It's a brand-new boat, and they want to make sure it doesn't sink." She laughed gaily.

The boat had no name on the stern. There were no curtains at the windows, no carpeting or furniture. All this would be added, Claire explained, after the boat passed its water test and went back to the yard. They didn't usually bring them all the way up here, but Porter felt like going out.

"I'm glad," Claire said. "He's always loved the water. A wonderful fisherman. Roger was too."

This close to the ocean the heat was bearable. Claire looked fresh in a crisp blue shirt and white walking shorts. Her legs were still shapely. She'd been a dancer, Anthony recalled.

She said, "We'll have lunch upstairs after the men are gone. Porter likes me to wave 'bye to him. Let's sit down for a minute." She took one of the molded plastic chairs, and Anthony pulled another beside her. She said quietly, "Nate told me everything. I haven't told Porter yet. Should I?"

"Of course a wife has a duty to confide in her husband." He added, "I leave that up to you."

A little smile tugged at a corner of her mouth. "I suppose that if you *wanted* Porter to know, you would have insisted on his being with us for lunch. No, don't answer."

One of the men picked up a cooler and carried it up the portable wooden steps, then went aboard through the gate in the side. The moment he set down the cooler, a heavy man sprawled on the bench seat opened the lid and pulled out a beer. Anthony recognized him as Porter's brother, Duncan, who had arrived at the condo with the news of Roger's death. He jammed his beer can into an insulated foam cover and popped the top. "Let's *go*. Hoist the mains'l, cap'n! All ashore that's going ashore."

From the bridge Porter shouted, "Hold your water, we're checking the GPS." He noticed Anthony sitting under the tiki hut and lifted a hand. A gold Cresswell emblem was embroidered on the front of his white captain's hat. "Hello! Claire said you'd be by. Come aboard."

Claire called back, "In a minute, honey. It's too hot." She crossed her legs and swung a foot, clad in a tennis shoe. "Porter says the police think Bobby Gonzalez killed Roger, but they can't prove it yet."

"With all respect to the police, they're on the wrong track.

Bobby is innocent." A doubt still lingered—Bobby had not yet explained his whereabouts after midnight—but to admit that now would be fatal to Anthony's purpose.

Claire exhaled. "I'm so relieved. Bobby is a delightful young man. They're going to promote him to soloist this season, you know. I *knew* Porter was wrong, and I made him promise not to gossip about it. What can I do to help?"

"We can talk over lunch," Anthony said.

"Tell me now."

The engines started with a deep rumble, and water splashed from exhausts at the stern. Anthony watched Porter Cresswell carefully make his way down the ladder from the bridge. He moved like an old man.

"Nate told you that we need to direct the investigation toward another suspect. To do that, I have to know your son. Who he was. His friends, his enemies. I'm particularly interested in his relations with those who were closest to him."

"You don't mean the family."

"For now, with regret, I can't rule anyone out."

The brim of her hat turned quickly toward him. "How can you ask me to accuse someone in my own family?"

"No, not to accuse, only to give me a direction. I wouldn't be here if I didn't believe that you care about Nate."

"Of course I do, very much, but you're wrong. No one in the family would have wanted to harm Roger. We're a very close, loving family. We take vacations together. Last year for Christmas we all went to Puerto Rico on our boat. We have a successful business. It wouldn't be that way if we didn't get along."

Anthony leaned a little closer. "I am sorry, Claire. I have to start with certain facts. Two months ago Roger consulted a lawyer about a divorce from his wife, Nikki. The night he was killed, he argued with your nephew, Jack Pascoe. Two weeks ago, you told me that Roger had problems at the company with Dub and Elizabeth. You said that the situation was so bad, Porter's mind had been affected. None of you revealed anything to the police, did you? But it exists, Claire. You know this."

She protested. "There were some disagreements, but no one had a reason to . . . to hurt Roger. That couldn't have happened."

With regret in his voice, Anthony said, "Very soon the police will see—as you do—that Bobby Gonzalez is innocent. When that happens, they will turn their attention to the victim's family. They will question everyone again, much more intensely. Your names will be in the news, and every detail of your lives will be exposed. The tabloids will send photographers."

"Don't threaten me like that. *Please* don't." Her sunglasses were not so dark that he couldn't see the accusation in her eyes.

"Then help me. If you care about Nate Harris, you'll do it. We were looking at Maggie's painting in your gallery, do you remember? You said you were grateful to Nate for keeping her closer to you, because she had spent most of her life in the Northeast. You said that before your daughter died, Nate gave her at least a little happiness. Are you going to turn your back on him now? For what? Are you so concerned about family image that you would let Nate be destroyed, and your son's killer go free?"

Claire's mouth opened, then clamped shut in a firm line. She pushed herself out of her chair and strode across the grass to the edge of the dock, where the motor yacht blazed white in the sun. Anthony followed. Through the long window of dark glass, he saw someone moving about inside. The bass rumble of the engines increased in pitch as the man at the helm played with the controls.

Duncan Cresswell's sunglasses shifted toward Anthony. The wind blew thinning hair across his wide, ruddy forehead. "Hey, we've met before."

From the dock Claire said, "This is Anthony Quintana, a friend of Nate's."

Dub didn't get up, but he leaned into a handshake. "Sure. I remember."

Anthony moved back to let one of the crew walk by on the side of the boat. Like the others, he wore a white Cresswell Yachts shirt. He stepped over the railing and jumped down to the dock, where he began to untie the lines securing the bow. His legs and forearms were corded with muscle.

It was time to leave, Anthony thought. His burst of impatience had only alienated Claire Cresswell. He had just lost his most valuable source of information.

Porter came out of the salon with a plastic cup. "Quintana! How about a drink?"

"Thanks, but I need to get back to work soon. I dropped by to express my condolences to the family."

"We appreciate it," Porter said. "This has been a difficult time for all of us."

Dub said, "Roger was a great guy."

A moment passed in which no one spoke. As if rousing himself, Porter said, "What about this boat? Isn't she something? Eighty-two feet, our latest model. We're going to go bigger next year. CEOs aren't afraid to spend money anymore on boats. Everybody wants to make a statement. Mine's bigger and stiffer." He gave a husky laugh, turning stiffly, head and torso in the same movement, to see if the man at the helm approved of the joke.

A laugh came down from the bridge.

"You got a boat? You should. Lawyers have money. I know because they've skinned me for enough of it."

Anthony said, "My law partner does. That's better than having one myself."

"You may be right," Porter said. "Damn pricey toys. Why don't you go out with us? Come on."

"Maybe next time."

"Got some news for you." Porter's crooked smile faded, and his jaw seemed to settle further into his neck. "They have a suspect in my son's murder."

"Nate mentioned it."

"A kid who used to work at the yard—Bobby Gonzalez, a friend of Dub's boy. Dub and Liz used to have him over to their house. What about that? You let someone in close and he turns on you. The kid attacked my son, threatened his life. Ted here saw it all. He told the police about it. Isn't that right, Ted?"

The man at the bow had tossed the lines to someone on the foredeck, and he walked toward the stern. "That's right."

Anthony asked him, "Why did he attack Roger?"

"Roger fired him for stealing."

Porter said, "This is Ted Stamos. Ted's our supervisor in the glass shop. Been with us since he was a kid."

Anthony inquired, "You install the windows?"

"*Fiber*glass. I build the boats."

"Your last name is Stamos. Is that Greek?"

"I'm an American. I was born here. What about you?" Stamos went to untie the lines at the stern.

Having heard such insults before, Anthony let it go.

The noise of the engines increased, and the smell of diesel exhaust hung over the dock. "All aboard that's coming aboard," Dub Cresswell said. "Come on, Cap'n. Make this baby scream."

"I'm going. Jesus." Porter grasped both sides of the handrail on the stairs to the bridge. He made a misstep and fell to one knee. His brother watched from the bench seat.

Alarmed, Claire called out, "Porter!"

"Leave me alone, I'm okay." He pulled himself up.

"Help him Dub! Help him get up."

Dub Cresswell said, "Have a drink, Porter. That's what you need."

Porter Cresswell laughed. "Who moved the fucking step?" He climbed the stairs and took his place at the helm. An air horn sounded a long, clear note that echoed on the buildings and gradually faded out.

Ted Stamos swung back aboard and closed the gate. The growl of the engines grew louder, and water frothed.

Dub Cresswell was swinging his beer back and forth. "Yo ho and up she rises, yo ho and up she rises—"

"Bye, Porter," Claire called out, cupping her hands. "Bye, honey."

Porter Cresswell snapped a salute off the brim of his hat and maneuvered the yacht away from the dock. It glided smoothly into the intracoastal, leaving a widening wake.

Claire waved for a long time, till the boat turned into a channel and headed out toward the Atlantic. Without looking at the man beside her she said, "We're taking Roger's ashes out to sea next weekend. I'd like it very much if you could join us."

* * *

Shortly after one o'clock, as Anthony's Cadillac sped south on the interstate, he held a microcassette recorder in his left hand, fingers on the buttons. He had become adept at simultaneously driving and dictating instructions to his secretary.

He pressed RECORD. "This is to be sent to Gail Connor. Her fax number should be in your files. Title it 'Memorandum' and put today's date. It goes . . . Today I met with Claire Cresswell at her residence in Aventura—"

He turned it off. Not at her residence, outside on the dock, watching her husband play boat captain.

"*Al cara'o con los* memos!" He tossed the recorder to the passenger seat, then half a mile later picked it up again and rewound to the beginning. He would give this to a courier for delivery to Gail Connor's office.

"Gail. This is your memo. If you want it in written form . . . well, you can type it yourself. I just had a meeting with Claire Cresswell."

He hit the PAUSE button, then let it go and said, "This was arranged quickly. Nate called her last night after you and I spoke. He asked her to see me today, and she agreed." The tape spun. "I didn't mention it this morning because you would have wanted to come along, and Mrs. Cresswell doesn't know you."

Anthony rewound, finding his voice saying *and she agreed*. Why the hell should he explain to Gail Connor his reasons for not telling her about the meeting? He would record over the rest of it.

When the tape was spinning again, Anthony told her that when he had gone to the Cresswells' apartment that first time, Claire had spoken to him alone. Anthony had realized that she was attracted to him. Today he had gone to see Claire intending to rely on those feelings, he couldn't deny it, but Claire had accused him of threats and manipulation. He hadn't intended to push her around, but he saw now that he had. This woman who had lost her son. Before that, a daughter. Had he been callous, using these tragedies to get what he wanted from her?

The tape spun slowly.

Anthony hit REWIND. If Gail were sitting in the passenger seat, he might have discussed his use of Claire Cresswell, and she would have commented, but on tape it sounded incoherent.

He said, "I leaned on her a little, but it couldn't be helped. She will do what she can, short of feeling like a traitor to her family."

He went on to say that Claire would tell Porter that she herself had hired Anthony Quintana to look into Roger's financial dealings at the company. Roger was dead now, but his crimes, if any, would survive him. Claire would say that Mr. Quintana didn't expect to find anything, but his investigation would at least allay Porter's fears. As cover stories went, it wasn't too bad.

"I noticed an odd thing today," Anthony said. "Porter slipped going up the stairs to the bridge, and his brother did nothing. I believe there is more malice in this family than Claire will admit, even to herself. She won't accuse anyone, but she will open the door. That's all I can ask of her."

Anthony turned off the recorder and idly watched the green interstate signs pass overhead. He didn't want to talk into this damned machine. He wanted to talk to Gail—the woman she used to be, before she turned into a chilly imitation of herself. He wanted *that* woman in the passenger seat. She would have understood what he wanted to say. She would have cut through to the point.

He wondered what would happen if he could play back the tape of their last day together and stop it before it went bad. They had awakened at dawn in a bed upstairs in his grandfather's house. He had felt her body beside him and pulled her closer. Had it been too rushed? She hadn't complained. Later that day, dozens of family and guests had converged on the house and the grounds, and then suddenly! She had run away, pushing through the gate, leaving the party, everyone watching. He'd run after her onto the golf course, demanding that she come back, finally begging, but by then she was out of control, no reasoning with her. That had set him off, and there had been nothing left but a smoking crater in the earth. No, the tape would have to be rewound more than a day. A week? A month?

Farther still. To before they had bought the house on Clematis Street. Yes, back to that point. She hadn't been enthusiastic, but he had wanted it, never mind the tens of thousands of dollars of repairs it had needed. An old house on a shady street, with tile floors and cool patios. Even fireplaces upstairs and down. He had talked her into it, then had let her spend everything she had, money she shouldn't have spent, trying to keep up with him. It had become a battle, a contest with two losers. He should have known.

He picked up the recorder. "I told Claire that you're working with me—or rather, you're working for Bobby Gonzalez. I said you'd acquired him as a client through the ballet, and I mentioned your mother's name. She knows Irene, and I believe that this helped put her on our side. As far as I know, none of the other Cresswells is aware that you're representing Bobby. Claire said she wouldn't tell them. I believe this includes her husband."

PAUSE.

RECORD. "Next weekend the family and a few friends will go out on the company yacht and scatter Roger's ashes at sea. It will be a small group. Claire suggested that you come too."

STOP.

Anthony rewound and replayed, going back and forth until he found the point just preceding *Next weekend* . . . His finger hovered above RECORD. He could press it and erase any thought of Gail's coming with him. He could tell her about it later. Do a memo.

But his finger moved over to REWIND, and the tape went backward, picking up speed until the beginning, where it stopped with a sharp click. He ejected the cassette and slid it into his breast pocket.

CHAPTER
15

As Dave was leaving Irene's house on Saturday, after dropping Karen off with her suitcases and bags, Irene ran out onto the porch after him and invited him to Sunday breakfast. He glanced at Gail. Quickly recovering, she smiled and shrugged. "Great." Her mother would have offered him the pull-out sofa in the den if he hadn't mentioned he was staying with friends. Selfishly, Gail wanted Karen all to herself. They spent the rest of the day with Irene looking at souvenirs and snapshots, trying on sarongs and shell jewelry, and catching up after a long month away from each other.

Just past eleven years old, Karen still had no hips, and her chest was flat, but the summer had made her glow. Giggling, she told Gail about the French Canadian boy she had met at the marina. Soooo cute. His parents owned a sailboat, and they'd be back to the islands next summer. He wanted to e-mail her. Could she write back? Could she? Karen fell asleep on Gail's bed, and the two of them slept curled up together.

On Sunday Irene fixed Karen's favorites—pecan waffles and bacon. She squeezed fresh oranges and opened a jar of homemade calamondin jam for the toast. Red-haired and sunny in a yellow dress with blue flowers, she fluttered around the kitchen like a brightly plumed bird, then settled down across from Karen, who chattered away about the things she had seen.

Gail gazed at her daughter. How beautiful she was. Sun-streaked brown hair. Long limbs, firm and tanned. Gail's eyes had some gray, but Karen's eyes were sky blue, like her father's, and her nose was his, and her square jaw and straight brows.

Dave dredged a piece of waffle through a pool of maple syrup. "Wow, Irene, I haven't eaten like this in years."

Not *years*, Gail replied silently. It had been Christmas a year and a half ago, the last one they'd spent together. It hadn't been much different from this morning, except that the topics of conversation had changed. Gail could almost imagine the scene after brunch: She and Irene would tidy the kitchen. Dave would be on the sofa, eyes closed, head back, the sports section sliding to the floor.

When the talk had run down, and Karen had begun to squirm in her chair, Irene reached for Dave's plate, then Gail's. "Does anyone want some more coffee? We could take it out on the back porch. It's not that hot today."

Dave stretched and looked at the black dive watch circling his wrist. "I would, Irene, but I told my folks I'd drive up there this afternoon. I'd better get going. This was super."

Gail said, "Would you like to take a walk with me?"

Their eyes met across the table. Knowing each other for sixteen years filled in the blanks. He said, "Okay, sure."

She smiled at Karen. "Sweetie, why don't you help Gramma clean up?"

They went out the front door, and the screen clicked shut behind them. The striped cat lying on the porch glider stopped licking its paws and watched them take the brick path to the tree-shaded sidewalk. Belle Mar was near downtown but walled off for security. Some of the houses were big two-story things with soaring roofs, but most were like Irene's, a ranch style about forty years old, getting a bit mildewed.

Gail had met Dave in college. He'd been two years ahead, a business major on a tennis scholarship. They'd married after her graduation, and Karen had come along midway through law school. Their marriage hadn't been passionate, but she'd been too busy with her career to be bothered by that. Too busy to notice Dave drifting away. With some effort she might have pulled them back together, but it was already too late. She had met Anthony Quintana, who had wanted her with a force she was incapable of withstanding. Looking back on it, she wondered if she hadn't been crazy, falling for a man of such extravagant passion.

Irrational jealousy had been the dark side of desire. He had feared that Dave would use Karen to lure Gail back, so he had ruined him. He had secretly arranged the failure of Dave's business and at the same time, a job offer at the other end of the Caribbean. That would have been bad enough, but a child had been separated from her father. It had been this harm to Karen, more than anything, that had shone a light on the truth: Anthony Quintana was remorselessly selfish, shamelessly cruel. Love had been a silken black mask over Gail's eyes.

The sidewalk led to a little park at the end of the street, a quarter acre of palm trees and grass on the bay. Gail leaned on the railing and looked out at the small islands between the mainland and Miami Beach. Dave waited. A patient man, he didn't push to know what had brought them here.

Gail said, "How's it going at the resort? Are you all right?"

"Sure. I like my job, the people I work with. They're talking about moving me up from marina manager to assistant resort manager. I'd be making twice the money, and working about four times as much, but the benefits are good."

"I'm glad. I wish you hadn't lost your business here."

"*C'est la vie.* A deal falls through, no point crying over it. I'm okay. Yeah, it took some getting used to, and I miss Karen, but other than that . . . Well, I'm about as happy as I've ever been."

"Scout's honor?"

He held up two fingers.

A row of coconut palms made moving shade on benches facing the water. Gail sat down and Dave sat beside her.

"So. What's up? Everything okay?"

"I'm pregnant."

For a few seconds his face was frozen, waiting for some clue how to react. "No kidding."

"Completely unplanned," she said.

"Wow." He made an uncertain smile. "What are you going to do?"

"I don't know. I keep making appointments, but things keep coming up, and I have to cancel. I have another one for Wednesday. Maybe I'll be car-jacked on the way, or Karen will get appendicitis. I shouldn't have told Mother. The way she looks at me. She doesn't have to say a word, she just gives me *the look.*"

"Jesus. Does Quintana know about it? He doesn't, does he?"

"Am I wicked?"

Dave shook his head. "No. On the other hand, he could help out. I mean, if you decide to keep it. Are you . . . asking me for an opinion?"

"I suppose I am, since this involves Karen, too. She's been through so much already, and this would be a major disruption in her life. She'd feel pushed aside. And I have to ask myself what kind of example I'm setting as a mother. She looks to me for how to behave. In a few years she's going to be dating. She'll want to have sex, and how can I legitimately tell her not to?"

"Because you're thirty-four, you were engaged, and this was an accident. Gail, I think she can figure it out."

"What about my practice? Just when I'm getting started again, I have this to deal with. Having another child right now would be the most irresponsible thing I could do."

"You're only thinking of the negatives."

"What else is there?"

"Karen might think it's neat." He smiled, and the lines deepened at his eyes. "A new brother or sister? Showing it off to her friends? Bossing him around?"

"Oh, Dave."

"Well . . . you always wanted another kid."

"Like *this*?" She laughed and dropped her head back. Above her, in slow motion, the huge palm fronds shifted in the breeze.

Dave patted her hand. "If you didn't want it, you wouldn't be talking about it. Would you?"

She closed her eyes. "I do. I don't. Oh, God, I don't need this now."

He sat forward, resting his elbows on his knees. His thighs were muscular and tanned, the hair lightened by the sun. "I'm sorry we didn't have another kid."

"Are you?" Gail smiled. "We did try, didn't we?"

"I guess it wasn't meant to be."

"What a mess. I'm so sorry for everything, Dave."

"Hey, come on, it's nobody's fault."

She leaned against him. His back was warm from the heat. "Do you still care about me? A teeny bit?"

"Sure I do." He shifted to put an arm around her, then kissed her forehead. "I always will, you know that."

"What if I came to St. John? You asked me once, after Anthony and I broke up, and I said no. I thought I could never leave what I had—a job, my mother, friends, all the familiar places I go, the things I do." She pulled away far enough to look at him. "I was afraid, maybe that was it. Afraid of change, of losing whatever I had. But I've found I really didn't have so much after all."

"You'd have the baby there?"

"Why not? This is so obvious! Nobody would care who I was, would they? Nobody would talk. Karen likes St. John, and she'd be closer to you. Charlene Marks could take over my cases. I have enough saved to make the move, and I could work there—it's U.S. territory. But not law, something new. A business. I'm good at that. Maybe we could start a business together."

He was staring at her, a crease between his brows.

Laughing, she held up her hands. "I'm not saying we'd get married again. A lot has happened. We'd have to take our time . . ." Her words trailed off, and she managed a smile. "It would be hard, wouldn't it? Another man's child."

"It's not that, Gail, I swear. The thing is . . . I've got to be up front with you. I met someone. We've been seeing a lot of each other. She owns a gift shop near the resort. Her name's Lori."

Gail looked for something to say. "That's . . . wonderful. It is. Really. Is she nice? Of course she is, what a stupid question."

He turned on the bench to face her. "But everything else, every-thing you said, it's a possibility. A definite possibility."

"I'm so embarrassed—"

"No, no, think how good it would be for you and Karen both. And the baby." Dave took her hands. "St. John is so peaceful and green. It's half national park, so it's never going to get overbuilt like St. Thomas. The job market isn't great, but we could find you something. I'm sure of it."

"What would your girlfriend have to say about your ex-wife moving to town?"

"She wouldn't mind."

With a little laugh, Gail said, "Only an idiot would let you get away with it."

"No, no, everything's different there, I'm telling you. So laid back and easy. The people are friendly. There's no crime. You don't need a car. You don't need fancy clothes. There's nothing much to spend money on. If you raise a kid there, you get him away from this maniac consumer society. You don't have a heart attack if he goes out to play. Irene could come visit. She'd love it, all those little gift shops. She could wear her sarong and straw hat. Listen. I'm going back next Sunday. Why don't you come down with me? Check it out, see if it's what you want to do. You know. Before you decide on anything else."

After a second or two, Gail said, "I'll think about it." She stood up, leaning down for a second to hold his face and kiss his cheek. "Thank you. Come on, let's go back. Don't mention this to anyone, all right?"

They started toward the house. Round black berries from the ficus tree crunched under her sandals. A small gray lizard scurried on delicate toes into the grass.

"Could we ever have made it work? Our marriage, I mean. If we'd been wiser, or more patient, or . . . something."

"You know, Gail, one thing I've learned is, the clock doesn't go backward. You just do the best you can based on what's in front of you."

*   *   *

Gail and Karen waved from the front porch as the rental car backed out of the driveway, and Dave tooted the horn. An ache formed in Gail's throat, and she took deep breaths until she was sure it wouldn't work into anything more. The car disappeared around a bend in the street.

"Are you going to miss him a lot, sweetie?"

"Sure, but I am *soooo* glad to be home." Karen turned her face up. "Can I go over to Anita's and watch a movie? She asked me to. Okay? Mom, it's so boring sitting around talking all day. No offense."

"Well, if you're *soooo* bored . . ." Gail kissed her. "Sure. Have a good time. I can find something to do with myself for a couple of hours."

When Karen was gone, Gail looked in her organizer for the phone number Diane Cresswell had given her. She had planned to go see her early on Monday, but this would be better. She sat on the side of her bed and made the call. Diane was at the cottage, and she told Gail to come around one o'clock.

In exchange for legal advice about a portrait, Gail would see the place where Roger Cresswell had been murdered. Gail thought briefly about telling Señor Quintana about it, but dropped that idea. He might want to come along. She found a notebook and pen, then went into the kitchen to fix herself a glass of iced tea.

Irene was on the back porch reading the newspaper and sneaking a cigarette. Gail could see her through the sliding glass door.

Two days ago Gail had told her about seeing Anthony Quintana. She wouldn't have mentioned it at all if she hadn't needed to know about the Cresswells. Irene had promised to find out what she could, but she'd been more interested in Anthony. What had he said? How had he acted? Gail had told her that nothing had changed between them, and the sooner this case was over, the better.

Gail slid open the door, and Irene hurriedly crushed out her cigarette as if Gail hadn't already seen it. On the patio, hanging baskets and big terra cotta planters of palms and bougainvillea cut the glare on white decking tile. Ceiling fans spun briskly, making a breeze. Water poured from the mouth of a decorative frog into the pool, and patterns of light danced on the screen.

Irene was wearing lime green half-glasses she had picked up at a gift store in Key West. A bit much with the red hair, but Irene had once said that God never intended everything in the world to be beige. She looked over the top of the arts section. "Did you and Dave have a nice walk?"

Gail put her notebook and pen on the patio table. "Lovely. We caught up on Karen, and he told me he's doing well. He's happy."

"He does seem to be." She turned a page. Her eyes were fixed on Gail.

Carrying her iced tea to the pool, Gail kicked off her sandals. She went down the steps at the shallow end till the water reached her knees. "Yes, I told him I'm pregnant."

The newspaper slowly sank to Irene's lap. "And?"

"And he was understanding and sympathetic. We discussed how it might affect Karen. Dave is a friend. I've known him all my adult life."

"You're not thinking of going back to him, are you?"

Gail laughed. "Of course not." She swung a foot through the water, which bubbled and curled.

"Be careful, honey. When a woman gets desperate, she grabs at whatever seems to make sense, whether it does or not. Dave Metzger is a sweetheart, and I love him to pieces, but that old saying about any port in a storm? It ain't so."

"Don't be so dramatic," Gail said. "You make me sound like Little Eva crossing the ice. I talked to Dave because I wanted his opinion about Karen. There's bound to be gossip, and kids would say things to her. Girls her age are so catty. I don't want her to suffer because of my mistake. I just won't allow it."

"Oh, for heaven's sake. People don't care. When I was young, it would have been a scandal, but not now. Where did you get such a conservative streak?"

"From you?"

"Well, you obviously misunderstood. I'm going to adore this baby when it comes, and so will Karen. What did Dave say? I bet he agrees with me."

"Dave can afford to. He's leaving next week. Let's not get into that, please. Diane Cresswell expects me in a little while. That's what I came out here to talk about—the Cresswells." Leaving wet footprints across the deck, Gail went over to the patio table and picked up her notebook.

Her mother looked at her over the top of the lime-green glasses. "You're going to have this child, Gail. Stop pretending otherwise. You'll have the baby, Anthony will find out, and you'll have to work it out with him, one way or another."

"I don't want to think about it." Gail sat down and uncapped her pen. "If I go over to Diane's, would you mind watching out for Karen? She went next door to see a video."

Irene rolled her eyes. "Of course I don't mind." She took off her glasses and swung her foot. "What are you doing, taking notes?"

"Yes, I'll have to do a memo on this. What did you find out about Roger?"

Irene Strickland Connor, third-generation Miami, belonged to half a dozen cultural and political organizations. She was petite and non-threatening, and her incisive intelligence was hidden behind a motherly smile. People would confide in her. She might repeat what she heard, but not to just anyone.

Irene had met Roger Cresswell only once, at a ballet gala last year that he'd probably attended to keep his parents happy.

"He was very good-looking, but he knew it. His wife was with him, falling out of her dress. Red hair out to here." Irene held her hands away from her head. "They were both smashed on champagne. This was *not* a marriage Porter and Claire approved of, but Roger played around for years on a trust fund, so you can see what kind of woman he'd go for."

Gail looked up from her notebook. "What did you find out about Porter's brother?"

"Duncan. Let's see. He drinks too much. He's a big joker, and it's his wife who wears the pants. Duncan has never been the bright star of the Cresswell brothers. In fact, nobody can figure out how he ended up as half owner. When their father died he left the business to Porter, and Porter isn't the kind of man to give anything away. Now, giving it to his *son*, I understand. When Porter got sick, he gave Roger ten percent of the business. I guess that wasn't enough for Roger."

"What do you mean?"

"He was like his father, they say. He just had to be in control." A friend of Irene's had told her that *her* husband, who was on the board of the Coral Reef Yacht Club with Duncan, had overheard Duncan's wife say Roger Cresswell's ego must be compensation for his pin dick.

"Mother!" Gail laughed.

"Well, I didn't say it, she did."

"Still."

Pausing to think, Irene said, "What is her name? Liz. She's from a blue collar family—not that there's anything wrong with that, but you'd think she'd have risen above it. They contribute scads of money to charity, and you see their pictures in the paper, but she doesn't get invited to the better parties."

Gail's pen flew over the page. More problems in the household. Their son, Sean, had been in trouble with the police. The older daughter, jealous of Diane. Diane leaving home as soon as she could, moving to Jack Pascoe's place, and who knew what was going on there? Jack had once been a reputable art dealer, but people said he'd been cheating his customers. Claire denied it, lending him money for a place in the Grove. Enraging Roger, of course. Name-calling between Nikki and Liz in the ladies' room at the Forge Restaurant, overheard by a friend of one of Irene's bridge partners. Hints of financial trouble at the company after Roger came in. Porter not happy. Claire in the middle, always smiling.

As a teenager, Irene had known Claire Pascoe. "We went to high school together at Cushman, but we were never friends."

"Why not?" Gail took a quick sip of iced tea. "Was she a snob?"

"No, I was younger and we were in different crowds. Claire was into dancing, and she practiced a good deal, so she was too busy to mix with other kids. Even when she did, it was like she was always onstage. She smiled too much, maybe that was it.

Everything was always perfect." Irene laughed. "Boy, did I get into trouble, but girls like Claire—honor society, prom queen. Beautiful clothes, never a spot on them. Her car was always so shiny. A little white Thunderbird that her parents bought her. They were members of the Bath Club and the Riviera Country Club, and her mother ran the debutante ball. What a bitch she was. She complained to my mother because I didn't wear stockings at the tea party. I think Mr. Pascoe was a deacon at the Presbyterian Church. They had the most immaculate house." Irene gave a little shudder, then was quiet for a while, looking out at the bay. "Maybe that explains it."

"Explains what?"

"I've lost a child too," Irene said. "I could hardly function for months—you remember how it was when your sister died. Claire just goes on, like closing a door, all the heartache locked behind it. She never complains, and I don't see how in hell she puts up with Porter. He had another woman for years, and she looked the other way. She didn't want a scandal in the family, I guess. Who *cared*? She has her own money, she could've booted him right out. What's she holding on to, I ask you? Can you imagine? Both children dead. I wouldn't be far behind, if that happened to me."

Eyes on the page, Gail continued to write, aware that she had fewer facts than inferences. Even so, she was left with a feeling of disgust for the entire Cresswell clan, except for Diane. So far, Gail had no reason to lump her in with the rest of them. As for Claire, was she anything more than a shell? Anthony had used the right words on the tape he had sent. *There is more malice in this family than Claire will admit, even to herself.* A family of wealth and position, to whom appearances meant so much. Families like that always had secrets. And how odd that both Roger and his sister had died on the same piece of property. One murder, one suicide. One family.

CHAPTER

16

The five colored glass numbers of Jack Pascoe's street address swung from an ornately twisted metal arch over his driveway that was hidden among so many untrimmed bushes that Gail went past twice before seeing it. The gate was open, and Gail drove through.

The house could have been transported from Key West—two stories of white clapboard, green shutters, and vines climbing up lattice trim. A garage was connected to the house by a portico, and under it was a little red Honda with a Miami City Ballet bumper sticker. It had to be Diane's. Gail couldn't tell if Pascoe was home or not. She pulled a compact camera out of her shoulder bag and took several pictures.

As instructed, she went under the portico to the back. She had worn shorts and a sleeveless linen shirt for the heat, but the sun blazed down with an almost physical pressure. Beyond an area of weathered picnic furniture and badly watered grass, a keystone walkway vanished into the shrubbery. Toward the far right corner of the property, dozens of palm trees soared above dense foliage. Their fronds moved in the wind. Roger Cresswell's body had been found among those trees. Everything corresponded to the hand-drawn map that Anthony had sent. Gail aimed her camera, then turned and took more photos of the rear of the house. Above the screened porch, the second-floor windows would give a stunning view of the bay.

Following the walkway another twenty yards or so, Gail found the cottage. It too was clapboard, build on a foundation of old coral rock, but the shutters were bright turquoise. Colored glass rotated on fishing line, sending flecks of light dancing across the front. Orchestral music was coming through tightly closed windows.

Gail didn't notice the black dog underneath the porch swing until he leaped out, nails scrabbling to gain a hold. She gasped, then froze in place while the animal stood at the top of the steps barking and growling. The music went off, and a moment later the door opened. From behind the screen a slender figure in blue tank top and white shorts called out, "Buddy, be quiet!"

The dog immediately shut up, wagged its tail, and padded toward the door. Diane Cresswell unlatched the screen. Her blond hair was on top of her head. "Come in. I forgot to tell you about Buddy. He's noisy, that's all." She reached down to pet him. "Hey, you silly old mutt, go back to sleep."

The cottage was air conditioned, and fans turned in the open-beam ceiling. A divider at one end marked the kitchen, and a door led to a small bedroom. Ballet posters and photographs decorated white-painted walls. The space seemed larger because the cottage was so sparsely furnished—tiny table and chairs, some floor pillows, an upholstered bench for a sofa.

Gail started to walk across the floor, then noticed the splashes of paint on the age-darkened pine.

"It's dry," Diane said. "I dance on it. Kind of neat, huh? Maggie took the paintings and left the drips."

Most of the paint was concentrated near the front windows, where an easel might have been placed. Rectangular shapes on the floor marked where canvases had been laid down, then taken up when they were finished. Tilting her head this way or that as she walked among them, Gail said, "It would be interesting to find out what she was working on. This one—all those little splotches of red and green. You could match it up to the painting."

"Jack says he ought to take out the floor and sell it." Diane laughed, then said, "Do you like carrot juice?"

Gail agreed to a small glass, and Diane walked to the refrigerator. She was barefoot. The big joint at the ball of her foot was enlarged, and her toes were reddened and callused.

"How long have you lived here?" Gail asked.

Glasses clinked in a cabinet. "About two years, except for eight months I spent in New York in the corps at the City Ballet. Edward Villella asked if I'd like to come back to Miami as a soloist, so I did. The cottage isn't exactly convenient, but Jack lets me have it for nothing."

"So you studied in New York?"

"No, here in Miami. Bobby Gonzalez and I took classes together. He stayed, I left. New York is wonderful, but there are so many great dancers it usually takes years to get out of the corps. So here I am again."

Setting her purse on the table, Gail noticed a gold picture frame on the wall beside the front door. She had missed it on her way in, and walked back across the room to see. "Oh, this is wonderful." Against an almost overpowering backdrop of black shadow and velvet curtains, a young dancer stood at the edge of a stage. Her tutu was a froth of net and gleaming pearls. The girl's small, rosy lips were parted, and her eyes were fixed on something out of view.

Gail realized that Diane was standing beside her. She looked back and forth, one face to the other. "It's really you. And the tutu! I could reach in and touch it. Is this typical of your cousin's style?"

Diane handed Gail the glass of carrot juice. "Well, the colors are sort of typical, but most of her paintings are abstract. She didn't do portraits, so this is special. That's what Jack says. He's an expert."

"And your mother wants it back. I don't blame her."

"She doesn't even like it. She'll have a cocktail party so she can show it off. 'Oh, yes, this was painted by our dear, departed niece, the famous artist. Isn't it just marvelous?' "

"You're her daughter. That could be another reason to want it."

"I wish that were true. One time, when I was a little kid, she got mad and said she'd found me in an orange grove. They were at Disney World when she went into early labor. I think she blames me for ruining her vacation."

Unwilling to argue, Gail said, "Tell me again how your parents acquired this. It was a gift from your uncle, Porter Cresswell?"

Diane shook her head. "Not exactly. Nate Harris gave it to Aunt Claire and Uncle Porter as a present, but then they gave it to my parents. Nate didn't want *them* to have it. He was Maggie's husband, and this was her painting, and he bought it for Aunt Claire and Uncle Porter."

"Wait. You say that Nate Harris gave it to them?" Gail wondered why Anthony hadn't mentioned this.

"Yes. He bought it from Jack. Jack's an art dealer. Nate came by here the night of the party and picked it up."

"You were here?"

"Not then. I was out with some friends and got home late. Earlier that day I saw it in Jack's study, and I said, what's this doing here? And he said Nate Harris was coming by to look at it. It wasn't in there the next day, so I guess Nate took it with him that night."

"Really. How did Jack get it?"

"From Roger."

Gail laughed a little. "Well . . . where did Roger get it?"

Diane looked to one side, then frowned. "I don't know, but Jack's had it for two or three months. It's been hanging in his gallery."

Lightly touching the gilded wood frame, Gail said, "How much is this worth? Just curious."

"Jack says a serious collector might pay fifty thousand. He was offering it for seventy-five."

"God."

"Well, Jack likes to bargain."

"Where is Jack, by the way?"

"He's home. I told him you were coming."

"And I suppose he knows I'm working for Bobby Gonzalez."

Diane tucked a strand of platinum hair into her stretchy black headband. "You don't have to worry about Jack."

"Listen, Diane. Do me a favor and don't mention this to anyone else. Don't mention me either. No one can know I'm working for Bobby. If your aunt and uncle found out, or your parents— Oh, great, I'm telling you to keep secrets from your parents."

"That's easy. I hardly talk to them anyway."

With another look at the portrait, Gail let out a breath. "Come on, let's sit down."

Diane went over to the little bistro table and lowered herself gracefully into a chair. The upswept hair made her neck seem long and fragile. The thin straps of her pastel blue top revealed the bones of her chest. Large eyes watched Gail approach, set down the glass of carrot juice, and pull out the other chair.

"It's a painting of *me*," Diane said. "Doesn't that give me some kind of right to it?"

"Afraid not." Gail thought for a moment, then said, "If Nate bought the painting for your aunt and uncle, and they gave it to your parents, you had no right to take it. But let's say for a moment that Nate hadn't paid for it. The sale wasn't final. If Nate didn't pay, and no one else along the line paid any money, then the previous owner, Jack, could in theory recover his property."

For a minute or two Diane looked blankly across the room. "Does that mean I could have it?"

"Well, if Jack would give it to you. And *if*—this is all very iffy—there was never actually a sale. I could find out, but honestly, no one ever wins in a family dispute. You should talk to your uncle. Are you on good terms with him? Maybe he'd persuade your parents to drop the issue, since he was the one who gave them the portrait."

"Well, my father doesn't really care. It's mostly my mother." Diane frowned in thought. "Uncle Porter has never been easy to talk to. He's kind of intimidating, especially since he got sick. He'd probably just tell me to go away and leave him alone."

"What about your aunt Claire?"

"She hates controversy, *hates* it, and she's such a mouse when it comes to Uncle Porter, you just want to scream. She might help, if I could convince her to do it. I know she likes me. She was a dancer in her faraway youth." Diane smiled. "That's what she says. 'My innocent and faraway youth.' "

Gail considered, then said, "Would you like for me to talk to Claire? She went to high school with my mother. What if I mentioned this, and said that I'd met you, and that we had talked about the portrait. . . ."

The pale blue eyes gazed back at her. "You could even ask about Roger. I mean, if you wanted to."

As before, outside the ballet, Gail had the sense of things being wordlessly conveyed. This girl would help Bobby Gonzalez as far as she could. "I could talk to Claire next weekend on the boat."

"What boat?"

"They're taking Roger's ashes to be scattered at sea. You hadn't heard?"

With a sigh, Diane nodded. "Jack told me. That's how I found out. My mother and father didn't say anything. You see how they are? But why are you going?"

"I'm working with Nate's lawyer. Claire invited him, and he got me onboard."

A smile dimpled Diane's cheeks. "Angela's father."

"Things get around, don't they?" Gail said, "Will you be with the family next weekend?"

The smile vanished. "I hadn't planned to. It would be awfully strained, wouldn't it? Everyone pretending they're sorry he's dead. I guess that makes me sound cold, but it's the truth."

"How well did you know your cousin?"

"Hardly at all. We saw each other at holidays or family dinners. He came to the ballet a couple of times, but only because Claire insisted."

Gail said nothing for a few moments, snagged on the awkwardness of asking Diane which of her relatives might have had a reason to commit murder. Her uncle, who had feared his son was destroying the company? Her own parents, who had clashed with Roger for pushing them aside? Diane's brother, Sean, had hated Roger for getting him in trouble with the police. And there was Nikki, who would have lost millions in company stock if her husband had divorced her.

Unable to find a thread to follow, Gail let her eyes drift across the room. Through the windows she saw the colored glass pieces slowly turning, catching the light. "Those are pretty, the pieces of glass. Did you put them out there?"

"No, they were here already. I think Maggie did."

"Did you ever watch her working?"

"I wish I had." She sighed. "I was too young to know anything."

"Tell me about her," Gail said.

"Well . . . she was brilliant, of course." Diane leaned forward on crossed arms. "Jack told me a lot about her. They grew up together. He says that when she was really small, she *knew* she was going to be an artist. It's sort of the same with me, actually. When I was little, I felt special, not like my brother and sister. Maybe that's why I don't get along with them, or with my mother. Anyway, Maggie ran away when she was still in high school and went north to study. She lived in a cottage on Cape Cod and was really happy there, even though she was alone. Sort of like me. I was a senior in high school, and one day Jack handed me the keys to this cottage, and he said whenever I wanted to come over here, it was mine. He let Maggie stay here too. I'm sorry now I didn't come over to see her. He says we would have been great friends. Isn't it sad how you always know something too late?"

Smiling, Diane softly said, "I feel that we do connect on another plane. She had a good spirit. I think that when someone with a good spirit dies, and you come into that aura, nothing bad will happen. Maybe that's why I've stayed here so long. It's like . . . she's watching over me. She sent Edward to bring me back from New York. I believe that, truly."

They were quiet for a minute. Gail could hear the hum of the air conditioner and the chain on one of the ceiling fans tapping on the housing.

"I almost forgot." Diane got up and walked to the bookcase. "Jack gave me this the other day, after I brought the portrait home. It's from a show in New York. Her last one."

Diane returned with a glossy exhibition guide from a gallery at Madison and Fifty-ninth. There was some text describing Margaret Cresswell's work, followed by full-color reproductions of her paintings. Gail turned the pages. So much black and brown, great swaths of it, pressing down on the more intense colors underneath, layer upon layer, as if pinning the heart of the thing far below the surface. Gail could see that the technique was excellent, but she felt no emotional connection. The portrait of Diane had spoken to her more clearly.

"Maggie's picture is on the last page." Standing behind her, Diane pointed, and Gail skipped ahead.

The black-and-white photograph took up the lower right-hand corner. The rest of the page contained her biography. Schools, degrees, major collections. Gail's attention returned to the artist. Margaret Cresswell had looked sideways at the camera as if it were intruding. Gail could only guess at the color of her long hair and pale eyes. Light brown and blue or gray? Gentle eyes, with faint shadows underneath. One brow a little higher than the other. No lipstick to define the small mouth, no blush to soften the sharp cheekbones. A woman who hadn't cared what people thought of her looks. Not defiance; irrelevance. *Why does it matter?* A man of some maturity and intelligence—a judge, say—might have found himself in the middle of a third or fourth conversation with this woman and have realized that he didn't want her to go back north. He would have persuaded her, somehow, to stay in the very place she had chosen to leave. Gail glanced at the date of the guide. Margaret Cresswell had been thirty-two years old. One year away from her death.

Gail said, "She killed herself. Do you know why?"

"They say it was clinical depression, which is the same as saying nobody knows." Diane turned her head toward the far end of the room. "There was a sofa under that window, and she took some pills and went to sleep."

"Who found her? Jack?"

"He was out of town. She left a note for her husband, and when he got home he read it and called the police, and they found her. It was too late by then."

"How sad. What did the note say?"

"It was just . . . 'Forgive me. I am at peace.' "

" 'Forgive me,' " Gail repeated softly. " 'I am at peace.' "

"I think she did it here because it's so quiet and peaceful. You don't notice it now but when the weather is cool, you can open all the windows and doors, and the breeze comes through, and you smell the ocean and hear the birds. It's perfect. I can turn up the music as loud as I want and not bother anybody."

Gail closed the exhibition guide. "May I keep this for a while?"

"If you want. Why are you so interested in Maggie?"

"Curiosity, I suppose."

"You feel her presence, don't you?"

With a laugh, Gail said, "No, not at all. All right, I'll tell you, and if this sounds weird, ignore it. I was thinking earlier today how odd it is that both of them—Maggie and her brother—died on this same piece of property."

Delicate blond brows lifted. "You don't think it has anything to do with Jack—"

"No, I don't mean that. I mean . . . I don't know what I mean." Gail wedged the guide into her shoulder bag. "This could be a complete dead end, but it bothers me." She took a small breath, then stood up. "Well. Could I see where you found Roger?"

"If I don't have to go with you."

Diane unlatched the screen and they went onto the porch. The dog opened his eyes and raised his head.

"Look straight across the yard. See that trellis? There's a path that goes under it, and you go about fifty feet, and you'll see a fountain. Roger was on this side of it." She paused, then said, "I haven't gone in there since that morning."

Gail recalled, "You were the one who found him. How?"

"I heard Buddy barking. I was coming from Jack's house about nine o'clock in the morning. We'd been up all night talking. I'd gotten home just as people were leaving the party, and Jack asked me if I was hungry. There was plenty of food left over. So I fixed something to eat, and helped him clean up, and we just kept talking and listening to old records, and then the sun came up, and we had breakfast. I was coming this way when I heard Buddy."

That had been more information, Gail thought, than she had asked for. "Will you be here the rest of the afternoon?"

"Yes, until around five o'clock, then I'm meeting some friends.

If you need anything else, just bang on the door. I'll have the music on." With some formality, Diane Cresswell extended a hand, allowed Gail to shake it briefly, then turned and went back inside.

Gail waited until the door closed, then looked down at the dog, whose tongue hung out one side of its mouth. "You want to show me the scene of the crime?" Knowing it had been spoken to, the dog padded over to Gail, nails clicking on the porch. She scratched the top of its head. "And where were you during the murder of Roger Cresswell? Not talking, eh?"

Tags jingling, the dog trotted after her down the steps and across the yard. Gail dug her camera out of her bag and turned to take a shot of the cottage, then swung the lens due east toward the bay. Bushes partially blocked the view, but as Bobby had described, there was a seawall across the rear of the property and a boathouse toward the left.

She walked toward the palm trees, which grew at so many heights, with tangles of foliage between, that it was impossible to see into them. The fountain was completely hidden. She took a wide shot then zoomed in on the trellis. A vine wound in and out of the cross beams, dropping tendrils with blue flowers into the dim and empty space underneath. Gail heard the dog panting beside her. She said, "I don't really want to go in there unless you go with me. How about it?"

Buddy gave a sharp bark and bounded away. Camera still at her eye, Gail turned to get a shot toward the house, of which only the shingle roof and second floor were visible. She pulled back the lens for a wide view, and a man in a white Panama hat appeared in the scene, striding toward her on the keystone walkway. The dog circled around him.

She lowered the camera. The stocky man was wearing hiking shorts, a loose shirt printed with game fish, and leather deck shoes. He had an enormous blond mustache.

Teeth appeared under it. "Ms. Connor. I'm Jack Pascoe. Diane said you'd be paying a visit. You didn't knock on my door."

"I'm sorry. Should I have?"

"It would have been considerate, since this is my property, and here you are with your little spy camera, clicking away."

Gail felt a flutter in her chest. "Yes, I suppose I should have asked permission." She closed the lens cover and dropped the camera into her bag. "Well, anyway, I'm glad to meet you. I'd hoped we could talk."

"About what?"

Uncertain what he knew, but suspecting he knew everything, Gail said, "I represent Bobby Gonzalez. The police suspect him of murdering your cousin, Roger Cresswell. I'd like to see the crime scene. That's why I brought the camera. I also need some background on Roger and his family, and his friends, if you know any of them. This is confidential, of course."

"Is that what you were pumping Diane for? She said she was getting advice on that painting."

"Mr. Pascoe, I'm being civil with you, am I not? Please don't be rude."

"I guess it ticks me off what you're doing to a good friend of mine."

"You mean Nathan Harris. I'm not happy about it either. Look. If I can get Bobby out of harm's way, Nate's in the clear too."

"That's enough. Nate's lawyer and I already had an extended discussion. He told me not to talk to anyone, except the cops, naturally. God forbid we get charged with obstruction."

"Oh, I see. And did Nate's lawyer happen to mention my name? As in, do not speak to this woman?"

Pascoe's smile revealed slightly crooked teeth. "A pleasure to have met you, Ms. Connor. If you don't mind, I've got a cold beer waiting in the fridge."

"One question. All right? Do you remember what Bobby was wearing that night? It's important. The police found a T-shirt in the trash outside his apartment, and it had Roger's blood on it, but from a fight two days before. The night of your party, Bobby wore a Hawaiian shirt. Do you remember it?"

Pascoe let out a breath and stared upward. The sandy mustache had some gray in it. "A green and white shirt . . . with pineapples. There. I've just eliminated a piece of evidence against him. Happy?"

"There is one more thing—"

"No, there isn't. It's hot out here, Ms. Connor."

"Let's stand in the shade. This is about the portrait. Diane asked me for legal advice, and I'm trying to help her."

Pascoe stared at Gail from under the brim of his hat, then exhaled. "All right. What do you want to know?"

They walked under a sea grape tree, where dried leaves the size of saucers littered the ground. Gail said, "You sold it—or gave it—to Nathan Harris. Did any money change hands? It's not an irrelevant question, Mr. Pascoe. I'm trying to establish ownership."

"Nate gave me a check for five thousand dollars on a total price of twenty. He owes me fifteen, which I may have to eat. It depends on where that painting ends up."

"I see. So you did actually sell it to him." That was disappointing, Gail thought. She would have to think of some other way for Diane to acquire the portrait. "I'm curious. You let Judge Harris have it so cheaply. Why was that?"

Pascoe was smiling at her again. "I'm a nice guy. Besides, it was for my aunt Claire."

Gail tugged one of the sea grapes from a long purple cluster. "Diane told me that the night Roger died, she saw the portrait in the study. Roger came to your house about nine-thirty, and you went into the study together to talk. Is that what you discussed? The portrait?"

Pascoe broke into a laugh. "Oh, yes, Anthony Quintana said you'd try to slip in a question like that. Just come out and ask me, Ms. Connor. Did you blow Roger away to get your hands on the portrait? No. I already owned it. He sold it to me in June."

"Where did Roger get the portrait?"

The only reply was an expansive shrug and upturning eyes. "God knows. Now off with you, I'm expecting company."

"Tell me about Margaret Cresswell," Gail said, not moving from where she stood.

"Why?"

"I'm curious about her. If I wind up defending Diane in a lawsuit over that portrait, I'd like to know about the artist. Diane said you grew up with Maggie. Is that right?"

Pascoe watched his black dog nose about under the leaves. "My parents traveled a good bit, and sometimes they'd leave me at Aunt Claire's house. Maggie was my age, so we spent time together."

"What was she like? I'd really like to know."

"Shy. Quiet. She read a lot. She drew constantly. You could see her talent even at age ten, eleven. A genius, but not in her schoolwork. She never cared about that. She created an inner life. She was the kindest person I have ever known. The sort of girl who would rescue baby birds."

"What about Roger?"

"He'd step on the eggs."

"How old was she when she ran away?"

"You've been talking to Diane." Pascoe fanned himself with his Panama hat. "I told her that because she needs to believe it. Maggie didn't run away. She tried to hang herself from the clothes rod in her closet. She was fifteen."

"Ohhh—"

"They sent her to a mental hospital up the middle of the state in Redneckville. She spent a few months there, then they shipped her to another happy farm in Vermont. She sent me a potholder. A joke, of course. I knew then that she was okay. Porter bribed somebody to get her into Bennington College. After that, she disappeared. She was cleaning hotel rooms on Martha's Vineyard. Winters, she painted. I didn't see her for ten years."

"My God."

Pascoe curled the end of his mustache around his forefinger. "Yes. Being a Cresswell would drive anybody crazy."

"Was she?"

"Certainly unhappy. Claire and Porter will tell you that Maggie was afflicted only with an artistic temperament. Thank God I'm not a Cresswell. Having had Cresswell cousins makes me only partially nuts. Does this help you? I can't see how it would. Sorry to be a grinch, Ms. Connor." He dropped the hat back on his head, covering a bald spot. "You should be running along now."

"Why did Maggie try to kill herself at fifteen?"

"I didn't ask. Sorry." He held out an arm toward the house as if to let her go first.

"I won't leave until I see where Roger died." Gail's hand had turned to a fist on the strap of her shoulder bag. "You don't have to escort me. I can find it on my own."

The cavalry-officer mustache lifted, but what Pascoe found humorous Gail couldn't imagine. "Okay." He indicated the direction with a nod. "Go through the trellis. The path curves a bit to the right. There's a fountain back there made of coral rock. You'll see a big brass manatee spouting water. Maggie designed it. If you've gone that far, back up. Roger was about ten feet this side of the fountain."

The timbers of the trellis had darkened with age or rot, and the vines that twisted around them had overgrown the lattice roof and climbed into the trees. Palm fronds rattled in a sudden gust of humid wind.

As Jack Pascoe walked away, he smiled over his shoulder. "Take some souvenir photos."

CHAPTER

17

Anthony followed Jack Pascoe's faded shirt and fraying khaki shorts through the long entrance hall that ran straight back through the house. French doors opened into a living room on one side, a study on the other. Books everywhere. Frames leaned up against walls. The oriental carpet was tattered, and upholstery sagged. Even thirty years in this country had not been sufficient to explain to Anthony why Americans from old money allowed their possessions—even their cars and their clothing—to appear so worn out.

On the screened porch, Anthony looked into the two tangled acres that made up the backyard.

"She's probably still in there, taking photos." Pascoe's mouth twitched with amusement. As if to lead the way, he reached for the door, but Anthony told him he was sure he could find it. He set off on the path that led due east toward the bay.

Five minutes ago, parking in front of Pascoe's house, he had noticed a silver Acura. His own reaction had surprised him: a pleasant buzz, a warmth in his chest like the beginnings of a laugh. This had been quickly replaced by curiosity: What was she doing here? Pascoe had supplied the answer to that.

Under the trellis the air was redolent of earth, rot, and re-growth. Plants pressed in from all sides and bent from their own weight. Red-throated bromeliads held small pools of water. Immense green and yellow leaves climbed across branches and tumbled down again, dangling in midair. Orchids clung to the trees. One of them shot out an immense spray of purple. Plants overflowed their pots, and ferns spilled across the path. Anthony's soft-soled shoes made no sound, and when he came around the final curve, Gail Connor didn't hear him.

She was pointing her camera at a brass manatee that seemed to rise up on its tail. A wall of rock formed the back of the thing, and water spurted from its mouth into a fern-draped, semicircular pond, ten feet in diameter, that glittered with bits of glass and broken pottery. Reflected sunlight dappled the trees.

The camera flashed, and Gail walked closer to the manatee, whose hippo-like face was level with her head of unruly dark blond hair. Slender arms lifted from a sleeveless shirt, and her sneakers were planted firmly on the path. A deceptively boyish figure.

Without speaking, Anthony waited for her to notice him. Finally she caught sight of him and jumped back a step, a hand at her heart. Recovering, she tossed her hair off her face.

"Well. Look who's here. Did Jack Pascoe send out the alert? What's the meaning of telling him not to talk to me?" She was steaming. "He wanted to kick me off his property, thanks to you."

Anthony made a slight bow. "How pleasant to see you, Gail. Is your cell phone on? No, never mind why. Just look and tell me if it's on." She took it out of her shoulder bag. "Turn it on. Now, does it show a message? That's from me. I called you to say I would be here at one o'clock, and to bring your camera. You cut my head off for nothing. First the ax, then the trial. And no, I didn't tell Jack Pascoe not to talk to you. Maybe he just didn't want to."

She dropped the phone back into her bag. "Sorry."

"What abuse I take from this woman. She comes here in secret, and do I complain?"

"Okay, don't rub it in."

He walked farther into the open. The keystone path widened

around the fountain, and three teak benches marked a semicircle. "What have you photographed so far?"

"The entrance, the path, the fountain." She turned and pointed. "I think Roger must have died over there. I wanted to save that for last."

Near where Anthony had stood were some broken and brown philodendron leaves, new shoots already uncurling. Any blood had been washed away by the rain. Sitting on his heels, he moved a leaf aside and saw a latex glove, likely dropped by the medical examiner.

Gail told him to move back, and while she took more photographs, he looked around. There were some small colored landscaping lights to illuminate the path and the fountain after dark. The full moon that night would have shone straight down through the opening in the trees. The killer had waited until his victim moved into this area by the fountain. Anthony glanced at the pond. An orange carp slid under the surface like a flash of blood. The level was low, and Anthony noticed a spigot connected to a garden hose.

Gail said, "Did Jack Pascoe tell you what I asked him?"

"Ah." Anthony turned. "Yes. You came to give Diane Cresswell some legal advice regarding the portrait in her cottage. You asked Jack about it."

She moved out of sight behind the fountain. "Why didn't you mention that you were with Nate Harris when he gave it to Porter and Claire?" Gail came out from behind the wall of coral rocks brushing some twigs out of her hair.

He shrugged. "It wasn't relevant. I don't see how it's relevant now." She had missed a leaf, and he reached out to pick it off. Her eyes followed his hand. "Why all the interest in a painting?"

"Because Roger used to own it, and it was here in Jack's study the night Roger was killed. Jack said he bought it from Roger last June. You don't know how Roger got hold of it, do you?"

Anthony flicked the leaf away. "Yes. I went by Jack's gallery yesterday, and we talked. I had no interest in the painting, only in asking what he and Roger had discussed in the study that night. He gave me a plate of bullshit. Supposedly Roger had dropped by to discuss buying something for his mother. Then Jack said he didn't know what to do about Nate's down payment. I asked what he was talking about, and he told me that Porter had given the portrait of Diane to her parents, and that Diane took it, and now it's in the cottage." Anthony smiled. "And you were here to talk to her about it. How things go around."

Sunlight came through the trees and moved on Gail's hair.

He went on, "Jack told me he would give Nate his money back, depending on what happens to the portrait. It came up in conversation that Jack bought it from Roger, and that Roger had been given the portrait by . . . Porter and Claire."

Gail laughed. "What? And Jack was sending it *back* to them? I bet he made money. How much did he pay Roger for it?"

"He didn't say. It didn't seem important, so I didn't ask. Nate doesn't know yet. I'll have to tell him, and he's not going to be happy with Jack, much less to find out what Porter and Claire thought of his gift."

"Yes, that was rude. Don't blame Claire, though. Diane says it was Porter's idea." Gail frowned slightly, then said, "Of course. Roger and Jack were arguing about the portrait. Diane told me it was in the study that night."

"And what would that prove?" Anthony asked.

"Look. Both Roger and his sister died on this same piece of property. He was shot; she killed herself. Don't you wonder about that? What connects them but the portrait? He owned it, she painted it. What if there's something going back to their childhood. Some secret that Roger was going to reveal, and someone—maybe Jack Pascoe—wanted to keep quiet."

Her mind was a garden of improbable theories. "Go on. What secret?"

She blew out a puff of air. "I don't know." In her excitement she lightly touched his forearm, and the hairs seemed to tingle. "Jack just told me something. Margaret Cresswell first tried to commit suicide at age fifteen. She tried to hang herself, and they sent her to a mental hospital. Did you know that?"

One tragedy on another. Anthony shook his head. "No. Nate never mentioned it. I'm not sure he knows. What an unhappy woman." The burble and splash of the fountain echoed in the thick enclosure of green. Anthony went over and rested a foot on the edge. Minnows darted under some lily pads. "Let's look at the facts. Roger went into Jack's study around nine-thirty. They talked for ten minutes. Roger slammed the front door when he left. He bought a fifth of whiskey at a liquor store around ten o'clock. He came back—we don't know what time. He parked along the road a block away, and he drank. He was either killing time or building up his courage. Then he came in through the gate—sneaking in. Why does a man do that?"

Gail walked closer. Her face shone with perspiration. "Well, why?"

"He's looking for his wife. We know that Roger suspected Nikki of adultery. Assume he came here to look for her. Jack said she wasn't here. Roger left, but he wasn't convinced. He came back. Someone was either following or waiting for him."

"Jack?" Gail wasn't convinced. "Why do you think he was sleeping with Nikki, of all people?"

"Pure speculation." Anthony laughed.

"Wait. This may be nothing, but . . . when I was talking to Diane, I asked her a simple question about finding Roger's body, and she goes into this long explanation about what time she got home, and the fact that she and Jack spent the night talking, and what they talked about. . . . When you hear testimony like that in a trial, what's your first thought?"

"Someone is lying."

"Maybe you're right about Jack and Nikki, but I don't know how we can possibly prove it."

Anthony took his foot off the edge of the pond. "Come on. Let's see how our killer got in."

A fence enclosed the south side of the property. The keystone walkway ended, becoming a soggy carpet of dead leaves. Anthony went first, sweeping away spider webs with a stick. They came to a rotting wood fence with vines twisting through broken boards. He found the gate and tugged on a rusting metal handle. The door opened silently. He motioned for Gail to go through, and in moving aside scraped his shoulder on the damp, fungus-black wood.

"*Coño.*" The shirt was a loosely woven Egyptian cotton with short sleeves, good for such sultry days. He brushed at the stain, only smearing it further.

He could hear Gail chuckling softly. "Next time wear an old one." She walked past him. Such a lovely view, the seam of her shorts tucking in just so under two perfect curves. Long legs. He shoved his thoughts away.

The unpaved street ended just to the left in a tangle of mangroves that hid any view of the water. Across the road was an overgrown vacant lot. Cars that had not fit in Pascoe's driveway the night of the murder had parked there. Gail took her photos, and they went back inside the fence.

She asked, "Why didn't the killer just shoot him outside? Why come in here?"

"Privacy. A car could have turned down that street with its headlights on." They walked back toward the fountain. Anthony said, "I don't believe that the killer was waiting inside. He would have had to know that Roger was coming back and at what time. Assume he followed Roger. There were two bullets in Roger's chest, which means that Roger turned around to see who was behind him. The police report indicates visible gunpowder on his shirt. The killer came close, possibly within a few feet, while Roger stood and waited. Why?"

"Because of the gun."

"No. Because Roger knew him."

Reaching the fountain, Anthony reconstructed the scene. "The killer calls Roger's name. Roger turns. He knows the voice and wonders why this person is here. He lets him get close. Then the gun comes out. The killer fires twice, directly into Roger's chest." Anthony touched his own chest. "Confused, Roger pulls away. A third shot hits him here in the upper arm at an angle as he turns. Now he runs. A fourth goes into his back. Blood is found on the path here . . . and here."

Walking slowly, Anthony pointed. "Roger falls. He instinctively lifts his hands to protect himself. A bullet goes through his wrist and into the ground. The killer stands over him, aims carefully, and— Two bullets through the left eye. The skull is cracked, and blood soaks the ground. The killer takes Roger's wallet, his Rolex—"

A faint moan made Anthony turn around. Gail was sitting on one of the benches, her head level with her knees. "Gail!" A few quick paces took him there, and he lifted her by the shoulders.

Her lips were bloodless. "I'm fine. Just . . . a little too much detail, I guess."

"*Ay, Diós,* I'm sorry." He looked around, remembering the spigot for the fountain. Taking out his handkerchief, he sprinted over and turned the handle. It came on with a rush and splashed mud on his linen trousers. Ignoring that, he took the wet cloth back to Gail and pressed it to her forehead. "Turn this way, *corazón.*"

A split-second after the accidental endearment slipped out, Gail took the handkerchief and shifted away from him on the bench. Anthony stared at the fossilized shells in the keystone pavement, gritting his teeth.

"Thank you," Gail said. She folded the handkerchief neatly on her bare thigh. "I'll wash this and get it back to you."

"Are you going to mail it?" he retorted.

She gave him a look. "You can pick it up at my office tomorrow."

He recovered his manners. "You're feeling better now?"

"I'm *fine.*" She took a breath. "Thank you. Really." She stood up and reached into her bag for a fresh roll of film. "Let's go, it's hot in here."

He was aware once again of that odd sense of dislocation, of time having slipped backward. This place was so quiet. A bird, the whisper of leaves. The sun dappling the path at their feet. She had worn those same sneakers when they'd walked together twenty times—five miles—around the deck of the *Sovereign of the Seas* last winter. He slowly raised his eyes. Up the curves of her legs, over her sharp-boned knees, snagging for a moment on her shorts. Cuffed hems, which had caught the sand on the beach at Captiva Island, Gail leaning back against his chest as they'd watched the sunset. Six months ago—or six days, it was all the same—he had unbuttoned that same shirt, such damnably small buttons, which now rose and fell on the curve of her breast.

His eyes lifted to her face. "Gail, I regret—so much—what happened to us."

She stared back at him, then looked down at her camera, which hummed as the film was pulled back into the cannister. She shook it into her palm and dropped in another. "No regrets. We're lucky to have found out in time, aren't we? I'm sure you feel the same way." The back of the camera closed with a sharp click. "Things have worked out quite well, actually. It looks like I'll be moving to the Virgin Islands. Dave and I think it would be better for Karen, having both her parents in the same time zone, so really, you shouldn't regret a thing."

Gail swung her bag onto her shoulder and walked toward the trellis.

Anthony stared into the unfocused tangle of greenery. Dimly, from deep underground, he heard bars rattling and howls, and he knew that if he opened his mouth, it would be the creature's voice, not his own. Anthony took a few slow breaths, then got up from the bench and followed the path.

She was waiting around the curve. She glanced at him as if to assure herself that he posed no danger. "I want to take some pictures of the seawall before I leave. Do you know where Nate and Bobby were sitting?"

How cold-blooded she was. Anthony's body ached from the effort of maintaining his composure. He had to repeat her question to himself before remembering the answer. "No, I don't. Why do you want the seawall?"

"I take pictures of everything."

They walked from under the trellis into the sun. Jack Pascoe's back porch was empty, a pair of ceiling fans slowly revolving. Anthony heard music, and realized it came from the small white house across the yard. A black dog lay on the front porch asleep under a swing. It lifted its head and watched them.

The path went into the shade of some sea grape trees, and their feet rustled through fallen leaves. Branches swayed, and Anthony felt the cool relief of wind on his face. He listened to Gail planning how she could speak to Roger's widow, what she might ask, and whether to do it before the family went out on the boat next weekend to scatter the ashes. She talked without a glance at the man beside her. Anthony allowed himself to ponder what Gail had told him back there by the fountain. Leaving for the Virgin Islands. Abandoning her law practice, her mother, her friends, her relatives, and her way of life to travel 1,500 miles to be with a man she had ceased to love. There was Karen, of course, but Anthony did not believe that any woman, had she a choice, would go to such extremes, even for her daughter. Round-trip airfare was less trouble.

Mentirosa. What games she played.

The wind tossed her hair. She wore no makeup today, but there was a pink glow on her face. She carried her small chin up, which had the effect of tilting her lashes slightly downward. Hiding from him.

They walked to the seawall. While Gail took photographs, Anthony sat on a bench in the shade of the boathouse, a wooden structure built over the shallows of the bay. A small power boat was up on hoists under the roof. Key Biscayne lay to the northeast, Elliot Key just south of it. Mangroves at Pascoe's property line hid the skyscrapers downtown. This spot could have been fifty miles away from the city. Water splashed softly against the pilings.

Anthony stretched out his arms along the back of the bench and put his ankle on the opposite knee. The warm buzz in his chest had returned. From ten yards away Gail turned toward him. "I'd like a shot of the boathouse. Do you want to move?" He smiled and shook his head, then waved at her as she looked through the viewfinder.

Gail closed her camera. "All right. I think that's everything."

"Come sit down for a minute. It's shady and cool here."

"No, I really have to go. Karen's waiting."

But she didn't go. She stood there looking at him. He said, "How is Karen? I am sorry not to see her anymore. May I say that without making you angry?"

He could see her let out a breath, then smile. Hang her head a little. "Yes, you may. Karen is wonderful, beautiful. She had a good time over the summer, and she's very glad to be home."

Ah-ha. This woman wasn't going to the Virgin Islands. Anthony raised his brows. "And your mother? Is Irene well? You must give her my regards."

"I meant to tell you." Gail stepped from the seawall to the dock, then under the eaves of the boathouse. She sat on the other end of the bench. "My mother has turned into a spy. She asked her friends about the Cresswells, and . . . well, I don't have any specifics, but you're right, what you said on that tape. They pretend to be close, but it's all an act."

Anthony let himself look at her. He smiled. "You can write me a memo," he said. "Ah. By the way, what did Bobby Gonzalez say about his alibi? Did you talk to him?"

It took her a second to reply. "Let's save that for tomorrow, when you see him at my office."

He continued to look at her, and her eyes became unfocused, then slid away from him. "You know, Gail, I can tell when something is going on. What is it this time?"

"Nothing is *going on*. We'll discuss it tomorrow."

She began to stand, but he held onto the strap of her shoulder bag. "Before I put one more hour of my time into helping that young jackass, I want to know where the hell he was when Roger Cresswell was shot to death." He looked directly at her, lifting his brows. "Where?"

"He was with a friend. We can discuss it later."

Anthony made a few little tugs on the strap. "What friend? We're working for the same thing, no? Why are you keeping secrets?"

She sighed. Deeply. Regretfully. "I'm so sorry about this."

It took him a few seconds before the impossible answer came to him. "Not . . . my daughter."

"Yes. Angela was supposed to have talked to you already. I see she didn't. Bobby's car wasn't working. She dropped him off here at eight o'clock and picked him up again about a quarter till twelve. All the times are the same, but he was with Angela, not Sean. They were together till about three in the morning, when she left him at his apartment on South Beach."

Anthony held up his hands. "No, no, I was at home that night.

She was upstairs in bed by ten-thirty. She couldn't have left. There's an alarm system."

"Girls that age can be very resourceful."

"*Coño cara'o.*"

"Bobby wanted to keep you from finding out, so he gave the police Sean's name as an alibi. It was foolish, but he did it for Angela."

"She told me—she *promised*—that she would stay away from him! How long have you known about this?"

"Two days. Bobby wanted to give Angela a chance to tell you herself. It was Angela who asked me to help Bobby. That was about a week and a half ago."

"*¿Por qué no me*— Why didn't you tell me?"

"Because I don't snitch on my friends."

"He barely graduated from high school! He's been arrested and he smokes pot. Do you think I want my daughter with someone like that? Do you approve of this?"

"Stop screaming at me, Anthony. If you so much as mention this to my client, I will throw you out of my office."

"*Voy a matar al hijo de puta.*"

"Oh, shut up. You're not going to kill anybody. Bobby is a decent young man, and Angela is in love with him. Deal with it."

A thought rocketed through his brain. "Have they . . . ?"

"How should I know?"

"You think this is funny, don't you?"

"I think you're being ridiculous."

Anthony opened his mouth to say something more, but could see there was no use in it. He put his elbows on his knees and his head in his hands and stared down at the rough boards of the dock. How had he failed his daughter? What secret life did she lead? What other lies was she guarding?

"I knew I would lose her someday, but not so soon. Not like this."

"Anthony. You haven't lost her." A sigh came from the woman beside him. "She's a normal teenage girl with a boyfriend you don't happen to like. This is so unbelievably *typical.*"

"Wait until Karen does it, then tell me it's typical."

"Good Lord."

"What do I say to her? That it's okay?"

"Just say . . . that you love her and you hope she'll be responsible." Gail followed that inadequate advice with a little shrug.

Anthony pushed his hair back with both hands. "Yes. You're right." He let out a breath. "This won't be easy, but . . . I'll talk to her. I will be . . . gentle. Like a saint."

Gail's laughter rippled like a light puff of wind on the water. "I think the heat is affecting your brain." She glanced at her watch. "I really have to go."

He stood up. "I'll walk with you to your car."

Her eyes went to his face, then away. She turned around and stepped off the dock and into the yard. He caught up. She reached into her bag and took out her sunglasses. "Did you ask Nate about smoking grass with Bobby?"

"Gail, listen to me. When you talk to Nate this week, stay away from that. It's not relevant."

"Are you setting limits on my questions?"

"I wouldn't put it that way."

"I would."

"*Ay, que pena.* Listen to me. Nate didn't follow Bobby from the house. Nate was sitting alone on the porch of the cottage having a drink. He was thinking of his wife and how she died. Nate saw someone walk to the seawall, he was curious, so he went to see who it was. That is *all*. And about the marijuana . . . Nate is embarrassed. He has no explanation, not much recollection, and as it isn't relevant, don't bring it up. I will not allow him to answer."

"Fine." Gail's long strides carried her quickly along the walkway to the house. She glanced at him. "I'd like to ask him about his wife."

"Maggie again. Do you really believe that a woman three years dead has anything to do with this?" Raising his hands, he said, "All right. You want to chase the painting. Go ahead."

They went under the portico, past a small red car, and into the front yard. Anthony's black Eldorado was parked in the shade, and he took out his keys. Gail rummaged around in her bag for hers.

She muttered, "Always at the bottom."

"What time should I be at your office in the morning?"

"I told Bobby nine-thirty. Is that okay?"

"I'll come a little early," Anthony said. "We can go over the case."

"Sure. You can read my memo on what my mother and I talked about."

"Memos. I'll bring you one of mine."

She laughed. "See you tomorrow."

He watched her get in and start the engine. The back-up lights went on. "Gail, wait!" He came around and tapped on the passenger door, then got in and closed it. Cold air was blowing out of the vents.

She stared at him through her sunglasses.

"I meant to talk to you about the house," he said. "I completely forgot."

"What house?"

"Ours. The one we own in the Grove. A decision to make."

The engine was running, and Gail's hands were clenched on top of the wheel. "I thought Raul was doing everything."

"He found a buyer. They can close immediately at four hundred thousand. If we wait we could get more."

"Wait? You wanted that house sold immediately, at any price."

"I did say that, but . . . what's the rush, after all?"

"Do what you want," she said. "As far as I'm concerned, it's yours."

Anthony shook his head. "You told Raul to make sure I was paid back the money I gave you. *Gave.* It wasn't intended as a loan."

"I think we should keep our relationship businesslike. When you gave—*loaned* me the money, we were engaged. Certain assumptions were made that are no longer true."

"Listen to me, Gail." He turned in the seat to look at her directly and with great effort restrained himself from taking her hands. "That house cost you everything you had. You wouldn't have signed your name on the contract if I hadn't wanted it."

"You didn't force me to do anything."

"When you had financial problems at your office, there was nothing left. I was glad to help you. I never calculated the cost. And then, when we broke up, everything you went through—I feel responsible for that. You had to move to a smaller space. You lost half your clients. I want to put you back in the position you were in before. It's the right thing to do. Isn't it?"

She was wavering.

"What about Karen's tuition? Private school is expensive. How long will it take for you to buy another house?" His voice was as gentle as he could make it. "Gail? You shouldn't let your anger at me hurt yourself and Karen."

Her hands let go of the wheel and fell into her lap. "Okay. We'll wait, then. If it's really no difference to you."

"None, I promise. Truce?"

A smile appeared. "Truce. I don't mean to be so . . . God, so *awful* sometimes."

He offered a handshake. Her fingers slid into his, and he felt the warm pressure of her palm. He lifted her hand and lightly kissed it.

It was nothing. A gesture between friends. He had done this hundreds of times, but his fingers refused to let go. He stared at her over the hand that seemed glued to his lips. Something shifted in his chest, like a knot being pulled loose. He felt a flame in his body, and it seemed to reflect in her face. Her cheeks reddened.

He grasped her sunglasses in the middle and pulled them off.

"Anthony, don't. Please."

If her voice hadn't wavered on *please* . . . He leaned toward her. She turned her head, and he felt the corner of her mouth, the softness of her cheek. He grasped her face with both hands and brought his mouth down on hers. He wanted to pour himself into her. Find the lever, lower the seat—

High-pitched vibrations, muffled words on his lips. Hands on his chest, pushing. He was barely aware of this. He thought of holding her there, showing her. Kissing her until the wall gave way, and the tidalwave surged through the breach.

She jerked her head away and looked at him as if facing a hard, stinging rain. "Take your hands off me."

"Gail—" He was out of breath.

"Get out of my car."

He reached for the door handle, wanting to rip it off. He ground his teeth together. "What is the matter with you? How long do you hold a grudge?"

She spoke through her teeth. "You have no idea what you've done, do you? And if I could possibly explain it, you wouldn't give a damn."

The air in the car was charged, and electrical impulses made his body so tense he thought his bones might splinter. He calmly smiled at her. "Why did you hand me that shit about going to the Virgin Islands with your ex-husband? I don't believe you. Why did you say it? To get a reaction?"

She laughed. "My God. What an insufferable egotist. You are beyond redemption."

"No, tell me. I am so curious. *¿De veras?* You're leaving?"

Her eyes were icy blue. "Yes."

"You want me to beg you to stay? Forget it. You should be with a man you can walk on."

"Get the hell out of my car!"

He got out and gave the door a hard shove. *"Olvídate. ¡Olvídate de todo!"*

The rear wheels of her car kicked up gravel, and dust hung in the air.

He was breathing through his teeth. "Idiot." He cursed himself for his generosity with the house. He would tell Raul to sell it immediately. She had played him on that one, hadn't she? "Fuck the house."

A fool to have loved her. He had said that to her their last day together, and it was still true. A fool to think that any love still remained, except as a last spasm of desire. She had ended that too, one sharp little knee in the *cojones.*

You are beyond redemption. Sins beyond forgiveness, as black as his soul.

Stanford Residence Hall at the University of Miami was a freestanding, blocky beige tower of twelve stories on the shore of a placid little lake with a fountain that shot into the air. The light was fading when Anthony drove onto campus. In no mood to go through red tape for a visitor's pass, and unable to find any sort of parking place, he parked beside a fire hydrant, half on the grass, half on the sidewalk.

He had inspected this building two weeks ago, but now it seemed different with students milling around. He went to the security desk in the lobby, said who he was, and that he'd like to see his daughter, Angela Quintana, a freshman who lived in . . . he couldn't recall the room number, but she was expecting him.

The guard asked for ID, gave him a paper to sign, and told him to wait.

Fifteen minutes later, the elevator door opened and Angela stepped out, looking around, a slender girl in jeans and a T-shirt. His blood, his life. He smiled at her and lifted a hand. His eyes stung. She seemed to take a breath before crossing the lobby.

He kissed her tenderly on the forehead. *"Hola, mi niña."*

"Hola, papi." She stared up at him. "You wanted to talk to me?"

He smoothed his hair, which had fallen over his forehead. "Yes. Can we sit over here?"

They sat in the most remote of the many groupings of green-upholstered chairs and couches. Angela folded her hands on her knees and looked at him across a low table littered with the UM newspaper, some crumpled paper, and an empty drink cup. He picked up the cup and the paper, saw no trash can nearby, and set them back down.

He nodded at the cartoon of the Hurricanes mascot—a white ibis—on the front of her T-shirt. "That's very nice. I see you're into the team spirit already."

"Dad? Are you okay?"

He felt his chin, remembering he hadn't shaved since early this morning, then noticed the mud on the bottoms of his trousers and the dirt across his sleeve. He brushed at the stains. "I was in some woods earlier today. A case I'm working on." He wished now he had suggested on the phone that they meet somewhere else. He reached over and laid his hand on hers. "I'm too busy lately. I've ignored you, haven't I? Maybe this is my fault."

She looked at him warily with her dark eyes. Her hair was a curtain pulled back on both sides with gold barrettes. He glanced around. There were other people in the lobby, but no one was paying attention to them. He leaned forward, keeping his voice low.

"Angela, you mean more to me than anything in the world. Don't you know this?"

She nodded.

"I was talking today with Gail Connor. You remember her, don't you? Of course you do." He paused to assemble his thoughts. "She told me something very disturbing. I couldn't believe it. She said you've been with Bobby Gonzalez. Is this true?"

Angela lowered her lashes.

"I'm not angry, but be honest with me. Is it true?"

"Yes."

"And you were with him the night Roger Cresswell was murdered?"

She nodded and seemed to shrink into her chair.

Gently, Anthony asked, "How did you get out of the house without my knowing? Did you turn off the alarm system?"

Another nod.

"And you were with him until three o'clock in the morning? Yes or no?"

A tear slid down her cheek. Her lips moved to form the word *yes.* She cleared her throat. "I—I was going to call you tonight anyway."

"Call me? Were you ashamed to see me face to face? To admit that what you did was wrong? I don't know what to say, Angela. You have disappointed me. Your mother will have to know about this too. What can I tell her?"

"*Papi,* please. You don't understand."

"Yes, I do. You're in love, but sweetheart, love is more than sex. Sex is a wonderful thing, of course, and necessary, or we wouldn't be here, but at the appropriate time and with the right person. The *right person,* Angela. That's important. Your mother and I have tried to teach you that you are too valuable to throw yourself away on someone who has nothing to offer. A young man with no education. No money. An arrest record. And who smokes marijuana. Don't you deserve more than that?"

"He doesn't smoke anything!"

"Shhh." Anthony held up a hand. "Yes, Angela. He does. Now I've thought about this a good deal, and maybe it's better, after this semester, if you go back to New Jersey and live with your mother. I have failed."

Her nose was running. Anthony started to reach for his handkerchief, then remembered where he had left it. He looked around the room, and several of the students glanced away, as if they'd been staring.

Angela wiped her nose on the hem of her T-shirt. "I won't leave! Bobby and I love each other."

His heart ached. "Sweetheart, listen to me. When a man is very young, he wants only one thing from a girl. He may deny it to himself—and certainly to you—but it's the truth. For him, it's not really love."

"How can you—" Her voice broke, and she took a deep gulp of air. "How can you get drunk and come here and tell me—"

"Angela! I am not—"

"Yes, you are! I can smell it on your breath. You didn't used to be this way! You drink when you're out, and you drink at home." She was crying. "You have no right to tell me how to live my life after what you've done."

"All right. I stopped by a bar. I had a couple of drinks. You're right, I shouldn't have done it, but don't change the subject."

She stared at him with red-rimmed, accusing eyes. "No! I mean what you did to *her*."

"Who?"

"Gail Connor. What you did."

"What I did?" He was blank for a second, then said, "You mean—sweetheart, we're adults. Please."

"You got her pregnant, didn't you? That's why you broke up with her, and she has to raise the baby by herself, or else get an abortion, so don't preach to *me* about morality."

"*¿Qué me estás diciendo?*" He glanced around the room. "Angela, why do you say such things?" He whispered, "This is impossible. We . . . took precautions. We were very careful about that. If anything had happened, she would have told me, you can be sure. Where did you get this crazy idea?"

She wiped her eyes. "Bobby told me."

"Bobby?" His mind spun.

"He saw her eating Tums and soda crackers."

Anthony laughed. "That doesn't mean anything. Just because a woman is eating an antacid—"

"And he overheard her on the phone talking to a doctor's office."

Anthony's hands were in midair until the solution came to him. "*Mentiras.* Don't you see? He's making up stories to make me look bad."

"He wouldn't do that! He wouldn't lie!"

"No? Didn't he lie about being with you? Didn't he tell *you* to lie? What have you become?"

"I'm sorry!" Angela stood up, and her chair tipped, then fell back on its legs. "I'm sorry I'm such a disappointment! You don't have to worry about me anymore. I'll get a scholarship, and if I can't, maybe I'll drop out, but at least I can live my own life. You hypocrite!" She ran a few steps away, then turned, and her hair whirled around her head. "And I'm auditioning for the ballet, too, and you can't stop me!"

They stared at each other. She burst into tears and ran for the stairs.

"Angela!" He started to follow, then noticed that there were two dozen pairs of eyes on him. All conversations had stopped. With dignity, he slowly turned, crossed the lobby, and pushed his way through the door.

CHAPTER

18

W here'd you get the money, Bobby?"

"I told you where I got it."

"No, I want a name. You gotta give us a name. Was it somebody at Jack Pascoe's party? I could go down the list for you."

Bobby Gonzalez folded his arms across his chest. The room was too cold. The gray color made it worse. Gray chairs, table, walls. He didn't know what time it was. Early. There wasn't a clock in here, and he hadn't put on his watch.

"When can I leave?"

"You ain't goin' nowhere, punk."

Detective Britton was okay, but the other guy, the skinny Latino with bad skin, looked like he'd enjoy grabbing a fistful of Bobby's hair and slamming his face into the table.

Britton said, "Take it easy. He can go as soon as he decides he wants to help himself. What's it gonna be, Bobby?"

Bobby stared at the things on the gray tabletop. Two mugs of cold coffee. Some glazed donuts on a paper plate. And a clear plastic bag with red tape on it and three one-hundred-dollar bills inside. The cash they'd taken out of his dresser drawer last Thursday.

A quarter to eight this morning, they'd come back, banging on the door, pissing off his roommates. *A small matter to resolve . . . a few minutes at our office.* Bobby had put on his jeans and T-shirt and got in the back of their unmarked car. He'd been sure he could handle this. *A couple of questions about the money we found in your room.* Bobby hadn't called Gail Connor because he didn't know what side she was on. She was working with Anthony Quintana, who would probably let Bobby go to prison if he had a choice about it. Anything to get him away from Angela. Bobby had spent some time last night listening to Angela cry into the telephone. She'd be over to his place at noon. He hoped he'd be home by then.

Sergeant Britton picked up the clear plastic envelope and held it up by a corner, let it swing. "Who gave you this, Bobby?"

"I don't remember."

"Who was it, we'll talk to him. A name. That's all you have to do."

Bobby could see it again—Sean Cresswell fanning out all those hundreds. He didn't think Sean had killed Roger. It had to be a mistake about the serial numbers. Or the cops were lying. Bobby thought about what would be better, to send the cops after Sean or keep his mouth shut. If he gave up Sean, that didn't mean his problems were over. Sean would say he didn't know anything about the money. His parents would hire a lawyer who would make Bobby look even guiltier, and he'd be right back here.

Britton was still talking in that hick voice of his. Looking worried, taking his glasses off, cleaning them on a napkin. "I don't know what to do about you, son. These hundreds are from Roger's wallet. Soon as that blood on your shirt comes back with Roger's DNA, the state attorney is going to draw up an indictment for murder one. I'd hate to see it happen."

The other cop put a foot on the chair and leaned into Bobby's face. "You jacked his wallet after you blew him away. He fired you from the company. You said, hey, the asshole owes me."

"I didn't touch his wallet. Did you find his wallet in my house? Did you find his Rolex?"

Britton held his glasses up to the light, then put them back on. "You goin' down for somebody else's crime? That's not smart."

Arms still crossed, Bobby stared at the opposite wall. "I want to call my lawyer."

The skinny cop laughed. "What a pussy."

Britton pulled out a chair and sat next to Bobby, leaning in close. "You're here, I'm here. Talk to me, son. This isn't going away. Are you protecting somebody? Is that what you're doing? You want to spend the rest of your life in prison? Come on, Bobby, I'm trying to cut you a break. Where did you get the money?"

Gail Connor glanced up from the pages on her desk—Anthony Quintana's latest memo. Anthony himself was still reading Gail's notes. It occurred to Gail that they'd done the same thing: written memos to avoid having to talk to each other.

She hadn't been certain, until the buzzer had sounded in her waiting room, that Anthony would show up. But he had, and so far they'd managed to discuss the case at a polite distance, each pretending that yesterday afternoon had never happened.

Gail noticed the clock on the bookcase. 9:42. Bobby Gonzalez was late. She thought of asking Miriam to call, then remembered again that Miriam wasn't here today. This was Labor Day. A holiday. Karen hadn't understood why Mom had run off to work. Gail had promised to be back around noon, and they would spend the afternoon on the beach. As if to underline this promise, Gail had left the house wearing jeans and a sunny yellow top.

She let her eyes drift to the man seated in one of the client chairs, elbow on the armrest, legs casually crossed, reading the pages on his thigh. She could see one laced shoe of gleaming brown leather. A finely woven sock that vanished under a cuffed pant leg. A dark green, double-breasted Armani jacket with subtle lines of midnight blue that matched the trousers. Emerald ring on his right hand, heavy gold on the last finger of his left. Perfectly white shirt, open collar. His hair was combed neatly off his forehead, curling into waves. Dark winglike brows, glowing skin. Sleek as a cat. He propped his cheek on extended fingers, and she saw that a button on his sleeve was missing, a thread dangling in the gap. How strange.

As if aware, he looked up, and for a second their gaze held before Gail returned to the memo he had brought. She forced herself to stare at the words, a jumble on the page. Not much sleep last night. An hour or two. She had lain in bed watching the numbers change on the digital clock, then reading a magazine, then throwing it aside. Unbidden, the memory of his kiss had intruded into conscious thought. The searing heat of his mouth, his tongue stroking hers, the hands imprisoning her face too tightly for escape. An assault, an invasion. But last night that kiss had replayed, over and over, and her body had traitorously responded.

A moment later she heard the rustle of paper as Anthony laid her memo on the desk. He draped an arm over the back of his chair. "You say a lot about the portrait of Diane Cresswell."

"She wants to keep it. I'm trying to help her."

"I still don't see how it relates to Roger's murder."

"It may not, but . . . isn't it odd how it keeps popping up? Porter and Claire give it to Roger, he sells it to Jack Pascoe, Jack sells it to Nate, and Nate gives it back to Porter and Claire, and *they* give it to Diane's parents, and now Diane has it—right back in the place where Maggie died. Don't you wonder?"

Dark brown eyes were focused over her head. He sighed. "No. It's interesting, that's all. Pursue it if you want, but I'd rather concentrate on Roger. Your mother found out some things that I doubt the police know about. Let's follow up on that. In my criminal cases, I've found that the most obvious motives are usually the ones that count. Greed and lust. Which of our suspects has both of those?"

This was a rhetorical question. Gail had seen it asked and answered in Anthony's memo. She replied, "Jack Pascoe."

Anthony lifted his hands. "Exactly. Nikki Cresswell now owns twenty million dollars' worth of company stock. Diane could have lied for Jack. From what you say of her, I think her motives were innocent—to protect him from suspicion of another kind. How guilty he would seem if the police knew that he was sleeping with the victim's wife."

"We have no proof whatsoever of that," Gail pointed out.

"Not yet."

"Why would Jack shoot Roger on his own property?"

"Who knows? We don't need to supply a reason. All we need

is a set of facts from which the detectives can reasonably infer that Bobby Gonzalez is innocent."

"Yes, I suppose that's true."

The pretense of civility was making Gail's head ache. With feet propped on a half-open desk drawer, she swiveled her chair slowly back and forth.

Anthony pulled back his cuff to see his watch—a gold Patek Philippe with a lizard strap. "You did say nine-thirty?"

"I told him to take a taxi. He should be here any minute." Gail made a little smile of reassurance.

"When did you speak to him?"

"On Friday."

"*Alaba'o.* That explains it. Last night I talked to Angela. God knows what she told him. That *papi* is going to break his neck the next time he sees him."

Gail inquired, "You didn't lose your temper, I hope?"

"Not at all. I never raised my voice. I was a model of fatherly concern. Even so, she started crying. She became angry. She said I had no right to tell her how to live her life. I've never seen Angela like that. I don't understand it."

"I wouldn't worry. She probably felt so guilty and defensive that she'd have cried no matter what you said."

"That could be so. I'll have to fix it with her somehow."

Gail looked at her telephone. "Maybe I should call Bobby."

"In a minute." Anthony made a slight smile, tapped his fingers slowly on his thigh, then said, "How are you feeling lately?"

"Fine. Why?"

"You almost fainted yesterday, and you were so pale." He gestured toward her face. "You look a little pale right now."

"Well, I . . . was up late with Karen."

"You haven't had a stomach virus, have you? The flu?"

"No. What a strange question."

His eyes were like beams of black light, moving over her face as if searching for something. His lips were pursed in concentration.

Gail pulled open her top drawer. "I nearly forgot. I washed and ironed your handkerchief. Thank you for lending it to me. And there's something else I've meant to return for a while." She set the handkerchief on the edge of the desk, then held out a small black velvet box.

He looked at the box in her hand. "What is that?"

"The earrings. The aquamarines. You should have them back. When I took them by your office last month, Raul said he couldn't accept them."

Anthony picked up his handkerchief. "No, you keep them. They look nice on you."

"I can't. Really, it wouldn't be right. They cost a lot of money. Give them to Angela." She set the box on the edge of the desk nearest him.

He straightened the corners of his handkerchief. "I don't want them back."

She dropped the box back into the drawer and slammed it. "Fine. I'll sell the damned earrings and give the money to charity."

He laughed. "What a childish response."

"So is yours."

The phone rang. Gail waited, then remembered that Miriam hadn't come in today. She picked it up. "Law offices . . . Bobby! Finally. Where are you? . . . Where? . . . Oh, God . . . Why didn't you call me?"

Anthony asked, "What's going on?"

"Wait. Wait a minute." Gail put her hand over the mouthpiece. "He's at the police station. Frank Britton picked him up, and he went with them. I can't believe he would do something so dumb!"

"Is he under arrest?"

"Bobby? Are you under arrest?" She looked back at Anthony. "They took him in for questioning. What should I tell him?"

Standing up and extending his arm across her desk, Anthony motioned with his fingers for the telephone. "Let me have it."

Gail stared up at him. "What are you going to do?"

"Give it to me."

She took her hand off the mouthpiece and said, "Bobby? Anthony Quintana is here. He wants to talk to you. . . . It's all right,

I promise. He's going to help you." She gave him the phone, praying she wasn't wrong.

He pushed back his jacket, put a fist on his hip, and walked slowly back and forth with the phone at his ear. "Bobby, this is Anthony Quintana. You're at Metro-Dade police headquarters, is that right? . . . I want you to listen carefully to what I'm going to tell you, and then repeat it back to me. 'My lawyer is on his way, and he has instructed me not to talk to you.' Now repeat that back to me. What did I just say? 'My lawyer is on his way . . .' "

The lobby of the Metro-Dade Police Department had shiny floors, an open reception desk, and glass cases with crime lab displays. Gail tried to look at them, but wound up pacing nervously while Anthony leaned a shoulder against the wall and read the sports section of the *Herald*. Finally a detective appeared—Frank Britton's partner, whom Gail had last seen outside Bobby's apartment after the search warrant had been served. He waited for the desk sergeant to issue visitor tags, then escorted them through a set of glass doors and into an elevator.

In the Homicide Bureau, Sergeant Britton stood talking to another man in a corridor running along a warren of open dividers upholstered in gray. Gail recognized the military haircut, wire-rimmed glasses, and beefy torso. The holster on his belt was empty, but the man and the surroundings were sending tremors into Gail's stomach. Britton broke off his conversation and watched them approach. He and Anthony shook hands.

"Frank."

"Look who's here," Britton said. "Hello again, Ms. Connor. My, my. Bringing in the big guns."

Anthony said, "I should complain about this, questioning a suspect without his attorneys present."

"Soon as the Supreme Court says not to, then I'll think about it. Bobby agreed to speak to us. He's not in custody. If we did things by your book, we'd never solve a single crime, would we?"

Gail asked, "Where is he?"

Britton nodded toward the plain gray door a few yards away. "Right there. We asked him about the cash we seized from his apartment. Brand new bills. Two of them are right in sequence with some others we found in a bank envelope in Roger Cress- well's car. Bobby says somebody lent him the cash. He won't say who. It would be in his best interest to tell us, you'd think. You want to go in there and see what his problem is?"

"Ms. Connor is going to take Bobby downstairs. Let me talk to you for a few minutes, Frank."

As they headed south again on the expressway, Gail glanced around at her client in the backseat. He was staring out the side window. His black hair was a mess, as if he'd been hauled out of bed. His faded blue T-shirt had a rip in the shoulder seam.

Anthony's eyes went to the rearview mirror. "We're going to Ms. Connor's office, then I'll make sure you get home. All right?"

"Fine." Bobby's knee was bouncing.

Gail exchanged a wordless glance with Anthony.

He said, "Bobby. While you were waiting downstairs, I ex- plained to Sergeant Britton that I'm helping Ms. Connor out as a favor. I didn't mention Judge Harris. Did they ask you anything about him, or did you mention his name?"

"No."

"What did you discuss with the detectives? The money? Any- thing else?"

"They wanted to know where I got it."

"And you didn't tell them."

"No."

"Are you listening? This is a high-profile murder, and they're under pressure to solve it, but Britton won't rush into an arrest. He admitted that the pistol they took from your roommates wasn't used in the crime. They're waiting for DNA results on the shirt. I told Britton you'd been in a fight with Roger a few days prior to the murder, and that he'd bled on your shirt at that time, and you were wearing a different shirt the night of the murder. Correct?"

"Yes."

"I told him we were developing some leads, and that in a week or two we'd share what we have, if he would keep our names out of it—Ms. Connor's and mine—for a little longer. There's a reason for this."

Bobby's wary and sullen expression hadn't changed, but he was listening.

"We're going to be talking to members of the Cresswell family, using a story about investigating Roger's financial problems. They won't talk to us if they think we're trying to point the finger at one of them. Do you understand so far?"

"Sure."

"This requires your cooperation. Does your friend Sean know that Gail Connor is your lawyer?"

"I never told him."

"Could his sister, Diane, have mentioned it to him?"

"I don't think so."

"Find out and tell her to keep it quiet. Will she do that?"

"Yeah, Diane's straight."

Anthony maintained the warmth in his voice, but Gail could tell from the occasional twitch of his jaw muscle that it wasn't easy. "I'm sure Ms. Connor has already told you, but don't talk about this case with anyone. Not your friends or your family. Or with Angela. Is that clear?" Anthony turned his head to look at him.

Bobby stared back. "Are you telling me not to talk to her?"

A couple of seconds went by. "I said don't talk to her about the case."

"All right." Bobby glanced at Gail, and she gave him a subtle smile.

Anthony continued, "We're looking for a better suspect than you to throw to the police. We might have one—Sean Cresswell. He gave you money that could have been taken from Roger's wallet. This doesn't prove Sean killed him. Maybe Roger gave it to him earlier that day. There are many possibilities. When we get back to Ms. Connor's office, you can help us sort through them."

"I could ask him," Bobby said. "I won't mention your name."

Anthony's eyes went to the mirror again. "Bobby. What did I just say? Don't talk about this case with anyone. That includes Sean Cresswell."

With a touch of defiance, Bobby asked, "Why?"

"Because, unless he is mentally ill, he would lie to you. Let us handle it. All right?"

"Fine." Bobby sighed and looked through the side window again.

The men took the client chairs, turned around to face the sofa under the window, where Gail sat with a legal pad on her lap. Bobby said, "Sean got the cash from his dad. That's what he told me. He said he had some mutual funds he couldn't get till he was twenty-one, but his father sold some shares for him and gave him the money."

"Do you believe that?" Anthony asked.

Bobby shook his head as if this were a particularly painful revelation. "No. Sean didn't used to lie, not to me. I mean . . . we were friends, you know, when we were kids. Like family. I thought so."

"Yes. But you didn't give the police his name. Why not?"

"I don't know. It didn't feel right."

A slight smile appeared on Anthony's lips. "I think it's called loyalty. But you can't keep any information from your lawyers. You know this, don't you?"

"I know."

Anthony asked if Sean had a .22 pistol.

"His father does. Sean took it one time, and we went target shooting. Dub has a gun closet. Handguns, rifles . . ."

For the most part, Gail let Anthony ask the questions. This was his meeting, arranged so that he could interview Bobby Gonzalez. Gail had said she would take notes.

Anthony wanted to know Sean Cresswell's whereabouts the night of the murder, starting from about ten o'clock.

"He was over at the Black Point Marina with his dad and his uncle, then later on, about midnight, he went over to South Beach. He said he was home in between."

"What was going on at the Black Point Marina?"

"They take buyers out to show them the boats, then they have dinner and get drunk. I went on a boat trip one time with Sean, and that's what they do. Dub makes Sean go along because he wants him to get a job in the company someday. Maybe that's why Sean never worries about school. His dad owns Cresswell Yachts. Half of it."

"What about the relationship between Roger and Dub?"

"It wasn't great. Roger was trying to take over, and Dub was ticked off. So was Liz, Sean's mother. They hated Roger. It's not like they said anything to his face, but I could tell. Not many people liked Roger at the company, unless they were brown-nosing."

"You didn't like him, did you?"

"No, I didn't. He fired me for stealing a disc sander. He set me up."

"Why?"

Bobby took a minute to answer. "To show he was the boss. Sean asked his dad to get me the job, and they hired me although Roger said they didn't need any more help. He put me to work laying down fiberglass in the molds. That's about the hardest job there. I was good at it, though, so he didn't have a reason to fire me. Yeah, I might have been rude, but Roger pushed people. He wanted you to bow down. Yes, sir. No, sir. Anything you want, Mr. Cresswell."

"Did you hear anyone make serious threats against Roger?"

"Like, 'I'm going to kill him'? No."

"Did he fire anyone else who might have carried a grudge?"

"Probably, but I couldn't name anyone. He wanted to fire the supervisor in the glass shop. That's Ted Stamos."

Anthony asked why.

"He wouldn't take his shit. Ted's been working there since he was in high school. His father worked there. Ted has this picture in his office of the first Cresswell boat. He said his father made it. He knows what he's doing, but Roger always wanted it done some other way. Ted had to come down and straighten out the mess a couple of times, and Roger didn't appreciate it, you know, everybody standing around watching Ted make him look like an idiot. Ted's a good guy. Roger told him to fire me, and he wouldn't do it. Then a few days later security found"—Bobby's fingers made quotation marks around the word—"They found the sander in my locker."

"At what point did you strike Roger?"

"The day he fired me, he took me up to Ted's office, but Ted wasn't there. Like he wanted to show him, you know? So I said I didn't take the sander, and he'd have to prove it. Then Roger called me a faggot, and I hit him. Ted heard the commotion and came in and pulled us apart." Bobby kept his eyes on Anthony. "I lost my temper, I guess."

Anthony lifted his hand from his thigh. The corners of his mouth turned down, the shoulders rose. No words, but the meaning was clear: Of course you hit him. He insulted your manhood. They went on to discuss Bobby's encounter with Roger at Jack's place. The shove in the shoulder, the heated words. Excluded from the club, Gail doodled boats and waves on her legal pad, thinking about what Bobby had said.

She wrote down STAMOS in block letters and underlined it twice. She had seen that name in Anthony's notes. He had met Ted Stamos on the dock behind the Cresswells' condo—a rough, uncommunicative type. Stamos had told the police that he'd seen Bobby attack Roger and threaten his life. This didn't match Bobby's version. Someone was lying. She put her money on Stamos. Gail penned the word WHY, then a question mark.

Anthony was asking if Bobby would recognize Nikki Cresswell if he saw her.

"Oh, yeah. Roger's wife. A red-haired chick. I met her a couple of times at family picnics and stuff Sean took me to."

"Did you see her at Jack's house the night of the party?"

"No. She called him, though. I forgot about it till now. It was about . . . ten-thirty? I recognized her voice. She asked to speak to Jack, and I couldn't find him, so I told her to call back later."

"Did she say anything else?"

"No, she just asked for Jack. She might've been in her car. I could hear road noises."

Anthony looked over at Gail, who had already begun to write it down.

Bobby explained why he had left the party early, even though Jack Pascoe had paid him to clean up. Angela had called him, so Bobby had told Jack to pay him only for the time he was there.

Anthony made no comments about Bobby's relationship with his daughter. They went off for some time, however, on a discussion of Bobby's family background, but by this time Bobby's confidence had been so restored that he spoke without hesitation. The poor Puerto Rican boy from East Harlem who had made a career in classical ballet.

Finally Anthony set both hands on the arms of his chair and announced that he was finished. Did Ms. Connor have any questions? Ms. Connor said she did not.

Gail looked at her watch and was astonished to find that nearly two hours had passed.

They walked Bobby to the door. Anthony said, "I'm helping you as a favor to Ms. Connor, but you should know that my first duty is to Nathan Harris. If there is any conflict between the two of you, you're on your own. It has to be that way. Do you understand?"

"Yes, sir, I do."

He wrote a number on the back of a business card. "Call me if you have any questions. In the unlikely event that you can't reach me through my service, try my pager. It's always on."

"Thanks. You too, Ms. Connor." Bobby shook their hands.

Anthony gave him two twenties and sent him in search of a taxi back to the beach.

Gail closed the front door. "Well. Who do we go after now? Jack Pascoe or Sean's father?"

"We can hand them both over. Not yet, but soon, I think. Yes. Did you hear what he said about Nikki?"

"You may be right after all," Gail admitted.

Anthony replied with a slight shrug.

"You were very good with Bobby. He likes you. He didn't want to, but he does, and he'll tell Angela how you saved him from the police interrogation squad, and how smart you are. '*Mamita,* I'm so surprised. He's not a monster. Why are you giving your *papi* such a hard time?' "

Allowing a smile, Anthony said, "Well, it's not so bad, then."

"And you didn't have that in the back of your mind, when you burned rubber all the way to the station?"

"I am doing this against my will. I should make him pay for it."

"Good luck." Gail laughed over her shoulder as she went back into her office. "Bobby gave me a hundred dollars. I'll split it with you. Oh, I plan to cash in when all the donors at the ballet find out what a great lawyer I am. I just hope nobody expects me to handle a criminal case. My God, if you hadn't been here."

"You would have managed."

"Oh, sure. After this, I'm sticking with civil practice."

They both stood at the edge of her desk. The moment went on, neither of them speaking. His eyes were still warm from his smile. Gail turned to flip a page in her desk diary.

"What about Judge Harris? When can I talk to him? My schedule is fairly open this week."

"I already asked him," Anthony said. "Tomorrow afternoon around five o'clock at my office. Is that good?"

"Yes, fine." She wrote it in the book, wondering what kind of gossip would start flying in the halls of Ferrer & Quintana when she walked through the door. She jammed her pen toward a can that Karen had decorated and got it in on the second try. He was standing a little too close, and the scent of his cologne entered her head. His hand rested on the desk, and he was drumming his fingers on its surface. Cheerily she said, "I'll write up my notes in the morning and bring them over. Remember what he said about Ted Stamos? It didn't match what Stamos said to you, did it?"

"Let me take you to lunch. Bring your notes. You know, we have a lot to decide with this case. Who talks to whom, what to do first—"

"I promised Karen I'd be home."

"An hour. You have to eat somewhere, no?"

"Oh, I can't. She's packing a picnic basket for the beach. If I'm late, she'll have a fit. It's our last day before she starts school tomorrow."

Acknowledging this with a nod, he said, "Of course, you should be with your daughter." When she reached for her purse, he put a hand lightly on her arm. "Gail, wait. There is something I need to ask you."

"I really have to get home," she said.

"This won't take long." He was looking at her in that same strangely intense way that had set her nerves jittering before. "Are you pregnant?"

Her mouth opened, but her brain refused to accept that he had asked this.

"I said, are you pregnant?" Same words, same soft intonation.

Impossibilities flashed in her mind. Her mother had called him. A friend had betrayed her. A soundless laugh finally came out. "That is ridiculous."

"Are you?"

"No. My God. Of course I'm not." She could feel the blood coursing into her face. "Anthony, that's . . . impossible. Birth control? Remember?"

"Sometimes it fails. So I've heard." His eyes shifted back and forth on hers, then narrowed slightly. "Look at me and tell me again. No, right here." He bent slightly to see directly into her face. "Gail? Are you going to have a child?"

"No! Anthony, stop it." She turned her head.

His fingers tightened on her upper arms. *"Jesucristo, es verdad."* She felt the words as a breath on her cheek. "You didn't tell me. Why?" He held her more tightly when she tried to twist away. "My child, and you didn't tell me? Why not?"

She closed her eyes, unable to speak.

"Last night I said to myself, no, that's crazy, she can't be pregnant. But what if she is? Why didn't she tell me? I didn't believe you, when you said you were going to live with your ex-husband. Maybe it's true. And maybe you didn't tell me because this isn't my child. Is it?" He grasped her face and turned it so he could see her. Color burned along his cheekbones, and his lips were tight against his teeth. "I asked you a question. Is it mine?"

How quickly rage ignited, incendiary and explosive. Her right palm connected before any conscious thought.

"Cara'o." He touched his fingers to his upper lip.

Trembling, Gail shook her hair out her eyes. "Go ahead. Call me a whore like you did last time."

"I never called you a whore."

"You did. A lying whore. 'Get out of my life, you lying whore.' " Her voice broke. "*Puta mentirosa*. What is that?"

He stared at her. "Gail—I don't remember, I swear to you—"

"You thought I'd been sleeping with my ex-husband. Engaged to *you*. In love with *you*—fool that I was—and sleeping with *Dave*? How *dare* you?"

"I was wrong." He reached for her, and she pushed him away.

"You ruined a man whose only crime was trying to be a good father. Destroyed his business, and sent him to work in a second-rate resort at the other end of the Caribbean!"

"Gail, I offered to give him whatever he wanted, and you refused. I offered to bring him back. I'll still do it. Is that what you want?"

"Never a thought what it would do to Karen."

"I'm willing to start over, to do anything. Gail, a child! How can you turn your back? This changes everything—"

"You had to control me, to lock me into your little kingdom, a petty tyrant like your grandfather, never mind who it hurt—"

"Did you tell me what you felt? Never. You drove me crazy with your lies and half-truths. What did you expect me to think?"

"You wanted me out of your life. Fine. I'm *gone*."

"Stop! Enough. Go ahead. Hit me again. Get it out of your system—"

She hit him again, more fist than palm.

"*Coño. ¿Qué me haces?*" He put a hand to his eye. "Do you hate me that much? I have a forty-five pistol in my car. You want to shoot me? No, this is better." He grabbed a letter opener out of the can on her desk, sending pens clattering and rolling across the surface. "Do it with this, why don't you? Stab me in the heart. I've been accused and found guilty. Now the execution." He held the point at his chest, handle toward her. "Take it. Go ahead. *Mátame*. Cut my heart out. Would that make you happy?"

She fell onto the sofa weeping.

"What do you want from me? What? *¿Me quieres mandar pa'l carajo? Ya estoy ahí.*" The letter opener clanged against the wall. "*No tienes corazón.* You are heartless. A cold and unforgiving woman. I pray to God you don't turn the child—*my* child—into the same piece of stone."

She heard his footsteps moving away. A few seconds later the outer door slammed.

Bobby called Sean's cell phone and found out he was over on the beach. Mustang just out of the shop, had a friend from school and a couple of girls with him. Bobby told him he had some coke and a few Roofies he could let go cheap because he needed to raise some cash. He told Sean to get rid of his friends and meet him back of the tire store on Miami Ave. Five minutes, straight over the causeway.

Bobby parked his car and sat on the front fender. Brothers from his street watching his back. Trees blocking the houses. Enough light to see the chain-link fence. Glass sparkling on the ground like stars. Bobby hadn't felt like this in a long time. No fear. His body running on some force outside itself.

He heard the Mustang before he saw it. A rumble, a throb in the air. Then it went off, and the car came around the corner, glinting under the streetlight before coming into the shadows.

Driver's door opened, shut. Sean doing the homeboy strut. Big shirt with horizontal stripes, baggy shorts to his knees. Silver ring shining on his eyebrow.

Bobby slid off the fender. The knife was behind his back, stuck in his belt.

"Yo, dog." Bobby held his hand up, and Sean slapped it.

"Whassup?" Sean said, "Sorry about the alibi, bro. Cops were leaning on me bad. Your woman can back you up, yo?"

"No doubt." Two silhouettes moving in behind Sean.

Sean said, "You want to go out?"

"No, I gotta hang here."

"Where's the stuff?"

"In the trunk." Sean came with him, running his mouth, already high on something. Bobby could see how it would go before he made the first move. Sean outweighed him fifty pounds, and he came crashing down in slo-mo. Hair bouncing on his forehead, and the leaves coming up, then falling back, and the elongated grunt. Then Bobby had him on his stomach, a knee in his back, arm pulled up tight.

He let Sean see the knife snap open. There was enough light for that.

"Oh, Jesus. Oh, shit, man, what are you—" Pressure on the arm made him whimper.

"I could cut you and leave you here. Rich white boy doing a deal, should've known better."

"Get the fuck off." Sean jerked. Bobby leaned his knee into Sean's back and stuck the point of the blade through the little ring in his eyebrow. He started crying. "Okay. Okay. I'm sorry. Bobby, I'm sorry, man. Don't. Please. Please don't kill me. Please. Take the money. Take it all. There's more in the car."

"That's not what I want." He leaned close to Sean's face. Sean was sweating, and leaves and sand were stuck to his cheek. His eye rolled. The stink of shit came from Sean's pants.

"You know that three hundred dollars you loaned me, bro? Where'd you get it?"

CHAPTER
19

The school bus from Biscayne Academy made stops in Irene's neighborhood, and Gail could have put Karen on it, but they had a ritual at the start of every new year: Mom and Dad would drive her there and stand outside watching while Karen ran into the building with her friends. Last year, Gail and Dave had gone through the divorce, and he'd been sailing near Puerto Rico, but he'd sent a postcard. Gail had told him he'd better show up this time, or Karen would be horribly disappointed. He wouldn't be flying back to St. John till next week, so there was no excuse. He promised to be at Irene's house by 7:30.

Gail looked at her watch, then shouted into the hall, "Karen! We're leaving in *ten minutes*!" With a guilty smile at Irene, she said, "It used to be so peaceful here, didn't it? Just you and the cats."

"I love having you girls around. Did you eat? Gail, you can't have just coffee." She opened the refrigerator. "What about some fruit yogurt? Eat something or I'll worry." Irene shoved a carton of peach and a spoon into Gail's hands.

Grasping the spoon to keep from dropping it, Gail winced. She had not known that hitting someone in the face could be so painful. She sat down at the table and scooted the gray cat away from her ankles. It was a struggle not to slump in the chair. She had hardly slept last night. The sound of a slamming door had replayed over and over in her mind. Anthony walking out. Telling her she was a piece of stone and *then* walking out. Several times over the past few weeks Gail had played with thoughts of what he might do if he found out she was pregnant. In her imagination he had usually done the same thing he had done yesterday—walk out—but always, before the door slammed, there had been that one glimmer of hope that he might turn around and rush back to her, saying he was sorry, that he loved her, that he could never leave her, or some other equally improbable shit. All Gail wanted now was to be rid of this damned case so they could deal with each other at a distance again.

"Mother? I need a favor. I'd like to meet Claire Cresswell. Could you introduce me? Is there a board meeting at the ballet you plan to go to?"

Irene dropped the last of Karen's breakfast dishes into the dishwasher. "Wednesday. I'm not on the board, but we could find some excuse. Do you think I should hang out a sign? Irene Connor, Private Investigations. I'll buy a trench coat."

Gail smiled at her mother's pink slacks and flower-printed top. "Here's another mission. I found out that Claire's daughter, Maggie, attempted suicide at age fifteen. It's been over twenty years, but I'd like to know what happened."

Irene turned around. "Oh, my. I heard she was a problem as a child, but not *this*. What did she do?"

"Tried to hang herself from the rod in her bedroom closet. They sent her to a mental hospital somewhere in Central Florida, then in Vermont, and she didn't come home for years. There was a gallery exhibition of her works here in Miami, and she met Judge Harris. Everyone says they were happily married. But she overdosed on pills in a cottage not fifty yards from where her brother was shot to death last month."

The telephone on the wall rang as Irene was saying, "Yes, of course, I'll find out what I can, but it won't be easy. Twenty years—" She picked up the phone. "Hello . . . Oh, hi, Dave, how are you? . . . Sure, just a second." She held it out to Gail. A look between the two of them asked the same question: Was he coming?

He wasn't. He and his friends had come back late from their fishing trip. A broken motor. He had forgotten to set the alarm. It would take him half an hour to get there.

"Dave, how could you? Karen was counting on this, especially since you missed last year. You promised . . . Being sorry doesn't help. . . . Okay, fine, never mind. Go back to sleep. . . . No, you explain it to her." Gail hung up and stared at the phone until her temper cooled. Such a stone-hearted bitch.

She found Karen sitting on the edge of the single bed in her room, buckling her shoes. This year Biscayne Academy had gone to uniforms—plaid skirts and white tops. Gail stared down at a pair of screaming green socks.

"Your dad called."

"I heard."

"Did you? Sorry. He said he'd call you tonight. Their motor broke, and he got in late." Gail sat on the edge of the bed. "You want to ask Gramma to come along?"

"Sure, she can come." Karen leaned down to do the other buckle, and her honey-brown hair fell over her shoulders. "Dad is like that, you know. I mean, I love him a lot, but you can't count on him. You sort of have to make plans for yourself."

"Oh, sweetie. I don't want you to grow up cynical and disappointed."

"I'm not." Flipping her hair back, Karen sat up. Her brows were sun-blond over bright blue eyes. "Who was that girl who tried to kill herself?"

"Do you eavesdrop on everything? That was a long time ago. The daughter of a friend of your gramma's." Gail put an arm around Karen and pulled her close. "She was unhappy and thought life had no meaning. But it does." Gail kissed the top of Karen's head. "Don't ever forget how sweet and precious it is, and how much I love you."

"Mom? Could we discuss this in the car? Please? I don't want to be late my first day." Karen got up and slung her book bag over her shoulder. She kissed Gail lightly on the cheek. "Really, Mom, you shouldn't worry so much."

*   *   *

Charlene Marks said, "You know what would show some real growth in this man? If he actually believed it was Dave's baby, and he could say, and mean it, 'Gail, I understand why you turned to Dave. I was such a jerk. This isn't my child, but I still love you, and I will pay loads of money to help you raise it. And I'll stay out your life until you call me.' "

"Not under threat of death would Anthony say such a thing."

"Then you should look for someone more civilized and forward thinking. You're not going to marry him, are you?"

"Oh, please."

"Here's a happy marriage. You're in bed on your honeymoon, and a 747 crashes through the roof and kills both of you. But my profession as a divorce lawyer has jaded me to some extent. Okay, what can I do for you?"

"I need to find Nikki Cresswell. I assume Anthony's investigator has a work address, but I don't want to call his office and ask. Did you write anything in the file besides 'ad agency'?"

Charlene led her into a storage room on the other side of the suite. She found the right file cabinet and pulled open a drawer, walking her fingers through the folders. "Cresswell, Cresswell . . . What are you going to do, ask her if she shot her husband?"

"A little more subtlety, I think."

"But why? According to Roger, she has the brain of a Barbie doll." Charlene opened a file. "Oh. Too bad. All I wrote was 'ad agency, Coconut Grove.' Well, how many can there be?"

There were six in the Yellow Pages. Gail got a hit on the second one, Bader-Miranda Advertising on Tigertail Avenue. Nikki wasn't in yet, but they expected her any minute. Leaving Miriam to reschedule the ten o'clock client for after lunch, Gail drove the six miles to the agency and found out that Nikki wouldn't be in till after eleven. She was having a pedicure at Biaggi.

The salon was a block away at the Mayfair Shops. Gail opened the door. The place had shiny wood floors, suspended halogen lights, silver walls, hairdressers in black, and a waiting area with red leather chairs, all occupied by women flipping through fashion magazines or chatting on cell phones.

Latin jazz played on hidden speakers. At the front desk a woman in leopard print tights was passing out espresso, blocking the receptionist's view. Gail slipped past the desk and around a frosted glass divider. Her nose was filled with the smells of coconuts and almond, hair conditioner and coloring, and the medicinal ping of nail polish remover. In the back a red-haired woman was reading a copy of *People* magazine. She was wrapped in a black salon robe, and her feet were in a vibrating foot bath scented with eucalyptus.

"Excuse me. Ms. Cresswell?"

The eyes, a green that existed only in contact lenses, made a quick, dismissive inventory: thin blond woman pushing thirty-five, tailored gray dress above her knees, shoulder bag, plain gold earrings, knock-off watch. She took the business card that Gail extended.

"My name is Gail Connor. Your office said you'd be here. Could I talk to you for a minute?"

A small exhalation of air—such an inconvenience. "What is this in reference to?" The voice was breathy and childlike. Her glossy pink mouth seemed designed to stay open, and the gaping vee of the salon robe revealed the curves of breasts as round and firm as grapefruit.

Gail didn't want to lie too blatantly. She would be seeing this woman again on the family yacht next weekend, the bereaved widow sprinkling her husband's earthly remains into the Atlantic. Whatever Gail said had to tie in with Anthony's cover story: He'd been hired by Claire Cresswell to look into Roger's financial dealings at the company.

She smiled down into the big green eyes. "My law firm is looking into the pension and profit sharing plans at Cresswell Yachts. We think you may be entitled to receive your late husband's account, but many of the records are missing. I shouldn't be talking to you, but . . . well, I'm not getting a lot of cooperation from management. I was hoping to talk to you in confidence. Could I sit down?"

"Sure."

Gail cleared some fashion magazines off a chair and pulled it over. "Love the nails. Are they acrylic?"

Nikki held up a hand and twiddled her fingers. A diamond ring sparkled. "Gel coats. They work really well with French manicures. How much money was Roger supposed to get?"

"We're not sure yet. The records are a mess. I was hoping that Roger kept duplicates at home?" Gail didn't think so. Charlene's notes said that Roger had taken some pride in the fact that he'd left his wife in the dark.

"The estate lawyer has everything," Nikki said, "but I could ask him to look."

Gail scooted the chair closer. She knew that Nikki Cresswell disliked her in-laws, and hoped to use that fact. "There's one little problem. Roger's father says that your husband was taking kickbacks from suppliers. That would mean the company wouldn't owe you anything—"

"What a liar. You want to know who was stealing? Porter's brother."

"Duncan."

"Right. Roger suspected, but he couldn't prove it. Dub is in charge of sales, and if anybody is getting kickbacks, it's him. Look at Dub's records, that's what you should do. Those people are all liars and cheats."

Gail put her elbows on her knees. "You don't mean Elizabeth as well."

"That bitch. I could tell you some things." Nikki pressed her lips together and her nostrils flared. "She's doing it with one of the men in the shop. Roger knew about it, that's why she stayed out of his way. And she called *me* a cheap little slut. To my *face!*"

Gail kicked herself for not bringing her tape recorder to sit slowly spinning in her pocket. "Who's the guy?"

"His name is Ted Stamos. Maybe you've met him, if you've been to the office, but he usually hangs out on the production floor. He's younger than her, and he's got a great body. I bet she pays him."

"No, I haven't met him yet." Gail remembered what Bobby

Gonzalez had said. "Didn't Ted Stamos and Roger have some trouble?"

"Ted thinks he runs the company, just because he's worked there all his life. So did his father. You want to hear something weird? Roger told me that Ted has all his dead father's tools in this little workshop, and he goes in there at night and polishes them. He won't let anybody else in. Roger needed the room for something else, and Ted pushed him against a wall and said if he touched the tools, he'd smash his face. Roger wanted to fire him, but Porter said no. It's like, no, Roger, you can't tell *me* what to do." Nikki nodded slowly. "With men, it all comes down to control. Power and control, Gail. That's why Porter is cheating me out of Roger's shares. He will grab and grab till they shovel the dirt on his grave. I mean, why would he *bother*? He's about there already. Roger and I went to see Porter in the hospital, and he was all yellow, even his eyes. It was awful. I'm sorry, but he's such a bastard."

"Wait," Gail said. "Porter is cheating you out of Roger's shares?"

"Yes! He says they have some kind of company plan where wives don't get shares. I mean, isn't that illegal discrimination or something? Porter wants my shares so he can have fifty-one percent again. After he gave Roger ten percent, he only had forty-one, right? He wanted the shares back so he'd have more than Dub again, who's got forty-nine. See, Roger and Dub were going to vote Porter out of office."

"And Porter didn't like that."

"He went crazy, are you kidding?" Nikki gripped the arm of the chair and came in close, whispering. "There was this family dinner at his and Claire's house, and Roger told him, and he turned purple! He's screaming, 'You little fuck, you can't take my company, I'm gonna kill you.' I thought he was going to have a heart attack right there. I wish he had."

"When? When was the dinner?"

"The day before Roger died. A Friday. That's the last thing Roger heard from his own father, that he wished him dead. So hateful."

A tiny, dark woman in a white smock came in and turned off the foot bath. The low-pitched humming stopped. The woman, who appeared to be of Central American Indian blood, settled herself on a stool and put a towel on her lap. "Foot, please." Nikki lifted one, dripping, and the woman patted it dry, then began working away with a pumice stone.

"Don't worry. She doesn't speak English. You know why I'm mad? It's not the money. It's how they acted, all of them. Liz and Dub laughing behind my back—I heard them! And Claire—Lady Perfect. I was never good enough for her. Porter called me a tramp. He threw me out of his office. He says I married Roger for his money. I did not. Roger was fun and we had a good time together. We were married four *years*! We had a good relationship. Roger loved me, and I loved him!"

The pedicurist finished with one foot, wrapped cotton in and out the toes, then fastened on a paper slipper. "Other foot, please." Nikki pulled the other one out of the water and put it on the towel on the woman's lap.

Gail hesitated, then threw away caution. "Nikki, are you involved with Jack Pascoe?"

Nikki stared at her foot, which the woman was rubbing briskly with cream. "No."

"But you used to be. Didn't you?" Gail said quietly, "Okay, look. I won't lie to you. I'm trying to find out who killed your husband."

"Are you a cop?"

"No. I'm trying to help someone. The police think he did it. He's innocent, but I'm afraid he might wind up in jail."

The green eyes turned. "Who?"

"His name's Bobby Gonzalez. He's a friend of Sean Cresswell. You've probably met him."

"Oh, sure. And I heard that, about him being a suspect, but I never believed it. He's a sweet guy."

Gail said, "I need to find out who killed Roger. Was it Jack?"

Nikki shook her head. "Jack was with me."

"You *were* at the party. What time did you get there?"

"A little bit before eleven. I had to drive from West Palm

Beach. Jack sent me upstairs, and he stayed down there with his friends till three o'clock in the morning, and I was waiting all that time . . . waiting and waiting. Jack never cared about *me*. He wanted to get back at Roger. He thought Roger was the one who ruined his reputation, but Jack is a liar and a thief. He tricked Roger out of a painting that his sister did. It was worth a lot of money, and he stole it for ten thousand dollars. Go ask him. He's down the street at the Pascoe Gallery. And while you're at it, throw a brick through the window."

The pedicurist leaned over to take some polish out of a rolling cart. She uncapped the bottle, keeping her eyes resolutely on her work.

Gail was afraid that if she asked Nikki to meet her later, the connection would be lost. She said, "Do you think Roger came that night looking for you? Did he suspect you and Jack?"

Nikki stared down at her hands, examining one of her glossy, white-tipped fingernails. "He knew. I didn't tell Jack, but . . . Roger guessed. I called Roger that night from my friend's house in West Palm and we fought on the phone, and I said, Wow, Roger, if you don't give a damn, then maybe I'll just go have some fun at Jack's party. He called me some names. He said he would kick Jack's butt. I guess . . . I wanted Roger to come get me. He came, but I wasn't there yet. He left a message on my cell phone and I didn't answer." Tears slid down Nikki's cheeks, and her mouth trembled. "I should have called back. I should have. I mean . . . he probably wanted to say he loved me. You know? Maybe."

The pedicurist nodded toward the box of tissues on the ledge behind the chair, and Gail stood up and pulled several out. "Here. I'm so sorry, Nikki."

"Is my mascara all over?"

"Not bad. Just a little. Look up." Gail dabbed at a spot while Nikki focused on the ceiling.

Nikki said, "Find out who killed Roger. You find out and let me know. They're such sorry bastards. Every one of them."

A minute later, Gail was sprinting for the legal pad in her car, trying to carry the words without spilling them out of her memory.

* * *

After Karen was in bed, Gail read her a story. Karen's eyes closed as the last page was turned, but Gail continued to hold her for a while. She lifted Karen's hand and spread out their fingers together, right hand to left. Karen had been premature, and her hands had been tiny, like doll hands, but so soft and sweet Gail had wanted to eat them. *Am I a stone? How can I love anyone this much and be a stone?*

She tucked the comforter around her daughter, turned off the light, and went to see where Irene had gone to. The kitchen was dark except for a glow over the stove. She saw a small orange dot moving on the back porch. A cigarette. Gail slid open the glass door. The tile was cool on her bare feet. Ceiling fans stirred the warm air, and insects tapped on the screen.

"Well, hello, you." Irene exhaled smoke to the side, then ground out her cigarette in the ashtray. "Don't lecture me. I'm down to three a day." She pulled her knees up, making room on the end of the chaise. "Sit down, talk to me. How's my girl?"

Gail lowered her cheek onto Irene's knees. After a while, her mother said, "What would you wish for, my pet, if you could have anything?"

"To know what to do."

"About what? Anthony?"

"He'll ask me to marry him. As soon as he calms down, he will. Except he won't *ask*. He'll have everything all worked out in advance. We'll have a small, private ceremony and move into an apartment till we found a house. Maybe something near the Pedrosas so we can go over there for dinner every other night. There will be a live-in maid and someone to watch the baby while I work, but of course my career is optional."

"Gail." Her mother's low laugh mixed with the night sounds coming through the screen.

"What if he only wants me because of the baby?"

"Do you really think that's the reason?"

"I don't know. He said the child changes everything. He said that, but there was nothing about *us*. Nothing about what we went through. Oh, forget that, it's in the past. He can compart-mentalize anything. There was nothing about . . . love. Excuse me for being so sentimental." Gail tried to laugh, but her throat was too tight.

"You still love him."

"I don't want to. Oh, God, I swear I don't." Gail closed her eyes. "I've never been so afraid in my life."

Irene stroked her hair. "Can I make a confession? Your father and I weren't as happy as I let on. How we fought. I nagged Ed for not being more successful. He drank way too much, and I thought of leaving him, but my parents swore they'd cut me off if I did. We made each other miserable, and after he died, the funny thing is, no one else ever measured up. I see now I shouldn't have spared you. Marriage isn't painless. No, it's agony, but you grow, and you learn, and eventually, if you're lucky and you stick with it, you have something very special. We were getting to that place, Ed and I. And then . . . well. People give up too soon these days. You go on to the next person, and it's no better, because your old self comes right along with you."

Gail felt a tap on her shoulder. Her mother said, "I found out what happened to Margaret Cresswell. You want to listen, or are you going to soak my knees all night?"

She sat up and blew her nose on Irene's cocktail napkin. "Tell me."

"This is capital-R rumor, you understand. Talk about favors. You owe me. I had to promise four seats to *The Nutcracker.*"

Irene resettled herself on the chaise and took a long sip of her drink. "I thought that if Claire had gone to Cushman, so had Maggie, and I was right. I know the secretary, Enid Lance, from the Garden Club. She's been at Cushman forever. She says that a week or so after Maggie dropped out of school, Claire came into the office and told the headmistress that the rumors weren't true. Maggie had *not* tried to kill herself, she'd had a nervous break-down. And no, she was *not* expecting. Enid says Claire wanted to squash the gossip. What gossip? Maggie wasn't one of the popu-lar girls, and when she left, they hardly noticed."

"She was pregnant at fifteen?"

"Who knows? Her mother went to great lengths to deny it."

"Protesting too much," murmured Gail. "I wonder what happened to the baby."

Irene could only shake her head.

"Anthony will tell me not to bring it up with Claire. He'll say it's completely irrelevant."

A little while later, Irene went inside to get ready for bed. Gail lay back on the chaise and watched the lights of boats moving across the dark water.

She could find no rational connection between an event that may not even have happened, and Roger Cresswell's murder. Even so, the facts of Margaret Cresswell's life and death continued to weigh on Gail's mind. Maggie had been only thirty-three when she'd shut herself in the cottage and opened a bottle of pills. *Forgive me. I am at peace.* Even the love of a devoted husband hadn't been enough to save her. What despair had made it impossible to go on? Gail wanted to know, as if by finding out, she could save her this time.

CHAPTER

20

Anthony had been almost certain that Gail Connor would leave a message to cancel the meeting, but she arrived ten minutes early. He could see her through the glass wall of the conference room. She sat calmly, as if waiting for a trial to begin. A glance at her watch. Aligning her pen on her notebook. She wore a pearl-gray suit, and her hair was brushed back from her face. Her reflection shone in the polished rosewood surface of the table.

Standing just outside, Anthony's own reflection came back to him, a somber, hollow-eyed ghost. He felt older, tired, and the dark suit matched his mood. She'd left her mark on his cheek, but the bruise was not visible, except to him—a tenderness at the bone.

He had decided to have the meeting here, not in his private office. He couldn't look at his sofa without remembering her pale body stretched out on black leather. Lights off, the sliding door to the atrium open, water laughing softly on the rocks. He had stood at a distance memorizing every curve and shadow before she'd reached out a hand. *Anthony. Come over here.* Had her body changed? Would her breasts feel heavier, fuller? He couldn't remember how these things progressed. That he would not know how *this* child progressed left him close to grief.

He shifted his folders to the other hand and opened the door. She looked around, acknowledging his presence. Walking around the table, he said that Nate Harris would arrive at six o'clock, not five, to allow time for discussion of other issues. Had she been offered something to drink? She said she didn't care for anything, thank you.

Anthony sat down across from her and placed two folders and a leather-bound notebook on the table. "I have good news. We have a buyer for the house, and the price is more than we had expected. It cancels the debt that you say you owe me, leaving an additional profit of around fourteen thousand dollars, which we'll divide between us."

He gave her a copy of a contract that showed the buyers as Jose R. and Beatriz S. Gomez of Miami. Totally fictitious. He didn't know where Raul had found the names. His old neighbors in Cuba, perhaps. "They want to close within two weeks."

At some point Anthony would tell her the truth: He was buying the house for himself. It would be gutted, repaired, made new. A pool, maid's quarters, a play room. A good place for his children to visit—all three of them. He would not be moving to New York.

She scanned the contract. Turned a page. "This is excellent. I didn't expect it to work out so well."

"Nor did I." He opened the other folder, hesitated only a moment, then said, "This is a draft of an agreement for paternity and support." He slid a copy across the table. "I agree to pay your medical expenses and all costs you may incur as custodial parent. In exchange, you allow me to participate fully in the child's life. You also agree not to take the child out of this area without my permission. There are other provisions. Life insurance on myself, medical expenses and education for the child, and so on. He—or she—will speak Spanish fluently. He will know his heritage. His last name will be Quintana."

"Not Pedrosa?" she retorted with a lift of her brows.

Anthony stared back at her for several seconds, matching her chilly disdain. "No. I have not seen my grandfather in two months. Ah. You seem surprised. The truth is, Gail, you were right. I was becoming too much like him. The power, the money— I told him I didn't want it. We argued. I told him to go to hell. He said the same to me. I swore on my life that I would never set foot again in that house, and I haven't." Anthony shrugged. "So. Don't worry about your child turning into a clone or a puppet of Ernesto Pedrosa or whatever the hell it was that you called me."

She released a held breath. "I shouldn't have said that."

"But you were right. You were also right that he contracted murder for me, but wrong to think I condone what he did. However, I cannot, as you suggested, turn him over to the police—"

"I know you can't," she said. "He's too old. I wonder if he was even rational, when it happened. He was afraid for you, I believe that. I hope you see him again. And I don't mind if . . . if you take the baby to see him. His great-grandfather."

Anthony felt that his head might explode. He lifted his hand from the table. Let it fall. "Perhaps. In the meantime, why don't you review the agreement? Take it to a lawyer if you wish. I think even Charlene Marks would find it generous."

She lifted the end of it and ruffled through the pages. He knew there were seventeen of them, plus a signature page. She turned the draft facedown and pushed it to one side. "I'm sorry you think this is necessary."

Anthony's cheeks burned. He had made a misstep. This was not the reaction he had anticipated. He had been prepared for war, a lawsuit, DNA tests—

He said, "You don't know which it is, do you? Boy, girl?"

"Not yet."

"When is it due?"

"The middle of February."

He had more questions, but swung his chair around and tossed his own copy of the agreement back into its folder. He was close to losing his temper, and could not isolate the source of his anger. His voice betrayed none of this. "We don't have much time before Nate gets here. I need to tell you about Bobby Gonzalez. He called me last night. I went to his apartment on South Beach to talk to him. He didn't call you today, did he? I told him not to."

Gail's eyes widened. "What happened to Bobby?"

"To Bobby, nothing. He held a knife at Sean Cresswell's throat and asked him where the three hundred dollars had come from.

Sean told him." Anthony leaned back in his chair. "Out of Roger Cresswell's wallet, which Sean took from Roger's dead body, which he stumbled over on his way into Jack Pascoe's yard from the side gate at approximately eleven-fifteen the night Roger was murdered. But not, I think, by Sean Cresswell."

Gail stared at him. "What?"

"Last night I said to Bobby, 'Have you lost your mind? You could go to prison for this.' 'No, don't worry, Mr. Quintana. Sean won't say anything. Besides, my friends will give me an alibi.' "

"Oh, my God. Do I want to hear this?" Elbows on the table, Gail dropped her head into her hands, fingers in her hair. "Go on, tell me."

Anthony could not decide whether Bobby Gonzalez was an idiot who'd been lucky or the most brazenly clever young tough he'd ever met. To have set up his ambush so neatly, every contingency anticipated. And to pull it off!

Where did you get the money? Simple question. And the answer had come quickly. Sean on the ground sweating, defecating in his pants. Bone-grinding fear. Expecting to die on the pitted asphalt behind a boarded-up tire store. One answer, then another.

"What Bobby told me ties in perfectly with the memo you faxed over about Nikki Cresswell. The times, the events. Bobby and I talked for three hours last night, but I think I can summarize it for you. The day Roger died, Duncan Cresswell took about a dozen potential buyers to Bimini and back. Roger went along, and so did Ted Stamos, who is in charge of boat construction. Sean always goes because his parents insist on it. They expect him to work for the company someday. He has to wear a Cresswell Yachts shirt and khaki shorts, and inevitably his cousin Roger made jokes about him. Roger treated Sean like one of the crew, making him bring drinks to the customers and cleaning up after them. You see the reason for this. Sean is the only other male heir, and Roger had to establish his dominance. Around seven-thirty the boat docked at the Black Point Marina, where a barbecue dinner was waiting.

"Shortly after nine o'clock, as everyone was preparing to leave, Roger got a call from his wife, Nikki, on his cell phone. Your memo mentioned the call. Roger became angry and said he was coming over there to, quote, 'kick Jack's fucking ass.' His uncle, Duncan, overheard this. He mentioned it to Sean. I imagine there were some winks and nudges. I imagine also that Duncan could have told Porter or Ted Stamos. None of them, obviously, mentioned it later to the police. This family protects its own.

"Claire arrived about nine-fifteen in the Bentley to take Porter home. She'd had dinner with friends. Sean didn't say where, and it doesn't matter. Sean's father and the rest of the men left in a caravan of cars. They were going to the Strip Mine, the very club, in fact, that Sean's father has promised to take him to on his twenty-first birthday. Roger was supposed to go with the others, but he drove out of the marina parking lot in a hurry, and there were a few more jokes about what he would do to Jack Pascoe. As we know, Roger got to Jack's about nine-thirty and left ten minutes later. He bought some liquor at a nearby store and came back. If he knew that Nikki had called from West Palm Beach, he also knew that she was unlikely to arrive before ten-thirty.

"Sean went home. He was still on curfew, part of his court-ordered probation for stealing Roger's car. Sean's mother and his older sister, Patty, were watching television. Sean sat in his bedroom drinking beer and playing video games until eleven o'clock. He heard his mother go into her room and close the door. She had his car keys, but he had a spare.

"It took him five minutes to drive to Jack Pascoe's house. He knew about the party from Bobby. Jack intercepted him at the front door and told him he couldn't come in. Bobby never saw Sean. Nor did he see Nikki, who had just arrived. Jack had sent her upstairs. We can probably assume that Roger saw her arrive and went around the side of the property to come in through the gate—you remember the one. Meanwhile, Sean got in his own car and started out for South Beach. A few miles up Old Cutler Road he realized he didn't have any money. He drove back to Jack's house and parked along the side street. He knew that Diane kept cash in the cottage. The music from the main house was loud, and he thought he could break a window without arousing attention.

"He came in through the gate, went around the fountain, and

tripped over Roger's legs. He didn't know who it was until he turned on his cigarette lighter. He saw the shirt from Cresswell Yachts. He saw the Rolex. He took that and the wallet, which contained a little over fifteen hundred dollars. He went to a club on South Beach—the Apocalypse, I believe. He remembers wearing the watch when he went inside, but he isn't sure what happened to it. He thinks he gave it to the girl who crawled under the table and unzipped his pants. He was very drunk at this point. Bobby didn't ask what Sean did with the wallet. Maybe he still has it, but if he isn't totally brainless, he got rid of it."

Anthony had sat listening to this until nearly three o'clock in the morning. The roommates gone. The place cleaner than he'd expected. He had accepted a *cafecito* to get him home. Leaving, he had asked, How do you know Sean was telling you the truth? Softly, and with certainty, Bobby had replied, I just know.

Bobby Gonzalez had laid the knowledge at Anthony's feet like a young wolf with a fresh kill. An offering.

"Sean thought Bobby had killed Roger. He says he never told the police or his parents because he was trying to protect him. I don't agree. A boy like Sean is motivated by fear, not loyalty."

When Anthony glanced at Gail, she was looking at him with both amusement and wonder. "You approve of what Bobby did," she said. "Go ahead, admit it."

He waved away the thought. "It was foolish. I told him that. He's lucky not to be in jail. Sean could still file a report. I don't think he will."

"What are you going to do now? Talk to Frank Britton?"

"Not yet. Sean would deny it. He'd say Bobby confessed, or that he saw Bobby run from the scene. No, we aren't in the clear."

Gail looked at her notes. "Well. Where was everyone else between eleven and eleven-thirty? Nikki was supposedly in bed waiting for Jack. Jack was with his guests. Porter was at home with Claire. Dub and Ted Stamos were at the strip club. Elizabeth was watching television with her older daughter. Everyone has an alibi."

Anthony smiled. "Everyone *claims* to have an alibi. Tomorrow morning I'll be at Cresswell Yachts. Claire arranged it. She says she was able to sell them on my cover story. Mr. Quintana has been retained to examine the books for evidence of Roger's financial crimes. Would you believe that?"

"It sounds plausible," Gail said. "We're lucky to have Claire's help. She agreed to meet me at the ballet on Thursday. I'd like to speak to Nikki again, but she probably won't let me come as close a second time."

The intercom buzzed. Anthony pushed his chair back to reach the telephone on the credenza. Extending an arm, he asked Gail, "How did you persuade her to tell you so much already?"

"She hates the Cresswells. Nikki may be as shallow as a saucer, but she doesn't like to have her feelings hurt."

He picked up the phone. "Yes?" Nate Harris had arrived.

Anthony went to get him, and when they came back into the conference room, Gail stood up and extended her hand. "Judge Harris, I am so sorry for everything you've had to go through. I had a client to protect, and I never intended—"

"No, no, don't apologize for doing your duty." He took her hand in both of his. "I understand completely." Looking around, Nate included Anthony in his next remark. "Are we ready for the latest, folks? Senator McCaffrey's office called. I have the nomination. They'll announce it tomorrow morning."

No one broke out in a cheer. This had come sooner than expected, putting more pressure on. Anthony gave Nate a one-armed hug and a slap on the back. "That's great." Gail smiled and shook his hand again.

Nate had left his jacket and tie in his car, and he wore a plain, long-sleeved white shirt and dark slacks. His gray hair looked windblown, and his eyes blinked behind his tortoiseshell glasses as if he were still trying to assimilate this news.

"It won't be easy. Jesus, the forms to submit—stacks of them. Every tax return since I was a paperboy. It will take them six months to a year to decide if I'm acceptable, and then the White House has to agree. Then the Senate. They'll want to know what brand of shorts I wear." He gripped the back of a chair. "This

Cresswell thing could blow up in my face. If you think there's going to be a problem, tell me. How are we coming?"

Anthony exchanged a look with Gail. "It's coming along faster than we'd thought."

"Good, good. Where do you want me to sit, Gail? Here?" He sat at the head of the table, Anthony and Gail across from each other. "Okay. You have some questions?"

Gail glanced at some notes she had brought with her. Anthony was prepared to break in if she steered the conversation onto forbidden ground—smoking dope with a young ballet dancer. Nate had told him there was no question off limits, but Gail didn't ask. There were a few general questions about the party, nothing awkward, no mention of a transvestite samba dancer, or the drunks, or the raucous music. She asked about times, places, who was there and who wasn't.

Her voice was soft and warm, and she had an easy rhythm to her speech. She was back from the table far enough for Anthony to see her stomach. It looked the same. Child due in mid-February. He counted backward. Conceived sometime in May? Perhaps in the house on Clematis Street. She and Karen had lived there, and he had planned to move in after the wedding. It was an old house with wood floors and a rarely used fireplace in the master bedroom upstairs. King-size bed. Ceiling fan over her head going around, around. Hands on his shoulders. The points of her breasts moving, hair bouncing on her forehead. Lower lip caught between her teeth. Eyes squeezed shut. Breathing in time with their rhythm. *Huhh. Huhh. Huhh.*

"How did you happen to choose this particular painting?"

"Jack suggested it."

Startled out of his reveries, Anthony said, "I must have missed something. What are we talking about?"

Gail lifted her brows. "The portrait of Diane. I asked Nate how he came to choose it for Porter and Claire, and he just said that it was Jack's suggestion."

Anthony spread his hands, assuring her: a slight lapse of attention.

She turned back to Nate. "A generous thank-you gift."

Nate said, "They deserve it. After my marriage to Maggie, they financed my reelection campaign. Porter used his political connections to make my name known, and it was he who suggested I apply for the federal bench."

"Really. May I ask how much you paid for the portrait?"

"Twenty thousand. Rather, I put down a deposit of five thousand when I picked it up at Jack's house. Jack tells me not to worry about the other fifteen, and that he hopes to get my five back to me when he sells the painting again."

Gail looked at him. With a touch of surprise in her voice, she asked, "Sells it to whom?"

"To whoever pays the price, I suppose. Jack's in the business of selling art. He said that title to the portrait is up in the air at the moment, but he hopes to get everything straightened out." A half smile creased Nate's cheek. "He tried to explain how he reacquired the thing, but it was too much for me to follow."

"Hmm." Gail tapped her pen on her notepad. Anthony could see the thoughts whirling around in her head like a cage full of birds. "Well, actually, Diane has it. Frankly, I hope she can keep it." She returned to her notes. "Tell me. Did you know that Porter and Claire had already owned the portrait once, and that they gave it to Roger, and that he sold it to Jack two months ago for ten thousand dollars?"

"Good God, no. Are you sure?" He looked around at Anthony, who nodded gravely. Nate sat back in his chair. "I knew none of this. I wish Jack had told me."

Gail said, "He was using you to cause trouble for Roger and double his money at the same time. Do you think so?"

The answer took a long while to arrive. "I don't want to think that of Jack." Nate's face bore an expression of chagrin. Disappointment. A friendship had just ended. Releasing a long breath, he adjusted his glasses on his beak of a nose.

"Did you ask Claire why they gave it away?"

"Yes, after Anthony told me about it. I was afraid I'd committed some faux pas, and she said no, Porter went into a senior moment and took it to the office to his brother and sister-in-law. She could only guess that he'd wanted Diane's parents to have it. I'm sorry for all this trouble Diane is going through with her mother."

Gail's pen was tapping on her notepad. "Roger originally got the portrait from his parents a year or so after his sister died. Do you know where Porter and Claire got it?"

He shook his head. "No. I'd never seen it at their house, neither where they live now nor their previous place in Miami Shores. I'm going to guess they bought it from a gallery or a collector. Perhaps . . . from Jack."

While Nate mulled this over, still stunned by his sudden glimpse into Jack Pascoe's nature, Gail glanced across the table at Anthony. He could see from her expression that she was moving in on something, and that he should stay out of it.

She cleared her throat and sat up in her chair. "Judge Harris, how much do you know about Maggie's childhood?"

"Her childhood?"

"Yes. Jack told me that at fifteen, Maggie tried to kill herself. Did you know?"

Anthony had to protest. "Gail, what is the relevance—"

"Did you know?" she asked again, ignoring him.

"Yes. Maggie mentioned it in an offhand way."

Gail smiled and tilted her head. "Offhand?"

"She didn't like to talk about it, and I didn't press her. But if you're curious?"

"Yes, I am, actually."

Giving up, Anthony leaned back in his chair and waited to see what Gail would do with this.

"Maggie said she'd had a crush on a boy, and it hadn't worked out. Porter and Claire hadn't approved, and Maggie had taken it badly."

"Apparently. Who was the boy?"

"Goodness, I don't know. A kid doing some fixup work at her parents' house. I think his father worked for the company. If she ever said his name, I've forgotten."

"Please forgive me if this seems like a strange line of inquiry," Gail said. "Did Maggie say she'd been pregnant? I think that might have been the case."

Another surprise. Anthony had to clamp his teeth together to keep from asking her where in hell she'd come up with that information. His eyes went to Nate.

"No, Maggie never mentioned a child. Are you certain? Well, you know, that makes sense now. She was only thirty years old when I met her, and she said she didn't want children. I thought it was funny, you know, a woman so young, but it was okay with me. I preferred it, in fact. We both had full careers. I sensed that something had happened in her past, and I asked her, but she didn't want to tell me. I said, whatever it was, I could overlook it. It wouldn't be an issue between us. But she never said, so I assumed it was of no importance. I don't think she actually gave birth. Knowing her parents, I'd say a termination would have been more likely. They're very practical people. So was Maggie."

"And your marriage was . . . happy?"

"I'd say so. We never had a serious argument. We were sexually compatible. Kind to each other. She respected my priorities, I respected hers. Her life was her art. Mine was the law. It worked out quite well."

"She traveled, didn't she?"

"Oh, yes, she spent most of her summers on the Cape, and she had a small place in Manhattan. I was often buried in trials for weeks on end, or I'd be off to this or that judge's conference. When we were home, she'd go out to the cottage to work, and I'd write my opinions. You know, being a judge is a sort of monastic existence, but she was great about it, and I understood her need to paint. Maggie was a genius. The last thing I ever wanted to do was hold her back from her calling."

"Do you have any idea why she ended her life?"

"Not to this day, I don't. Toward the end she became more depressed and remote. I'm sorry I couldn't save her. Nothing could have."

Gail laid her pen on her legal pad. Silence stretched out. Finally she said, "I have no more questions. Thank you."

Nate stood up, stretching a little. "Well, if there is anything else, just ask. Anything I can do. I'm grateful to both of you. Anthony, you're going to give me an update on everything so far?"

"Yes, I'll call you tonight."

Gail stood up, and she and Nate shook hands. "Good luck with the nomination, Judge Harris."

"Oh, well, we won't know for a long time. And call me Nate."

Anthony escorted him out. They talked for a few minutes in the empty lobby. Everyone had gone home. Nate said he hoped for the best with Gail. Maybe they could work it out. A terrific girl, wasn't she? Anthony nodded.

He went back to the conference room and found Gail standing by the window, looking out. "What a bloodless man. How did you ever become friends?"

Her words contained more than a hint of accusation. He searched for a reply. "We never talked about his life. Only about the law. He's a good judge. A brilliant legal scholar." Anthony shrugged. "I don't know."

"I would have killed myself, too." She pushed away from the window and went to the table to sort through her papers.

"Where did you learn about Margaret Cresswell becoming pregnant at fifteen?"

"It's a rumor my mother unearthed. We don't know whether she had the baby or not. I imagine it was taken care of—one way or the other—at the mental hospital. If it was a mental hospital. Wherever this alleged institution was."

"Why are you pursuing this?"

"I can't even say anymore. It seems to have less and less to do with her brother's death, and yet I can't leave it alone." She waved it all away. "I need to get home."

Anthony wanted to keep her there, to make some excuse. There was more to say, too much more. Maggie and Nate went through his mind. Bloodless. Dead.

"I talked to Angela again. We had breakfast together. I told her about the baby. She took it better than I had expected." Anthony remembered his daughter's sudden smile, the arms thrown around his waist. And the question he'd had no answer for: What next?

"What will you tell Karen?" he asked.

Gail laughed. "I have noooo idea."

The top edge of the paternity and support agreement protruded from her leather-bound folder, which she held loosely in one hand. Anthony slid it out. "You're right. This is too complicated. Why don't you tell me what you want? That would make it easier."

She picked up her bag. "I'll ask Charlene to handle it, if you don't mind. I don't want to think about it. But you should know that this may all be for nothing. I have a history of miscarriages."

"No." His breath stopped. "What does your doctor say?"

"I don't have one yet."

"Why?"

"I don't know. I—I've been . . . too busy."

Anthony put a hand on her arm. "Well, get one immediately. The best, I don't care what it costs. Will you do that?"

Eyes averted, she made a quick nod and went toward the door. "Let me know what you find out at the company tomorrow."

"Gail?"

She stopped and looked over her shoulder.

"Why were you afraid to tell me about the child?"

"Probably because . . . I needed to be free of you."

It was said with regret, not rancor, but no words could have injured him more, a final thrust into a heart already bleeding.

CHAPTER

21

Porter Cresswell growled, "Ask me what you need to, but make it quick. Claire's running me to the doctor's office for a little checkup. I had a close call a few months ago. I'm okay now, but she keeps me on the straight and narrow. Don't you, honey?"

Her eyes looked over the top of her magazine, then back to the page.

Anthony said, "I'm not an accountant, Porter. I'll have to send a team to go over the records. They'll need full access to anything Roger was working on. Will I get cooperation from your brother and his wife?"

"I told them to give you whatever you need. Open the books, show you around. I said, 'If Roger was screwing with the accounts, I want to know before the IRS does.' You shouldn't have any problems."

"Good. I understand that Roger's wife, Nikki, is unhappy about distribution of shares. She's accusing you of fraud. Is that anything we should worry about?"

"Jesus, no. I tried to tell her. The shares reverted to me when Roger passed. That was my dad's idea. He and his first wife went through a bad divorce, so when he set up the corporation, he made it so shares stay in the family. We can't sell them or give them away unless everybody consents to it, and spouses don't inherit, only kids. I told Nikki that. She's a nitwit."

"I'd like to review the original documents," Anthony said.

"What for? That was set up over fifty years ago."

A voice came from the corner. "Porter? If Anthony says he needs it, I'm sure he does. He's trying to help."

"Okay, okay." Porter was leaning sideways in his chair with his weight on an elbow. He waved a hand. "Tell my secretary I said to give you a copy. It's out there because I was about to write a letter to the lawyer handling Roger's estate, show him what I'm talking about."

"Why did you give Roger ten percent?"

"I was being a good father, bringing him into the company. Shit, it was going to be his anyway, wasn't it? Then he turned around and bit my hand. I think of that cretin out there running it someday, I get sick. Dub's boy. I'll sell the goddamn company before I see that happen. This is sad. Very sad. A fine company, falling apart. I told Roger to marry some nice girl and have a couple of kids, but they kept putting it off. Selfish, both of them. Having too much fun, to hell with the family. My son was the biggest disappointment of my life."

Anthony wondered what Claire had thought of her husband's outburst, but he didn't want to turn and look. He said, "Dub and Roger could have pooled their shares, correct? Did they?"

"They planned to. They were going to vote me out of office. I wasn't going to go gently into the night, as the old saying goes. I should've left it the way my dad set it up. Doesn't pay to be nice." One corner of his mouth rose. "My dad gave me seventy-five percent. You know why? Because he knew I had the brains to run this corporation, goddammit, not that lazy ass in the next office."

From the corner of the room came the rustle of a magazine page turning.

Anthony pulled some facts from his memory. "And now you have fifty-one percent. Dub has forty-nine."

"And that's as far as it goes. It stops right here. You put two heads on one body, you're asking for trouble." He pushed himself out of his chair. "You tell my secretary to give you whatever you need."

Anthony stood up. "Porter, one question. Why did you make Dub half owner? Rather, a forty-nine-percent owner?"

Porter straightened his lapels. "That's between my brother and me."

"The accountants will want to know."

"Fuck the accountants. Claire? Put that magazine away. Let's go."

The sign on the half-open door said DUNCAN CRESSWELL, EXECUTIVE VICE PRESIDENT, SALES.

The executive VP himself was on the telephone, leaning back in his chair and passing one hand slowly over his head, again and again. Discussing a boat show in Savannah. A steak house on the wharf. Best fuckin' ribs outside of Memphis.

Anthony knocked. The big executive chair swiveled around. Still talking, Dub Cresswell motioned for Anthony to come in. The walls were paneled in maple halfway up, then covered with vinyl printed with regatta flags. An immense swordfish took up the wall opposite the desk, the shelves were lined with fishing trophies, and under the windows were a series of glass cases containing scale models of Cresswell boats. Anthony spent some time reading the labels, certain that the conversation would have ended already if he were not there.

To prod it along, he took a card from his wallet and laid it in the center of Dub Cresswell's desk. A minute later the handset dropped onto the telephone. "Quintana. How's it going? Porter said you'd be dropping by."

Not having been asked to sit, Anthony remained standing. "A favor for Claire. If I may be candid? She's afraid for Porter's health. Their son's death has put stress on him, physically and mentally. You understand. On Monday the accountants will come to look into Roger's transactions with the company. A simple matter."

"Yeah."

The faces of the Cresswell brothers were similar in the square shape and cleft chin, although the younger man's features were heavier, more flushed with blood. He didn't get out of his chair, and his navy sports coat rode up on his shoulders.

"If Porter wants you to look at the operations side, that's fine," Dub said. "Sales and marketing is a whole 'nother department. Roger didn't have anything to do with it, and I can't give out sales figures willy-nilly."

Anthony acknowledged that with a nod, but said, "Your business secrets would remain confidential. I can assure you of my complete discretion."

"I don't see the point to this. Roger's dead."

"But the IRS is alive. Roger owned ten percent of the company. He had a direct connection, in that way, to everything that goes on here."

"Yeah, well, I'll talk to Porter."

"I'm confused about one thing," Anthony said. "Your ownership. You have forty-nine percent, correct?"

"That's right."

"How much was your share originally? I infer from your brother that it was less at some point."

The man was politely being asked to say what value his father placed on him. "Twenty-five percent. Porter had the MBA, and he showed an interest. I wasn't sure I even *wanted* into this business, but Dad twisted my arm."

"Ah. And when did you acquire the other . . . twenty-four percent from Porter?"

"Oh, it's been quite a while. Twenty years, maybe more. The IRS won't care about that, will they?"

"Probably not. I was simply trying to get it straight in my own mind. And . . . why was this done? Why did Porter nearly double your interest in the company?"

Heavy hands rose for a moment from the arms of the chair. Then he laughed, his cheeks making ruddy circles. "I'm a damn good salesman."

Anthony knew it would be useless to ask further questions. He expected to have a report from his accountants within ten days. Excellent men. Former FBI. He expected it to reveal that Duncan

Cresswell had been looting the sales accounts. The next problem would be proving that Roger had known about it. Nikki Cresswell had alleged this, but did she have evidence? Or had she only repeated to Gail Connor what her husband had told her?

Hands in his pockets, Anthony walked over to the swordfish, which took up eight feet of wall space. The creature had been turned into blue plastic. One glass eye looked back at him. "You're a fisherman."

"I pulled him in, but my wife hooked him and fought him for two hours. Lizzie insists that this is her fish. Big sucker, isn't he?" As if in testimony, a framed photograph on a shelf underneath showed a woman in fishing hat and sunglasses grinning up at the fish hanging by its tail from a crossbeam, boat in the background.

Anthony turned around. "Where could I find her?"

"Probably out in the yard somewhere. Get someone to page her."

Porter Cresswell's secretary pressed the appropriate button on her telephone and spoke into it. "Elizabeth, call the main office, please. Liz, main office." While Anthony waited, the secretary made a copy of the original articles of incorporation and the resolution regarding distribution of shares, which Anthony folded and put into the breast pocket of his suit coat.

A pudgy young man around twenty years of age sat at a worktable going through papers, sorting them, writing notes. This had to be Sean, Anthony thought. His brown hair was short on the sides, longer on top, and he wore a white company shirt. No earrings in sight. He glanced over at Anthony, holding his gaze for only a few seconds. Sullen, bored. He returned to his work. There had been nothing in his gaze to tell Anthony that Sean Cresswell knew of his connection to Bobby Gonzalez.

Within minutes, an elevator opened, and the brunette who had hooked the swordfish stepped off it. Her breasts filled out her shirt, and khaki shorts came to mid-thigh. Good legs, firm and tanned. She had a two-way radio on her belt. She looked around, then spotted Anthony, who walked over and shook her hand.

"Hi. I'm Liz Cresswell." Her dark hair was tied back in a scarf, and heavy bangs went straight across her forehead. "I've been ex-pecting you. Come on, I'll show you around the facility. We'll ride in my cart."

In the elevator, he said, "Who was the young man at the table, your son?"

"Sean." She beamed. "He works here part-time while he's in college. We'd like for him to hurry up and graduate, but he takes his time. Maybe he plays a little too much. They all do. Not like it used to be, isn't that the truth? Kids." She led Anthony through the lobby on the first floor. Big photographs of boats decorated the walls. "Porter told me why you're here. Is there some way I can help you?"

"Tell me about Roger."

"He was a smart man. Not easy to get along with, but he had the right ideas." Elizabeth pushed through the glass doors into the blazing white sun. "Roger and I had some fights about *how* it ought to be done, but we usually agreed on the goal. I'm sorry he's gone. God knows what's going to become of the company now. No, I don't think he was stealing. He didn't have to. He was making good money. He'd have wound up as half owner some-day. I question Porter's sanity."

The cart was on the walkway under a canvas awning. A tag on it read, E. CRESSWELL, VP OF OPERATIONS. Anthony laid his folded coat on the seat. He put on his sunglasses and held onto the bar supporting the roof. The cart took off with a jerk.

"We've got ten acres here, and you can find anything from a plumber to an electronics engineer. All the trades are represented. It's like you're building a house, except the damn thing has a point at one end and a couple thousand horsepower at the other."

As the cart hummed over the asphalt, Elizabeth Cresswell pointed out the assembly building, the various warehouses and shops. Her bangs blew back from her face in the breeze. She went through the front entrance, waving to the security guard, then sped down a short street to the Miami River. "This is where we put the boats in the water." There were three shiny new craft un-der a shed, and she called out to the man in the stern of one of them. "Carlos! *¿Cómo se van los cables?*" The man shouted back in Spanish that the cables were working now, no problem, *señora*. She waved back at him and turned the cart toward the main yard, fishtailing the back end. "We test them in the water first, then do the finish work, and off they go."

It occurred to Anthony, as he braced one foot on the dashboard to hold himself steady, that if Elizabeth Cresswell had been Dub's sister, not his wife, she would have been running this company. Perhaps she already was.

She braked the cart to a stop in the shade of an open building with a metal roof. A hot wind came across the lot.

"See that? That's the polishing shed. See those girls in the face masks and smocks? That's me, twenty-five years ago. I worked seven in the morning till four in the afternoon. I had to, or I wouldn't eat. My dad died when I was fourteen, my mother was a drunk, and I was on my own. The other girls were Cubans, and so were the men in the shop. Cubans made the boat industry in Miami, Mr. Quintana. They came here and took jobs nobody else would want. I learned Spanish and sweated right alongside them, so I know how it was. But you don't look like you came up that way. Not saying you couldn't handle it. I'd say you could handle anything."

Dark pencil outlined her eyes, and a reddish brown tint lay across sharp cheekbones. There was a scar at one corner of her upper lip. Anthony could feel the sexuality of this woman as clearly as the heat boiling up from the asphalt. She turned toward him and put her left foot up on the dashboard and swung her knee. White canvas deck shoes. A tanned, muscular leg. With each slow swing of her knee, a gap appeared between her shorts and her thigh.

"What are you doing here? And don't tell me you're putting Porter's mind at ease, which is the line Claire gave me."

"But it's true." Anthony smiled at her. "She's a devoted wife."

"I know something about you, Mr. Quintana. I know from my son that your daughter is dating Bobby Gonzalez. Angela, right? Sean says she's adorable. So maybe you are here helping Porter find his lost marbles, but I also think that you have an interest in helping Bobby. I hope you do. He's a sweet kid."

Anthony let this information settle, then said, "Do you have any idea who wanted Roger dead?"

"I have a guess. The person who had the most to gain was Jack Pascoe. You know Jack?"

"Claire's nephew. We've met," Anthony said. "He was sleeping with Roger's wife. Is that what you mean?"

Liz's mouth opened as if a laugh might come out, but none did. "Jack didn't want Nikki. What he really wanted was for Roger to find out. Sleeping with Nikki was payback. You see, Roger told stories about Jack's double-dealing and put him out of business. But that's not the reason Roger's dead. I mean, what's the fun of having someone *dead* if you want to see him suffer? No, Jack did it for Claire's money. Porter won't last much longer, and everything will be hers. Millions of dollars and all those paintings. And Jack is her only heir."

Under his shirt, Anthony could feel sweat trickle down his side. The heat was like an open oven door. "Jack won't inherit the company, will he? Porter's shares are worth around a hundred million dollars, and at his death they go to his brother. Your husband."

Her exotically penciled eyes flared with comprehension, then amusement. "Dub? He didn't kill Roger. He wouldn't know what to do with this company."

"But you would."

Liz's knee swung back and forth. "That's true, but it isn't mine, Mr. Quintana, and it never will be. In fact, Porter will probably force a sale. The company is a burden to him now, and if Porter can't control something, he gets rid of it."

"Could that apply to his own son?"

"My God, what a thought." She made a low laugh. "Not that I didn't consider it myself. No, Porter was home with Claire on the night in question. Dub was with friends, and I was with my daughter Patty. Like I said, you should be looking at Jack. As soon as the company is sold, it turns into cash, and who inherits Porter's money? Claire does."

A clang of metal on metal arose, adding to the steady whining noise from the polishing shed. Another golf cart went by, vanishing into the enormous door of the assembly building. Anthony looked back at Liz Cresswell. "What do you know about Ted Stamos?"

"He runs the glass shop. He's one of our best men. Why? Are you saying Ted might have murdered Roger? There is no way."

"They had problems on the job, no? I was told that Roger wanted to clean some old tools out of a workshop that Stamos's father had used, and Stamos threatened to break his face. Is that true?"

"You were told? Meaning you won't say who told you. It doesn't matter. Everyone knows about it. Yes, they had problems, but not to that extent. Anyway, Ted was with my husband and about twelve other men the night Roger was shot. The police checked out everyone's alibis, believe me. So. Looks like you've struck out." Her knee was swinging again. "Give me your card. You never know. I might want a good attorney someday. We should stay in touch."

Anthony lifted his hands. "I am sorry, but I gave my last card to your husband. I wonder if you could show me where the production supervisors are. I'd like to talk to them."

Still looking at him, Elizabeth Cresswell leaned down to turn the key, and a moment later the golf cart jerked forward. There were four supervisors on the list that Porter had given Anthony, but only one he wanted to meet—Theodore Stamos. Liz Cresswell's lover.

The glass-enclosed offices looked down from a catwalk thirty feet above the floor of the assembly building. Hoists in the roof carried heavy parts and equipment, and the boats were lined up end to end, two rows of them in various stages of completion. Big fans roared, moving air through the building.

Anthony grasped the railing with both hands and leaned over. Directly under him half a dozen men in rubber gloves were moving around inside an empty hull, laying down sheets of fiberglass, adhering it tightly with resin guns and rollers. The guns were attached to long hoses that fed from a stainless steel tank. Sparks flew from a welding torch in another part of the building. A drill whined, and metal clanged. An odd chemical smell drifted up toward the catwalk.

"I wouldn't lean on that railing. It's loose. Guess I better have it fixed."

Anthony glanced to his left. A man in jeans and work boots stood a few feet away. The plaid shirt reminded Anthony of a cowboy, and the man's arms were heavy with muscle. Straight brown hair stuck out over his forehead, and caution showed in his eyes. He had a thin-lipped mouth bracketed by deep creases. Anthony knew the face.

He extended his hand. "I'm Anthony Quintana. We met last weekend at the marina behind the Cresswells' condo. They've hired me to look into company records."

"Yeah, Porter told me."

"What is that smell?"

Ted Stamos raised his head, testing the air. "Resin, probably. I don't smell it anymore. The chemical composition changed some years back, but used to be, men would die of acetone. That's what killed my father. Liver cancer."

"Could we go inside your office? It's noisy out here."

The noise receded when Stamos shut the door. The office was jammed with file cabinets and stacked with papers. In/out boxes. Lists, schedules. Machine parts whose purpose eluded Anthony. He handed Stamos his card.

"Criminal law?"

Anthony let go a small sigh. "Porter is afraid that Roger may have committed financial crimes here at the company. Embezzlement, kickbacks. This is probably untrue, but to erase the doubt is worth something. You worked with Roger. Perhaps you have an opinion."

"I only build the boats," Stamos said after a moment. "How they get sold, and to who, I wouldn't know. It's not my concern. I keep my eye on the production costs, sure, but I don't know what goes on over at the main office. I don't think I can help you."

Anthony knew he would get nothing further. He noticed on the wall behind the battered desk a framed black-and-white snapshot of a man standing in front of a power boat, hands on his hips. "Who is this?"

"My father. Henry Stamos. He built that boat." The son leaned casually against the desk with his arms crossed.

"Yes, I recognize the boat from a photograph in the lobby. The prototype of the first production model."

"Sure is. He'd never worked fiberglass before, but look at it. He was raised in Tarpon Springs, and he'd only built fishing boats out of wood. The man was a genius."

Anthony agreed that it was an impressive piece of work. He studied the small face in the photograph. The man was dead, but his tools were still in his workshop, polished and sharpened. "I'm curious about ownership of the company. The shares of stock and so on. Did your father ever own any shares?"

"Nope. Charlie Cresswell never got around to that. He died first."

"But he intended to make your father a part owner." Anthony looked at Stamos. "How long has Cresswell been dead?"

Still leaning on the edge of the desk, Stamos crossed his scuffed work boots at the ankle. "About thirty years, I guess. Why?"

Anthony allowed a shrug to indicate lack of any good reason to know this. He said, "Twenty years ago Porter transferred shares to his brother, making their interests approximately equal. Do you happen to know why this was done?"

"No. I didn't know it was. What they do in the office doesn't concern me. You know, I need to get back to work."

"Of course." Anthony lifted a hand. "There is one other question." He hesitated for a moment, then decided that Ted Stamos already knew, if he had been talking to Liz Cresswell. "It's such a small world. My daughter is dating Bobby Gonzalez, who used to work in your department. Do you remember him?"

Stamos's expression didn't change, but he took a moment to answer. "Sure, I remember Bobby."

"And you know he's a suspect in Roger's death. Angela asked me to help him. I can't say no to her. She would never forgive me. Bobby says you stood up for him with Roger. You refused to fire Bobby when Roger told you to. He told me about his fight with

Roger here in your office. He said that you came in and broke it up, correct?"

"Yeah, that's right."

"And that you weren't here when it started, but you heard the noise and came in. Is that so?"

"Yeah."

"But when I met you at the marina, Porter Cresswell said that you had seen Bobby attack Roger for firing him, and then threaten his life. Porter asked you if that was true, and you said yes. That's what you told the police as well. Who asked you to lie to them? Porter?"

Stamos shifted, uncrossing his feet, standing up straight. He was smiling, but not as if he had found the question amusing. "The man owns the company. He said Bobby did it."

"No. He was with my daughter at the time. He's completely innocent."

"No kidding. Good. Glad to hear it." Stamos went over to the door and opened it so Anthony could leave. "If you don't mind, I've got some work to do."

Around ten o'clock that night, Anthony went by the Strip Mine, a one-story concrete-block building with a flashing sign showing a pair of *tetas* in a martini glass.

He ordered a drink, leaving the bartender a twenty as a tip. A little later he asked about the party of men who had been come in the night of August 16, and he laid twenties on the counter until the man slipped the pile into his pocket. Anthony showed him some photos his investigator had taken with a telephoto lens.

The bartender leaned on his elbows. "Yeah, I know Dub Cresswell. He's always in here. I remember that night because the guys he brought in were speaking French, from Quebec, and the girls got a kick out of it. Mr. Cresswell is a good customer. Don't mention I talked to you, he might not come in here no more."

"What time did they come in that night?"

"My shift starts at ten o'clock. They had their first round on the table already. I'm guessing nine-thirty."

The bartender recognized Ted Stamos as well. "He always

SUSPICION OF MALICE 269

comes in when Mr. Cresswell brings a group like that, but he drinks club soda. I guess he's the designated driver or something."

"Did Mr. Cresswell leave early?"

"No, he stayed and signed the bill. It's a company account. Like I said, he's a good customer."

"What about Stamos? When did he leave?"

"He left when the rest of them did. I remember he had to help Dub get out of his chair."

"Could either of them have gone out during the night, then returned?"

"Oh, jeez. We're jammed on Saturdays. I can't remember. You want to talk to the parking lot attendant."

It cost Anthony sixty dollars. "*Sí, por supuesto, yo recuerdo a ese hombre.*"

The attendant remembered that the man had come with the others, but he had wanted to leave his Jeep Cherokee by the entrance. It had taken some explaining, because the attendant didn't speak English, and the man—*Este, ¿verdad?* The American had been forced to speak Spanish, and not well. *No movar el camión. Estoy aquí en cinco minutos.* Don't move the truck. I'll be back in five minutes. Ted Stamos had come out, and his rear tires had squealed taking off on the highway, heading south. He had returned a couple of hours later. About one-thirty in the morning he and the other men had come out of the club. He had helped *el gordo*—the fat man—into the passenger seat and had driven away.

"*Muchas gracias,*" Anthony said.

CHAPTER

22

Gail's mother introduced her to Claire Cresswell in the staff lounge at the ballet. Claire had just attended a board meeting, and she had an hour or so before she was expected home.

"We're having people over for cocktails," Claire explained, "or else I might let Porter fend for himself." They talked for a few minutes about what ballets Gail should see this season, then Irene went out and left them alone.

Windows in the lounge gave a view of the fourth-floor terrace and the placid turquoise of the Atlantic a few city blocks to the east. Interior windows at right angles looked down into one of the practice studios with its wall of mirrors and shiny wood floor. Gail and Claire took their cups of coffee to a grouping of chairs in a corner.

Not having met her before, Gail could not tell what marks Roger Cresswell's death had left on his mother's face, but she was arrestingly beautiful. For women with money and taste, years were irrelevant. Claire Cresswell fought back with a stunning wardrobe, elegant jewelry, and glowing makeup. Platinum hair was fastened at the nape of her long neck in a flat black bow. A deep rose silk jacket whispered against flowing trousers. Her nails were the same shade of pink, and a loose bracelet of pink amethysts clicked against the gold band of a diamond-faced watch when Claire picked up her coffee.

"Of *course* I remember your mother in high school. Irene was so well liked by everyone. Has it been forty years? Can it be?" Claire lightly touched fingers to her cheek and made a mock grimace. "More than forty. Uggh."

Gail sat at right angles, holding her cup on her knees. "I told Anthony to be here at five-thirty so we could talk first. I'm so grateful for your help. I know this is a terrible time for you, losing a son, but you may have saved Bobby's career. And Nate's too."

"It's very kind of you to say so, Gail." Claire smiled. Her glossy lipstick matched her jacket. "Well. What's on your mind?"

"Diane asked me to help her with a legal matter. It's about the portrait that your daughter painted. You know it's at the cottage now, don't you? And that Diane took it from her parents' house."

"Yes. Nate told me all about it. I was so mad at Porter. I said, 'Porter, you're giving Nate his down payment back.' Porter promised he would. This might be one of those things we'll all laugh about later."

"Diane would like to keep the portrait," Gail said. "She feels a special attachment, as you can understand. She says her parents don't care about it, except for its monetary value. Even so, she doesn't have much chance of acquiring title unless they give it up. I thought you might be willing to help, to persuade them somehow."

Claire leaned to set down her cup. "Of course, I'd be happy to help. I can't guarantee what Liz would say, though. Does Diane want it that much? Maybe I could buy it for her. If Liz won't give it to her voluntarily, then I'll just make an offer. Is that a good idea?"

Gail laughed, surprised. "Diane never expected this, but I'm sure she'd accept. You might just shame her mother into giving up, since they paid nothing for it. I'm curious about something. Before Roger sold it to Jack and all this started, you and Porter owned it. Where did you get it?"

"From Maggie."

"Really. I asked Nate, and he said he never saw it at your house."

"We never hung it up. Can you believe it? I meant to get it framed, but we went on vacation, and I stuck it aside and completely forgot. We have so many paintings. When did Maggie do that one? It's been a good eight years. One day we were redecorating a guest room, and there it was. We gave it to Roger and Nikki for Christmas."

"Why not to Diane's parents?"

"Oh. Well, we decided that since Roger didn't have any of his sister's works, it would be a nice gift."

That was hardly an answer, but Gail went on. "Nate told me that when Maggie was fifteen, she was in love with a boy who worked at the boat yard, but you and Porter didn't approve. Maggie was so upset that she attempted suicide. Is that what happened?"

"I'm afraid so. We don't like to talk about it. It was a terrible time for everyone."

"Your nephew, Jack, says he and Maggie were close as children. He loved her very much, I think. He says that she was sent to a mental hospital farther up the state, and she stayed there a few months. Where was it?"

"Outside Orlando. They got her stabilized, and then we sent her to a place in Vermont. Porter has family there. We visited, of course. I practically lived on airplanes."

"How old was she when she went away?"

"Sixteen. We hated to do it, but they had excellent facilities for girls her age."

"When she attempted suicide . . . was she pregnant?"

"Pregnant? No." Claire laughed, blinking heavily mascaraed lashes. "Of course she wasn't pregnant."

"So many years later, and she's gone. It wouldn't matter now if you told me."

"I just did. You know, I don't see the reason for these questions. How is this helping Nate? How is it helping Bobby?"

"I'm looking for the reason Roger was killed. Perhaps it was because of something he knew." Allowing some time to gather her thoughts, Gail shifted some ballet magazines aside on the table and set down her coffee. "This is what I see. Diane told me that her mother was on vacation at Disney World when she went into early labor. That's near Orlando, where you first took Maggie. If she'd had a child, it would be twenty, the same age as Diane. Diane doesn't look like her parents. She looks more like you. She's a dancer. So were you. And there's the portrait. Maggie never painted portraits, but she painted Diane. The longing in it is overpowering. It says . . . this is my child."

Claire Cresswell, who had been stunned into silence as Gail recited these facts, blurted out, "That is completely untrue. I hope to God you haven't repeated this to anyone else."

"No, I haven't, not even to Anthony. I wanted to talk to you first—"

"This has *nothing* to do with Roger's death. Do you find some strange satisfaction in picking through my family's past?"

"I didn't mean to—"

There was a knock on the door, and both women turned. One of the staff showed Anthony in. He saw them and smiled.

Claire walked to him, lifting her hands so he could take them. "Look who's here. And aren't you just gorgeous? What a lovely suit. Did you see Nate's interview on TV this morning? Wasn't he wonderful?"

For a second Anthony's eyes met Gail's. She made a subtle shrug. He said to Claire, "My secretary taped the interview. I was in court all day. Am I late? I hope you haven't waited long." He bent to allow Claire to brush his cheek with hers. "Come, let's sit on the couch. Gail, I think Claire left her coffee over there on the table. Would you bring it, please?"

She said prettily, "May I get you some coffee, too?"

"Would you? Cream, no sugar." He looked up and smiled, and she read his thoughts clearly. *Give me a few minutes with Claire.*

Claire said, "The break room is down the hall to the left. And if you could bring me a fresh cup? Black is fine. Thanks."

Gail walked down the corridor and back again, looking through the windows into the open studios. A class of little girls in one of them. Older dancers in another. Then to the break room for the coffee.

When she returned, they were in a discussion about the lawsuit that Roger's wife had threatened. Whether to settle. Claire thought they should.

Gail set the cups on the coffee table, feeling a nudge of annoyance that he had been able to calm this woman so quickly. Claire Cresswell was chattering like a schoolgirl. And why wouldn't she be smitten? That resonant voice, the big brown eyes, the slight frown of concern. His warm, subtle sexuality had put a blush on her cheeks. *Aren't you just gorgeous?*

Claire was smiling, and her face had relaxed. Gail took that as a good omen for her own chances of not being kicked out again. She took a chair at the end of the couch, facing Anthony.

"Porter just hates to be pushed around, but I said, Porter, you don't want to be in litigation for years, do you? Our lawyer has him pretty much convinced it's the right thing to do, just let it go. I'm going to call Nikki and say there are no hard feelings and we're so sorry. We *have* to make up before Sunday, don't we?"

"Sunday?"

"When we go out to scatter Roger's ashes. There won't be many of us. Just the immediate family and a few friends." Claire turned to smile at Gail. "You're coming too, aren't you?"

Gail nodded, relieved that Claire Cresswell had forgiven her.

Anthony patted Claire's hand, then squeezed it. "Claire, I am sorry to raise such painful issues, but when Ms. Connor and I talk to the police, they will ask us certain questions. I want to have all the answers for them. You understand. There was a family dinner the night before Roger died. Some disagreements between him and Porter. Could you tell me what it was about?"

"Roger wanted Porter to resign, and he wouldn't do it, so Roger and Dub said they'd vote him out. Porter was the angriest I have ever seen him. He threw things. It took me forever to get them calmed down."

Anthony leaned over to put his empty cup on the table. The expensive fabric of his suit rustled softly, and Gail imagined a little cloud of cologne wafting around Claire's head. "The next night, Saturday, Porter was at the Black Point Marina after a cruise to Bimini," Anthony said.

"No, Porter didn't go on the cruise. He just hasn't got the strength. I dropped him off at the marina and had dinner with some friends."

"You picked him up again around nine o'clock. And then?"

"And we went home. He was in bed by ten-thirty." Claire laughed. "Believe me, Porter's not going to go creeping around in the dark."

"Another difficult question," Anthony said. "Ted Stamos told the police that Bobby attacked Roger without cause and threatened to kill him. This never occurred. I asked Stamos about it, and he said, indirectly, that he lied because Porter told him to. Was Stamos afraid of losing his job? Or was it simple loyalty? What do you think?"

Claire took her time. "I'm sure Porter didn't ask Ted to lie. Ted misunderstood. But it's true that Ted and Roger didn't like each other. It goes back some years. Ted had a crush on my daughter when they were kids. Roger knew about it, and he'd promised not to say anything, but he told Porter on them, and Porter threw Ted off our property. Ted and Roger never liked each other from that moment on. Remember what I told you before? No one in the family could have killed Roger."

Gail could read Anthony's thoughts. It was comfortable for Claire to blame Ted Stamos for murder. Anthony said, "Not liking someone isn't a motive I would suggest to a homicide detective. Let me ask you about the corporation. You recall that yesterday I asked Porter about the shares, and he said that about twenty years ago, he gave Dub additional shares of the business, up to forty-nine percent. Why did he do that? Does Dub have some hold on him? I am thinking of blackmail, and perhaps Roger found out—"

"No!" Claire protested with a laugh. "They're *brothers*. It was just the fair thing to do. Dub had been working so hard, and he wanted some compensation for it. It doesn't *mean* anything. Porter still has the controlling interest. It was for appearances."

Anthony nodded, apparently letting it go.

Gail leaned forward, elbows on knees, hands clasped. "Was it for Diane?" In the corner of her vision she could see the flicker of surprise on Anthony's face. "Was it because Porter wanted them to take Maggie's child?"

Anthony was openly staring.

Claire Cresswell's face paled as if someone had struck her.

Gail said, "Claire, it's true, isn't it? Porter promised his brother more shares of the company if he and Liz would adopt the baby." This was the only reason that made sense to Gail. She had guessed, but Claire's reaction had just confirmed it. "Please, Claire. This could be the reason Roger died. Did he know? Was he going to tell?"

The facade began to crumble. Lips pressed together, then trembled. Eyes shone with sudden tears. "He couldn't have known."

"Are you sure? Claire, he was old enough to see what was going on. Maggie might have said something."

"Maggie never told anyone. She hid it. Even from me." Claire's voice became husky. "We didn't know until . . . she tried to kill herself. The maid found her, and we called an ambulance, and at the hospital the doctor told us. Porter wanted it aborted, but it was too late. They wouldn't. We had to decide what to do. We couldn't let Maggie keep it. She was only fifteen. Her life would have been ruined. Something shameful like that? All the gossip, the whispering—" Sharply Claire said, "You think it shouldn't have mattered, but you weren't *there*. It was awful for all of us."

Gail thought for a moment of backing away from a topic so clearly painful to this woman, but she said, "So you decided to keep the child in the family by giving it to your in-laws."

"Porter decided. I wanted to put the baby up for adoption, but Porter wouldn't allow it. He said . . . hell no. 'Hell no. It's my flesh and blood.' He decided the baby would live with Dub and Lizzie. A little sister for Patty. So we drove Maggie up to Orlando. I have a cousin there. Liz came up and stayed until it was over. She doesn't have family, so it wasn't hard to do. We had a private doctor, and he put Dub and Liz's name on the birth certificate.

"Porter told Maggie to sign the consent. He said the baby was going to be adopted by a nice couple in another state, and she shouldn't talk about it again, ever. He said, 'What you did was bad, but it's behind you. Don't think about it anymore.' Porter had to go back to work, but I stayed with her. After the baby was born, Porter and I took her to his cousins in Vermont, and they put her in a hospital there. The doctors were wonderful. It was the only solution. It's the only thing we could have done. She got better. We sent her to school up there. She became an artist, and she was famous. Her paintings are in museums. She was on the cover of *Art in America*—"

Claire's exhalation turned to a sob, and she pressed her fist against her mouth. Anthony gave her his handkerchief.

After a minute, Gail leaned closer and said softly, "Claire? Who was Diane's father? Did Maggie tell you?"

Taking some time to answer, Claire pressed the handkerchief to the corners of her eyes. "No. Maggie kept so much from me. Porter said to let it be. I didn't press her to talk about it."

"Did she ever find out about Diane? Did she guess?"

"She must have." Claire took a shaky breath. "Eight years ago Maggie spent the winter with friends in Key West, and she came through Miami. That's when she painted the portrait. I'm sure she knew. Before she went back north, she gave it to us. She came to the house and set it on a chair for us to look at, and she didn't say anything, and nobody said anything, and Porter walked into another room and closed the door. When she was gone, he came out and said . . . 'Put that thing away.' "

Claire's mouth trembled. "I didn't see Maggie for four years. Oh, we'd write, and there were some phone calls, but she never visited. Then she met Nate, and they got married. He was so kind to her. He didn't know any of this, but he tried to patch things up. He kept after her, and we started visiting again. She even saw Porter a few times. We spent Christmas together.

"A week before she died, Nate said, 'Maggie, go visit your mother, go see the new gallery.' We'd moved to the condo by then. She came over, and we had a nice lunch, just the two of us. Porter was at the office. And afterwards Maggie got up and walked around the house, and she asked me, 'Mama, where's the portrait that I gave you? Where is it? I don't see it anywhere.' I didn't remember what she was talking about. I didn't remember at first. She tore the house apart looking everywhere, and I was running after her, crying, begging her to stop. She found it in a box under the bed in the guest bedroom. I tried to tell her. I said, 'Your daddy wanted me to give it away, but I didn't, I kept it.' I said, 'Maggie, I'll have it framed and hung in the gallery, I will. I promise.' She didn't say anything more. She pushed the portrait back under the bed and she left.

"We spoke on the phone a couple of times that week. I wanted to say something, but she didn't sound upset. I thought everything was all right. A few nights later Nate came over and told us she was gone. She'd killed herself in the cottage with her sleeping pills. After the funeral, I didn't think about it anymore. I put all those thoughts away in a box. Never looked, not for three years. It was Porter's idea to give the portrait to Roger. He didn't care who had it. He just wanted it out of the house. Then Nate bought the portrait. It wasn't a mistake. Jack sent it back to us because somehow he *knew*. Or he guessed. He loved Maggie so, and he blames us for what happened to her. He hates us. Maybe he should."

Claire clutched the handkerchief in her fist. Mascara was splotched around her eyes. Breathing deeply, she gazed out the window. "Diane should have her portrait. I'll talk to Liz. I'm sure, very sure, I can persuade her. I may talk to Diane someday. Maybe after Porter is gone. He would be so furious if he knew I'd told you."

Anthony said, "You can rely on our discretion. No one will know."

"Thank you. Oh, my. What time is it? I should go. It's late, and we have some people coming over for cocktails." Claire stood up, tottering a little, and Anthony steadied her with a hand on her arm. Her lipstick was gone, and her face sagged. "It's been lovely seeing you both again. Don't forget Sunday."

They walked her out of the lounge and across the hall to the elevator. She took gold-framed sunglasses out of her purse and put them on. She waved goodbye as the door slid shut.

Gail stared into the brushed metal surface. "Oh, my God."

Turning her toward the lounge, Anthony said quietly, "Let's talk for a few minutes." He closed the door. "Why did you suggest that Roger was killed because of what he knew? It's doubtful he knew anything."

"I suggested it to see what would come next."

"It worked," Anthony said.

"Then why do I feel so rotten?" Gail wandered to the windows looking down into the studio. Dancers had come into the room. Some stretched their legs, others practiced their steps. They wore the same patched or faded clothing that Gail had seen the last time she'd been here, with Bobby Gonzalez.

Standing beside her, Anthony said, "It does seem clear, however, that Ted Stamos is Diane's father."

"Does it?"

"Who else could it be? Based on what Jack Pascoe told you about Maggie, I don't think she was promiscuous."

Gail was silent for a while, then said, "Claire was so evasive. And didn't you pick up on that hideous undercurrent of shame? Porter told Maggie what she did was 'bad,' and Claire was afraid of gossip."

"Ah. You think Jack was the father. He was Maggie's cousin. There's the shame you noticed. This explains why he sent the portrait to Porter and Claire, no? He used Nate to make a point."

"I wasn't thinking of Jack," Gail said. "He loved her, but not like that."

"Who, then?"

"Porter."

Anthony made a short laugh of disbelief. "No."

"Think about it. Porter refused to put the baby up for adoption because it was his flesh and blood."

"But that's true. Diane is his granddaughter."

"But look at what he did with the portrait. He walked out of the room when Maggie brought it to them. 'Nobody said anything.' Why not? What were they so ashamed of?"

Anthony shook his head. "I don't know. Ted Stamos is more likely."

"You're probably right," Gail said. She leaned heavily against the edge of the window. "Why did he kill Roger?"

For a minute Anthony looked at the dancers below them. "For

money. Let's say his relationship to Diane is irrelevant. If Nikki was right in what she told you, Roger knew that Dub was embezzling from the company. Say that Dub paid Ted Stamos to get rid of Roger. Or we could assume that Porter paid Ted to do it. Porter thought his son had betrayed him. Or Ted did it for Elizabeth because he's in love with her, and Roger was threatening her position."

Gail watched the dancers working in the studio below. One of the male dancers made a leap, twisted, and came down without a wobble. He did it again, not as steadily. "Imagine taking a child to get a bigger share of the company. What greed. God, I feel sorry for Diane. How could Claire have looked the other way all these years?"

There was no music. The voices were muffled, and the only noise was the occasional thump of a foot coming down on the wooden floor. One girl held onto the barre and raised her leg past her shoulder, then leaned slowly into an arabesque. Another watched herself in the mirror. On pointe, then down, then up, plié, relevé, plié . . .

Anthony touched Gail's arm. "Look. It's Angela."

"Where? Oh, I see."

She was the girl in the pink leotard and tights. Her long hair was pinned into a bun at the back of her head, and she wore a hip-length wrap skirt tied at her waist. She stood at the barre, arm raised, back perfectly straight, leg moving quickly in and out and in.

"She's auditioning tonight for *The Nutcracker*," Anthony said, moving back from the window a little. "Can they see us up here? I don't want to embarrass her."

Angela turned the other way and saw someone across the room. A black-haired male dancer came into view. Bobby Gonzalez was beautifully masculine, even in tights and an old T-shirt with a hole in it. It hung off his broad shoulders. He walked around Angela, holding her hand while she balanced on pointe as delicately as a porcelain doll. Then she pirouetted, and the little skirt fluttered at her hips. As if showing off, Bobby ran and vaulted himself into the air, legs perfectly extended in front and behind, arms open to the sides, hair flying. He landed, spun, and dropped to one knee, a hand on his hip, the other arm in a flourish.

"Bravo," Anthony said.

Rising, Bobby did a quick turn on one foot, steadied himself, then walked with Angela toward the front of the room and gradually out of view.

Gail continued to stare, unseeing, into the studio for another minute, then another. No one spoke. Her chest had become constricted, leaving her short of breath. She was afraid she would start to cry if she didn't leave quickly. Her legs stiffly carried her to the purse she had left on the table.

She managed to say, "Do we have enough to take to Frank Britton?"

"We should go with the family on Sunday," Anthony said. "Maybe we'll push it a little and see what kind of response we get. After that, we'll see Britton."

"He'll leave Bobby alone, won't he?" Gail asked.

"I think so. He'll have other leads to pursue."

"Then we've done it." Gail looked at her watch. "Past six. I should go." She took a breath. Then another. The things in the room blurred out of focus. Of Anthony she saw only his shoes, the legs of his trousers, and a hand at his side.

"What is going to happen to us, Gail?"

She shook her head. "I don't know. We should try to be friends, I suppose."

He laughed. "*Ay, mi Diós.* Is that what you want? Yes, friends. We'll be civil to each other. For the good of the child, no? I will tell you this now. I can't be your friend, like Dave. I can't walk away and forget it. That's what Nate suggested. 'Let her go. If it was meant to be, it will.' I'm not like Nate. What do you want me to do? I can't forget you. I can't have you. You will marry again someday, but the thought of you with another man—to think of my son or my daughter in another man's house—I would go insane."

She looked at him. His eyes were black and hollow, as if he had been consumed from inside, and nothing was left but ashes.

"No. I won't marry again," she said.

"Why? You're a beautiful woman. You won't stay single for long."

"Because . . . you'd always be there. In one way or another, you would be there. In my bones, my blood. In this child."

"I'm not a good man, Gail. Don't think I am."

"Please don't say that." She placed her fingers lightly on his cheekbone. The skin seemed tight and fevered. "You are. I didn't see it."

His eyes closed. He took her hand and pressed it to his lips.

CHAPTER
23

The faint whisper of waves came through the sliding door. They had left it open a little, and the curtain belled inward, gauzy white. Warm, salt-laden air drifted into the room, carrying the smell of the ocean ten floors below.

Exhausted, sated, but unable to sleep, Gail had watched daylight fade, watched stars appear, barely visible in the wash of light from the moon. The things in the room had become shadows—the armoire, the sofa and chairs, the lamps, Anthony's suit on the chaise by the windows. The entire east wall was windows, and the curtains were drawn, except for that one place they had slid the door open.

Anthony's hair looked black on the pillow. One arm was below her breasts, and the other hung off the side of the bed. He lay as if he had run for miles, then collapsed facedown. She could hear him breathing, slow and deep.

Their bodies touched at chest, hips, thighs. There was just enough light to see the long curve of his back. The sheet was down there somewhere, and the air conditioner was almost too cool, but Gail couldn't bear to move. She wound a strand of his hair around her finger. It was still damp, smelling of the herbal shampoo they had found on the marble vanity in the bathroom. Two kinds of shampoo. Stacks of towels. A basket of lotions. Two soft terry robes in the closet, both of which now lay in a heap on the floor.

The first time—before they had filled up the immense bath-tub and floated around in the perfumed water—the first time had been excruciatingly slow. Finally she'd had to tell him she wouldn't break, nothing would happen, for God's sake, do it, please—

How cool she had once been. How perfectly balanced, pro-tected by layers of pretense, manners, and professional caution, like calluses. Not anymore. She was a greedy slut. Hands and mouth all over him. In bed their bodies had still been slick from bath oil, and she had crawled on top of him, Anthony groaning in pleasure. She'd finally straddled him, bearing down so hard she felt him probing the mouth of her womb, and her body had flamed. Not a polite and bloodless love.

The mattress was soft and deep. Pillows like clouds. Gail would see a client in the morning, and Anthony would be back at Cresswell Yachts, but all that was years away. She had called her mother last night to say where she was, and with whom, and she might be late . . . Her mother had said if she came home before dawn, she was an idiot.

What would Karen think of this? Gail wasn't sure what she herself thought of it. In the space of a few hours the world had shuddered to a stop, creaking on its axis, then had slowly begun to revolve in the other direction.

In the staff lounge at the ballet he had kissed her hand. She had felt the heat in his mouth, and if he had thrown her to the car-pet she would have let him do it. He had simply suggested they go somewhere else. Quickly. Even in this extreme state, Anthony had chosen well. No noisy Art Deco relic but a suite at the Fontaine-bleau. The heavy door had thudded shut. They had stared at each other as if neither had the least idea how this had happened. She remembered being horribly frightened. Then he had kissed her. Held her face and kissed her so gently she had started to cry. His hands had been cold. In bed it had taken awhile to get warm. And then the fire had caught.

In the bathroom mirror she had seen fingertip-shaped bruises on her butt, bite marks on his neck. Then starting all over again in the bathtub, sloshing the water onto the floor. Then back to bed, and she would have been content to lie snuggled against him, but he had wanted more and, she discovered, she did too.

The sun had finally gone down, and it had become dark as he slept.

She lightly stroked her fingers on his temple. His beeper went off, a vibrating buzz on the nightstand. He stirred, took a breath. A deep sound in his throat. The one eye she could see came open halfway. Then he dragged himself up and looked at the clock. "*Nine-fifteen?* You shouldn't have let me sleep so long."

"I needed the rest," she said.

With a soft chuckle, he kissed the corners of her mouth. Stroked his hand over her breasts, moving down to kiss each one, biting softly, then doing wonderful things with his lips and tongue.

"I'm not sure. Are they bigger?" He weighed one in a palm. "I think so."

"I hope so," she said. His shoulders were smoothly muscled. She loved looking at him, the way muscle joined tendons, the fit of his skin.

He slid his hand across her belly and caressed her between her legs.

"Ow. It's sore."

"*Lo siento.*" He gently kissed her in the same spot. "Is this better?"

"Oh, yes. Perfect. Right . . . there."

The beeper buzzed again. "*Cara'o.*" He sat up and reached for it, squinting to see the illuminated panel.

Gail said, "Don't let it be a client calling from jail."

"No, it's Angela. I should see what she wants. Close your eyes, I have to turn on the light." He reached for the telephone, but before dialing, he pulled the sheet up to his waist and smoothed his hair with his fingers.

"*Hola, Angelita, es tu papi, ¿qué pasa?* . . . Ohhhh, *que bueno,* congratulations. That's a good part, no? . . . I'm very proud of you, sweetheart. . . . Be sure to call your mother. I'll see you this weekend. Wait." He looked around at Gail. "Guess who's here with me—in the kitchen. We're having a late dinner together. . . . Right. . . . Yes, I'll tell her. . . . *Te quiero mucho, preciosa.*" Anthony hung up. "Angela says to tell you hello."

"What about the ballet? She got a part?"

"They made her a Flower. She wanted to do the Chinese dance, but they said maybe next time. If she does well—of course she will—and if she studies at the school for a little longer, she might get into the company as an apprentice."

"Are you going to take me to *The Nutcracker?*"

"*¿Qué va?* I'll buy two rows of seats. We'll see it every performance."

Gail propped herself on an elbow. "Your grandparents will want to come. You might have to speak to Ernesto."

"Ah, well. It would make Nena happy." He pulled Gail close with an arm under her neck. She played with the hair on his chest, lifting it with closed fingers. He said, "You want to hear something funny? Alicia told me the other day that Ernesto wants me to take him to Cuba. Yes. To Cuba. He wants to see it one more time before he dies."

"Oh. That isn't funny, it's so sad."

"He must be getting senile. He attacked me for years for going to see my father and my sister. He called me a communist. But now it's different. He wants to see Cuba again, and I have to take him—in secret. If they caught him in the country, after what he's done, they could charge him with treason. No. If they're smart, they'd put his picture in the newspaper and laugh about it, then send him back to Miami. That would be worse than prison, for his friends to know where he'd been. I didn't expect such cowardice from the old man. He knows he was wrong all these years, but he can't admit it."

"Are you going to talk to him?"

"No."

"Not at all?"

"I'm not going to take him anywhere. He could die on the way. And what would he see if he got there? Nothing's left. The house, the farm, the stables. All gone. Alicia wants me to lie to him! To tell him I'll take him, just to make him happy."

"Maybe you should. A lie could be the kindest thing to do."

"Gail, I'd rather not talk about this now. Every time I think of that old man, of that house, of the fights we had . . . Look. I break into a sweat even thinking about it." Anthony swung his legs off the bed. "Are you hungry? I am starving to death."

He walked to the desk across the room to find the room-service menu. He was wonderful in clothes, more so without. Gail stretched out like a cat, arms above her head, and watched him. His back in three-quarter profile, the front of him in the mirror. The desk lamp shining on chest hair, darker at his groin. Lean legs, a taut stomach. Not bad for almost forty-three. He flipped through pages. "A big steak and baked potato. What do you think?"

"God, yes. No, I want a lobster, dripping in butter, and a whole loaf of French bread. I haven't had an appetite like this in months. I'll get fat."

He turned to smile at her. "I would love to see you fat. *Mi gordita.*" He called room service and gave the order, adding that they should bring a bottle of champagne. Something nice. He hung up and came back, looking at her lying across the rumpled sheets, one leg crooked over a pillow. Under the heat of his eyes, her skin tingled.

He patted her hip and sat down. "When are we getting married?"

"We don't have to."

"What do you mean? To have a child without a father?"

"I thought it had one."

"Gail, please, no jokes. We have to get married. It's better. You know it."

"For the baby? Or for us?"

"Of course for us. For the baby too. Are you being difficult?"

"If I weren't pregnant, would you even consider it?"

"Yes."

She laughed. "You would not."

"Okay, maybe not as soon, but the fact is, you *are* pregnant, and I love you, and here we are, together again. Aren't we? Gail?"

"I don't want to think about it right now."

"*Ay, no me digas eso.* When will you think about it? In the labor room?"

"We have one night together, and everything is suddenly different?"

"One night? *One?*"

"Anthony, please don't push me."

"Okay, okay." He sat for a moment with his hands in his lap, then leaned over to kiss her between her hip bones. He whispered, "*Oyeme, bebita. Dile a tu obstinada mamá que se case conmigo.*"

"What was that?"

"I told her she has to convince you herself because I can't get anywhere."

"She?"

"I hope it's a girl. I want her to have your face. When I see her, I'll think of you." He leaned over and whispered into Gail's navel. "*Ya te quiero aunque no te he visto.* I just told her, 'I love you already, without having seen you.' "

"You're sweet. What if she is a he?"

"A boy? Well, that's all right too."

"You'd better not make him too macho."

"No, but we can't allow him to be lazy or disrespectful. You know what boys are like these days. This one won't get into trouble, I promise." He spoke into her navel again and patted her belly. "Hey. Wake up. Are you listening to me, *hijo*? This is your father speaking. You be a good boy, don't make problems for your mother."

Gail's throat tightened and ached. She pressed her hands to her face and felt tears on her fingers.

He sat up. "What is this? *¿Qué te pasa?*"

"It's real, isn't it? It hasn't been until this very moment. Please, Anthony, don't make me want this too much. What if I lose the baby?"

Murmuring softly, he picked her up and held her tightly. "No, that won't happen. Shhh. Don't cry. You'll see a doctor next week, a specialist, the best in Miami."

She wept into his shoulder. "I didn't want to be pregnant. I thought I would miscarry, but it didn't happen. Then I made an appointment for an abortion, but I couldn't do it. The baby wasn't *real*. Now it is, and you're here, and I'm afraid of losing both of you."

"*No llores. Todo va a salir bien.* Everything will be all right, I promise."

"If I lost the baby, would you still want me?"

"Oh, Gail." He made her look at him. "How can you say that? Of course I would." He kissed her tears.

Scooting away, she said, "I remember what you told me a few months ago. You wanted me, and you loved me, but you didn't need me. Is that still true?"

Anthony smiled and shook his head. "I can't believe I said such a stupid thing. *Sí, mamita, te necesito.* I need you, I love you, I want you. Now come here." He lay back on the bed and pulled her down beside him, cradling her head on his chest. She could hear his heart beating, steady and strong. He held her for a while, then said, "I bought the house on Clematis Street."

"*You* did? Then who are the Garcias?"

"Raul made them up for me. I didn't want to let the house go. We can live there after it's remodeled, but that could take a year or more. Do you mind living in an apartment until then? We should start looking for something right away."

"Wait. I didn't say I would marry you. I didn't even say I would live with you."

He shifted down in the bed until they were looking eye to eye. He smiled. "You know you will. Don't play these games with me."

She avoided his kiss. "I am totally serious. We shouldn't rush."

"Listen to what you're saying! You're afraid of losing me, but you don't want to live with me. Does that make sense? What do you want me to do, come visit the baby at your mother's house? That's crazy. Gail, *corazón*, be reasonable."

"After everything that's happened, we have to take it slowly."

"Okay." He gently kissed one corner of her mouth, then the other. "As slowly as you want." His hand moved between her thighs. "*Muy despacio.*"

She drew back and stilled his hand. "Anthony, please."

His heated breath was on her lips. "Don't run away from me anymore. Please don't."

"God, I'm so afraid of loving you." She laughed. "It was so much easier to hate you."

"Oh, yes, I know."

"Just don't lie to me. Promise."

"I promise. *Te juro.* You don't have to be afraid of anything. I love you. Let me touch you. Don't be afraid." She felt herself falling, and Anthony holding her, then filling her with himself, and her body became liquid fire, consuming all conscious thought. *"Siempre te amaré, te quiero, amor mio. . . ."*

CHAPTER
24

Leaning on the railing, wrapped in the hotel's white robe, Anthony looked out at the ocean. Immense, boundless. There were still stars, but they were beginning to fade in the east. The beach was deserted. He could see lines of beach chairs, some folded umbrellas.

The ocean was black in the distance, a vague gray motion nearer the shore. The waves were paler gray where they broke on the sand, an irregular shush and thud.

He heard a noise behind him, then Gail's sleepy voice. "Hi. What are you doing?" She had put on the other robe, but it hung open crookedly, and he could see her body. Beautiful. And her stomach was not as flat as two months ago.

He said, "The sun will be up soon. *Amanecer.* Dawn."

"You should have woken me. I like to see the sunrise."

"You didn't sleep much. I don't want you to get too tired." He held out his arm. "Come here." Yawning, she belted the robe as she crossed the terrace. He pulled her next to him.

A slight breeze came up, warm and salty. He could feel, more than see, the darkness diminishing. The foam on the sand was whiter, the railing more visible. The horizon showed clearly.

He kissed her forehead. "There's something I'd like to do right now, before it gets any later." The words seemed to snag on their own implausibility.

"Tell me," she said.

"My grandfather always gets up at dawn. He has his *café con leche*, and his *tostada*, and he sits on the balcony outside his room and watches the sun. He used to read two or three newspapers. I don't know if he still does."

"You want to go see him."

"Yes."

"Go. It's all right. I'll sleep for a little longer, then drive home."

"Will you come with me?" He could see her smile fade. What must she be thinking? The last time she'd been there, such a scene. Walking out of the Fourth of July party. Running onto the golf course, Anthony running after her, everyone talking about it.

"Ernesto wouldn't want me there. Or your grandmother—"

He put a finger on her lips. "They aren't as unforgiving as you think. I would like you to come with me, but if you can't, I understand. I won't say anything else about it. It's up to you."

He understood because it was the same for him. Worse. Going back into that house again. Claustrophobic and old, heavy with the weight of history and lost dreams. He had to go back, but she didn't. Even so . . .

She was looking at him intently, and the light had changed even more. Her eyes caught the color of the sky. "All right. I'll come with you."

Anthony called the house, and Aunt Fermina answered in the kitchen. She had just started the coffee, and she would set out extra cups for him and Gail.

By the time they arrived, the wide iron gate was open. He drove in and parked, sitting for a moment with his hands on the steering wheel, looking at the house. The fountain and cobblestone driveway. The bougainvillea climbing the twisted Moorish columns under the portico. The second-floor windows with their iron balconies and heavy curtains. Shafts of sunlight slanted across faded stucco. Someone had come out to pick up the newspapers.

Gail tugged at his arm. "Come on. They're expecting us."

As if they had never left. Kisses on the cheek from Aunt Fermina for him and for Gail. She apologized that Uncle Jose was still in bed. There were some visiting cousins asleep in the guest house. His sister came downstairs as Fermina was going on and on, and there was another round of kisses and embraces. Alicia offered them breakfast, but Anthony said he would go straight up and see Ernesto, if the old man hadn't fallen asleep again.

They spoke in Spanish, but Gail knew enough, he thought, to follow the meaning.

Anthony asked Alicia, "Does he know I'm here?"

"I told him."

"And that Gail is with me?"

"Yes, he knows."

Gail's fingers were tight around his. They went up the wide stairs, then turned at the top toward the front of the house. Sconces illuminated the long carpeted hall, and their footsteps made no sound.

Alicia tapped on the door and led them into Ernesto's room. To the left, beyond the four-poster bed, the French doors were open, and Nena saw them come in. Ernesto was in his wheelchair. He turned a page in the newspaper.

The old man was not deaf, he was making it difficult.

Nena crossed the room, holding out her arms to Gail, and Anthony could see that his grandmother had already put aside every negative thought she'd had for this *americana*. Gail smiled, kissed Nena's cheek, and tightened her grip on Anthony's hand.

"Who is there?" The voice from the terrace was strong. Ernesto customarily wore his pajamas and robe to read the paper, but today he had put on a guayabera, crisp and fresh. Mockingbirds sang raucously in the trees. A small table held the remains of breakfast.

"It's Anthony. Gail is with me. Good morning."

"Good morning."

They looked at each other across the room.

"Come here, let me see you." His glasses tilted, catching the light. "You are looking well." He smiled at Gail. "And you are as pretty as ever."

She stumbled a little over the words. "Thank you. It is a pleasure to see you."

The old man smiled at her, then said in English, "I'm happy to see you too. Alicia, tell Fermina to bring them something to eat. Digna, my love, where are two extra chairs?"

The conversation on the terrace was less strained than Anthony had feared. He told his grandparents about Angela's winning a part in *The Nutcracker* and promised good seats for opening night. He did not mention the child. Gail had asked him not to. Not yet.

The sun came through the trees in shifting splashes of light that fell on the silverware, the crystal glasses of juice, the red filling inside the flaky guava pastry. Crumbs dotted the front of Ernesto's shirt, and Nena brushed them away. The old man was breathing slowly. A pause, then a breath.

When Gail set down her cup, empty, Ernesto reached over to take her hand. "My dear. May I beg you a little favor? I need to speak alone to my grandson. A few minutes. Then you come see me again."

With a nod, Gail stood up. "Of course." Ernesto pulled her closer and kissed her cheek. "Digna? Show Gail the new orchid that bloomed yesterday in the back garden. *Gracias, mi vida.*"

When the women had left the room, Ernesto Pedrosa gestured toward the chair, and Anthony sat down again.

In elegant, formal Spanish, he said, "I am dying. Not today, not tomorrow, but soon enough. Much begins to fade away as one approaches death. Anger. Pride. I wish to tell you that I make no apologies for taking you out of Cuba, away from your father. I despise his politics, but even more, I despise his ignorance and his coarse manners. He was far below your mother, and I didn't want my flesh and blood to be like that, so I brought you here. I don't always agree with you, Anthony, but overall, you have turned out well. The second thing. I was wrong to tell Hector to get rid of that man who was threatening you. That was a mistake. He was a very bad man, but—" Ernesto shrugged, the corners of his mouth going down. "I told Hector to take care of the problem, and he did. At least you are safe, thanks to God."

"Where is Hector now?"

"Still in New York. Or perhaps Puerto Rico. I am not sure. He gave me a number to call if we need him. He knows that after I am gone, his loyalty is to you. I will leave the information in an envelope with my attorney."

"I don't want Hector around me."

"You say that now. When you need him, you will think again. Don't interrupt. My breath is short, and I am tired. Alicia told you that I would like to take a little trip."

"To Cuba. Were you serious?"

Ernesto looked at him sharply from under tangled white eyebrows. "I am not afraid, my son. I am not afraid of what might happen to me there, nor am I afraid of what people would say of me here. To hell with them. However, if they knew, I would be used for political reasons, and that would be wrong. Do you understand?"

After a moment, Anthony nodded.

"You remember your promise? You promised you would take my ashes to Cuba. Sentimental shit. You can throw my ashes out with the garbage, I don't care. I want to kneel down and pick up the earth, to smell it."

"And what if you died there?"

"You would bury me." He lifted an arm toward the door. "That flag over my desk downstairs. We'll take it with us. If I die, put me in that and roll me into the ground. Bring a little piece back for Digna. That and some of the dirt."

Anthony stared at him.

"Why are you looking at me that way? You don't have the guts to do it? Are you afraid of getting caught?"

Unable to sit still any longer, Anthony walked to the edge of the terrace. Bracing his hands on the wrought-iron railing, he looked down into the yard. A brick path wandered between the oak trees. "It isn't that. Don't tell anyone else. Gail is expecting a child."

"Is she?" The old man laughed. "Imagine that. Congratulations. She isn't far along, though, is she? We'll be back before the child is born."

"I promised I wouldn't go anywhere until afterward. That includes Cuba."

His grandfather said, "Ah. We'll wait, then. I hope I can live that long. I am going to go, whether you or someone else takes me. I want you to do it. I want you with me. You, Anthony."

The voice was suddenly thin and weak, and Anthony knew if he turned around he would see his grandfather crying. *Lie to him*, Alicia had said. *He needs hope.* Yes, a lie was sometimes the right thing to do.

Anthony said, "Arrangements would have to be made. Where and how to enter. It wouldn't be easy. You could go in on false papers, but I suppose they have your photograph."

"In every *Guardia* office."

"Naturally. You made quite a nuisance of yourself. Is it true that they sent agents to kill you?"

When Anthony finally looked around, the old man was smiling. "Oh, yes. Fidel sent his agents three times, but each time I was warned, or I saw something that alerted me, and they failed."

"And it would be a satisfaction to you, wouldn't it? Getting in and out of Cuba under their noses."

His grandfather laughed. "I would send the Beard a picture of myself on the Malecón. Well? Are we going or not? I want an answer."

Anthony said, "Yes. I'll take you."

"Good. Good." Ernesto Pedrosa pulled in a long, slow breath and leaned back in his wheelchair, touching his side.

"Are you all right? Do you want the nurse?"

"No, I want to lie down for a few minutes." He wheeled his chair around, and Anthony pushed it into the room. "Do you remember the orchids in Soroa? I would like to see that again. And the waterfall? Do you remember?"

"I remember." His grandfather slowly stood up, and taking him by an elbow, Anthony guided him to the edge of the bed, then knelt and took off his shoes. The socks were thin, outlining his big, knobby feet. Men in Cuba wore socks like this years ago. He set the shoes by the bed.

When he bent to kiss his grandfather's cheek, the old man was already snoring. Anthony pulled a blanket over him. *"Duérmete bien, viejo."*

CHAPTER

25

It was nearly sundown, and the office had been deserted for hours. Everyone liked to leave early on Friday. Passing by the workroom, Elizabeth Cresswell happened to glance inside. Fluorescent lights buzzed in the ceiling. Her son was at a computer desk tapping on a keyboard.

"Sean? Are you still here, honey?"

He kept his eyes on the screen. "I'm just finishing some stuff for the website."

"It's Friday night. Aren't you going out?"

"No. I'm kind of tired. I might watch some videos."

Liz nodded, hardly knowing what to say to this. It pleased her that Sean was working so hard, but his mood worried her. He had been home every night this week. He didn't listen to music or play his video games; he read. She wondered if he was depressed. Young men who became depressed could do terrible things to themselves. He had come home late Monday night with scrapes on his face, which he'd refused to explain. This worried her, but she was aware that most things worried her these days.

She smiled at her son. "Okay, you choose the movies. Your dad wants to order a pizza. Would you like that?"

"Fine."

"Good. I'll see you at home later." She patted the door frame, then continued walking around the corner to Dub's office. The door was open, and she could see papers scattered on his desk. He'd been staying late ever since Porter had ordered him to turn over the sales figures to the accountants by Monday. Dub didn't have the backbone to refuse, even if the request was as crazy as the man who'd made it. Porter had been complaining about Roger all week. Betrayal and sabotage. Selling boats right out the back door, pocketing the cash.

Dub reached to pick up his bourbon and saw her in the doorway. "It's my lovely helpmate. Hello, lovely helpmate." He lifted his drink in her direction.

Liz nodded at the papers. "What's that, Porter's project?"

"Yeah, what a fucking waste of time."

She came in, closing the door. "You and Porter had some kind of meeting this morning. Nobody told me about it."

Dub widened his eyes and put a fingertip to his mouth. "A secret shareholders' meeting. As you aren't a shareholder, I shouldn't talk."

"Don't play with me, dammit, I've had a horrible week."

Dub's belly stretched the front of his green knit shirt. He leaned back, sipping his drink, making her wait. "Broward Marine made an offer. Porter had the papers on his desk already. We went over them."

"That can't be true."

"Oh, come on, Lizzie. They've wanted to buy us for a long time. They make bigger boats, and they're talking about keeping the Cresswell name. I think that gives Porter a hard-on for the deal."

"Tell me he didn't sign the contract."

"Not yet. We want our tax lawyer to look at it, and we have the red tape with the corporate resolutions and so on. What do you want to do, buy Porter out? We don't have the money, Liz. We can't get a loan fast enough. Broward is hot to go. Yeah, okay, they'll probably close down the yard, but they'll take some of the guys up to Fort Lauderdale, those that want to make the move."

Liz screamed, "How can you be so damned *indifferent*? You can't let him do it."

"Porter has fifty-one percent. He can outvote me. Basically, he can do what he wants." Dub sat in his chair watching her explode. Enjoying it, the bastard.

"Stall him! All we have to do is *wait*."

"Yeah, I've been hearing that song for months now. The cancer's in remission. Porter could outlive both of us."

"Remission? Is that what he told you? No, Dub. No." Liz sat in a chair and rested her elbows on the desk, supporting her head in her hands. "Do you know what an unresectable tumor is? That means they can't operate. He has one in his liver. Chemo won't do any good. He may not last out the month."

Dub stopped swiveling his chair back and forth. "Jesus. Who the hell told you that? Claire?"

"God, no. Claire will deny he's even sick. A few weeks ago I asked the insurance agent for a favor—call Porter's doctor. He's going to die, Dub. Don't let him sign anything. Call Broward Marine and give them some excuse. Say we've got loans outstanding that don't show up on the books. Say our orders are off."

"I can't do that."

"Why not?"

"If he found out—"

"Screw if he finds out! Do it first thing Monday morning." Liz picked up a stack of computer printouts and slammed them back down on his desk. "And I want those goddamn accountants out of here. Can't you see what Anthony Quintana is after? Can't you?"

Dub stared up at her. "Yeah, Porter is nuts, and he thinks Roger was ripping him off, and he wants—"

"No! It's Claire. Claire hired him, not Porter. That crap about Roger is bullshit. Claire wants this company sold. She's the one, not Porter. She must have *known* Broward Marine was going to make an offer. Claire wants this company valued by someone from outside."

"Why?"

"The money! Are you blind? If Porter dies, the shares go to you. If he votes to abolish the corporation and sell the assets, and *then* he dies, all the money goes to Claire. Not you, Dub. Claire. All you get is your fucking forty-nine percent."

"Minus our corporate liabilities," he said, "but it's still a nice piece of change. Lizzie, I don't *want* the company. I'm sick of it, to tell you the truth."

She was speechless for a minute. "*How* can you say that? It's for your family. For Sean. The girls aren't interested, but Sean is. He'll run the company someday. Sean and his children. It's for them, Dub. Stop thinking about yourself for once."

Dub was laughing. "My God, this is too much. Too much. Elizabeth, you were born in the wrong century. You'd be a match for Lucretia Borgia any day. I'm just a way to get your son on the throne."

"*Your* son, Dub. Yours too."

"No, he's all yours. You've seen to that. He thinks I'm dog shit. Come on, Lizzie, why don't we sell the company? We'll have plenty of money. How much do we need?"

Anger boiled up inside her, making her vision blur. She clenched her fists. "The money isn't the *point*. I've been poor, and I could be again, but I absolutely refuse, I will not allow, our children to have no sense of who they are. They will have a place. They will see the name Cresswell on a boat and know it means something. Yes, Sean, because the girls don't care. You know where your son is right now? In the computer room still working. He *wants* to take part. This is his birthright, and you would let it go?"

Dub was rubbing his forehead, and his eyes were hidden behind his hand.

She stood over him. "You know I'm right. You know I am. Kill the deal, Dub."

"Okay, fuck it." He dropped his hand to the arm of the chair. "You handle it, Liz. I leave it all up to you."

"Porter doesn't trust me. You have to do it."

"How?"

"We'll figure it out over the weekend." She wanted to drop to the floor and weep with relief, but her voice was calm. "All we have to do is put him off till he's too sick to sign anything. It won't be long."

Dub came out of his chair so fast Liz had to move back. He stacked the records and correspondence and put them in a drawer. He grabbed his jacket off the end of the desk.

"Where are you going?" she asked.

"Out. Don't wait up."

"I was hoping we could all have dinner together."

"Not tonight."

"What do I tell Sean? He's expecting you. We're having pizza and watching movies. All of us."

"Baby, he won't even notice." Dub patted her cheek. "You two have a good time. Don't wait up."

After he left, Liz stood like stone in the center of the room, then went to the window, looking down into the nearly empty parking lot. A few seconds later Dub came into view and got into his shiny red Corvette. A ridiculous car for a man his age. He drove too fast in it. He sometimes drove drunk. She imagined his car going over an expressway embankment, bursting into flames. She knew that one day he would leave her. Knew it. And knew she would have to do something, but not yet. Just wait. Wait.

The guard at the entrance waved from the shack, and the chain-link gate rolled back. The Corvette braked, then turned and vanished at the corner. Still staring out the window, regathering her senses, Liz saw someone else come out from under the awning at the front of the building. A solidly built young man. His shadow stretched out in front of him. He crossed the parking lot and at the street turned left toward the river, going out of sight behind the warehouse at the edge of the property. A hundred yards farther on was the long tin roof of the boat shed. The setting sun had turned it deep orange.

Feeling a nudge of panic, Liz ran downstairs and got into her cart, still parked by the front of the building. She whirled it around and went across the lot. The guard saw her coming and opened the gate. She waved at him and went the same way Sean had gone. There were no other vehicles on the dusty dead-end street, only a couple of trucks parked off to the side. A line of palm trees marked the Cresswell docks.

Sean was walking with his head down, staring at the pavement. Liz stopped the cart just ahead of him. "Hi, honey. Where are you going?"

"Nowhere. Just taking a walk."

"Not in this neighborhood. It will be dark soon. Get in, I'll take you back."

"Jesus, Mom, I've been inside all day! I wanted some air, okay?"

"Get in. Please. I need to talk to you."

He scowled at her but did as she asked. She pulled ahead a few more yards and parked between two of the palm trees. Turning to look at him directly, she said, "Sean, something's wrong. What is it? You know you can tell me anything."

"Nothing's wrong."

"I can see it, honey. What happened? Some trouble with a girl?"

Sean stared straight ahead.

"Please let me help. Whatever's wrong, it's between you and me. You know I have never betrayed you." As she watched him, his face reddened, then twisted. His eyes squeezed shut. His chest rose and fell in great, heaving sobs, a man's sobs. "Sean? You're scaring me. What happened?"

He told her, and her breath stopped. He had gone to Jack's the night of the party, going in the back way to find Bobby Gonzalez and borrow a few dollars. He had stumbled over Roger's body, still warm. He had taken the wallet out of Roger's pocket, the Rolex off his wrist.

Sean inhaled a breath through clenched teeth. "I don't know why I took the stuff. That's all I did. I didn't kill him. I didn't. You've got to believe me."

Liz put her arm around his shoulders. "Yes, of course I believe you. Did you see anyone?" When Sean shook his head, she asked, "What did you do with his things? Where are they?"

"Somebody stole the Rolex. I went to South Beach that night, and I was wearing the watch. About five guys jumped me in an alley. They had knives and said if I didn't give up the watch, they'd kill me."

"Oh, God. That's where you got the bruises on your cheek. I was afraid of something like that." She touched his face, which he rarely permitted. Razor stubble rasped under her fingers. He was only nineteen, but too soon a man. She said quietly, "What about the wallet?"

Sean reached into his pocket and withdrew a black leather wallet that Liz had never seen before. She took it from him, opened it. Roger's face looked back at her. Blond, smiling. She felt her stomach tense. She shoved the wallet into her pocket.

"I was going to throw it in the river. I'm sorry I took it. I'm sorry. I don't know what to do." Sean wiped his nose on his shoulder, dampening his shirt. "Don't make me talk to the cops. Please, Mom. They might revoke my probation. I'd go to jail."

"I won't tell the police."

"What about Dad? Are you going to tell him?"

"No. We're going to forget this ever happened. Now listen to me. You never went to Jack's house. You never saw Roger. You must keep this the darkest, deepest secret in the world. All right? You left our house that night around eleven o'clock, just as we told the police, and you drove straight to the beach. You never went anywhere else. Do you understand? Okay, now tell me. Where did you go? After you left our house, where?"

"I went to the beach."

"That's right." She squeezed his hand. She wanted to hug him, but he would be embarrassed. "I'll take care of everything. Don't worry. Nothing will ever hurt you. I swear. Whatever happens, I'll take care of you. You believe me, don't you? Sean?"

"Yes. I believe you."

"I love you very much, Sean. No one will ever love you as much as I do." Liz turned the key in the golf cart. "Come on. I'll take you to your car. I want you to go home now."

"What are you going to do?"

She turned the wheel, and the cart hummed back toward the boat yard. "I have to finish some paperwork. Do you have any money with you?" He said he did. "Why don't you go pick out two or three movies and order a pizza? I'll pay you back when I get home. I won't be long."

Liz didn't know what she would do, but something would come to her. It had to.

She found Ted Stamos moving boxes out of his office in the assembly building and stacking them up on the mezzanine floor they called the catwalk. He would start his new job next week. Porter had arranged for Ted to have his own secretary and a company car. His office would be in the executive suite. Ted had said he wanted to set it all up tonight so it would be waiting for him when he came in on Monday.

Ted was maneuvering a hand truck under a stack of cardboard boxes that he had set by the railing on the catwalk. Each was marked STAMOS in his uneven handwriting. At a distance, he could pass for a man in his twenties. Wide shoulders and narrow hips. Brown hair sticking out over his forehead. Seen closer, his lean, sun-browned face showed the lines of thirty-seven years.

Liz pulled the wallet out of her pocket and dropped it onto the top box, flipping it open. Ted leaned over, curious, frowning at the picture on the driver's license. "What— Holy shit." Liz went into his old office and Ted followed, closing the door. The air conditioner rattled away in a corner.

As if someone might hear them in this deserted place, he whispered, "Where the hell did you get that?"

She told him.

Ted fell heavily into his desk chair, an old brown relic on casters. "Did your boy see anything?"

"No. You were damned lucky. Give me your handkerchief." Liz intended to clean off the wallet and every piece of plastic inside it. "I told Sean never to mention this again."

"What are you going to do with that?"

"Nothing. *You* take care of it. Burn it. Bury it. Throw it wherever you threw the gun. Damn you for being so stupid. Why didn't you take it? I *told* you to. His wallet, his watch. It had to look like a robbery. And why did you do it *there*?"

"Shut up about it, all right? We've been over that already. I did the best I could."

His feelings were hurt. Liz pressed her fingers against her forehead, then said, "Okay. I'm just nervous about Sean. I'm crawling out of my skin."

Ted put everything back into the wallet and slid it into the front pocket of his jeans. "I'll take care of this for you. Don't worry about it."

"Thanks. Be careful, will you?"

Liz knew already, but it hit her again with sickening force. Ted Stamos was a dunce. He had barely graduated from high school. He knew what to do with his hands and his body, and he made her feel good. She had ignored everything else. *She* was the stupid one. She wondered why Porter had given him a promotion at all. Ted didn't fit the part of executive. He was gloomy and coarse. Why had Porter done it?

Ted smiled at her. His face tended to look vacant when he smiled, as if this expression were foreign to him. Deep creases appeared on either side of his mouth. "You are so sexy."

She smiled back, then said, "I need to talk to you, Ted."

"I don't feel like talking." He ran his hands up her arms. "I want you. I must be crazy to want you so much." He pulled her shirt out of her waistband, then in another motion her bra went over her breasts, and he buried his face between them. She bit her lip not to shout at him to stop it. She had no time for this. No time.

He was sucking at her, pulling her into his mouth. Alarmed, she looked through the glass that ran on three sides of the room, from waist level up. "Ted, not here. The security guard will be by in a while."

"I don't give a damn." He unzipped his pants and forced her hand inside.

"We can't, not now."

Her skin scraped painfully on the teeth of the zipper. Ted backed her into the desk. "You haven't let me touch you since Roger. Don't you think I'm entitled?"

"Ted, stop! It's too dangerous. For God's sake, will you *think?*"

He let her go, taking some time zipping back up, letting her see what she'd missed. While she readjusted her clothing, he started tossing things from his desk into an empty box. His radio, a clock, the charger for his telephone. "I ought to put this shit in my truck and keep going. Get the hell out of here, far as I can go. Is that what you want?"

Ted Stamos needed his hand held.

"Please, Ted, don't say things like that to me." Liz felt tears scald her eyes, the result of weary frustration. "Oh, darling, please don't." She put her arms around his waist, pressing herself against him. "As soon as it's safe, we'll be together. I'm yours, you know that, but we have to be careful. Do you love me? You just said you want me, but do you love me?"

His *yes* came out on a laugh. "I love you more than any man ought to."

"I have to know I can trust you completely. That you'll do anything for me. Prove you love me, Ted. Or are you using me to get what you want out of this company?"

"No, that's crazy, Elizabeth. You know how I feel."

"I need you, Ted. Now more than ever." She brought her face close to his, whispering against his cheek, "We're in danger of losing everything. I couldn't stand that, after all we've been through. I want you so much, but we have a problem. One I never anticipated. We have to do something."

"What problem?"

"Listen to me carefully. Diane is not my daughter. It's true. Her real mother was Maggie Cresswell. She got pregnant at fifteen, and by the time Porter and Claire found out, it was too late. They told Maggie the baby was put up for adoption, but the truth is, Porter gave it to Dub and me. I didn't want to, but he promised Dub half the company, and Dub said yes. Nobody knew the truth. But Diane has been asking questions lately. She said, 'Why do I look like Aunt Claire and not like you?' My heart stopped! She's going to find out. She's Porter's only heir. Porter will be dead soon, and if she makes a claim, she'll get all his shares in the company. Fifty-one percent. She'll sell it to Broward Marine. They've made Porter an offer already! What would happen to us? Everything we've worked for would be gone. We have to do something about Diane."

Ted stared at her.

"We *have* to do it, Ted. There's no other way. It can be an accident. A fall. She could slip off the seawall. She doesn't swim. Don't look at me like that. She isn't my daughter! She hates me. She said so in those very words. She calls me horrible things. Porter made us take her. I am so afraid of what she'll do when she finds out. And she will. Oh, she will, Ted, and then we are lost."

As if in pain, Ted went over to the desk and sat heavily on the edge of it. "Maggie had a baby?"

"Yes. Diane is hers."

Ted laughed. He tried to hold it back, but he exploded in laughter, falling into his chair, laughing until Liz wanted to hit him. "Stop it! What is the matter with you?"

"I knew Maggie when we were teenagers. I went over there to do some carpentry work, and we had sex in the guest room over the garage. Diane could be my kid."

"That's impossible. She isn't yours."

"She might be. I could take a DNA test. Jesus Christ. If she was my daughter . . . I'd have to help her run the company, wouldn't I?" He started laughing again. "I'd have more than you. Wouldn't that be a kick in the ass?"

"Shut up, Ted. She's not yours. She's Porter's."

His grin disappeared, and he stared up at her. "Porter's? What do you mean?"

"What do you think I mean?"

"That's sick."

"I know it's true because I know Porter. I know what he is. I thought something funny was going on when I first met him, when Maggie was only eleven. I know because Roger told me when he was a kid that his father liked to read bedtime stories to Maggie with the door shut. I could see the way he looked at her, the way he touched her. I know because my father did the same thing to me!" Liz was unable to repress a shudder of disgust. "She isn't like other people. She shouldn't have been born."

Ted got out of his chair. His face had flushed red. "I'm not going to murder a twenty-year-old girl. Are you crazy?"

"We have no choice. The minute Diane suspects she's Maggie's daughter, we'll lose everything!" Sensing the conversation spinning out of control, Liz put her hands on Ted's shoulders. "I couldn't bear being without you. You feel the same way about me, don't you? Say you love me, Ted. Say it."

"Oh, Jesus." He pushed her hands away. "I'm getting out of here."

"Where are you going?"

"I don't know. I've got to think."

"You can't leave. Ted, I love you."

"Let go of me." He walked out the door, arm still raised as if warding her off.

"What do you want? You can have anything." Running onto the catwalk, Liz stopped him with arms around his waist. She pressed her cheek against his back. "Don't leave me, Ted. Be with me. You know I love you. I need you so much."

"What you want me to do . . . it's too much. Roger was one thing—he deserved it. But this. Oh, Jesus. You're sick. You're one sick bitch."

What happened next unfolded clearly and slowly, and Liz could see her mind processing the facts like watching a mathematical solution worked out on a computer screen. Her body responded and all she could do was watch it happen.

It didn't take much. A quick jerking motion toward the edge of the catwalk, hands between the shoulder blades, a strong push.

Ted hit the railing hard at hip level, and the momentum was enough to send his torso over the edge and pick up his feet. He balanced, arms flailing. Liz could have caught the fabric of his shirt. She knew there was time, a split second or so, and her hand was poised to reach for him. And then the railing gave way. With a loud snap the horizontal bar broke from one post and swung from the other. Ted dropped, and the space in front of her was empty.

There was a crashing of wood and the deeper thud of a body.

Twisted metal hung from the railing post. Moving away from the gap, Liz steadied herself on the unbroken portion of the railing and peered over the edge. Ted had landed in a boat hull thirty feet below her, facedown. She scanned the assembly floor, the quiet lines of boats. The big doors at either end had been rolled shut, and the far corners of the building were dark. The windows under the roof were pale gray, and long fluorescent tubes in wire cages pressed their weak light into the enormous space. No one was running toward the noise. There were no footsteps, no demands to know what had happened. The security guard would come by, but he wouldn't be able to see into the hull. Unless someone noticed the broken railing, Ted Stamos wouldn't be found until Monday morning, when the men came to lay in the next layer of fiberglass.

With the toe of her sneaker Liz tipped over a box as if Ted might have stumbled over the contents. Things slid to the floor—a stapler, a desk diary. A black-and-white photograph of his father standing in front of a boat. Pens, pencils, a jar of paper clips.

She heard a moan and looked over the side again. Ted's hand lifted from the boat hull. He was alive. She turned and ran down the stairs, coming out on the ground floor.

The mold was supported by a scaffolding of lumber three feet above her head. There was a ladder allowing access for the workers, and Liz climbed it. The hull was made of overlapping layers of fiberglass, an inch thick at the bottom, less at the top. A long box-shaped form gave strength to the keel, and heavy ribs supported the sides. Ted lay facedown across one of them in the bow of the boat. His knee had broken, and his leg was bent at an odd angle. His face was toward her, cheek pressed against the hull. Blood oozed from his mouth and darkened his teeth. He struggled to raise his forearm, and the skin made a sticky popping sound as it pulled free from the resin.

"Eliz—Elizabeth. Please. Help. I can't . . . move." He hit the boat hull with his open palm. "Elizabeth!"

The men had just laid down a new layer of glass, and the resin was drying. Brownish red, sticky, glistening like an open wound. Within an hour or so it would be completely set. They would have to tear Ted loose to get him out of there. The thought made fire leap across her skin.

"Help me. Help. Please."

Liz went down the ladder and sat huddled in a ball on the concrete floor. She pressed her hands over her ears. If he would only shut up. The guard would be along soon, and Ted would tell. He would tell everything. His hand was beating slowly on the hull.

Thud. Thud. She got up and ran from one place to another, look-ing for a bar, a rod, a two-by-four. Something heavy. They would say his head cracked on the gunwale.

"Be quiet. Be quiet, damn you."

The moans diminished in volume as she ran farther down the line of boats. The carpenters had been working in one of them. She opened a tool chest and found a twenty-ounce claw hammer. She tested its weight, her fingers tight on the rubber grip. She thought she could reach him. If she leaned down, she could reach him. How many blows would it take? But it would be obvious. A hammer. And what if she dropped it? Her fingerprints—

"Somebody! Somebody, help. Please."

His voice was getting stronger, and it echoed on the high walls.

Liz clenched her teeth. "Shut *up*." Quickly she put the hammer back and closed the drawer. She had seen the resin tanks near the hull where Ted lay. The stainless steel tanks were on wheels, and a hose ran from each one to a resin gun. There was a rusty fifty-five-gallon drum used for trash, and in it she found some old paint-brushes and rollers. She pulled out a brush. The resin had hardened on the handle, but the bristles had some play in them. She flipped a switch on the tank. The compressor motor came on, and Liz snapped it off after a few seconds. She squeezed the resin gun. The liquid came out, the color of honey. She wet the brush with it, hoping there would be enough.

Sick with fear that someone would see her, she climbed the lad-der again. Ted was four feet below. His eye followed her move-ments, focusing on the brush coming closer. She leaned over as far as she could reach.

"Don't. No. Elizabeth. God's sake—"

She touched the brush to his nose, dabbing the resin into his nostrils. Not too much. They would say it happened that way when he fell into the hull. Then she placed the brush firmly against his mouth. His eye rolled, and she looked away. She could feel him trying to push the brush away with his tongue and lips, and she pressed it tighter. *Mmmpphhh. Mmmfff.* His palm hit the hull. *Thud, thud . . . thud. Thud.* Each time he lifted his arm she heard the popping noises of drying resin.

She was leaning over the gunwale, and she felt the vibrations in her hipbones. *Thud . . . thud.* He gasped in a breath, and she adjusted the brush, pressing harder. Her arm shook from the strain. She thought about the extra shirts in the office storeroom. She would have to put one of those on and throw away this one.

"Oh, no!"

Roger's wallet was still in the front pocket of Ted's jeans. They would find it. Liz wondered about climbing in to get it, then realized what they would think. They would think what was already true—Ted had killed him.

She looked around the assembly building again. Still no one. The thudding had stopped. Ted was quiet now, but Liz counted off another full minute on her watch. Finally she looked down at his face. His eye stared at the hull. She slowly pulled the brush away. Waited. Nothing.

As she went down the ladder she wiped off her fingerprints with the hem of her shirt, which was already ruined. Then the handle of the brush. The bristles touched her shirt, leaving a red smear of blood on the white fabric. She wrapped the brush in a piece of newspaper and tucked it under her arm.

Unseen, Liz ran across the darkening boat yard to the office building, punching in her access code at the back door. The halls were eerily quiet. She found the box of company shirts and put one on in the ladies' room, then washed her hands, using nail polish remover to clean off the resin. She saw herself in the mirror, astonished that she recognized her own face. She stashed the old shirt and the brush in her tote bag and went out the front entrance to her car. She smiled and waved at the security guard on the way through the gate.

It was late, and Liz felt the pressure of time, but she made a detour off the expressway. Behind a Cuban shopping center south of the airport she found a green dumpster, opened the lid, and tossed her shirt and the now stiffened brush inside.

Once that was done, she used her cell phone to check in with Sean. On my way, she cheerfully told him. They chatted for a couple of minutes about what movies he'd picked up, and she told him to keep the pizza warm.

CHAPTER

26

The weekend weather was typical for late summer in Miami: temperatures in the mid-nineties, humidity over eighty percent. Conditions like these accelerated the decomposition of flesh, and so security at the boat yard noticed the smell before they finally located the body around eight o'clock Sunday morning.

The matter might have remained a routine Miami P.D. accident investigation, except that when the victim was finally cut out of his clothes and freed from the fiberglass, a wallet was found in the front pocket of his jeans. The M.E. opened it and saw the face of a young blond man, Roger C. Cresswell, age thirty-two. Recognizing the name from a county case, he put in a call to Frank Britton of Miami-Dade Homicide.

At 1:45 Anthony Quintana turned his car onto the short dead-end street leading to Cresswell Yachts. He and Gail Connor were planning to board the *Lady Claire* with family and friends of the late Roger Cresswell, whose ashes would be scattered at sea. Roger's mother had instructed them to park close to the dock, but Gail pointed out the activity going on in the yard. Several city and county units were clustered around the open end of the main assembly building.

Anthony parked in the lot and they got out. Yellow tape strung between sawhorses barred entry through the wide door. As they walked closer, Anthony spotted Frank Britton talking to a crime-scene tech with a camera. Britton finished his conversation and came over. Sweat dampened his blue sports shirt, and his collar was open.

"Well, Tony Quintana, don't you turn up everywhere," he said. Light slid over the lenses of his sunglasses as he turned to Gail. "Hello again, Ms. Connor. Y'all just happened to be driving by?"

Anthony said, "We're meeting the Cresswells at the dock. They're taking Roger's ashes out to sea in the family boat. What's going on, Frank?"

"Oh, yeah, I heard about the boat trip. What happened is, one of the construction supervisors fell and killed himself. You want to guess what we found in his pocket? Roger Cresswell's wallet."

"*Ay, mi Diós.* Which supervisor?"

"Ted Stamos. His office overlooked the floor, and he took a dive over the railing. We think it had to be Friday because he landed in one of the molds where they'd just laid down some fiberglass. He was stuck like a fly on flypaper. Security had to call the owners for permission to saw him out. They got here a little while ago with their families. We took some statements and sent them over to the boat. They're pretty shaken up. Stamos worked here all his life. So did his father."

Anthony exchanged a glance with Gail, hoping she read the warning in his eyes not to say too much. "Do you think he shot Roger Cresswell?"

"Damned if I know." Hands on hips, Britton swung around to look into the building. "A few weeks ago we interviewed Stamos along with everybody else connected to Roger, and he said he was with Duncan Cresswell and a dozen other guys at a strip club from nine-fifteen till one o'clock a.m. Half an hour ago Duncan says, 'You know, Detective, I'm just not sure Ted *was* there the whole time. I'd been drinking. I don't remember.' And I go, 'Well, did Ted have any problems with Roger?' 'Oh, yeah, all *kinds* of problems.' 'Well, why the fuck—' Excuse me, Ms. Connor. 'Why didn't you tell me that before?' 'You didn't ask, Detective.' Jesus. So now I've got a new suspect we had to peel off a boat hull. That throws all my pet theories into the can. A very confusing situation."

Anthony gazed into the assembly building. Lines of sleek white motor yachts extended to the other end of the long, vaulted space. Ted Stamos lay unattended fifty yards away under a yellow plastic sheet. Confusing indeed. If Sean Cresswell had taken the wallet, then how in the name of God had it wound up in Ted Stamos's pocket? Anthony could not raise this question without implicating Bobby Gonzalez in an assault.

He checked his watch. They had a little time. "Could you could show me Stamos's body?"

Britton hesitated, then nodded. "Sure. I'll warn you, it's not pretty."

To Gail, Anthony said, "Do you want to come with us?"

Her lips tightened as she looked at him—she resented his suggestion that it might be too much for her. Then her eyes shifted to the body, and she shook her head. "No, I'll wait here. Don't be long. It's almost two o'clock."

Britton lifted the crime-scene tape, and Anthony bent to go under. The half dozen officers on the scene watched them walk deeper into the building. Fans stirred the air, but not enough to waft away the sticky-sweet aroma of rotting meat. Anthony asked if they had found the pistol used to kill Roger Cresswell.

"Not in Stamos's office, and not at his apartment. I sent a detective over to check. He didn't find the Rolex either, but Stamos could have pawned it."

Anthony knew that if Sean Cresswell had told Bobby the truth, the Rolex had vanished under a table at Club Apocalypse the night of Roger's murder.

They passed three unfinished boats to get to the one where Ted Stamos had landed. Lumber from the scaffolding had been pulled out of the way. The front end of the hull lay in pieces on the floor, and one section about six feet in length had been propped up against the next boat in line. Tattered remnants of blue jeans and a plaid shirt made the twisted outline of a man.

Britton pulled back the tarpaulin. Stamos lay face up on the bare concrete. Bits of fabric still adhered to his chest and thighs.

The decaying skin had turned several shades darker, and chunks of it were missing. One leg bent sideways at the knee. A piece of fiberglass was still attached to his hair and cheek, and the one eye in view was a narrow slit. His tongue had turned purplish brown, protruding through broken teeth.

Dropping his tinted clip-ons into his pocket, Britton said that the medical examiner had just left, and that the van would arrive shortly for the body. "Stamos fell from right up there, where you see the boxes. He was working late, moving some stuff out of his office."

There was a gap in the railing above them. The horizontal bar had come loose. Anthony remembered leaning on it to watch the activity on the floor. Stamos had warned him that the railing was rusty, and that he should stay back. Why had Stamos disregarded his own advice?

Holding his breath, he circled, taking a closer look at Ted Stamos's head and chest. There were no suspicious holes, no dents in his skull, no blood matted in his short brown hair.

"I didn't see anything, either," Britton said, "but the autopsy is this afternoon, and the M.E. will let me know."

Anthony looked at him. "You aren't calling this an accident."

"I'm not calling it anything yet."

"Who was here after hours besides Stamos?"

"Nobody in this building. Over at the office, Duncan Cresswell and his wife and their son were working late. Duncan left about six-thirty, Elizabeth around seven-fifteen, and the kid sometime in between. We don't know when Stamos went over. No idea."

"Have you interviewed them yet?"

"They have a boat ride to go on. I said I'd be in touch."

Anthony stepped back from the body, but the smell was pervasive. "Did you mention to any of the Cresswells that Bobby Gonzalez had cash from Roger's wallet?"

"No, I didn't. You asked me as a favor not to. Remember that? You said to keep it quiet and you'd call me with information, and I ain't heard squat from you." Britton stood with his feet apart and his fists on his hips. "If you know something, I want to hear it."

Anthony let a shrug convey his regret. "I'll call you this week."

Britton was unhappy. "Far as I'm concerned, finding Roger Cresswell's wallet on Ted Stamos doesn't prove Stamos killed him. You still haven't explained where Bobby Gonzalez was between eleven and midnight, and you haven't told me how he got the cash. In fact, I want to know where he was on Friday night, when Stamos took a swan dive off the edge."

"I can't talk to you yet, Frank, but I will."

"Tomorrow."

Leaving Frank Britton to cover the body, Anthony turned and crossed the assembly floor. Gail was a slender silhouette at the end of the building, a long-legged woman in a narrow dress above her knees. Anthony ducked under the crime-scene tape and walked into the sunlight, pulling in a lungful of fresh air.

He felt a hand on his shoulder. "Are you okay? How was it?"

"Not too bad."

"I bet." She had worn pale blue today. Her skin was smooth and fresh, and the wind played with her hair. She pushed it behind one ear. "What did you say to Frank Britton?"

"As little as possible. Come on, let's sit in the car." As they walked, Anthony explained the broken railing to Gail and the un-likelihood that Ted Stamos had fallen through it on his own.

Her mouth opened, a smile of comprehension. "Someone pushed him. That's what you're saying. Ted Stamos didn't kill Roger on his own, he did it for somebody else. And this same person made sure the wallet was in Ted Stamos's pocket first so the police would blame him for Roger's death. Bobby's in the clear."

"No. Frank still wants to know why Bobby had cash from Roger's wallet. He says Bobby could have been working with Sta-mos. I don't think Frank believes that, but he wants information. I said I'd call him tomorrow. I hope we have a name by then. Otherwise, I don't have much to give him."

Anthony opened the passenger door for Gail, who stood wait-ing until he had the engine going and the air conditioning blowing cold. She got in and pulled the door closed with a solid *thunk*. "Do we reconsider Sean?"

"Possibly. He was here late on Friday night, and so were his parents. They all left separately at different times. Put on your seat belt, sweetheart."

"We're only going half a block."

"Yes, but it makes me worry."

"Would you please stop being so overprotective? And another thing. The only reason I didn't want to look at Ted Stamos's body was because I thought I might throw up. Funny smells make me sick. It wasn't because I was afraid to."

"Gail, please. No arguments. Put on your seat belt."

"Fine."

He heard a satisfying metallic click and leaned over to kiss her. "I don't want anything to happen to you." Her mouth was sweet, and it melted under the soft pressure of his lips.

She pulled back a little, smiling. "We have some bad habits to break, don't we?"

"No. Well, a few. *Te quiero.*"

"I love you too. Let's go, or they'll leave without us."

CHAPTER
27

Sorry for making a fuss over a seat belt, Gail reached out to put the back of her fingers on Anthony's cheek, a mute apology. He glanced at her, shook his head, then turned to put a quick kiss on her fingers.

Forgiven.

This would not be easy, reversing course. It would require throwing aside all the resentment and fear she had built up in two months. Everything was new again. New and frightening.

Two days had passed since they had been together. Gail had made excuses when he asked to see her for lunch. She had cut their phone conversations short. *Please, Anthony. I need time. We both do.* Time to think, to recover her balance. Gail had said little to her mother, and nothing at all to Karen. Not yet. She was too afraid that something would go wrong.

She had driven to his office today, leaving her car there, letting him drive. Still in the parking garage, nearly deserted on a Sunday, they had fallen into a kiss so thorough and deep it had set them afire. The engine had been going, and cool air blew through the vents. He had slid his hands under her dress. She had heard her own soft moans. Then the hum of the electric seat going back, rapid breathing, and the click of his belt buckle, coming undone. Anyone could have walked by. No one did.

Gail wondered if there was a way to love rationally, not risking so much. How easy it had been with Dave. Easy to love, easy to walk away. Loving Anthony was to throw herself off the edge of a precipice.

She blinked, roused from these thoughts, when the car nosed up to a chain-link fence at the end of the street and the engine went off. A sign on the side of the one-story white concrete block building announced CRESSWELL YACHTS, INC. There were already several other cars in the parking spaces, and a security guard in the shade of a golf umbrella.

They got out and walked around the building.

This was not a marina but a working dock made of concrete and creosoted pilings. Two Cresswell boats were in slips, ready to be taken to customers, Gail assumed. The *Lady Claire*, with its gleaming white sides and curves of dark glass, waited at the dock. Gail guessed her length at nearly a hundred feet, with one open aft deck and a smaller one below it. A narrow walkway went from the stern to the pilothouse. The captain would navigate from there or from the open fly bridge on the top level. A line of portholes indicated staterooms below. Engines rumbled, and the smell of diesel exhaust hung in the air.

Anthony stopped walking and pointed out people Gail had heard of but had never seen. Duncan Cresswell was the heavyset man standing on the aft deck with a drink in his hand. His wife, Elizabeth, was the brunette in the green dress who had just come out of the salon. On the flybridge at the top of the boat, a dark-haired young man sat with his sneakers propped on the helm. He tipped back a long-neck beer.

"Is that Sean?" Gail asked.

Anthony said that it was.

For a while they silently gazed at the boat and the people moving about, some on deck, others seen dimly as shadows through the dark glass of the salon and pilothouse.

Anthony again asked the question that most puzzled both of them. "If Sean took Roger's wallet, how did it get into Ted Stamos's pocket?"

Gail shook her head. "I can't think why Sean would give it to him. Unless Sean and Ted were friends, and Sean asked him for help."

"And then killed him?"

"Well, what if Sean had the wallet in his room and his parents found it? They took it and planted it on Ted Stamos."

"They?"

"All right, one of them. Elizabeth or Duncan."

"Stamos fell facedown, so if the wallet was planted, it was done before, not after he fell."

"Or was pushed."

"Exactly."

"Liz did it," Gail said. "She and Ted Stamos were lovers. She used him to kill Roger, then framed him with the wallet."

"Possible, but it's too convenient. How could she make sure the wallet was in his pocket, then make him stand close enough to the railing so she could push him over? It makes more sense that someone knocked him out, planted the wallet, then lifted him over the railing, which broke under his weight. That isn't something a woman could easily do."

Gail followed Anthony's eyes to the upper deck, where Duncan Cresswell was in a conversation with another middle-aged man. They heard his booming laugh. He slapped the other man on the back. If not Liz, then Dub. The list had dwindled to two. Gail wondered if they had missed someone. All their assumptions could be wrong.

Anthony was giving her reasons to suspect Duncan Cresswell. "Roger knew that Dub was embezzling. That's a motive for murder. We know that Ted Stamos acted as a bodyguard when Dub took customers out to nightclubs. Let's assume that Dub paid Ted to get rid of Roger, and Ted's own hatred of Roger made it easy for him to accept. You remember what Bobby told us. Dub owns a .22 pistol. He could have let Ted use it. When Ted had done his job, he was more of a risk than an asset." Anthony looked at Gail. "What do you think?"

"Oh, let's just go ask him." Gail kept her voice low, although there was no chance anyone would hear them. The engines on the boat were rumbling steadily. "This is hopeless. What are we doing here? I feel like an intruder."

"No, no. We're friends of Claire's. She invited us." Anthony took Gail's hand. "We're simply going to observe. I'm counting on your intuition."

"Mine?"

"You are the one who guessed that Margaret Cresswell was Diane's mother, no? Come on."

A set of stairs had been placed at the open gate in the side of the boat. Beyond was a door, and Claire Cresswell appeared in it. "Hello! I was just in the salon and saw you through the window. Welcome."

Letting Gail go first, Anthony kept a firm grip on her arm. Claire waited on the narrow, teak-finished walkway. Gold buttons and loops of braid relieved the stark white of her linen jacket. The boat would be taking her son's ashes to sea, but Claire had requested that no one wear black.

When Gail and Anthony had both stepped aboard, she drew them closer. "Have you heard the news?" Her face was flushed with excitement. "They know who killed Roger—one of our own employees."

Before she could go on, Anthony told her that they had stopped by the boat yard on the way and Frank Britton had given them the details.

"I still can't believe it," Claire said. "Ted has been with us all his life! We knew his father, Henry, so well. How could he have murdered my son after all we did for him? You see? I told you it couldn't have been one of us. Nate's all right now, isn't he? And Bobby? They can put it all behind them. I wish I could. I just want to go *do* this and come back, get it over and done with." Claire leaned past them to look up and down the dock. "I think we have everyone now. I'll go and tell Porter. He's playing captain today, so hang onto your life vests. There's some food in the salon and plenty to drink. Look at the boat if you wish, then come and meet everyone."

Claire went through a polished teak door, which she left open for them. Cool air drifted through it.

Gail and Anthony remained behind for a while watching the departure. A man in a shirt with a Cresswell emblem stood at the bow to catch the rope tossed by another man on the dock. Someone else hauled in the lines from the stern. The engines throbbed, and the long bow of the boat swung away from the dock, propelled by a bow thruster. The *Lady Claire* glided smoothly into the river, which would carry them past the skyscrapers downtown and into Biscayne Bay. This part of the river was lined with freighters and marine-repair facilities. There was no beauty to this river. Trash, tattered sea grass, and rainbows of oil floated in the water. Rusting Haitian or Panamanian freighters were tied along the opposite side of the narrow river, and dark, bare-chested men worked on their decks.

A drawbridge went up as the *Lady Claire* approached. They had both worn cool, light clothing, but the wind was sticky and hot, and after a few more minutes of this, Gail suggested they go inside. Anthony held the door, then shut it behind them.

The interior was paneled and carpeted, and frosted glass sconces lit their way. The main salon was aft, the pilothouse forward. "Let's see what's down here," Anthony said. "Be careful on the stairs." They had to move aside for some people coming up, doing the same thing they were, exploring the Cresswells' yacht. On the lower level they went through the kitchen—the *galley*, Gail reminded Anthony. It sparkled with brushed steel and ceramic tile, and Gail groaned with envy. Farther aft they walked out onto a small deck with bench seats and a table affixed to the floor. The city went in reverse motion, unfolding backward as they passed out of the river and into the bay. The engines changed pitch, and the boat picked up speed. Fat, graying clouds were piling up overhead, and the humidity was too much to bear.

They went forward, discovering the master stateroom with its mahogany cabinetry and private bath tiled in marble. There were three smaller rooms, then the forward stairs that led to the pilothouse, finished in teak, with more dials, lights, and screens than Gail thought remotely necessary. She could see through the wraparound windows that they were already parallel with the southern tip of Key Biscayne. The bow dipped slightly, and spray shot up on either side. Gail steadied herself on Anthony's shoulder.

Porter Cresswell sat at the wheel in one of two high captain's chairs bolted to the deck. He wore white pants and a blue blazer with gold buttons. Cigarette smoke curled from an ashtray fastened to the helm.

Anthony introduced Gail, and Porter took her hand. His grip showed some strength, but his shoulders were curved, and his skin was cool and slack. Gail saw at once that he was ill. His color was wrong, and his belly was distended. This was the man who had banished his daughter to another state for getting pregnant. Gail could not put out of her mind what other damage he might have done.

She tugged out of his handshake. "I'm so sorry about the loss of your son."

"Thank you." His smile was slow, lifting one side of his mouth, exposing smoker-yellow teeth. A deep cleft divided his square chin. Hooded eyes lingered on Gail's face, then shifted to Anthony. "Claire says you heard about Stamos. That was a real shocker. I'm glad he's dead. Saves the state the trouble of putting him on trial."

Gail remembered what Roger's widow had said about her father-in-law. How he had hated his own son. How he had yelled at him, "I could kill you."

She asked, "Do you have any idea why Ted Stamos did it? Why he killed Roger?"

Anthony glanced at her.

Porter Cresswell's ropy hands turned the wheel a fraction. "Roger was trying to take over the company, and Ted wouldn't have it. That's what I think." He reached for his cigarette, tapped off the ashes, but didn't smoke it.

A few drops of rain slid across the glass. The horizon seemed to rise and fall, and Gail stood with her feet farther apart and held onto Anthony's arm.

He asked, "How far are we going?"

Porter glanced at the instruments. "We'll stop about ten miles south of Elliott Key. Roger liked fishing down that way. He won a trophy when he was thirteen, a ninety-two-pound swordfish. I thought he'd like to go back there."

Gail exchanged a look with Anthony, who made an almost imperceptible shrug. It had been a strange remark, but it didn't mean Porter was crazy.

Porter glanced around when two men in their early thirties maneuvered through—Roger's friends, Gail thought. He nodded and smiled, accepting their condolences on his son and their compliments on his boat. Of the son and the boat, she had no doubt which he valued more highly.

The boat shifted, and Gail reached out for the back of the other chair, aware that more than the ocean had unsettled her.

Porter laughed at the expression on her face. "Don't worry, honey. This boat could ride out a hurricane. The pastor will say a few words, we'll give Roger back to his maker, and then we'll head home. You don't get seasick, do you?" He laughed again. "Miami girl like you? Tell Claire I said to get you some Dramamine."

Gail forced herself to smile. "Thanks."

"Porter!" Duncan Cresswell came through the door from the salon. He stopped dead, looking at Anthony. His eyes seemed too small for his heavy face. "What are you doing here, Quintana?"

"He's here because Claire invited him, and he's brought his lovely lady friend along," Porter said.

Turning his back on them, Dub Cresswell stood beside Porter's chair. "Have you looked behind us? It's raining like hell, and it's coming this way."

"I've got radar. Of course I know. We'll run right out from under it."

"So you say. Let's stop here and get it done with. You can't scatter ashes in a storm."

"It's not going to storm."

"We ought to stop here, Porter."

"Who's running this goddamn ship? You or me? I'll tell you when we're stopping."

Fury reddened his brother's cheeks. He stepped back, fists clenching. With a quick heated glance at Gail and Anthony, he left the pilothouse.

Porter lifted his cigarette from the ashtray, rolling it between his fingers. He saw Gail watching him and smiled at her. "Claire won't let me smoke anymore either. Can't smoke, can't drink. I can still appreciate a pretty woman. If this guy can't do it for you, come see me." He laughed. "Quintana, can't you take a joke?"

Anthony's hand clamped onto Gail's elbow, and he turned her toward the door on the port side. He closed it firmly behind them, and they walked aft to a point beyond view of the pilothouse windows.

Gail made a theatrical shudder. "What a reptile." She kissed Anthony on his jaw, which still was knotted. "Don't worry. I like you better."

He let out a breath. "Porter wasn't as crazy as that when I first met him, I assure you."

The boat plowed steadily through the water. The wind was blowing from the other direction, and the rain fell only in intermittent drops.

Gail took her lipstick and compact out of her small shoulder bag. "Anthony, what if we're wrong? Maybe Dub and Liz had nothing to do with Roger's death. What if it's Porter?" She put on her lipstick, then looked at Anthony. "Well?"

"No. Porter wouldn't have the strength to throw Ted Stamos off the catwalk, and he wasn't there late on Friday."

"What if Ted just *fell*, and we're following a dead end thinking that someone pushed him?"

"Anything is possible," Anthony said glumly. "It is possible that whoever did this is going to get away with it. We have no proof of anything." He put an arm around her. "Why don't we go have a drink and forget about it? No. I'll have a drink, you can have a club soda. No alcohol for you, *mamita*."

Gail leaned against him. "Did I apologize yet for avoiding you the last two days?"

"Is that what you were doing? I thought you had changed your mind."

"No. I wouldn't do that. I can't." She turned her head to kiss him, savoring the moist warmth of his mouth, the adjacent roughness of beard under his skin. And then he was embracing her with a ferocity that took her breath.

He held her face and rested his forehead on hers. "How long do you have to *think* before you stop being so afraid?"

"When you kiss me, I can't think of anything."

"Good. Then you should let me do it more often."

The boat plunged again into a wave, and water sprayed into the air. Gail shrieked a laugh. There was salt on her lips.

"Let's go inside," Anthony said. Walking single file, they made their way toward the rear deck. Coming around the corner, they felt the force of the wind. Afternoon clouds, born over the Everglades, were piling into gray masses. A few of the guests had come outside to watch the slow-motion thunder heads in the distance and the silent flashes of lightning. The flag snapped and fluttered on the fly bridge.

Gail noticed Jack Pascoe in one of the chairs, sitting with his ragged leather deck shoes crossed on the stern. He held his fishing hat down with one hand so it wouldn't fly off his head.

Anthony reached for the salon door, but Gail hesitated. "Go ahead. I want to talk to Jack Pascoe."

"Why?"

"Just a couple of questions. I'll be there in a minute."

Anthony acquiesced with a shrug, and Gail dragged another chair across the deck to sit beside Pascoe.

His eyes turned toward her. "It's Ms. Connor. Did you bring your spy camera today?"

"No, I did not. Anthony and I are here as friends of the family."

"Oh? Did Claire let you onboard?"

Gail's temper flared. "After what you did with that portrait, sending it back to Porter and Claire after they gave it away, I'm surprised she let *you* onboard."

Jack Pascoe smoothed his mustache down, pressing outward with thumb and forefinger. "So am I. I showed up and apologized, and she forgave me. Porter is another matter. That's why I'm out here, to avoid running into him. He said he would throw me overboard. I hope he was kidding."

"I have a question."

"What a surprise."

Gail pressed her lips together on a quick retort, then said, "You've heard about Ted Stamos."

"Who hasn't? It's all they're talking about in there."

"The police suspect that Ted Stamos shot Roger, but until they're sure, they could come back to Bobby Gonzalez. Otherwise, I could just let it go. When I came to your house that day, I thought that Roger's death and Maggie's suicide might have been connected somehow. I haven't completely discarded that idea."

Pascoe gazed past her at the city on the horizon. The wind was strong enough to move the curled ends of his mustache.

Gail leaned close, not wanting to be overheard by anyone else on deck. "Shortly after Porter became sick, he gave Roger ten percent of the company. Why would he do that? From what I know of Porter, he hates to give up control. I was thinking, What if Roger had been able to pressure his father somehow? What could he have bargained for a share of the company? What might have gotten him killed if he'd threatened to reveal it?"

Pascoe's eyes shifted to focus on Gail.

She said, "I know who Diane's mother is. Don't worry, I'm not planning to tell her or anyone else. I won't have to. I think one day she'll figure it out herself. But that's only half the picture. I think you know who her father is. Or was. I think Maggie told you everything because you were the only person she ever really trusted."

"Ms. Connor." Pascoe tugged on one end of his mustache. "Some things in the world are not meant to be known, and if they are known, they are best forgotten." He returned to gazing at the black horizon, and Gail knew she would get nothing more from him.

She stood up, holding onto the back of the chair. The deck was moving, and she walked with her arms outstretched toward the salon door. She had begun to despair of ever finding the truth. The facts seemed to swirl, unsettled and elusive.

The door to the salon was of tinted glass, like the windows on three sides. She pushed it open, and the low buzz of conversation entered her ears. There were thirty or more people, seated on upholstered chairs and sofas. Anyone standing had braced himself against something steady. The carpet was thick, and fresh flowers adorned the side tables. Indirect lighting glowed on a gold-toned ceiling, and spotlights picked out one of Margaret Cresswell's originals, this one in shades of blue. Ice cubes clinked in a pitcher on the bar, and the water level shifted. Gail glanced around to find Anthony. He was talking to Claire Cresswell. Gail might have joined them if she hadn't seen Diane. She sat curled up in the corner of a sofa, cheek in her palm, watching the ocean. Her long blond hair fell over her shoulders. She looked around and smiled when Gail bent down to give her a hug.

"It's good to see you," Gail said. "I thought you weren't coming."

Diane scooted over so Gail could sit down, then tugged her denim skirt back into place. "Aunt Claire asked me to come. Family togetherness and all that. I saw you arrive with Angela's father. Are you back together again? Angela said you were."

Wondering how much Angela had told her, Gail said, "We're taking it slowly."

"I hope it works out for you." Diane ducked her head closer to Gail's. I have some news. My mother said I could have the portrait."

"Wonderful."

"Well, it was Aunt Claire's idea. My mother wouldn't be so generous. Aunt Claire promised to give her something else to replace it, one of more value, so really, Mother should be happy."

Gail let her eyes drift over the crowd. She had only glimpsed Elizabeth Cresswell at a distance when Anthony had pointed her out, but she had no trouble finding her. Dark, shoulder-length hair framed her face, and her cheekbones were made more prominent by accents of brick-red blush. The hem of a narrow green dress came several inches above her knees. Her legs were worth showing off.

She stood beside a chair in which sprawled her son, Sean. As she talked to one of her friends, she put a hand on Sean's shoulder and played with the collar of his shirt. Sean looked away, bored.

Gail continued to watch them as Diane said, "Remember I told you that I feel Maggie's presence in the cottage? It's more so ever since I brought the portrait there. Do you know what I found out? Maggie didn't run away. They sent her away because she had a breakdown. Aunt Claire told me. I want to know things, but no one will tell me."

Looking around again, Gail saw Sean's father at the bar, pouring another drink. He made his way through the people in the salon, passing his wife and son without so much as a glance at them.

"It's like they're hiding something. Why is Maggie such a taboo subject?"

Gail was aware that she had not been paying attention to Diane, but the questions had not been intended to elicit an answer. As Diane continued to complain about being left in the dark, Gail glanced back at Dub Cresswell, whose laughter reached across the salon. He had just told a joke.

The truth hit Gail with a chill that made her shiver. There was no connection between father and son. It was all between Sean and his mother. If he had given Roger's wallet to anyone, it would have been to her.

At the first break in the conversation, Gail touched Diane's hand. "I should go find Anthony. Would you excuse me?"

"Sure." Diane smiled at her. "And good luck with everything."

Standing up, Gail felt her stomach shift. She breathed deeply, then steadied herself on one chair, the next, making her way across the salon. The door opened, and two women blew in on a gust of wind. Gail looked out the windows. The sky was a mass of clouds. Jack Pascoe still sat in his chair, staring out at the storm.

Gail felt Anthony's arm go around her. "Are you all right?"

"A little queasy. They say to keep your eye on the horizon, but I can't see it."

"You should sit down."

"No, I'm okay. It's better when I stand up."

The boat was not rocking terribly, but she felt as though her insides were being poured from one bowl into another and back again.

Gail heard Liz Cresswell say, "Claire? If you don't mind, I'm going to check with Porter and find out what we're doing." She waved a hand. "Everyone have a drink."

Liz went out the door toward the pilothouse, and Gail saw Diane get up from the sofa and follow.

The room was too warm. The bulkhead creaked, and from deep below, the engines made a constant muffled noise.

Claire rang a spoon on a glass. "Everyone? I'm so sorry about the weather, but Porter says he's trying to get past the worst of it. When we stop, we won't stay long. Our pastor, Bill Hardwick, will conduct a short service." Claire nodded toward the man seated in an armchair by the salon door. "I'm grateful to you all for coming. It means so very much to Porter and me. What I thought I'd do, if you don't mind, is to ask if anyone has something to say about Roger, maybe a funny story, or some way in which you remember him. If so, please share it with us."

Gail tried to breathe slowly through her nose.

Claire cleared her throat. "Well, I guess I can begin by saying how much Roger would have liked to be with us. Ever since he was a little boy, he loved the ocean. . . ."

Gail felt the sweat on her neck. She whispered to Anthony, "I'll be back." He mouthed the words *Are you sick?*, and she nodded.

She quietly went out the door. Hardly daring to breathe, she hurried down the stairs, then steadied herself on the bulkheads as she ran along the companionway. She went through the nearest door, ran into the bathroom, and leaned on the edge of the sink. Nothing came up. She had not eaten more than a slice of toast and some juice six hours ago, and her stomach heaved uselessly. She leaned on both hands and spat bile into the sink, then took a paper cup from the holder and ran a little water into it.

She was gradually aware of muffled voices. Women's voices. Gail drank the water and listened. For a moment she was confused about where the women were, then looked at the bulkhead of the bathroom, where the wallpaper was a pattern of tropical fish. The voices were coming from the next stateroom. She recognized Diane's voice, but the other woman spoke too softly to be heard.

The walls were thin, and Gail could hear Diane crying.

Never told me . . . all my life was a lie!

There was only a murmur in reply, but Gail knew who it must

be. Diane's mother. As if confirming this, Liz Cresswell's voice became clearer. *Maggie's baby was born dead . . . a coincidence . . .*

Diane answering. *That's a lie . . . want to know the truth. I'm not your daughter!*

The reply was only a laugh.

Diane spoke again. *. . . to ask Uncle Porter.* Gail pressed her cheek to the wall.

You will do nothing of the sort.

I will . . . my uncle or my grandfather?

"Oh, my God," Gail breathed.

Come back here!

There was only silence for several long seconds. Liz's voice again, only a low murmur. Then nothing. Nothing.

Gail heard the click of a door opening. A few moments later, it closed. There were footsteps, fading away.

She pushed away from the wall and caught sight of her own face in the mirror, pale and wide-eyed. She put her purse strap back over her shoulder and crossed the stateroom. She opened the door and looked into the corridor. It was empty. She walked toward the stairs and was about to go up when she heard a metallic clatter from the galley, as if a pan had been dropped.

The engines were below this deck, and their muffled roar made it impossible for Gail to be sure what she had heard. Vibrations came through the floor. She walked around the corner into the galley and saw a small metal trash can on its side. She peered into the corridor leading to the deck at the stern and saw light coming through the door. It was suddenly cut off when the exit door closed.

There had only been a split-second's glimpse, but the incongruity had been enough to imprint it on Gail's vision. A blond woman lying on the deck. Then Gail remembered the denim skirt. Diane.

She ran for the door and pushed it open.

Diane was sliding away, and in another instant Gail saw the cause. Frozen with disbelief, She watched Liz Cresswell pull Diane by the wrists across the rain-soaked deck. Diane's head lolled back, and her hair flowed out behind her. A waist-high wall surrounded the deck on three sides. Liz dropped Diane to unlatch a small door at the stern. It swung outward, and water frothed and sprayed. The rear of the boat rose over a wave, then dropped. Liz lurched against the side, then regained her balance. The green dress was halfway up her thighs, and the wind swirled her dark hair around her head. She bent to pick up Diane's wrists.

In an instant Gail knew what would happen.

"Stop! Leave her alone!"

Liz Cresswell spun around and saw Gail. Brown eyes widened to become points of darkness in her face.

"Help!" Gail's screams tore at her throat, but she barely heard them above the growl of the engines.

She turned to run, but it was too late. A hand clenched in her hair and snapped her head back. Gail held onto the door frame. "Somebody help!"

"Shut up!" Liz crooked an elbow around Gail's throat and lifted. Gail's feet were off the deck, thrashing. She dug into the arm around her neck.

The boat pitched at an angle. Diane rolled toward the open gate, and the door swung free.

Twisting madly, Gail freed herself and fell to the floor, crawling under the table. Liz's fingers scraped her arm. Gail came out the other side, picked up one of the white chairs, and flung it off the back of the boat. Then another one. Someone had to see. "Please! Help!" She threw the third chair at Liz, who turned and deflected the chair off her shoulder.

Like a limp doll, Diane lay across the opening. The stern lifted, then sank, and Diane rolled closer. Her head and arms slipped through.

"Somebody help!"

Liz charged at Gail, and they fell to the floor, hitting each other. Gail yelled, "Bitch! I know what you did, and I know why you did it!" On all fours, Liz grabbed Gail's arm and pulled her toward the open gate.

Gail became aware of other shouts not her own. Voices came from above them.

The boat dipped, and Diane vanished.

"No!"

A split second later a man hurtled past holding onto a life preserver. Gail saw a fishing hat fly off his head.

Liz stared. Comprehension flooded her face, and she howled in despair, a cry like a mortally wounded animal. They had found her. She would not escape. She pressed herself into the far corner of the deck, half sitting on the gunwale. Her eyes were wild.

Gasping for air, Gail staggered to her knees.

Footsteps came closer, and men rushed onto the deck. Liz pressed herself away from them. The engines quieted to a low growl, and the boat slowed, moving ahead on its own momentum.

"Mom!" The yell came from above. Gail leaned out. She could see Sean above her. "Mom!" His voice was shrill, terrified.

Liz Cresswell looked up at him. Her mouth moved. *I love you.* She closed her eyes and pitched backward.

"Mom!" Sean howled and beat his fists on the boat, and someone held him back.

A voice shouted to lower the dinghy, get the dinghy over.

Anthony pushed past two other men to reach Gail. He dropped beside her and pulled her close. "Gail! *Ay, Diós mío.* Oh, Jesus, are you all right?"

"Where is Diane? What happened to her?"

"Jack Pascoe has her."

"Is she alive?"

Anthony was brushing Gail's hair off her face, touching her arms, running his hands across her ribs. "Your knee is bleeding. Can you bend your leg?"

"Yes. Anthony, is Diane alive? Please let her be alive."

"I don't know, sweetheart." He helped her stand. "Come on. I'll take you upstairs."

"Where's my purse? I lost it."

"We'll find it later. Here, lean on my arm." He shouted for people to move out of the way. The corridor was jammed, and Gail felt eyes staring at her. A chorus of voices asked what had happened. Was she all right? Did someone jump off the boat? Who was in the water?

Gail buried her face in Anthony's neck. "I need to lie down. Please." Her back had begun to ache, a deep, twisting pain.

"Come to the salon. I'll help you up the stairs."

"No. Let me lie down."

Dub Cresswell's face appeared in view, red and shiny with tears. He wanted to know why Diane had fallen into the water. Why had Lizzie jumped? Gail opened her mouth. Nothing came out but a moan. She closed her eyes.

Anthony murmured something in Spanish, then said he needed to take Gail to one of the cabins. He asked someone to open a door, then he scooped Gail up, one arm under her knees, the other around her back. Gail heard voices diminish. A door opened.

"Thank you," Anthony said. The door closed. He put Gail on the bed, and she lay on her side, curling up.

"Anthony—"

"Gail! What's wrong?" He lifted her face. "Look at me. What is it?"

The pain was low in her belly, taking her breath.

"What is it?"

"The baby . . . I'm losing the baby."

"*Jesucristo.* No. No, this won't happen."

"Please go get me some towels . . . in case. Please." Her breath caught on another wave of pain. "Hurry."

He shouted to her from the bathroom. "It's going to be all right." She heard the panic in his voice. "Maybe it's nothing."

"It's the same as before. Oh, God. It hurts so much."

He dropped to his knees beside the bed, looking into her face. "*Corazón, todo va a salir bien.* I promised you. Don't you remember? It's going to be all right." He pulled her closer, murmuring prayers she couldn't understand.

She cried into her hands. "I wanted it so much."

"It's going to be all right. I won't let anything happen to you." His voice broke. "I promise."

"I'm so sorry."

"*Shhhh.*" He kissed her forehead and circled an arm around her.

The vibration of the engines changed, and Gail felt a shift in weight as the boat accelerated. They were moving again.

"We're going back, you see? Full speed. They must have Diane onboard." He stood up. "I have to tell them to radio ahead for a doctor."

"Don't leave."

"It won't take long. You need a doctor. Maybe they can stop the contractions."

Gail knew that there wasn't time. She reached out her hand. "Please stay."

He knew it then, too, and he hit the door so hard the bulkhead shook. "I wish you had never seen what you saw. I would rather Diane had drowned than this happen. God forgive me for saying that." When he looked back at her, his eyes were tortured. He knelt beside her again and buried his face in the pillow alongside hers.

Gail gritted her teeth against the pain, and when it had subsided a little, she took a breath. "I have to tell you something. Anthony, I've never said this to you before, and I'm not sure I know how. I used to be happy before I met you. At least I thought I was. You made me so miserable and so alive at the same time. I've never hurt as much with anyone else, and I've never loved anyone as much as you. When it was over between us, I died a little, just enough not to hurt anymore, and then you were there again, and all I could think of was how afraid I was that I'd lose you."

"You won't." He gently pressed his cheek to hers.

"I'm not afraid anymore. Whatever happens . . . I'm not afraid, but . . . I do love you. So very much."

"I will never leave you." He grasped her hand and brought it to his lips. "I swear it on my life."

The pain clawed at her again, and she felt that she might be pulled down into it, but Anthony was holding on tightly.

"*Te quiero tanto. Te juro, no te dejaré. Nunca.*"

CHAPTER

28

Claire closed the magazine on her lap. She had read the same page over and over. She turned back her cuff.

From his bed Porter asked, "Why do you keep looking at your watch?"

"Well, if the nurse gets here, I thought I might go to Diane's. She's having a housewarming for her new condo."

"You told me." He coughed. "I don't like that nurse."

"You liked her last week, Porter."

"Well, I don't like her now! I don't want that damned woman in here." His tongue moved inside his cheek, under his lip. "Give me some water. I'm thirsty."

Claire got up. He opened his mouth, waiting for her to bend the straw exactly right. His eyes rolled to look at her. They were yellow, and she hated to see them, but she thought it was important to maintain a pleasant expression.

"What are you laughing at?"

She sighed. "I'm not laughing at anything. There is nothing to laugh at."

"That's for damn sure." He sucked up some water, and Claire stared past him out the window. The ocean was pretty today, bright turquoise. The light came in so that Claire could see a vague reflection of herself in the glass. *How old I look. Old and ugly.*

Diane had invited her, but surely she had done it to be polite. Claire did not believe that Diane would ever forgive her.

When Porter finished, Claire patted his lips dry and set the glass and the straw back on his bedside table.

She stole another look at her watch. Two-thirty. The invitation had said to drop in between two o'clock and five. Claire supposed that everyone would be there, all Diane's friends.

If only the nurse would come. Porter wouldn't let her leave until the nurse came. She sat down and opened her magazine, staring at the page. A little while later Porter started to whimper. "Claire! I'm hurting. I need a shot."

"I can't give it to you, Porter. The nurse has to."

"Goddamn it, you know how."

The room smelled like a hospital. Claire slept in another room now, although Porter had protested about that. He liked to see her there all the time. She dreamed that he would never die. That she would grow old with long white hair, waiting for release. Maybe it was her punishment.

"Give me a goddamn shot!"

"I can't."

"You're still mad at me, aren't you? Come on, now. I didn't tell Ted to do anything. He construed it the wrong way."

Claire shouted, "Then why did you give him a promotion?"

"Services rendered." Porter laughed. "Go on, call the police. They could take me away. I could die in jail. You'd like that, wouldn't you? You never saw what a bad son you had. He hated me." Porter touched his belly. "Oh, Jesus. I'm eaten up with it. Make it stop, Claire."

He started crying, and she looked at him without pity. She could tell what she knew, but they would say he was sick and crazy. They already blamed Liz. Let it stay that way. Liz had seduced Ted, and he had killed Roger for her. Ted had done it for Porter, too. And maybe for himself.

Gradually the whimpering stopped. Porter said, "Stop looking at me that way. I know what you're thinking. I never touched Maggie! Roger lied. I never touched her, and you know it. She was a little tramp with all the boys at school."

"No, she wasn't, Porter."

"Shut up! I know what I'm talking about. A tramp. Claire! I want a shot. Now!"

Claire stood up and laid the magazine on the nightstand. "The nurse will be here in a little while. Go back to sleep."

"What are you doing?"

"I want to see Diane's new apartment. I won't be gone long."

"You're not going anywhere."

"Yes. I'm going to Diane's. My granddaughter." The idea made her heart leap in her chest with such force that she thought she might cry. "My granddaughter is waiting for me."

"I'm hurting. I'm in pain!"

"I'll be back soon. Lie still, Porter."

He was still yelling as she shut the door.

CHAPTER

29

The ocean stretched out below them in variegated bands of blue, from crystalline turquoise to deepest cobalt. This time of year, in early winter, the perfectly clear skies and slanting light made the water uncommonly brilliant, as if diamonds had been scattered across the surface.

Anthony leaned his elbows on the railing. "This is a fantastic view."

Gail agreed that the view was nice, but Karen wanted a yard.

"You know you can come to Clematis Street, both of you, anytime."

She smiled at him. "I know."

They were still dueling over that and other things. She was elusive. She liked to see him suffer. Anthony drew her closer, wrapping her inside his jacket. Thirty-two stories above the ground, the air could be chilly. The wind played with her hair. He breathed in the sweet, fresh scent of it.

This condominium belonged to Diane Cresswell. Diane's father had bought it for her before moving to the French West Indies. Diane still called Dub Cresswell her father. The woman she had once called mother was forever cast out. Anthony had never met or heard of a woman of such brazen confidence, one who would attempt murder under the noses of three dozen people. Who would ever suspect that Elizabeth, such a loving mother, had a motive? Unfortunately for her, the truth had already begun to rattle its cage, and she had not heard it.

Unfortunately for the truth, too much of it would remain with the dead.

The walls of Diane's new living room were pale blue, and on one of them Diane had hung the painting of herself done by Margaret Cresswell and lit it with small spotlights. Maggie had guarded her secrets well.

Still looking through the open doors, Anthony noticed his daughter sitting on Bobby Gonzalez's lap. This annoyed him, but he had learned to hold his tongue. Complain, and it would drive them closer. He had at least persuaded Angela not to move in with Bobby. The line had to be drawn somewhere.

Gail's daughter was no less of a challenge. He watched as Karen tried ballet steps in a pair of Diane's pointe shoes. Oh, Karen. Anthony needed the wits of Machiavelli, the patience of a saint. And on occasion, some discreet bribery. So far Karen had accepted him back. If not, her mother would be impossible.

Diane looked out onto the terrace and waved at them, then separated herself from her guests. She slid the door shut and the noise level dropped.

"I haven't properly thanked you both, have I? I owe you so much."

Gail smiled at her. "No, just be happy."

"Do you want to hear something odd that I've never told anyone else? I believe that Maggie was looking out for me that day on the boat." Diane made a small laugh. "I keep calling her Maggie. It's just too strange to call her my mother. Maybe I will someday, but for now she's Maggie. When I was in the water, I heard her. She told me she would hold me up until someone rescued me. Do you believe in things like that?"

"Anything is possible," Anthony said.

Diane turned to look at the portrait of herself. "I invited Aunt Claire to come today. I want her to see this. I hope she comes, but it's hard for her to leave Uncle Porter now that he's so sick. I look like her, don't you think? I can see it so clearly now. Aunt Claire and I have been talking a lot about the past. I know who my father is."

They looked at her, waiting.

"He was a French boy who was over here on vacation one winter with his parents. His name was Jean-Louis. Maggie never told them his last name, but Aunt Claire remembers he was from a good family. He father was a wine maker in Bordeaux."

Gail nodded and glanced at Anthony. They both knew that her grandmother had spun a story where reality was too grim to bear. It was more likely that Diane was either the product of incest or the child of a murderer.

Anthony smiled at her. "A French boy. Yes, I can see a certain . . . French influence in your face. But after twenty years it would be impossible to find him."

"I'm afraid so." Diane looked from one of them to the other. "I'm sorry for what happened to you, too. Losing the baby. I hope someday you try again. Is that all right to say?"

A shadow passed over Gail's face, then vanished in her smile. She kissed Diane's cheek. "Yes, of course. Thank you."

When Diane had gone back inside, he put his arm around Gail and said, "We could do that, if you want."

He had expected a quick no, but she walked to the railing and looked out to sea. "I don't know. Maybe we could just wait and see how it goes."

"Would you take that risk?"

She looked over her shoulder at him. "Maybe."

"Maybe." He sighed. Across the space between them he said, "What are we going to do with ourselves, *corazón*?"

She smiled. Her eyes caught the blue of the sky, the blue of water behind her, and the aquamarines at her ears.

ACKNOWLEDGMENTS

I depend on practicing lawyers (and a judge) to help me remember what it was like: Milton A. Hirsch, Bruce H. Fleischer, Alfonso J. Perez, Juan Ramirez, Eugene W. Sulzberger, and David Waksman. For details of police procedure, I am grateful to crime-scene technicians David Gilbert and Gerald J. Reichardt; Detective Ramesh Nyberg, Miami-Dade Homicide Bureau; and Reinhard W. Motte, M.D., Associate Medical Examiner. Physicians Jodie Boggs and Aysegul Ozbek provided medical information; Jill B. Shave and Ken Rampone shared their knowledge of boats; Leslie Curtis and Shari Little made the world of ballet come alive; and Jill Cannady and Bob Sindelir helped me create the art gallery at Coconut Grove. Many thanks to you all. For correcting my Spanish, *gracias* to Alicia Abreu, Liced Abreu, and Vivian Llanos. Teté Portela gave me lovely details about Anthony's grandmother. And finally, Bobby Gonzalez sends his appreciation to James, Jennifer, and Valerie, who put the words in his mouth. Any errors of fact or interpretation are mine.